Sign up for our newsletter to hear
about new and upcoming releases.

www.ylva-publishing.com

Other Books by Quinn Ivins

Worthy of Love
The Love Factor

Something's Different

Quinn Ivins

Acknowledgments

I wrote this book during a rough year, and some of my stress unfortunately leaked into the first draft. Characters indulged in excessive self-pity and complained about many topics at length. My beta readers and editors slogged through the griping, and their feedback spared readers from doing the same.

I am grateful to my beta readers—Faith Prize, Amy Bright, and Melanie—for early feedback that greatly improved the manuscript. The mood, accuracy of the setting, and likability of the characters all benefited from their comments.

Sandra Gerth edited this book as if a single mistake or missed opportunity would result in her execution. The time and care she put into the manuscript went far beyond her obligation, and I am so thankful for both the results and the opportunity to learn. If anything is wrong with this book, I probably added it during a later stage.

Sandra is also a twin—a fact I shamelessly used to secure her as the editor in the first place—and her insight added depth and authenticity to Caitlyn and Chloe's relationship.

Another twin, who wishes to remain anonymous, also provided valuable feedback.

Thank you to Sheena Billett for polishing the manuscript and to Daniela Hüge for formatting the book. Thanks also to Jenny Spanier and Glendon from Streetlight Graphics for their work on the cover, Karen Reno-Cobb for and extra proofread, and to Lee Winter for writing a fabulous blurb.

I love Ylva Publishing and our international family of authors. Thank you to Astrid Ohletz for giving me the chance to join Ylva and for supporting my work ever since.

Finally, thank you to my wife who just looked over and asked, "Am I in the acknowledgments?" In the immortal words of Vanessa Williams, I saved the best for last.

Dedication

For my kitty

Chapter 1

WHEN HER SISTER CALLED INSTEAD of texting, Caitlyn's twin sense prickled. *Something is wrong.* Then she realized it was a video call, and sirens blared in her mind. *Oh no.* Her hand shook as she swiped to answer.

Chloe's face appeared on the screen, almost a mirror of Caitlyn's own, but her brown hair was shorter with shaggy bangs. Her heavy eye makeup looked smudged. "Hi."

"What's going on? Is Mom okay?" Caitlyn dropped onto the futon.

"Huh? Of course she's okay."

Thank God. Caitlyn took a deep breath and blew it out slowly. "You scared me."

"Sorry. I should have known you would think someone died when I called." Chloe's lips quirked into a half-smile.

"You have to admit it's unusual. I can't remember the last time we did a video call."

"I do. It was when you found that spot on your foot, and you thought it was cancer."

"Right." Caitlyn's foot twitched. "In my defense, it looked exactly like the pictures online."

"Sure, until it came off in the shower." Chloe's grin was teasing, yet affectionate. "Oh, and the time you thought you found toxic mold in your apartment."

"If you had seen the documentary, you'd be worried too."

"Uh-huh." Chloe chuckled, but then she turned serious. "Anyway, nobody died. But I want to ask you something, and I thought video would be best."

"Okay." Caitlyn tightened her grip on the phone. "What's up?"

"Mom said you're coming home on Friday."

"That's the plan." Caitlyn gestured at the boxes behind her. "My lease expires tomorrow, so I have to leave. I'm almost packed."

"And you don't have a job lined up, right?"

Caitlyn winced. Chloe knew perfectly well that she had struck out on the academic job market. Everyone knew.

"Oh no—no. That's not what I meant," Chloe said quickly, as if reading her thoughts. "I know you didn't get a professor job. Sorry, I didn't mean to bring it up. I meant a *summer* job. Weren't you talking about teaching online classes or something?"

"I'm looking at online tutoring, but I don't have a job yet. Why do you ask?"

Chloe chewed her lip, gaze darting back and forth. "I'm in a jam, and I was hoping—well, I was wondering if you could help." She sighed as though resigning herself to a bad reaction in advance. "It's about my boyfriend."

Boyfriend? Caitlyn searched her memory. Chloe often fell in and out of love in the span of a few weeks, making it difficult to keep track. "Do you mean the guy you've been talking to online? The one who lives in Colorado?"

"Yes. Nick. He bought me a plane ticket to visit him so we can finally meet in person. We're going to spend the week together."

"That sounds…nice." Alarm bells rang in her mind. "Um, you've seen this guy on video and verified his identity, right?"

"He's not a catfish." Chloe huffed. "I'm not idiot. We chat on video all the time."

"Okay, that proves his age and gender. But what if you get there and he turns out to be married? Or an axe murderer?" A shiver ran through her at the thought of Chloe knocking on the door of someone she'd never met in person.

"You've met people online before."

"Sure. But usually it's for a brief date in a public place. You're flying to his city for a week." Caitlyn frowned. "Are you staying at his place?"

"Of course I am. We've been talking for four months. He's a normal person who works in accounting, not some monster from your anxiety dreams." Chloe seemed to catch herself and adopted a more conciliatory pose. "It's sweet of you to be concerned, but I'm sure about him. The problem I'm having is with my job."

Caitlyn tried to recall Chloe's latest employer. It was easy to lose track of her ill-fated stints in various unrelated occupations. "This is the one at the college?"

"Yeah, at Pulaski. I'm the president's *executive assistant*." Chloe made air quotes. "It's a really good job. I mean, my boss is kind of awful, and it's extremely boring. But I've never made this much money in my life—and the benefits are awesome. I have an actual retirement savings account for the first time ever."

"Oh wow. Those benefits are great." Caitlyn had never had a retirement account, a consequence of spending her twenties in graduate school. She shook off a pang of bitterness that her free-spirited twin had one first. "So what's the problem?"

Chloe took a deep breath. "They won't let me take time off. I'm out of vacation days and sick days. I'm out of everything."

"Why are you out of leave?" As far as Caitlyn knew, Chloe had been perfectly healthy.

"Because I just started two months ago, so I only had a handful in my bank. That's hardly anything."

Typical Chloe. She'd probably used the days on impulse, not bothering to consider if she might need them in the future. "So why can't you wait until you've earned more days?"

"Nick surprised me with the ticket. I can't ask him to pay a big fee to change the date—and besides, it would take months to earn enough vacation days. I don't want to wait that long to see him."

"What are you going to do?"

"Well…" Chloe drew out the word. "If I go to Colorado, I'll lose my job. But I really, really need to go on this trip. So I was thinking, since you're coming home anyway, and you won't have anything to do… I was wondering if maybe you could cover for me."

"Cover? You want me to impersonate you at work?" Caitlyn nearly dropped the phone. "You can't be serious. These people *know* you. They'd figure it out, and they'd probably have me arrested." Didn't Chloe remember the pranks they'd played as teenagers? Sure, they had fooled a few teachers, but most of their friends had guessed within minutes.

Chloe rolled her eyes. "They don't know me at all. Ruth, my boss, barely looks at me, and the faculty treat me like an airhead. I'm one of the little people—the help. I don't think they'd notice if I grew a second head."

"Well, I wouldn't know how to do your job." The mere thought of trying to fake her way through someone else's workday made Caitlyn's blood pressure rise. It would be like walking into one of her stress dreams with no way to wake up.

"But it's easy. I answer the phone and do menial office tasks. Sometimes I take notes in meetings, but you just write down whatever they say. I'm sure my genius sister can figure it out."

Caitlyn noticed that Chloe said *genius* without the usual animosity, probably because she was asking for a favor. "Well, I appreciate your confidence, but I'm not going to pretend to be you."

"Fine." Chloe slumped. "I don't know why I even asked."

"Look, I'm here for you. You can ask me for anything else. But taking your place... If we got caught, we would get in so much trouble. You would lose your job for sure. Besides, I can't take a risk like that, especially when I'm going on the job market again in the fall."

"Sure." Chloe tugged at her hair. "I understand." Her bitter tone said otherwise.

"Anyway, it might not cost very much to change the ticket. You could reschedule for—um, when will you have five vacation days?"

"Five months from now."

Caitlyn winced. "Ouch. Well, maybe a long weekend..."

"Uh-huh." Chloe looked past the camera, apparently done with the conversation. "I should go. I'll see you when you get home."

"Okay. Love—" The call disconnected. "...you." Caitlyn hated to disappoint Chloe, who rarely asked for anything. But what else could she say to such a reckless proposal?

Just go in.

Caitlyn stood on the porch of her childhood home, hesitating at the final step after four hours of driving. She had already told her mother about her job-market failure over the phone, but she wasn't ready to see the disappointment and worry on her mom's face.

Chloe would offer condolences, but with a hint of satisfaction that only Caitlyn could detect. After a lifetime of resenting her reputation as the underachieving twin, Chloe probably viewed Caitlyn's misfortune as validation that her freewheeling approach to life wasn't so bad after all. *Look where Harvard and a PhD had gotten Caitlyn—absolutely nowhere.*

Caitlyn just hoped Chloe wasn't still mad that she had shot down her outrageous twin-switch idea. She didn't want to deal with tension between them on top of everything.

There was only one way to find out. She opened the door. "Hello?"

"Mom, I love him!" It was Chloe's heated voice.

"You can't be in love with someone you've never met!" their mother said.

Oh no. Caitlyn cursed her awful timing. She glanced back at the sleepy residential street behind her, tempted to take a long walk before coming back to the house. But she'd already disappointed Chloe by refusing to cover for her. She couldn't abandon her twin now.

Caitlyn closed the door behind her, dropped her suitcase, and slipped off her shoes.

"You just don't understand," Chloe said. "Everyone meets online these days."

Bracing herself, Caitlyn rounded the corner and entered the kitchen.

Chloe and their mom stood on opposite sides of the table, where dirty dinner plates sat untouched. While their mom gripped the back of a chair, Chloe's arms crossed her body like a shield.

Caitlyn cleared her throat. "Hi."

Their mom turned her head. "Oh! You're home." She reached Caitlyn in two strides and enveloped her in a snug hug.

"Hey." Chloe walked over, dressed in yoga pants with a pink spaghetti-strap top. "Good to see you." Her hug was quick and loose. When she pulled back, tension creased her forehead.

There was no point in pretending Caitlyn hadn't heard the argument. "You were talking about Nick?"

"Yes." Her mom sank onto a kitchen chair with a weary *thud*. "Your sister wants to quit her job."

"What?" Caitlyn's head whipped back to Chloe. "I thought you were going to cancel the trip."

"No," Chloe said. "That's what *you* said I should do. But I can't do that to Nick. He spent a lot of money on the ticket."

"What about your money?" Caitlyn asked. "Your job is worth a lot more than a plane ticket."

"Your sister is right. It has health insurance." Their mother ran her fingers through her gray bangs. "When was the last time you had a job with benefits?"

"I'm perfectly healthy." Chloe tossed her hair. "We should have Medicare for All anyway. It's not my fault that America sucks."

"Still, you can't change America," Caitlyn said. "Can't you visit another time, when you have more vacation days?"

"Honestly…" Chloe's bravado faltered as her gaze drifted to the floor. "I'm not sure how much longer he'll wait for me."

"What do you mean, he might not wait?" Caitlyn asked carefully.

"Long-distance has been hard for him. He cares about me, but he has said a few things like—you know, if we can't see each other in person, what's the point? Of course, I don't want to lose my job. But Nick is more important."

Her mother balled up her napkin. "If this guy cared about you, he wouldn't want you to give up your financial security. A woman needs her own income. When your father left…" She closed her eyes, then shook her head and refocused on Chloe. "Well, I was grateful to have a job. I know your boss annoys you, but you should hold on to this opportunity."

"I have to make my own choices. I'm not turning down the trip. And there's no way I can go without getting fired." Chloe glanced at Caitlyn. "Well, actually, I did think of a way, but Caitlyn said no."

"What are you talking about?" Their mom frowned. "Wait. You don't mean…?"

"I asked Caitlyn to cover for me. But, of course, she wouldn't do me this one favor."

"A favor?" Caitlyn's voice rose. "This is so much more than a favor. We'd be risking—"

"Yeah, I know." Chloe dropped her gaze and tapped her phone. "I'm going outside. Nick wants to FaceTime." As Caitlyn and their mother watched in silence, she walked out.

"Um, wow." Caitlyn rubbed her eyes. "I didn't think there'd be drama the minute I got home."

"I'm sorry, sweetie. That's not how I wanted to greet you. Are you hungry? Thirsty? There's pasta on the stove." Her mom got up.

"I'll get some in a bit." Caitlyn sat at the table. "I filled up on snacks an hour ago."

"Okay." Her mom sat back down and rested her chin in one hand. "I'm concerned about your sister."

"Me too. Doesn't sound like the best decision, to say the least."

"I don't want this to become another Jacqueline situation."

Caitlyn winced at the memory of the ex-girlfriend who had persuaded Chloe to accompany her ska band on a tour of North American dive bars. "Yuck. I hope this guy is a better catch than Jacqueline. All Chloe got out of that relationship was credit card debt."

"Well. I already told her I can't bail her out this time. I can't—" Her mom shook her head. "I can't be her safety net forever."

"Are you okay?" Caitlyn asked. "Financially, I mean? I know you said not to worry about paying rent, but I don't want to take advantage of you."

Her mother gave her a reassuring smile, but her eyes held a worried expression. "You're always welcome here. And I have enough money for my expenses. But if something were to happen to you or Chloe, some emergency—well, I don't have much extra."

Caitlyn's heart ached. Her mom had worked so hard to raise them, and the toll was written in countless lines on her pale forehead. The last thing Caitlyn wanted was to add to her mom's stress. "We'll all be okay. Chloe will come back and get a new job."

"If she comes back," her mom said quietly.

Caitlyn wanted to reassure her mom that Chloe would return, but the promise died on her lips. They both knew Chloe would follow her heart even if it led her straight off a cliff.

"I'm afraid she'll stay out there and become dependent on him."

"Yeah, that's a possibility." Caitlyn hated the idea of her sister stranded in Colorado with a stranger paying the bills. Chloe would feel obligated to continue the relationship even if her feelings changed.

Her mom looked at her seriously. "If Chloe had a stable job waiting for her, she'd be more likely to come home."

"Yeah, it's a shame that... Wait." Caitlyn's stomach dropped as she realized the implication. "Are you suggesting that I do what she's asking? Pretend to be her?"

"You have to admit it would work. People used to mix you two up all the time. You have longer hair, but you could hide it with a headband or a scarf."

Caitlyn's heart rate accelerated. "But it's such a ridiculous idea. I mean, what if I get caught? I'd get in so much trouble. We both would."

"Caught how? If you think about it, how could they prove that you're *not* Chloe?"

Caitlyn rubbed her temples. She supposed that if she carried Chloe's ID, anyone who checked would conclude that she worked at Pulaski. "But five whole days of pretending? I can't just wing something like that. I'd have to learn everything about her job, her coworkers, the college—plus all of the little things like her computer password." Just thinking about it was overwhelming.

"You don't have anything to do next week," her mom said quietly.

The words stung. Whatever Caitlyn might think of Chloe's choices, the reality was that she had returned home to mooch off her mother. Guilt flooded her chest. *I let her down.*

The front door opened, then closed. Chloe started up the stairs without acknowledging either of them.

Pulse pounding, Caitlyn pushed her chair back and stood. "Chloe, wait. Come in here."

After a pause, footsteps descended the stairs. Chloe entered the kitchen with a wary gaze.

Caitlyn took a deep breath. "I'll do your job next week."

"Seriously?" Chloe's eyes widened. "You really mean it?"

"Yes." Caitlyn gulped. Was she really doing this? "But I have conditions. I want the money you'll earn for the week—I think that's only fair—and I'll use it to buy groceries and other things for the house while I'm staying here.

I also want you to give me your driver's license. You can use your passport to get on the plane."

"That sounds okay, doesn't it, honey?" Her mom looked between them, eyes shining with hope.

Caitlyn wasn't finished. "And I want you to spend the rest of the weekend telling me every single detail about your job, no matter how irrelevant it might seem."

Chloe broke into a smile. "Of course! I'll tell you everything. We can even look at photos online so you'll recognize everyone." She surprised Caitlyn with a fierce hug. "Thank you so much. You're amazing."

As Caitlyn hugged her back, anxiety churned in her gut. Maybe it would all turn out okay, but getting through a week as Chloe would be hell on her nerves.

Thank God for my Zoloft. Next week, she'd need every milligram.

Caitlyn stood in the center of her childhood bedroom, contemplating the boxes and bags that she'd hauled from her car. The sight of all her worldly possessions piled at her feet made her realize how little she'd accumulated in St. Louis. Her entire wardrobe fit in three bags, each containing a mix of well-worn outfits from high school, preppy basics she'd bought on her grad student budget, and pajamas with stains and holes.

What she had was a lot of books. The stacks of compact boxes with labels like *methodology* represented the bulk of her spending aside from food and shelter. The only item related to a hobby was her guitar, ensconced in a hard-shell case with colorful stickers she'd applied back in college—the last time she'd had time to practice.

"Knock knock." Chloe appeared in the doorway, bearing her laptop. "Is that all you brought home?"

"Yeah, this is everything. My furniture wasn't worth the cost of transportation."

"You're lucky, in a way." Chloe gingerly stepped over boxes, making her way toward the bed. "I have so much stuff, there's no hope of getting organized. Like, I can't reach for my hairbrush without toppling a pile of accessories."

"I believe it." Caitlyn could picture it perfectly, thanks to growing up across the hall from Chloe's chaotic bedroom. "You know, Marie Kondo would not approve."

"Who?" Chloe tilted her head.

"Oh, she's an expert on home organization. You're supposed to ask yourself whether an item sparks joy—and if not, you get rid of it."

"I see." Chloe tapped a box labeled *political sociology* with her bare foot. "So do these books spark joy?"

"Um." Caitlyn could imagine joy—clutching her phone to her chest after receiving a job offer, glowing with satisfaction that her struggle had been worth it. *Maybe next year.* "You came to show me some things about your job?"

"Yes." Chloe opened her laptop. "While you were getting settled, I made you a PowerPoint presentation."

"Really?" Caitlyn sat next to Chloe on the bed.

"Of course. I've got some computer skills." Chloe angled the laptop toward Caitlyn.

A map of the Pulaski College campus filled the screen. One of the buildings was circled in red with a text box reading *Dictator's lair* along with a devil emoji.

"Uh, what's that?"

"That's the president's office. Which brings me to the next slide." Chloe tapped the arrow key. "Say hello to Ruth Holloway."

Under the heading *BOSS* was a portrait of a woman with short, blonde hair and striking blue eyes, so vibrant they must have been digitally enhanced. With her arms crossed in her navy blazer and her chin raised, she appeared defiant, as though daring the viewer to challenge her authority. Instead of the amiable smile most college administrators wore in official photos, Ruth's lips curved into the slightest hint of regal satisfaction.

"Um. Wow." Caitlyn couldn't stop staring. "She looks…" *Smoking hot.* "Intense."

"That's a nice euphemism." Chloe smirked. "You mean she looks bitchy."

As a feminist, Caitlyn didn't use the word *bitchy.* Besides, it was inadequate. Ruth Holloway looked sharp and powerful, like every no-nonsense teacher or professor who had turned Caitlyn's guts to mush during her many years of school. Caitlyn searched Ruth's oval face. She looked young for a president, about forty, but it was hard to guess from an official portrait—some combination of foundation and Photoshop had smoothed away pores and any fine lines she may have had. "So what is she like?"

"Let's see. She's always making these exasperated sighs that I can hear from my desk." Chloe made a huffy sigh and rolled her eyes, apparently mimicking Ruth. "She thinks she's smarter than everyone around her, and she doesn't bother to hide it."

"Charming." Caitlyn's attraction wilted. Ruth sounded like one of those arrogant academics who belittled others to boost her own status. *I'll feel right at home.*

"But sometimes that's a good thing," Chloe said. "Ruth doesn't trust me to do very much, which makes my life easier."

"I suppose that's good for me." Caitlyn studied the woman for another moment before ripping her gaze away. "What's next?"

Chloe tapped the computer, revealing a bulleted list. "I typed up everything you'll need to know, like my login and password, and how to handle requests."

"Requests?"

"Yeah, meeting requests. People are always trying to get on Ruth's calendar. They'll email you because they're afraid to ask Ruth directly, but you're supposed to forward the requests to her. She'll respond and let you know what to do. Usually, she just writes *No.* Then you write back to the person and say, you know, unfortunately, Ruth isn't available. Something like that."

"So she doesn't meet with anyone?" How could Ruth run a college without holding meetings?

"Oh, she does. She meets with her friend Piper all the time and the senior staff. Here, I grabbed their photos from the website." She flipped to a slide with eight headshots. "If you memorize their names, you'll be fine."

"That's it? You must know more people than that."

"Not really. Sometimes faculty stop by the office, so I put some of their pictures on the next slide—the ones who come most often. But you won't need to remember their names. Just tell them Ruth can't talk because she's in a meeting." Chloe grinned. "See? I told you it would be easy."

"Easy," Caitlyn echoed. The job itself sounded simple, assuming Chloe's account was accurate. However, Caitlyn had the impression that tolerating Ruth Holloway for five days might be the hardest part of all.

Chapter 2

CAITLYN FIDDLED WITH THE BUN that hid the true length of her chestnut-brown hair. *I should have cut it.*

At home in the bathroom, Caitlyn had thought she'd done enough to copy Chloe's style. Now, standing before the imposing building that housed the Pulaski administrative offices, doubt nagged at her.

A pair of Chloe's false lashes weighed down her eyelids. Caitlyn had even borrowed her sister's snug charcoal skirt and low-cut pink blouse, although she drew the line at the impractical high heels Chloe wore to the office. If anyone asked, her comfy flats were due to rapid-onset plantar fasciitis.

Aside from the frumpy shoes and unflattering hairstyle, she looked like Chloe. Didn't she? Growing up, they'd been mistaken for each other more times than she could count. Most people didn't notice the slight differences in their bodies and faces.

Her heart pounded as she pushed through the heavy door. In her head, she chanted reminders in an effort to calm herself down. *We're twins. We're identical. It's fine.*

A custodian nodded at her. "Good morning."

"Good morning." Caitlyn forced a smile as she strode past his trash bin.

The hallway was quiet, just as she'd hoped. Arriving an hour early had been the right call. No one saw her gaze dart around as she searched for the correct hallway, and while she could only imagine how her face looked—pale and terrified?—she was grateful to be alone.

Tall glass doors loomed at the end of the hall, matching Chloe's description. A sign reading *Office of the President* hung from the ceiling, removing all doubt that she was headed in the right direction. Instead of reassuring her, the sight made her nauseous. This wasn't some obscure clerical role; Chloe's boss ran the entire institution. If Caitlyn was caught intruding, the penalty would be high.

As she reached the doors, she peered through the glass. A sleek wooden desk occupied the center of a spacious reception area. *Chloe's desk.* Could she really sit there for an entire week without anyone catching on?

Caitlyn dug in her purse until she closed her fingers around her key chain, now equipped with a stainless-steel key to the presidential office suite. As she held it up to the lock, her hand shook so badly that she missed the keyhole by half an inch.

This is a crime. Caitlyn Taylor had no right to enter the office. If she unlocked the door and walked in, she'd be trespassing. The badge dangling from her collar constituted identity fraud. Somehow, she'd made it through the weekend without backing out, but now the risk had become real.

Her lungs tightened until it was hard to breathe—a sensation she might have interpreted as cardiac arrest if she hadn't spent a lifetime experiencing it every time she risked getting into trouble.

It was the same feeling she'd had when her college roommate had persuaded her to try marijuana at a party. Afterward, while Shannon snored in the next room, Caitlyn had stayed up googling criminal penalties and researching how long the drug could be detected in urine and hair.

She'd had the same feeling in grad school after deducting bogus "school supplies" from her taxes until her burden no longer exceeded her bank balance. As the envelope with her tax return had slipped from her grasp, she'd jammed her fingers into the mail slot, hyperventilating as she desperately tried to retrieve it. But the steel box was secure, condemning her to months of worry that a SWAT team would descend on her apartment to haul her to jail over six hundred dollars.

Every time she broke the rules, she regretted it. *So what the hell am I doing?*

I can't do this. Caitlyn dropped the unused key into her purse. Her breathing slowed as her panic waned. Soon she would be safe in her car, driving away from the world's worst decision at forty-five miles per hour.

Footsteps sounded in the hallway, causing her to jump and whirl around.

A tall blonde strode toward her, wearing a teal blazer with beige pants and functional brown loafers. *Ruth Holloway.* Her short, layered hair had grown since the photo portrait, and the waves were mussed. She also wore considerably less makeup. However, her blue eyes were even more vivid in person, the color popping even from several yards away.

As Ruth approached, she squinted at Caitlyn. "Who are you, and what have you done with Chloe?"

Oh God. "I…um…" Caitlyn trembled.

Ruth stopped a few feet away. "You've never arrived even one minute before nine, and now you're showing up at eight? On a Monday, no less. I should alert the *Gazette.*"

Relief washed through Caitlyn, full-on meltdown averted. But now she was trapped. "I had an early appointment." Her voice cracked.

"I see." Ruth's forehead creased beneath errant wisps of hair.

Shit. Caitlyn was already fucking up. Chloe would never schedule an early appointment. She'd been last out of the womb and late to every engagement ever since.

"Are you all right?" Ruth studied her. "You look flustered."

Caitlyn flushed under the scrutiny. Chloe had described Ruth as so indifferent toward her that she wouldn't notice if someone literally replaced her for a week. But the concern in Ruth's gaze appeared genuine.

"I'm fine." Caitlyn took a breath. "Thank you for asking."

"Good." Ruth continued to stare.

Caitlyn dropped her gaze to break eye contact, only to be confronted with the sleek curve of Ruth's neck and the silky white blouse that drooped to bare a hint of cleavage. Ruth's clothes fit, but they weren't tailored, as though she'd grabbed her usual size at a department store and decided *good enough.* Still, the functional outfit couldn't hide Ruth's hourglass curves. Ruth was gorgeous and powerful with obvious intelligence behind her probing gaze. Caitlyn struggled to control her breathing as the vision in front of her, combined with the high-stress situation, overloaded her brain.

"Well?" Ruth gestured at the door. Her clear nail polish gleamed under the florescent lights.

"Right. Of course." Caitlyn fumbled for the key. Avoiding eye contact, she unlocked the door and held it open.

As Ruth whisked past her, Caitlyn detected the faint scent of lavender. It didn't smell like perfume. More like soap or shampoo. Ruth probably didn't bother with fragrance. She had the clean, polished look of a professional who maintained impeccable grooming with as little effort as possible. Minimal makeup, sturdy shoes.

Oblivious to Caitlyn's staring, Ruth disappeared into her office, leaving the door ajar—probably so she could yell to summon Caitlyn, a habit Chloe had warned her about.

This was her chance to run, to let Ruth think Chloe had arrived early and then split for good. But despite her wobbly stomach and rapid heartbeat, something drew her forward until she stood beside the assistant's desk.

She wanted to know more about Ruth.

The portrait hadn't lied. Ruth was young for a president, with intense and captivating eyes. How had she achieved so much at her age? Especially if she was as unpleasant as Chloe claimed.

Caitlyn was curious. Yet the brief encounter had driven home the point that she was deceiving a human being who would no doubt be horrified to learn the truth. Whatever Ruth's flaws, she didn't deserve to spend her day working with a fraud.

And she'd hang me if she knew. Meeting Ruth in person had left little doubt that she'd be livid if she found out the truth.

"Chloe?" Ruth appeared in the doorway. Her hair had been tamed into place. "Jack is stopping by at nine for a quick meeting. I assumed you'd still be arriving. But since you're already here, I'd like you to take notes."

"Oh sure. Absolutely." Caitlyn's head bobbed while she searched her memory for the name. *Jack Downey, Budget Director.* Chloe's presentation had included a photo of an Irish man in his mid-fifties, along with a note that he met with Ruth regularly. It had to be him.

"Thanks. See you soon." Ruth disappeared into the office again.

Caitlyn gulped. How could she leave now? If she wanted to avoid suspicion, disappearing before the meeting wasn't an option.

Jolted out of her indecision, Caitlyn plopped into the swivel chair. She located the power button and started the computer on the desk. As it whirred to life, she caught her reflection in a small mirror that Chloe had left on the desk, next to a slouching makeup bag. Aside from the headband, she looked like Chloe.

Holy fuck. I'm really doing this.

Something is wrong with Chloe.

The thought had nagged at Ruth ever since she'd arrived. Now seated across from Chloe at the table in her office while Jack prattled on about the budget, Ruth grew even more suspicious.

What Chloe lacked in ambition, she made up for by being predictable. She usually arrived five minutes late, checked the voice messages, and then spent most of the day on her iPhone. As a receptionist, she was decent—personable, nice to everyone—but rarely lifted a finger outside of her assigned duties. Her notes were adequate, but minimal.

This morning, however, Chloe's typing was rapid, almost frantic. When she wasn't taking notes, her gaze shifted between Ruth and Jack as if she weren't sure which one would strike first. She also kept scratching her arms. It was unnerving.

Then there was her appearance. Chloe typically styled her hair in ringlets, crisp from a curling iron and frozen with hair spray. Today, she wore a cloth headband at her hairline, and the rest was knotted into a bun. Ruth wondered if the conservative hairstyle and skittish demeanor were related to Chloe's early arrival on campus and the supposed *appointment* she'd mentioned.

"One more thing," Jack said. "The VP came to see me."

Ruth's lips twisted into a sneer. "Oh? What did Alice want?"

"Another faculty position. The math department wants to hire, and she's supporting them." He held out his palms. "Hey, don't shoot the messenger."

Ruth scoffed. "Oh, come on. Another hire in math?"

"Well, they lost a full-time faculty when Donnie retired. They want to replace him."

"For God's sake." She rolled her eyes. "They lost a grouchy, old crank who was out on medical leave every other semester. Now they're pretending it was a devastating loss to the department?"

Jack cracked his knuckles. "I hear you. But the argument they'll make is that we could hire a new tenure-track professor for less than half of what we paid Donnie, so we'd still save money."

"God, some of these full professor salaries are obscene. He made almost as much as a dean." Ruth shook her head. "Remind me, how much does a new tenure-track professor make?"

"Sixty thousand, plus benefits—so, eighty-five thousand."

"And how much would we pay an adjunct to cover his courses?" She asked the question slowly, as though prompting a small child.

Jack chuckled. "About twelve thousand per semester."

"Exactly. You'd think the *math* department could arrive at that point on their own, but I suppose I'm expecting too much. Anyway, we need that money in ten other places. Student services, for one." She glanced over to make sure Chloe wasn't transcribing her frank comments, then did a double take.

Chloe sat with her back straight and her fingers clenched into fists, eyes flashing with unmistakable fury.

"What's wrong?" Ruth asked.

Startled, Chloe dropped her hands into her lap. "Nothing." She softened her scowl into a more neutral expression, but her jaw remained tense.

Was Chloe angry on behalf of the math faculty? Why would she care? Ruth sat back and leveled a stern gaze at her. "If you have an opinion about our budget discussion, I'd be fascinated."

"I don't have an opinion." Chloe looked down at her lap.

Ruth pushed to her feet with a heavy sigh. Why even bother? "Okay. I'll deal with the math department. Keep me posted on summer revenue. Chloe, please send me the notes and then delete them."

"Okay." Chloe closed her laptop, slid out of her chair, and scrambled to the exit.

Jack jerked a thumb at the door. "What's up with her?"

"No idea." Then a sudden thought occurred to her. The scratching, the odd behavior, the irrational anger. Was Chloe on drugs?

Ruth massaged her temples. She had vowed to wait until noon before taking her second aspirin of the day, but she already knew she wouldn't make it.

When Piper stepped into her office, Ruth took one look and knew there was bad news. Piper's inability to hide her true feelings was her only flaw as a public relations director.

"Oh God, what?" Ruth rubbed her forehead. "Just tell me."

"Okay." Piper wheeled a chair over to the desk. "The *Tribune* called, seeking comment about various faculty complaints." She sat with her notepad and crossed her legs.

Great. "Which complaints? There are so many—you'll have to be more specific."

"Enrollment is down, blah blah blah. The administration only cares about numbers and money. I gave them the usual spiel about our recruitment initiatives, but the reporter didn't seem interested. He asked about canceled summer classes, which makes me think he's been talking to Steve Stubbons."

"Of course." Ruth dug her fingernails into her palms. "Steve probably made a big deal about being faculty council president, as if that means he speaks for the entire faculty. Meanwhile, he only got elected because no one else wanted the job."

Piper consulted her notes. "The reporter said something about an arbitrary enrollment cutoff, basically that you canceled any class that fell below a certain threshold regardless of the circumstances."

"Oh, come on. Do you know what that arbitrary cutoff was? Five. Faculty wanted to run courses with *four students.* Meanwhile, the college is bleeding. We can't lose money year after year and stay in business. Why am I the only one who understands this?"

"They don't want to understand." Piper gave her a sympathetic smile. "If they engaged with the facts, they'd have to accept that no amount of ranting will make everything how it was twenty years ago. I think deep down, they know that, but it's easier to blame you."

Ruth shook her head. "Did you know math wants to hire? They want a new tenure-track position to replace Donnie."

Piper frowned. "Isn't math over budget?"

"They're all over budget," Ruth snapped, then instantly regretted her tone. "Sorry, it's not your fault. I suppose the *Tribune* needs money too. 'College president tries her best' doesn't generate clicks."

"I know you're trying." Piper's thick glasses magnified her kind eyes.

The sound of laughter drew Ruth's gaze to the window.

A group of students clustered in the center of the footpath outside her office, having an animated conversation. One young woman gave her friend a playful push on the shoulder.

"Have you ever heard of the iron law of institutions?" Ruth asked, still watching the students.

"What do you mean?"

"Math cares about math. Steve Stubbons cares about Steve Stubbons. A nuclear bomb could wipe out the campus tomorrow, and the union's first priority would be a raise. Everyone cares more about their own interests than the success, or even the survival, of this college." Ruth turned back to Piper, determination welling in her chest. "So that's my job. I'm going to get us through this enrollment crisis even if it makes them all hate me."

"I'm not here to *make friends*." Piper drawled the last two words in a twangy accent.

Ruth gaped. "Huh?"

Piper blushed. "It's what they say on reality shows."

"Ah. Your guilty pleasure." Ruth picked up a pen and twirled it between her fingers. "Well, the saying is apt. A college president has no friends. Only adversaries and a handful of sycophants on the administrative staff—present company excluded, of course. I know you're on my side."

"Of course I am." Piper patted Ruth's arm. "So much is out of your control. The press may not understand that, but I do. All you can do is your best." It was the kind of thing Piper would say because their friendship predated Pulaski by fifteen years.

A notification appeared on the computer screen, announcing an email from Zachary Thomas, the chair of the board. The subject said, *Call me.* Ruth knew the body of the message would be blank, but she clicked anyway to be sure.

"What?" Piper asked.

"It's Zachary demanding a phone call. Which means he's mad about something."

"Ah." Piper stood. "I'll give you the room." She squeezed Ruth's shoulder, walked out of the office, and closed the door behind her.

Ruth leaned back and shut her eyes. She'd call Zachary in a few minutes. First, she needed a moment of calm.

The stress was getting to her. She knew what her doctor would say. *Work less. Get more exercise. Take a vacation.*

On the desk, her iPhone buzzed. Ruth opened her eyes and checked the screen: Zachary Thomas.

Her break was over.

Chapter 3

"OKAY, THANKS. I'LL MAKE SURE Dr. Holloway gets the message. Goodbye." Caitlyn plunked the phone into the receiver, willing it to stay silent so she could fume in peace.

Two hours after the meeting, she still hadn't calmed down. Of course, she was well aware of the practice of hiring cheap adjuncts instead of full-time faculty, but she had never imagined she'd hear an administrator—a president, no less—speak about the cost savings in such callous terms. It was infuriating.

How dare Ruth mock the faculty for wanting to hire a full-time professor instead of offering poverty wages and zero security to someone with an advanced degree? People like Ruth were the reason Caitlyn and most of her classmates couldn't find permanent jobs.

Her righteous anger washed away any guilt she'd felt about lying to Ruth. If this was how she governed the college, she deserved an indifferent assistant who sent a stand-in to cover her duties—but that didn't mean Caitlyn could tolerate four more days assisting a woman who represented everything she despised. If the stress of impersonating Chloe didn't give her an ulcer, the rage she felt in Ruth's presence would eat her from the inside.

I'll finish the day, and then I'm done.

Peppy footsteps interrupted Caitlyn's thoughts. A tall man with wavy, black hair and a well-trimmed beard came through the doors.

Caitlyn flinched and averted her gaze. She didn't recognize him, and she had no idea if he expected her to know his name. Hoping to appear busy, she typed a string of gibberish on her keyboard.

"Hi there." He waved a hand to get her attention.

Act natural. Caitlyn straightened her back and looked up. "She's in a meeting." So far, two different people had entered the office, seeking "a few minutes" with the president. Per Chloe's instructions, she had told them no—except for a woman named Piper Flemming, who had unrestricted access.

Ignoring her words, the man walked right up to the edge of the desk and grinned at Caitlyn with twinkling brown eyes. "Oh my God. We need to talk about Brenda."

"We do?" Caitlyn squirmed. *Who the hell is Brenda?*

"I always knew she was hiding something, but damn. Defrauding her own grandma?"

"Yeah… Wow." Caitlyn was utterly lost. "That's awful." It seemed like a safe response.

"I can't believe Nikolai hasn't dumped her yet. Do you think he just wants a green card?"

Caitlyn blinked at him. "Maybe…? I mean, it's possible."

He narrowed his eyes. "What's wrong?"

"Sorry, I'm a little out of it this morning. Could you just remind me— um, what are we talking about?"

His eyebrows shot up. "*90 Day Fiancé.* You haven't seen it yet?"

"Ah, right! Of course." Caitlyn laughed, but it came out false and near hysterical. "Wow, I totally spaced on that." She swished her hand. "One of those days. No, I haven't had time to watch it."

"Well, I came to grab you for lunch. Not a moment too soon, I can see." He gestured at the door. "Shall we?"

"L-lunch?" Whoever this guy was, he clearly had a personal relationship with Chloe—one she'd neglected to mention. How could she fake her way through an entire meal with someone who expected her to be conversant in Chloe's pop culture interests? "Thanks for the offer, but I'd better stay here and get some work done."

His jaw dropped. "Seriously?"

Oops. Wrong thing to say. "Er, what I mean…" Her voice cracked. *Oh God, I'm blowing it.*

"Okay, what's wrong? Did something happen? Are you possessed?"

"No." It came out in a squeak. "Of course not."

"But something's going on. You even look different. Your hair…" He gestured at the headband.

Shit! He was getting suspicious. She had to distract him. *Say something. Do something.* Caitlyn jumped to her feet. "I'd love to go to lunch." She swayed and caught the desk as she processed the words that had popped out of her mouth. *Oh no.*

"Great! Do you need to call Gary?"

Gary? *Gary.* Caitlyn knew that name. He was the vice president's assistant, and sometimes he covered Ruth's phone line while Chloe was away from the desk. "Of course." She plopped back down in the seat.

"I'm sure he'll oblige." Miguel's mouth quirked as though they were sharing a joke, one that was beyond Caitlyn.

"Uh-huh." Caitlyn consulted the list of extensions on the desk, then tapped the speaker phone button and dialed.

"My dear Chloe," Gary answered within seconds. "How may I be of service?"

"Hi." Caitlyn frowned at the odd greeting. "I'd like to take a lunch break, so would you mind answering Ruth's line until I get back?"

"Anything for you, fair maiden." Gary spoke in an accent that was clearly American, but with an affected lilt. "May I ask what is on the menu?"

"Um, I'm not sure yet. Thanks. Bye." She hung up and looked at Miguel.

Miguel smirked. "I guess he still isn't over his creepy crush."

"Guess not." Caitlyn wrinkled her nose. Chloe's briefing hadn't included anything about Gary's weird behavior. What else didn't she know?

"Let's go." Miguel inclined his head toward the door. "The usual joint?"

Oh God, something else I'm supposed to know. "Of course." Caitlyn followed him out of the building, taking deep breaths as quietly as she could manage. *Be calm. Act natural. There will be plenty of time to panic in prison.*

Miguel led her across the small campus past clusters of modest brick buildings. It was nothing like the research university where she'd spent the past seven years, which had majestic buildings with arches, plus glistening structures that advertised the wealth of the business and medical schools.

Pulaski's campus reflected what it was—a small liberal-arts college with a modest endowment.

"So how did Nick take the news?" Miguel asked.

Caitlyn's footsteps faltered. Miguel knew about Nick? And the trip? They had probably talked last week, before Caitlyn had agreed to step in—but the question was so vague, she was afraid to assume any specifics. "Oh, about how you'd expect."

"That's too bad. I hope you'll find a way to meet up soon. Maybe he can come visit you here."

"Yeah. Maybe." Caitlyn's fingers twitched as she fought the urge to scratch her arms. Chloe had told her all about Pulaski College—well, minus the detail of her good friend Miguel—but she hadn't prepared Caitlyn to talk about Nick. Maybe she could steer the conversation into less dangerous territory. "Honestly, I'm still bummed, and I don't really want to talk about it. How are *you* doing?"

Miguel let out an exaggerated sigh. "I spent the whole morning on last-minute course prep. Then the copier ate my syllabus, and it took half an hour to find the jam. I really needed a break."

Course prep? He must be a professor.

"Sorry about the copier. How's the course prep going?" Caitlyn asked, careful to not use any terms Miguel hadn't used himself.

"Not bad! We're starting with Sylvia Plath and then Anne Sexton."

Poetry. Good to know. "That sounds great."

"It's nice to start in the twentieth century. Students are less intimidated."

"I bet." Caitlyn rotated the campus map in her head as Miguel turned a corner. She'd memorized each building and how to navigate between them, but traversing the campus in person was another matter. She kept her footsteps just behind Miguel's, hoping he wouldn't realize she had no idea where they were going.

They arrived at a small café attached to an academic building. It was deserted with one bored-looking employee hunched over the counter, immersed in his phone.

"Do you want to just eat here?" Miguel asked. "Since it's not crowded."

The thought of conversing as Chloe on campus, when anyone could walk in, made her squeamish. But a trek to some other location she was supposed to know could present more pitfalls. "Sure. Sounds great."

Miguel grabbed a flatbread sandwich and a Diet Coke, while Caitlyn selected a Caesar salad and a root beer. She'd been trying to drink less soda, but today wasn't the day to forgo all of her vices.

They sat across from each other at a small, square table, each starting with their drinks.

"So," Miguel said as he unwrapped his sandwich.

Dread curled within her as she waited to hear what he wanted to ask "Chloe."

"Did your sister get here okay?"

Caitlyn choked on her root beer. Coughing, she grabbed her napkin and hid her face behind it.

Miguel knew Chloe had a sister? Did he know they were identical twins? Keeping her cover would be even harder if Miguel was aware that someone else in town looked exactly like Chloe. The day just kept getting worse.

Regaining her composure, Caitlyn took a throat-clearing sip and set down her root beer. "Sorry. Wrong pipe. Yes, Caitlyn arrived this weekend."

"Cool. How's that going?" Miguel's expression was open and curious, providing no indication of what he already knew about Caitlyn and Chloe's relationship.

What would Chloe say? "Oh, you know—Caitlyn is still wallowing about the academic job market. I guess a fancy sociology degree isn't worth as much as you'd think."

"Whoa, did something happen?" Miguel looked startled.

Caitlyn frowned. What had she said wrong? "What do you mean?"

"Well, last time we talked you were a lot more sympathetic. Like, you seemed genuinely heartbroken that it didn't work out for her, and now you sound a bit…callous. Did you two have a fight?"

The words squeezed Caitlyn's heart. Chloe had said all the right things, but she'd had no idea Chloe cared so much. Caitlyn was ashamed that she'd assumed otherwise. "I didn't… Yeah, you're right." Caitlyn shook her head. "Of course I'm sorry for her. I guess I'm just in a weird mood." She shoved a forkful of lettuce into her mouth, still reeling at Miguel's words.

After a minute of awkward silence, Miguel checked his phone. "Oh, you texted me. It must have been while I was coming to see you."

I did? Caitlyn straightened and sucked in a breath. She hadn't texted Miguel, obviously—she didn't even have his number. Chloe must have done it from the airport. *Oh no.*

Miguel's eyes grew wide as he read the text. He looked up at Caitlyn, face contorted in shock. "Holy shit. You're Caitlyn?"

Caitlyn's chest heaved as she struggled to breathe. "What do you mean?" It came out in a dry rasp.

Wordlessly, Miguel slid the phone across the table.

Caitlyn picked it up and read the message:

Hey darling just wanted to let you know I'm on my way to Colorado! Caitlyn agreed to cover for me, so if you see me at work it's not really me! Shhh don't tell anyone. And don't say anything to Caitlyn because she would freak out.

A series of emojis followed, one with a finger to its lips and a few different smiles followed by a heart.

Hand shaking, she dropped the phone on the table. *I'm going to kill Chloe.* Then she remembered what Miguel inadvertently told her—that Chloe really did care about her job search. Chloe could be impulsive and reckless, but Caitlyn loved her. *I have to get through this for both of us.*

"I should have known something was wrong!" Miguel said. "You look identical, but your personality is obviously different. And Chloe would never miss *90 Day Fiancé*. Damn, I can't believe this."

"Okay," Caitlyn whispered. "I'm not denying it, but I can't talk about this here." She glanced behind her. They were the only ones seated, but a small line had formed at the register.

Miguel pushed back his chair and stood. "Come on, we can go to my office. Then you have to tell me everything!"

Miguel led Caitlyn down a hall of faculty offices, past overflowing bulletin boards and a poster of William Shakespeare, to an office at the back of the building. The nameplate on the door said *Miguel Fumero, Assistant Professor.*

"Sorry, it's a bit chaotic. I'm getting ready for summer session." Miguel closed the door behind them. "We can finish eating here." He dropped his sandwich on a small, circular table in the corner and sat on one of the chairs. "All right, I can't stand it any longer. What's going on? When is Chloe coming back?"

Caitlyn sank into the opposite chair. She placed her salad in front of her, but she'd lost her appetite. "How much do you know about Nick? And Colorado?"

"I know that Nick bought her a ticket, but she couldn't get time off work and she was thinking of quitting. I told her to stay here and visit another time, but she was obviously conflicted about it. Anyway, I haven't talked to her since last week."

"Well, when I got home, she was determined to go on the trip. She was going to quit her job—but somehow, against all reason and sense, I agreed to take her place for the week. Honestly, I still can't believe I got talked into it. I was in a bad place, and my mom piled on the guilt, and I caved. I promise I don't normally do things like this."

"Ah, that's genius!" Miguel didn't look even slightly upset or judgmental. "So she can visit Nick and keep her job! Wow, it's really nice of you to do this for her."

"That's one word for it. I've been feeling like I lost my head." Caitlyn looked him in the eyes. "You can't tell anyone. Not a single soul. Please promise me."

"I would never!" Miguel held out his palms. "I promise. Chloe is my best friend at Pulaski. I wouldn't do that to her—or to you."

"Okay. Thank you. So how do you know Chloe?"

He brightened. "One day I had to drop something off at Dr. Holloway's office, and when I got there, Chloe was watching one of my favorite makeup artists on YouTube. We got to talking, and she's really sweet and hilarious. So we started hanging out."

"Cool." Caitlyn had a hard time imagining that Ruth Holloway tolerated her assistant watching YouTube on the clock. She supposed this was additional evidence for Chloe's claim that Ruth didn't pay attention to her. "So what do you think of Chloe's Internet boyfriend?"

"He sounds nice." Miguel shrugged. "I just hope they get along in person. And even if they have a good time together this week, long-distance is tough." Sadness passed over his face.

"It's none of my business," Caitlyn said slowly, "but you sound like you're speaking from experience."

"Yeah." Spots of color appeared on his cheeks. "I'm in a long-distance marriage. My husband lives in Vancouver."

"Oh wow. That's so far away. I'm sorry to hear that, although I can't say I'm surprised. A lot of academics are in the same situation. So his job is in Vancouver?"

"Well, yes, but that's not the problem." Miguel's teeth caught his lip as he seemed to debate whether to trust Caitlyn. "He's not eligible to come to this country."

Caitlyn resisted the impulse to ask why. "That's a rough situation."

"You're not going to ask what he did?"

"It doesn't matter to me. Besides, you just met me, and I'm actively committing fraud. I'm not in a position to judge your husband—not that I would anyway."

"I appreciate it, and that's why I'll tell you." He took a deep breath. "Preston had a difficult childhood. Well, that's an understatement. He got into drugs, and he caught a trafficking charge when he was eighteen. After that, he got help, went to college, and became a nurse. But even though he's been clean for a decade, the US won't let him in. So that's why he couldn't move here." Miguel watched Caitlyn closely as he spoke.

"That's awful. They shouldn't ban him for a teenage mistake." Caitlyn hoped her face conveyed her sincerity and her lack of condemnation. "I'm on your side. Truly. He should be able to come with you."

Miguel nodded sadly, the strain written all over his face. "We have one of the best immigration lawyers, but the authorities won't budge. And the only job offer I got was here, so that's why we're long distance."

"What are you going to do?"

"I really don't know. Last year, I applied to every listing for poetry faculty in Canada—all two of them. I'll go on the market this year too. But if nothing changes, I might need to choose between my marriage and this career."

"That's horrible. You shouldn't be in this situation. I'm sorry."

"Thanks. Um, I didn't mean to get so personal when we just met. Maybe it's because you look like Chloe."

"That's reassuring, I suppose—that I look like her. I've been so been terrified that someone will find out."

"I promise Dr. Holloway won't know the difference. Now that you know your way around, you'll be golden for the rest of the week."

The rest of the week. Caitlyn recalled her earlier vow to quit at the end of the day. In the heat of her rage, she'd been certain, but now she wasn't sure. Meeting Miguel had reminded her why she was there in the first place—for Chloe, who really did care about Caitlyn's job search. She didn't know what to do.

Caitlyn sloshed her root beer back and forth. "You keep calling her Dr. Holloway. Does everyone? When Chloe talks about her, she always says Ruth."

Miguel laughed. "I think Chloe likes to imagine she's on a first-name basis with everyone. Most of us wouldn't dare, at least not before tenure."

"Yeah, I already have the sense that she's not too friendly with the faculty."

"No, and it's mutual. She's smart, and I guess she works hard, but she doesn't care what we think about anything. Faculty want shared governance. They expect a seat at the table, not to be informed after she already made a decision."

"She must think she knows better than the people who actually do the work." Caitlyn rolled her eyes. "Typical administration. They should all be shot into the sun."

"Don't let Dr. Holloway know you feel that way." He grinned and took a big bite of his sandwich.

"I won't. I plan to avoid her for the rest of the day, and honestly…" She braced herself for Miguel's disappointment. "I'm not sure how much longer I can do this."

Miguel covered his mouth. "Oh no. Why?"

"How can I spend a whole week as Ruth's assistant? She's awful. It's bad enough that I'm surrounded by everything I can't have. On top of that, I'm supposed to fetch coffee for a stuck-up administrator who is actively damaging the labor market. Chloe made her job sound boring. I didn't know it would be torture."

"But four more days won't be so bad." Miguel anxiously twisted and pinched his straw. "Anyway, the job comes with some perks. Like—like you can use the library for your research!"

"I can?" Caitlyn hadn't considered this. "Chloe can check out books?"

"Absolutely." He nodded vigorously. "Staff have the same privileges as students. You can access loads of journals online!"

"I have been worried about keeping up with research now that I've lost my grad school credentials." Caitlyn frowned. "It figures that Chloe would have access to academic journals but not me. What a world."

Miguel beamed. "But if you cover for Chloe, you can read all the sociology you want!"

It wasn't that she *wanted* to read more sociology. After grad school, her brain was fried. But she'd need resources to work on new papers for conferences and journals. "I'll think about it."

"Good. Plus you can see how administration works from the inside. Who knows, maybe you'll learn something that helps you on the market next year."

"So far, I'm learning what I already know—adjunct labor is cheaper than hiring faculty, and administrators don't care." She stabbed a mound of lettuce with too much force. "Ruth certainly doesn't."

"Well, maybe you can meet some sociology professors. You could even come to department events if they've got any scheduled this week." He was like a telemarketer desperate to stop her from hanging up. "Maybe it could even help you get a job *here* one day! You can network as Chloe and talk up your sister. I mean yourself. You know what I mean."

Caitlyn had zero plans to mention her existence to anyone else at Pulaski. "Yeah, I don't think that's a good idea. I'm trying to stay under the radar until I can go home in a few hours." *And I probably won't be back.*

———————————

When Caitlyn entered the house, her mom was waiting at the kitchen table, clasping her mug with both hands. "Well? How was it?"

"I don't even know where to begin. At first, it was terrifying. I was ready to turn around and get my brain examined for even considering this ridiculous plan. But then Ruth—Dr. Holloway, whatever—saw me, and I had to stay for the day."

"Did everyone think you were Chloe?" The tremor in her mom's voice betrayed her anxiety. She'd probably spent the whole day worrying about both of her daughters.

"Yeah. No one suspected—well except for her friend Miguel, but only because Chloe flat out told him." Caitlyn grabbed a glass from the kitchen cabinet and filled it with tap water.

"Oh yes, Chloe mentioned him once or twice. The gay poetry professor."

"Yes. He's a sweet guy. But Ruth is awful. She's arrogant and insensitive and personally responsible for replacing full-time faculty with adjunct labor. I don't know how I can stand to be her assistant for four more days."

Her mom's thumb moved up and down the handle of the mug. "Oh, honey, I'm sure it will go by faster than you think. And it means a lot to me that you're holding the job for Chloe."

"How is Chloe? Have you heard from her since she landed?"

Her mom pointed to her phone. "She texted us. Didn't you get it?"

Caitlyn pulled her phone out of her purse and saw the notification. "I must have been driving." She swiped, revealing a selfie of Chloe with a man in his thirties. He had black, curly hair and big eyes. They beamed at the camera, his arm around her shoulders in a side-hug while their heads touched.

Who are you, really? Caitlyn scrutinized Nick's face, searching for some sign of his true intentions. Had he been honest with Chloe when they'd talked online? Did he really care about her? "Well. I'm glad she got there safely."

"Yes, but we need her to come back." Her mom trapped Caitlyn with a pleading gaze. "You're not quitting, are you?"

Caitlyn looked down at the photo again. Chloe looked bright and happy—the way she looked when she threw herself into some new adventure without a care in the world. If it didn't work out, she'd be crushed.

The first day at Pulaski had been harrowing, but she'd survived. She'd fooled everyone, even Miguel. A few more days could give Chloe security.

This is something I can do for my sister, for my family. Determination swelled in her chest. *Screw Ruth Holloway.* "No. I'm not quitting."

"You'll go in the rest of the week?" Hope filled her mother's voice.

God help me. "Yes."

A relieved smile spread across her mother's face. "Thank you, honey."

She took a big swig of water. "You're welcome. I'm going upstairs."

Caitlyn went upstairs to her childhood bedroom. Every time she entered it, she felt transported in time. Most of the decorations were from her teenage years—posters of pop stars and photographs taken with friends who had since moved far away from Linvale.

She walked over to her closet door, where she'd hung a photo of her and Chloe at their sixteenth birthday party, grinning with identical tiaras atop their heads. A sadness passed over her. She and Chloe cared for each other, but they hadn't been close since high school—the last time they'd been in the same place.

Caitlyn could spot herself in any photo taken with Chloe, but she wondered how many of her friends and acquaintances would mix them up. Ruth hadn't clocked her as an impostor, but what if she saw them side-by-side? Would she be able to spot her real assistant?

These days, the most obvious difference was their hair. Caitlyn walked over to her mirror and pulled off her headband, letting her grown-out bangs flop into her face. Then she pulled out the hair ties and let her hair fall to her shoulders.

Her boxes and suitcases were still on the floor in a heap. She opened the box containing items from her bathroom and dug around until she found her shears. Thanks to her meager stipend in grad school, she'd been cutting her own hair for years.

She yanked Chloe's ID badge from her shirt and set it on the edge of the mirror for reference. Chloe had sparse bangs that skimmed her eyebrows, with a few longer strands near her ears. The rest of her hair was about an inch shorter than Caitlyn's.

Growing out her bangs has taken years. But she couldn't walk around with longer hair if she expected to last another four days in Chloe's place. And despite her better judgment, she'd committed to seeing it through.

Holding her breath, she pinched a lock of hair between her fingers and lifted the shears. She snipped one strand and then another. As her reflection slowly morphed into one that more closely resembled Chloe, an unexpected feeling of loss stabbed at her chest. The unique identity she'd worked so hard to establish was falling around her on the floor—and the worst part was that no one would wonder where Caitlyn had gone, since she lacked a place in the world to vacate.

Twenty minutes later, a rough approximation of Chloe's haircut stared back at her. She blinked, feeling the weight of the false eyelashes. As long as she didn't look closely, she could imagine it was Chloe's reflection.

Four years of college, seven years of grad school, and I'm back here playing pretend.

Caitlyn took a steadying breath and reminded herself that the gig would be over by the weekend. When she was done living Chloe's life, she could get back to dealing with her own.

Chapter 4

WHEN RUTH REACHED HER OFFICE, the suite was dark, and there was no sign of Chloe. Yesterday's early arrival must have been an aberration. She hoped Chloe's foul mood was also in the past. Whatever the reason, it was unsettling when her assistant radiated hostile energy throughout the day.

As she unlocked the double doors, rapid footsteps approached behind her. She turned to see Jenn Christiansen marching toward the suite.

Jenn wore a button-down shirt and faded blue jeans, the uniform of tenured faculty who hadn't bothered with their appearance in decades. Beneath her short-cropped, gray hair, tension creased her forehead, and her mouth was a grim line.

What now? Ruth took a deep breath and smiled. "Good morning, Dr. Christiansen."

Jenn ignored the greeting and held up a folded piece of paper. "I'd like a word about a memo we received from student services."

"Of course. Please come in." Ruth held the door for Jenn.

They walked past Chloe's vacant desk into Ruth's office, where Jenn immediately plopped down at the conference table. She crossed her legs and sat back as though she owned the place.

That's how they think. Tenured faculty run the college, and I'm their glorified subordinate.

"It's hot in here," Jenn said. "Is the AC broken?"

Ruth set her purse on the desk. "I've put in numerous work orders, and they assure me it's all in my head." She took a seat across from Jenn. "You said this is about a memo?"

"Yes." Jenn smoothed the paper on the table. Most of the sentences were underlined in red pen. "It says that starting with summer classes—meaning, next week—all faculty are required to record attendance in GradesFirst."

"That's right." Ruth shot her a questioning look. *And?*

Jenn jabbed the paper. "We want to know why you're making it mandatory."

Ah. That was an easy one. "Because we already tried making it voluntary, and less than forty percent of you participated."

"What I mean—"

"Look, Pulaski's retention rate is abysmal. Only sixty percent of our freshmen come back for sophomore year. We need to intervene early, when there's still time to help, but we don't know which students are at risk of dropping out unless the faculty tell us."

Jenn scoffed. "Well, that sounds noble, but we know what you're really doing."

"What am I really doing?" She didn't have the faintest clue what Jenn meant.

"Spying," Jenn spat. "You're monitoring faculty so you can punish the ones with poor attendance rates. That's why you want us to put every little thing in your computer system."

Ruth ground her teeth. Why did faculty always assume she had ulterior motives? "I am trying to keep students in class so they come back and take more classes next semester. Weren't you all just complaining about the summer schedule? Your department had three courses canceled because there weren't enough students enrolled."

Jenn straightened her back. "Our enrollment is down because of the career center."

"The—excuse me?" That was a new one.

Jenn flapped her hand. "You know, the administration's glistening monument to capitalism—complete with lounge chairs and a Keurig machine—where glorified guidance counselors tell students not to take philosophy."

For God's sake. "They don't tell them not to take philosophy."

"Oh please. I wasn't born yesterday. The whole enterprise is an affront to liberal-arts education."

Ruth squinted. "Helping students to get jobs is an affront?"

"All I'm saying is that enrollment is down for many reasons that have nothing to do with our teaching—and more administrative intrusion isn't going to fix anything. My whole department feels this way, and I know we're not alone. Alice Stewart agrees with us."

Of course she does. It was no surprise that Alice had undermined the initiative behind her back—anything to be the faculty's favorite. "Dr. Stewart works for me. I decide policy, and recording attendance is now mandatory. If there's nothing else, I have some more intrusions to cook up."

Jenn narrowed her eyes. "I don't think that's funny."

"I'm not laughing." Ruth pushed her chair back and stood. "Thanks for stopping by."

Scowling, Jenn got up and faced her. "You know, presidents come and go. I've been through five of them. The ones who ignore the faculty don't last long." With that she walked out, probably on her way to report an embellished version of the conversation to her faculty friends.

Ruth sank into her desk chair with a weary sigh. *Maybe an early exit would be a blessing.*

Okay, she didn't really feel that way. It was a good job—a chance to implement policies that would make a real difference for vulnerable students. She didn't want to fail, and she didn't want it to be over—especially not because she couldn't handle cranks like Jenn.

I need coffee. The clock indicated it was a few minutes till nine, probably too soon to count on Chloe.

Ruth got up and strode out of her office—right into Chloe, who was rounding the desk.

"Oh my God." Chloe reeled backward, her purse falling to the floor. "Sorry!"

"My fault." Ruth knelt to pick up Chloe's purse. A tube of lipstick had spilled out along with a bottle of prescription pills.

"I got it!" Falling to her knees, Chloe made a clumsy grab for the bottle. Instead, she sent it rolling toward Ruth.

As Ruth reached for the bottle, her gaze caught the label: *Sertraline*, along with *YLOR*—the end of Chloe's last name—wrapping around the translucent red bottle. She snapped her hand back, realizing belatedly that Chloe didn't want her to see it.

But it was too late to unread what she'd read, and she couldn't help that she already knew what it meant. Sertraline was the generic version of Zoloft. *Chloe takes antidepressants.*

Chloe stuffed the bottle into her purse, followed by the lipstick, then looked up. Her cheeks flamed bright red, and her gaze was cagey, as if she'd been caught.

Guilt tumbled through Ruth. Chloe had no way to know she took her own antidepressant every night. She was well aware of the stigma, but she would never judge anyone for taking care of their mental health.

Still on her knees, Chloe fumbled with the clasp on her purse as she watched Ruth with palpable fear.

Ruth wanted to say something reassuring, but a comment would confirm that she'd seen the bottle and recognized the drug name. It was best to pretend she hadn't seen anything. "My apologies."

"That's—that's okay." Chloe wobbled to her feet.

As Ruth stood, she tried to remember why she had left her office in the first place. *Coffee.* "Could you get me a coffee from the lounge, please?"

Chloe gave her a strange look, then glanced away. "Sure. I'll go now."

"Good. Thank you." Ruth wandered back into her office.

Chloe's prescription was none of her business, but Ruth couldn't help speculating about what she'd seen. Sertraline could be prescribed for depression. Or perhaps she took the drug for anxiety. A week ago, Ruth never would have guessed Chloe suffered from either one—but for the past two days, Chloe had acted nervous for no apparent reason. Perhaps there was more to her than the carefree persona she'd exhibited since she started the job. Ruth resolved to pay more attention in the future.

Caitlyn fidgeted in her chair as the senior staff filed into the conference room. She hadn't seen Ruth since leaving the coffee on her desk—stuck on a conference call, Ruth had nodded and shooed her away—and she couldn't stop obsessing over the morning's mishap.

Rationally, Caitlyn knew that if Ruth had seen the name on the prescription bottle, something would have happened by now. At minimum, Caitlyn would be in Human Resources, stammering some explanation for why she had pills belonging to a "family member" in her purse. Nothing like that had occurred, and the logical conclusion was that nothing would happen, yet she spiraled over the possibilities.

Would her lawyer advise her to plead guilty or go to trial? When she inevitably landed in prison, would it be a local facility or hundreds of miles away?

Fuck. Maybe I should have let my doctor raise my dose.

"Hi, Chloe." A woman with pearl-white hair waved at her.

Caitlyn waved back, mentally reciting the woman's name and title. *Beverly Clyburn, dean of students.* Perhaps Beverly would be present when the campus police hauled Caitlyn away in handcuffs.

Ruth strode into the room, her presence bringing all idle chatter to a halt. She sat primly at the head of the table and crossed her legs before scanning the room. "Good afternoon."

Caitlyn twitched when their eyes met, but Ruth's unblinking gaze swept past without the slightest hint of suspicion. *Thank God.* The tension in her chest deflated as she realized her catastrophic fears were unfounded. Ruth hadn't seen anything.

Still, dropping an item that said *Caitlyn Taylor* at Ruth Holloway's feet was a damn sloppy mistake. Not to mention the contents of the bottle—her psych meds. Of course, she didn't feel ashamed of her anxiety disorder, but she preferred to keep it private. People had all sorts of prejudices and misconceptions about mental health, and she didn't want Ruth to think poorly of her—or, rather, of Chloe. From now on, she'd leave the bottle at home.

"How is everyone?" Ruth asked.

No one answered, a moment made more uncomfortable by the small size of the group: The vice president, four deans, Jack, and Piper were in attendance. Caitlyn would have expected a larger team, not that she had any basis for comparison.

When no one responded, Ruth clicked her pen. "Fine. We'll start. Summer classes begin next week—I hope that's not a surprise—and we're piloting the new retention initiative. All faculty have been informed that recording attendance in GradesFirst is mandatory, so I expect—"

"They're not happy about it," said a fair-skinned woman with braided gray hair.

Alice Stewart, the vice president.

Ruth shot her an annoyed look. "I heard."

"They feel we're overstepping and telling them how to run their classes." Alice folded her hands primly. "They also worry their attendance numbers will be used against them—and frankly I don't blame them. There's also the technology issue."

"Excuse me?" Ruth asked.

Alice raised her chin. "Some of them don't know how to use GradesFirst. Our older faculty, in particular."

"I see." Ruth's tone was civil, but her eyes were ice-cold. "Our IT team has conducted *five* separate trainings for GradesFirst. There is a recorded session on the intranet. If people with PhDs can't learn how to mark absences on a computer screen, I will personally escort them to Human Resources to file retirement paperwork."

Caitlyn stifled a laugh. Ruth might be wrong about everything else, but she was right about this. Caitlyn had learned two different programming languages in grad school, and academia had no room for her. If older faculty couldn't manage to learn simple software, they *should* retire.

"First week attendance is critical." Ruth's voice rose. "If students don't come to class, they get dropped and charged full tuition—unless they withdraw in the first ten days. How are they supposed to pay those bills? You can't use financial aid for a class you didn't take. I have *begged* the board to change this absurd policy, but evidently, they'd rather chase bad debt than help our students come to school. So, the advisors are going to call every single person who doesn't show and get them to withdraw before they get charged."

Yet again, Caitlyn found herself on Ruth's side. It was horrible to think of students owing tuition for classes they'd never taken. If attendance records could spare students from debt, shouldn't that be a priority for everyone?

"I'm not objecting to that," Alice said, growing flustered. "It's the GradesFirst—"

"How are we supposed to identify the students without GradesFirst? Hmm?"

Caitlyn squirmed in her seat. If anyone spoke to her like that, she'd already be in tears.

Several people at the table shifted or glanced away, but nobody looked shocked. Did Ruth quarrel with Alice often?

"Any number of ways," Alice snapped. "Faculty could email a list or drop it off at advising. They don't need to take attendance all semester for you to catch students in the first week. It looks like you want to spy on the faculty."

"This college has an *epidemic* of students withdrawing after midterm," Ruth said. "Not to mention the ones who don't bother to withdraw—they just flunk. So yes, I want the information every day, all semester. As for the faculty, I don't give a damn about their concerns. If they're good teachers, they don't need to worry about us having the data."

Ugh. Ruth was back to sounding like the worst stereotype of an interfering administrator. Attendance rates could vary for reasons that had nothing to do with the quality of instruction. The faculty had a right to be concerned about how the administration planned to use the resulting data—particularly an administration led by Ruth Holloway, who obviously had contempt for instructors.

"Well." Alice let out a huffy breath that could be heard across the room. Instead of responding, she clamped her mouth in a crooked frown.

"Any other thoughts? Comments?" Ruth surveyed the room with a stony scowl, not finding any takers.

Caitlyn looked at her laptop screen. Underneath the date, the blinking cursor stared back at her. Was she supposed to document all of that? Or were public reprimands left off the record?

Ruth drew an enormous check mark on her notebook with dramatic flourish. "Next item. The top deck of the parking garage will be closed for repairs starting next Wednesday."

As the conversation continued, Caitlyn typed.

All faculty are required to record attendance on GradesFirst. Advisors will contact students who miss the first class. VP Stewart shared that some faculty have concerns.

Good enough. Besides, according to Chloe, Ruth would review and edit the minutes before they were finalized. If Ruth wanted to add commentary, that was up to her.

Half listening to the ongoing discussion about parking, Caitlyn thought about Ruth's argument with Alice. She was still surprised to find herself on Ruth's side—on the merits of the initiative, if not the implementation.

So Ruth had at least one redeeming quality; she cared about students. Maybe she wasn't a completely horrible president. However, Ruth wouldn't get far if she treated the faculty like the enemy. Her success would depend on her ability to work with them.

Not my problem. Whether Ruth figured it out or not, Caitlyn wouldn't be there to see it.

When the meeting came to a close, Caitlyn's goal was to exit the conference room without getting sucked into small talk. Every conversation was a risk to her cover, so it was best to keep to herself as much as she could.

Instead of following the others to the door at the front of the room, Caitlyn tucked her laptop under her arm and power-walked to the rear exit. She glanced back to ensure no one else was following as she stepped through the door—and found herself in the dark.

The heavy door had closed behind Caitlyn, but enough light came through the bottom crack for her to confirm the unfortunate fact that she'd walked right into a closet.

Shit. Maybe nobody noticed.

A knock sounded on the door. "Chloe?" It was Beverly's voice. "Are you okay?"

"Fine!" Caitlyn called out. "Thanks!" *Go away, go away.*

There was a beat of silence. "Are you coming out?"

"Yes. In a second." Caitlyn squeezed her eyes shut and wished she could disappear, but when she opened them, her situation remained the same. She cracked the door and peeked out.

Beverly stood before her, but she wasn't alone.

Alice, Jack, and—oh God—Ruth all stared as Caitlyn emerged from the closet, attempting to appear dignified even though she knew her face was flaming red.

"I thought I heard something," Caitlyn said. "So I thought I should check it out. But it's fine—er, I mean, it's a closet. Just like always. I'm fine."

Jack shrugged and walked away, while Beverly lingered a moment longer before following.

Ruth continued staring at Caitlyn with a furrowed brow and bright, analytical eyes that seemed to see through her. "Everything okay?"

"Oh yeah. Great. Excuse me." Caitlyn ducked her head and slipped past Ruth. Her heart pounded as she walked down the hall to the women's restroom.

Inside, she splashed her face with water. "That could have gone better," she muttered to herself. No one had accused her of not being Chloe, but they probably thought she was losing her mind.

When Caitlyn returned to the office, Ruth still wasn't back. Deciding it was important to behave normally, she turned on her computer and scanned through her notes. They were thin, especially since the meeting had ended ahead of schedule. She shouldn't care if Ruth thought her notes were good— this wasn't even her job—but the perfect student inside her couldn't help wanting to submit something respectable.

She added a few details and cleaned up the formatting. Then she added a link to the policy document Ruth had referenced. Finally, she checked for typos before saving the document and sending it off.

Ruth still hadn't returned, which was unusual. Her Outlook calendar indicated the location of all of her meetings, and most of them said *President's Office*—probably because she preferred to be on her own turf, staring down her long glass table at whoever dared to appear before her with a request.

Caitlyn was browsing the *Chronicle of Higher Education* when Ruth whisked through the doors with pink cheeks and tousled hair. There was something undeniably alluring about Ruth when she was flushed and disheveled, adding a raw element to her otherwise professional appearance.

"I went for a walk." Ruth gave her an odd look.

Oops. Caitlyn was staring. She shifted and clasped her hands, attempting to look like someone who hadn't been ogling her sister's boss. "That's cool."

Ruth continued to scrutinize Caitlyn as she passed the desk, then disappeared into her office with the door left ajar. A few minutes later, she called out, "Chloe?"

Caitlyn jumped up, expecting a coffee order. She entered the office to find Ruth at her desk, contemplating her computer monitor. "What's wrong?"

"I got the minutes you sent." Ruth steepled her fingers and tapped her chin with her thumbs.

"Oh." Caitlyn shifted her weight. "They're bad?"

"No, they're excellent."

Caitlyn had been so focused on turning in decent notes, she hadn't considered that what she deemed adequate might count as overachieving for Chloe. *Act like it doesn't mean anything.* "Cool. Thanks. I mean, that's good, right?"

"Yes. It's good." Ruth sat back. "If you could write them like this in the future, I'd appreciate it."

Uh-oh.. This could cause trouble for Chloe, but saying no wasn't an option. "Yes. Sure." Caitlyn wondered why Ruth hadn't told Chloe what she wanted in the first place. A college president shouldn't spend her time editing and formatting notes.

"Your summary of the GradesFirst discussion was…diplomatic." The corner of Ruth's mouth quirked into something resembling a smile.

"Yeah." A nervous laugh escaped Caitlyn. "For what it's worth, I agree with you—well, about this. Recording attendance shouldn't be some big imposition, and if it might improve retention rates, why not try it?"

Ruth studied her. "Thank you. I agree."

"Was there anything else?"

"No. I just wanted to say good work."

Caitlyn couldn't shake the feeling that Ruth was holding back a question, but she turned and left quickly, afraid she wouldn't know the answer.

Miguel thought Caitlyn's closet story was hilarious. "Oh no!" He guffawed. "I can't imagine what Ruth thought."

"Har har." Caitlyn rolled her eyes.

He chuckled again and then sank his teeth into his greasy burrito. Mirth danced in his eyes as he chewed.

"So what's the deal with Ruth and Alice?" Caitlyn asked, eager to change the subject. "It seems like they hate each other."

"They do. I shouldn't be surprised you already picked up on it. They don't bother to hide their mutual disdain."

"How can that be? Didn't Ruth pick her vice president?"

"No way." He slurped his soda. "Alice has been here for a decade, maybe more. The board hired Dr. Holloway two years ago, and now they're stuck with each other."

"Is that why they don't get along?" Caitlyn stirred her salad. "Alice wanted to be president, and they picked Ruth instead?"

"Nah. Alice knows she'll never be president. They don't get along, because Alice is an old-school academic. She taught for twenty years, considers herself a scholar—you know, one of those. She's aligned with the faculty, and that's why the board will never choose her for the presidency. They want someone like Dr. Holloway, who represents reform."

The word *reform* raised alarms. Caitlyn associated it with pompous technocrats interfering in the classroom and blaming instructors for poor outcomes. "What kind of reform?"

"All sorts of things. More online classes, beefing up student services to improve retention rates. For example, Holloway wants to do more teaching evaluations—and then mandate extra training for the faculty who don't meet her standards."

"Yikes. No wonder faculty aren't on board. The whole point of tenure is that you don't have to deal with administration telling you how to teach."

"Exactly. You should hear what they say about her behind her back. Especially some of the old guard. They call her a bitch and worse." Miguel made a face. "They can be nasty."

Caitlyn cringed at the word *bitch*. "Well, I don't like her politics either, but they shouldn't be sexist. She's..." Caitlyn stopped herself from saying *demanding*, another gendered word. "She's focused and doesn't tolerate excuses. If she were a man, they'd probably respect her for being tough."

"Maybe." Miguel looked doubtful. "Well, it's true that they're not used to having a woman in charge. Did you know that she's the first female president we've ever had?"

"Yeah, I read that on the website. I'm sure they hate that a woman is trying to change things. It doesn't help that she's attractive and young for a president."

"Attractive, huh?" Amusement glittered in his eyes.

Caitlyn coughed. "I didn't mean she's attractive to me." She sipped her water and mentally shooed away the image of Ruth returning from her walk with flushed cheeks. "I'm simply applying the standards of Western beauty conventions and forming an objective conclusion."

"Uh-huh. Of course." He winked. "So are you bi, like your twin?"

Caitlyn's fork faltered. "What?"

"Sorry if that's too forward."

"It's okay. You just surprised me. I've been away for so long that I'm not used to people knowing Chloe and comparing me to her."

"I bet that's weird. Sorry again. You don't have to answer."

"No, it's fine." Caitlyn hesitated, then decided that as a fellow queer academic, Miguel would likely understand her past anxiety. "The other thing… I don't know if it's like this at Pulaski, but labels were sort of fraught where I went to grad school. Many sociologists are deep into gender theory and queer theory, and it can lead to a lot of arguing and problematizing."

"Oh yeah." He punctuated the words with a heavy nod. "We have all that discourse here too."

"Anyway, I used to spend a lot of time analyzing my sexual orientation and worrying about what to call it until my therapist finally convinced me that it wasn't productive. To be honest, I think she was tired of hearing about it—but I learned to stop worrying so much about labels. So yeah, you could call me bi or queer. I seem to lean more toward women than Chloe." Caitlyn suddenly remembered why she'd started rambling about her sexuality in the first place. "That doesn't mean I'm into Ruth!"

"Uh-huh." His teasing smirk told her she wasn't off the hook.

Caitlyn wanted to ask if Ruth liked women. She found the prospect strangely intriguing, even though she obviously had no personal interest— but Miguel would no doubt seize on the question to further torment her. Instead, she took another bite of her salad and hoped for a change in topic.

"So do you have a girlfriend or boyfriend?" Miguel asked.

No such luck. "No, not for a couple of years. Toward the end of grad school, I thought there was no point in dating because I was going to move away to whatever school hired me." Caitlyn slumped at yet another reminder that it hadn't worked out how she'd planned.

"Okay, so what's your type?"

Her cheeks warmed. "Um, intelligent."

"Hmm. Someone, perhaps, who shares your education level?" He tapped his chin in mock thoughtfulness.

Caitlyn pointed her fork at him. "Someone who is *not* an evil administrator working to undermine everything I value in academia."

"Okay, okay. I guess Ruth Holloway is out of the running."

"Yes." Caitlyn rolled her eyes, then turned serious. "Honestly, everyone in this town is out of the running. I'm going on the job market next year, and if things work out, I could land anywhere. Maybe even another country." She winced as she heard her own words. "I'm sorry. I didn't mean to be insensitive. For me, it's all hypothetical, but you're actually dealing with a geography problem keeping you apart from your husband."

"Don't worry about it," Miguel said, but there was a hint of sadness in his eyes. He sipped his drink. "Speaking of relationships, Chloe seems to be happy with Nick. Did you see pictures?"

"Yeah, she sent me one. I'm glad he's not a catfish or anything. I just hope she comes back when the week is over. It's too soon to move in with this guy."

"I think she will. And hey, if she doesn't, you can quit for her." His eyes lit with mischief. "Maybe on your way out, you can tell Dr. Holloway what you *really* think about her policy agenda."

Caitlyn nearly choked on her water. "Oh my God." She imagined the look on Ruth's face if "Chloe" walked into her office and announced she was quitting over ideological disagreements on how to run the college.

Miguel chuckled. "Wouldn't that be a shock?"

"Well, I hope it doesn't come to that. But the look on Ruth's face would be something to see."

Chapter 5

THE WIND RUSTLED CAITLYN'S BANGS, and her hair bounced lightly against her back as she walked up the path to the administrative building.

When she reached the glass doors to the suite, a glimpse of her reflection confirmed she still looked like Chloe even though she wore her own clothing—a fitted button-down shirt and a black skirt that swished around her ankles instead of her thighs.

After two days without issue, her confidence was growing. *Maybe tomorrow I can ditch the false eyelashes.* They were cumbersome and itchy—she had no idea how Chloe tolerated them every day.

Smoothing her hair, she pushed through the door.

"Hi." A voice piped up from the side of the room.

Caitlyn whirled to see two young women seated in the waiting area. One wore a fitted tank top that said *Pulaski* in block letters, along with leggings, flip flops, and sunglasses pushed up to her hairline. The other wore a loose maxi dress and ballet flats. They had to be students.

"Hello." Caitlyn dropped her purse on the desk. "Do you have an appointment?"

"Yeah," the woman in the dress said. "I'm Priyanka Sen. The student council president?"

"And I'm Samantha, the vice president. We have a meeting with Dr. Holloway at nine."

"Okay, let me take a look." Caitlyn sat at the desk and logged into Chloe's computer to check Ruth's calendar. Sure enough, there was a meeting with Priyanka Sen and Samantha Rivers scheduled for nine o'clock. "Yep, you're on the schedule."

"Sorry we're a little early." Samantha shifted in her chair. "Dr. Holloway is always punctual, so we didn't want to risk being late."

"That's okay." Caitlyn glanced at the closed door behind her desk. "So, you've met with her before?"

"Of course. Lots of times." Priyanka looked at her oddly. "It's okay if you don't remember. I'm sure you've got people coming in and out of the office all the time."

Oops. They knew Chloe. "Ah, right. I remember you now. Sorry, I'm a little slow first thing in the morning."

"No worries." Priyanka smiled. "We're on summer break, so this is the earliest I've been up in days."

"May I ask what you're meeting about?" Caitlyn asked. "If you can't tell me, it's okay."

Priyanka shrugged. "Nothing major. Student council doesn't have formal meetings in the summer, so we're updating Dr. Holloway on what we're hearing from students. Like, the library closes early in the summer, and a lot of students want it to stay open later. We also want more vegan options in the dining hall next year. Things like that."

"Cool." Caitlyn found it hard to believe that Ruth would block off an entire hour to listen to complaints about the library and the dining hall. Perhaps the students would be booted out early.

The door opened behind her, and Ruth stepped out of her office, wearing black dress pants and a sleeveless silver top.

Caitlyn's gaze swept over Ruth's freckled shoulders, then down to the curve of her breasts beneath the shimmery fabric. Ruth looked entirely too sexy for the office. It wasn't the amount of skin showing—the top had a high neckline—but the absence of a stodgy blazer. Without it, Ruth could have stepped into a swanky bar and fit right in.

Or maybe I'm just overly fixated on her body. Caitlyn straightened and attempted an indifferent expression. "Good morning."

"Oh, you're on time. Good morning." Ruth dropped her gaze to Caitlyn's skirt.

Caitlyn fought the urge to fidget. The skirt was more conservative than Chloe's usual outfits, but she'd hoped Ruth wouldn't notice.

Ruth blinked hard and shook her head as though shaking off sleep, then turned to the students. She broke into a wide smile. "Ladies. So glad you could make it."

Priyanka and Samantha stood. "Hi, Dr. Holloway," Priyanka said. "I like your top."

"Thank you." Ruth looked down. "It goes under a blazer, but it's at least eighty degrees in my office. I hope you don't mind."

"No way," Samantha said. "We sure didn't dress up."

"Well, you're students." Ruth chuckled. "You've got the rest of your lives for frumpy office clothes."

Caitlyn gawked at Ruth's friendly demeanor. Was she always like this with students?

Ruth ushered them into her office. "Come on in. I'm so glad we found time to catch up." She closed the door behind them, leaving Caitlyn alone.

Animated voices sounded through the wall, punctuated with frequent bursts of laughter. Caitlyn couldn't make out the words, but they sounded like friends catching up.

A few minutes before ten, two older men walked into the suite. One was tall with wavy, white hair, while the other was bald and stocky.

The tall one helped himself to a seat and rested his feet on the table.

Um, okay. Make yourself at home.

"Hi, Chloe," said the other man, who remained standing.

Caitlyn's heart rate ticked up. Was she supposed to recognize them? "Hi. Good morning."

They both wore T-shirts and shorts. Among academics, personal style tended to degrade as one rose in the ranks, so they were probably tenured faculty.

She checked Ruth's calendar again, finding a ten o'clock meeting with Dan Toscano and Eric Krebitz. *Aha.* But she had no idea who was who.

A quick web search brought her to the physics department's home page. There was a photo of Dan—the tall one—with the caption *Department Chair.* So the other one had to be Eric.

"This is such a waste of time," Dan muttered.

Eric's lips curled into a sneer. "Probably. We know Ruth doesn't care about science."

"That's what we get for hiring a failed academic," Dan said.

"With a PhD in nonsense," Eric said.

Nonsense? What did that mean? And why did Eric call her a failed academic?

Caitlyn returned to the web browser and looked up Ruth's biography. The college's website stated that Ruth Holloway held a PhD from the University of Pennsylvania—an Ivy League school. So what was the problem?

Oh. Realization dawned as her gaze fell on the word that explained it. Ruth's PhD was in education. Some academics looked down on the discipline because it relied on a mix of methods from other fields. Not to mention, education attracted a lot more women than, say, physics.

Recalling Dan's comment—*failed academic*—Caitlyn wondered if they viewed Ruth as a career administrator who hadn't spent enough time as faculty. After all, Ruth was young for a president. Caitlyn skimmed the bio. Ruth had only taught at the University of New Mexico for seven years before becoming a dean of careers in Chicago.

The door opened behind Caitlyn.

She jumped and quickly closed the browser.

The students emerged first, all smiles, with Ruth trailing behind them.

"Keep in touch," Ruth called to Priyanka and Samantha as they left. When her gaze landed on the two professors, her warm expression vanished, but she stepped forward with a smile fixed on her face. "Good morning."

Dan and Eric stood. "Hello, Dr. Holloway," Dan said.

Caitlyn noticed the difference in how he addressed her privately—*Ruth*—and to her face, where he used her title.

"You're here about the lab equipment?" Ruth asked.

"That's right," Eric said.

"Please go inside and have a seat. I'll be there in a moment." After they passed her, Ruth pulled a slim wallet out of her back pocket. "I'm going to need espresso for this. Could you please get me an iced latte from Kravings with an extra shot? And get yourself one of those whipped milkshake concoctions you like so much."

"Oh—thanks." Caitlyn couldn't hide her surprise. Not only did Ruth remember Chloe's favorite drink, she was buying her one?

Ruth held out two bills. "Tip the rest."

"Sure." Caitlyn watched Ruth walk away, eyes dwelling on the contours of Ruth's shoulders and back. Would she don the blazer now that two sexist men were there to see her?

Focus. She grabbed a sticky note and jotted down Ruth's drink order before it could slip her mind.

Outside, the temperature had jumped ten degrees. She walked slowly along the path, using a map on her phone to find the campus coffee shop. By the time she arrived in the student union building that housed Kravings, beads of sweat trickled down her chest, pooling in her cleavage. An iced drink would be a relief.

While she waited in the short line, she studied a bulletin board with multicolored fliers advertising various clubs and events. The sight made her wistful. *This could be the last time I work at a college.*

The word *sociology* jumped out at her on a flier promoting an *Interdisciplinary Colloquium on Inequality.* It was sponsored by several departments, including the sociology department. First Wednesday of every month...*as in, tonight?* Even in the summer?

Caitlyn moved closer and saw that the current date was included in the list—a lecture by a political scientist named Will Czerwinski on voter participation rates.

I could go. The chance to learn something interesting lifted her mood. Perhaps attending an academic lecture would motivate her to get to work on her research. Or at the very least, maybe it would make her feel more like herself.

Why not? As a staff member, she had every right to go—well, Chloe did. She could sit in the back and blend in with the students. No one would even notice.

She pulled out her phone and snapped a photo of the flier. As long as she was doing Chloe's work, she deserved all the perks.

Someone was in trouble. Caitlyn didn't know who was on the line, but Ruth was letting them have it.

"He can't order a damn transcript, because... Yes, I know. You said that already. And if repeating it could solve the problem, I'd be in heaven."

Caitlyn caught herself smiling. There was something endearing about Ruth in boss mode. She was focused and relentless, and she didn't bother to hide her exasperation when subordinates didn't deliver.

"So what, I'm supposed to tell this young man that because we don't have our shit together... No, that's not an option. You need to try something else." There was a pause. "Well, then why don't you call me back when you think of something." The crack of plastic smacking plastic indicated that Ruth had hung up—with considerable force.

"Chloe!" Ruth called.

Caitlyn jumped up and scrambled to the open door. "Yes?"

Ruth sat with both elbows on the table, chin propped up in her hands. She'd removed her blazer, and her hair was slightly frizzy, but the fire in her eyes left no doubt that she was in boss mode.

"Could you please..." Ruth closed her eyes, composing herself, then opened them. "Could you please search the website at the US Department of Education and see if you can find a phone number for a sentient human being who is empowered to make an actual decision?"

Caitlyn swayed in the doorway, hoping Ruth would elaborate. "Sure. But if you can tell me a little more, it might help me to find the right department."

Ruth huffed. "Do you know what's happening in Tigray? Ethiopia?"

"Um." Caitlyn knew, but would Chloe? "I'm not sure." She took a few hesitant steps into the office.

"Sit." Ruth gestured to the empty chair next to her desk.

"Okay." Caitlyn sat and waited.

Ruth pushed her foot against the desk to swivel her chair so that she faced Caitlyn. "Our student, Amari, came to the United States to escape the war. Now he can't get financial aid because he wrote on a form that he already has a degree from Ethiopia. But it was only a one-year program, so he should be entitled to aid for a bachelor's degree. Anyway, they won't let him correct it without an official transcript. But his old university shut down because of the war."

"Oh wow. What can he do?"

"Jeff submitted paperwork explaining the situation, but the Department of Education denied the appeal. Apparently, Jeff accepted it as the final word." Ruth blew out a frustrated breath. "I don't accept it. This student survived *a war*. He has no other way to pay for school, and I'm not going to tell him—" Her voice cracked.

Was Ruth going to *cry?* Caitlyn held her breath.

Ruth did not cry. She set her jaw and stared past Caitlyn with a steely gaze. "I am not going to tell him that no one in this country is prepared to listen to him and make a reasonable decision. I don't accept it." Determination flashed in Ruth's vivid blue eyes.

The raw passion on display was like nothing Caitlyn had ever seen from an administrator. Ruth looked ready to punch through walls if it would help the student. *I'd hate to be the one in her way.*

Ruth placed her hands on the desk, seeming to steady herself. "So. If you find me a phone number, I will call them myself, and I will keep calling until this is resolved."

"Got it." Caitlyn nodded firmly, hoping to show her commitment. "I'll start looking right now."

"Thank you. I appreciate it."

Caitlyn got up and walked to the door. Compelled to say more, she turned around. "I think it's great that you're fighting for him."

Ruth gave her an odd look. "Well, of course I am. He's our student."

"Of course. I'll see what I can find." She returned to her desk, feeling disoriented.

At first, Caitlyn had assumed Ruth's uncompromising leadership style was the product of an oversized ego. Now she saw something different. Ruth sincerely believed she was on the side of the students. Some of her efforts were misguided, but her heart was in the right place—at least some of the time.

The chance to help filled Caitlyn with a heady sense of purpose. She navigated to Google and found a phone number for students filling out their FAFSA forms. But a help line wasn't good enough. Ruth needed someone with the power to overrule whatever policy had resulted in the current impasse.

Twenty minutes later, Caitlyn hadn't found anything useful. She supposed staff with authority weren't eager to receive calls from the general public.

Caitlyn slouched in her chair until a jolt of inspiration caused her to sit up straight. *The Harvard alumni network.* Surely someone who went to

Harvard worked at the Department of Education or at least knew someone who did. She navigated to the Harvard website in her browser and began to type her login information, then stopped.

Oops. She couldn't log on as Caitlyn Taylor—not on a Pulaski computer, where IT surely kept records of web traffic. No one would notice in the short term, but still. She had to be careful.

Reluctantly, she pulled out her phone. Using her thumbs, she navigated to the alumni message board, entered her credentials, and tapped out a new post.

I need contact information for someone in the Department of Education who works in the area of financial aid. My sister is seeking to help a student who has issues with his paperwork due to conflict in his home country, and the standard process is getting us nowhere. Please help!
Caitlyn Taylor

As she clicked submit, she prayed Harvard would come through. She didn't want to let the student down. It had nothing to do with pleasing Ruth. Nothing at all.

Caitlyn set her phone down and returned her attention to her desk when something moved in her peripheral vision—an enormous cockroach right next to her chair.

She shrieked and jumped up. Breathing hard, she backed up to the wall while her gaze remained locked on the hideous bug.

"What?" Ruth called from her office.

"There's a…a huge… Oh no."

The bug skittered under the desk out of sight.

Her panic rose. She couldn't work there, knowing the hideous creature was lurking inside.

Ruth walked out and looked Caitlyn up and down, her eyes wide. "What?"

Caitlyn swallowed. "There's a cockroach the size of my hand under my desk." She pointed with a shaky finger.

Ruth narrowed her eyes. "You're afraid of bugs."

"Yes. Um, just the big ones." Surely the admission wouldn't compromise her cover. Chloe was just as squeamish around crawly things. "This one is *huge*."

"That thing there?" Ruth pointed to the other side of the desk. The bug had crawled out and stood still on the carpet.

"Yes!" Caitlyn shrunk back even farther.

Ruth scoffed. "It's an ordinary cockroach." She approached the desk and plucked a letter opener from the cup of pens and pencils. Then she flung it at the roach like a dart, spearing the bug right in the center. A gob of puss oozed onto the rug.

"Holy shit." Caitlyn stared at her. "How did you do that?"

Ruth shrugged. "I've got good aim."

"I'll say." Caitlyn watched in awe as Ruth turned to walk back to her desk as though she hadn't done anything extraordinary.

"Leave it there and call Eugenia," Ruth called over her shoulder. "She doesn't believe we have a bug problem—maybe some freshly stabbed evidence will make the case."

"Oh. Okay." Caitlyn searched her brain. Eugenia, the director of facilities. Chloe had mentioned that they often bickered.

She returned to her chair, replaying Ruth's effortless slaying in her mind. Gross bug aside, it was incredibly hot.

The afternoon stretched on with no response to Caitlyn's message and nothing to do besides field emails and phone calls. Ruth's day was crammed with meetings, but Caitlyn hadn't been asked to take notes.

Caitlyn wished Ruth would call her into a meeting, partly to escape the phone—but also because she found herself increasingly fascinated by Ruth. She wanted more opportunities to observe before her stint as Chloe came to an end.

A few minutes before one o'clock, a young woman with curly, red hair and freckles entered the suite, clutching a Manila folder to her chest. She slowly guided the door to the closed position as though the glass might break, which was completely unnecessary. People marched in and let the doors swing behind them all the time.

At last, the woman turned to Caitlyn. "Hi, Chloe. I'm here for the meeting. I'll just wait here." She sat in the far corner of the waiting area and crossed her legs.

Caitlyn checked the next meeting on Ruth's calendar. The attendees included Beverly, Piper, and Maggie Simone, the director of research. So this had to be Maggie—but the woman before her looked too young and insecure to be a director of anything.

A quick search brought up Maggie's LinkedIn profile, confirming the woman's identity and title. Maggie had received her bachelor's degree four years earlier, so she was probably about twenty-six, which seemed quite young to be a director of anything.

Beverly and Piper strolled into the suite together.

Piper pointed at the door. "Is she in there?"

"I think so," Caitlyn said. "Unless she stepped out through the back door." As the words came out, she realized she wasn't sure the door behind Ruth's desk was an actual exit. *I hope it's not another damn closet.*

Piper didn't indicate that Caitlyn had said anything amiss, however. She walked right into Ruth's office without knocking and closed the door behind her. A moment later, she returned. "Ruth said to come in and sit down. Chloe, she'd like you to take notes."

"Oh, okay." Caitlyn glanced at the phone. If she didn't ask Gary to cover, she'd have to deal with voice messages when she returned to the desk, but she wasn't in the mood for his weird flirting. Instead, she typed a fast email:

Please cover Dr. Holloway's line for the next hour. Thanks.

After making sure to close Maggie's LinkedIn profile, she picked up her laptop and followed the others inside.

Ruth sat at the head of the conference table, now wearing her blazer even though her office was as warm as it had been earlier. "Okay. Let's get started. We're going to review retention rates for our high-risk courses and make note of any that have gotten worse since last year—or better. I suppose it's possible that by some miracle or fluke, *something* has gotten better."

Piper snickered at the comment, but no one else reacted.

Ruth turned to Maggie. "You said you have data for us?"

"Yes, ma'am." Maggie's head bobbed as she pulled a slim stack of paper from her folder. She passed a copy to Ruth first, then quickly distributed them to everyone else.

Caitlyn scanned her copy. It was a printout of a spreadsheet. Each row listed a course name, the percentage of students who had stayed in the course until the end of the term, and the increase or decrease from the previous academic year.

Ruth tapped the table with her pen as she examined the handout. "Well. As I anticipated, we still have retention problems in most of these courses. But there was a big improvement in Math 110." She furrowed her brow. "What's going on there?"

"It's Maria Stafford," Beverly said. "She taught multiple sections in the spring. The students love her, so they're more likely to stick it out. The year before, she was out on maternity leave."

"Well, that's impressive," Ruth said. "An 18 percent increase."

Caitlyn started to type the information in her notes. She checked the table to record the exact numbers and then stopped. *Wait a minute.* That wasn't an 18 percent increase.

While the group discussed math courses, Caitlyn studied the table. A pattern quickly emerged. Maggie had simply taken the difference between the two percentages.

Beverly circled something on her handout. "The English department is getting worse. Look, they had a 12 percent decrease in retention for English 201."

No, they didn't.

"That's almost as bad as history," Piper said. "Fourteen percent."

As the meeting plodded along, Caitlyn grew agitated. Every time someone said *percent decrease*, it was like nails on a chalkboard.

It wasn't Caitlyn's place to speak up. She was only there to take notes—and to pretend to be Chloe, who certainly wouldn't spot a math error. Besides, there were four other people with advanced degrees at the table. One of them should notice.

Nobody did. The conversation grated on her until she couldn't hold it in. "Um, it looks like there's a typo on the table."

All four heads turned to look at her.

"Where?" Maggie asked.

Caitlyn pointed at the handout. "The column header says *percent increase or decrease*, but that's a different calculation than what you have in the column."

Maggie blinked rapidly. "No. It's the difference between the two numbers."

"Yes, but you calculated a difference in percentage *points*. That's different from a percent increase."

Ruth scribbled in the margin and looked up. "Chloe is right. It's not a percent increase."

"Hold up," Beverly said. "Are you saying sixty-eight minus fifty-seven *isn't* eleven?"

"No." Caitlyn shook her head. "Think of the first number like a pie—"

"What?" Maggie said.

"She's saying to subtract fifty-seven from sixty-eight," Piper said. "Or… Wait."

"Oh, for the love of God." Ruth smacked her forehead with her palm. "You take the difference between the two numbers and divide it by the original. *That's* a percent increase. Chloe is right."

"Oh. I see." Piper gave Caitlyn a curious look. "Good catch, Chloe."

Maggie's face was as red as her hair. "Well, that's obviously what I meant. It's the percentage point increase."

Caitlyn felt sorry for her. *Shit. I shouldn't have said anything.* "It's an easy mistake to make—very common. If you tweak the heading to say percentage points, it will be correct."

"Yes," Ruth said, "but I'd prefer the actual percent increase from now on." She arched an eyebrow at Caitlyn. "Perhaps Chloe can show you after the meeting."

"I know how to do it," Maggie snapped. "I was just doing percentage points. That's all."

Ruth studied Caitlyn for another moment, then shook her head. "Let's move on. What happened in Music 105?"

Caitlyn looked down at her laptop, regretting that she'd said anything. She'd upset Maggie. Ruth seemed to be wondering about her. On top of that, she'd have to teach Chloe how to calculate a percent increase over the weekend.

Ruth watched in silence as her employees vacated the room.

Maggie wore a dark expression, no doubt brooding over Chloe's correction of her handouts.

Meanwhile, Chloe fled without making eye contact with anyone.

Piper stayed behind, probably sensing that Ruth wanted to debrief. When everyone else had gone, she closed the door and sat back down. "Thoughts?"

Ruth held up Maggie's handout. "How is it possible that my institutional researcher doesn't know how to calculate a percent increase?"

"Well, Maggie isn't really a researcher. That's her title, but she was hired to pull data for simple requests. From what I understand, that's all your predecessor ever asked of her. She's not an analyst."

"Fine. But please tell me why *Chloe* is the one who caught it."

"That was a surprise. Still, a percent increase isn't too complicated. I'm pretty sure my daughter studied percentages for the SAT. Maybe Chloe did the same thing. She went to college, didn't she?"

Ruth searched her memory. "I believe she has an associate's degree from LCC. But that's not the point. Why was she checking the math in the first place?" She got up from her chair and began to pace. "There's something off about her. I've noticed it all week."

"What do you mean?"

"First of all, she's punctual—hasn't been late for three days. Then yesterday, she gave me beautiful notes from the senior staff meeting. You should see them. They were organized with bullet points and links to relevant documents. Usually, she sends a couple of paragraphs, and I clean it up it myself."

"Maybe she's taking her job more seriously." Piper shrugged. "That's good, right?"

"Perhaps." Ruth sat on the edge of her desk and crossed her arms. "But it's more than that. She looks nervous all the time."

"Sounds like your ideal employee." Piper winked. "Seriously, you should talk to her. Maybe she'll tell you what's going on."

"I'm not sure that's any of my business." The thought made her warm and somewhat itchy. She tugged on her shirt and scratched her neck.

"Okay, but work is your business—talk to her about that. See how it's going for her and if she needs anything. You're her manager, so that would be perfectly appropriate."

Work. It's about work. "You're right. I'll talk to her sometime this week. But not today. I've got back-to-back meetings, and then I'm going to this colloquium...thing." She drew circles in the air in lieu of remembering the name.

"The what?"

"It's a series of talks put on by the social science faculty. I'm overdue for an appearance."

"Okay." Piper stood. "But don't put it off too long. There's no reason to be afraid of your own assistant."

"I'm not." The suggestion was absurd. There was just something about Chloe that threw Ruth off-balance, particularly in the past couple of days. "I'll talk to her," she said again. Maybe if she gained some insight, she'd feel more at ease.

Chapter 6

CAITLYN REALIZED HER MISTAKE AS soon as she walked into the room. The colloquium had attracted a crowd she could count on one hand—four older people who looked like professors, plus a fifth man plugging in a laptop. The others were busy arranging tables into a small square, apparently not expecting anyone else to attend.

She should have known. Of course an academic lecture in early June would be nearly deserted, especially at a liberal-arts college that didn't have graduate programs. *So much for hiding out in the back of the room.*

Caitlyn started to walk out when one of the professors said, "Chloe?"

Shit. The middle-aged man who approached her was a complete stranger to Caitlyn, but he obviously knew Chloe.

"You're attending the colloquium?" He kept his tone neutral despite the confusion in his gaze.

"Well, I thought—I mean, I didn't..." Caitlyn scrambled for an excuse.

His eyes widened. "Oh goodness, you don't have to explain yourself. Staff are welcome at all of our events, and we're always delighted to have new people. Especially during the break, when some of our regular members are away."

"Oh. That's good." Caitlyn slid another glance at the door. *So close and yet out of reach.*

"Here, come have a seat." He gestured to the tables. "It's an intimate group today. Kimberly brought cookies."

"O-okay." Caitlyn's heart raced as she followed him. Why hadn't she said she was in the wrong room? Now leaving would only draw more attention to the fact that she had come at all.

She gave the other faculty a tight smile as she sat at one of the tables. Was she supposed to know them? She prayed none of them had interacted with Chloe at length.

"Welcome," a tall woman with frizzy auburn hair said. "Have some cookies!" She pointed to a box of sugar cookies with rainbow M&Ms.

"Thanks." What had the man called her? *Kimberly.* Caitlyn committed the name to memory as she selected a cookie and put it on a napkin. Perhaps in a pinch, she could stuff it in her mouth and pretend to choke.

"Have as many as you want. Joe already had two." Kimberly shot a playful smile at the man who had greeted Caitlyn.

Joe. Now only two names remained a mystery, assuming the presenter was Will.

"I'll probably be good with one." The cookies were almost the size of her hand. "But thanks."

An older man peered at her through round spectacles. "I don't think I've seen you before. Are you a student?"

"This is Chloe," Joe said. "You know, Dr. Holloway's assistant."

"Hmm." His bushy white eyebrows moved up and down as he appraised her. "Welcome. I'm Ted Kahill."

"Nice to meet you." As the faculty turned their attention elsewhere, Caitlyn began to calm down. She'd made it through the greetings without raising suspicion. All she had to do was sit through the talk, remain silent during the discussion, and get out as soon as it was over. What was the worst that could happen?

"Dr. Holloway!" Joe jumped from his chair.

Oh dear mother of God.

Ruth Holloway strode toward them, a polite smile adorning her face—until she saw Caitlyn. She did a literal double take, then approached with a baffled expression.

Caitlyn's stomach lurched. "Hi."

Ruth fixed a penetrating gaze on her. "What are you doing here?"

"Um. I saw a flier, and—" Caitlyn's gaze fell on the cookies. "I heard there would be food." She looked helplessly at Joe. "It's open to staff."

Oblivious to her misery, Joe gave her a warm smile. "We're delighted to have two representatives from administration here."

"Yes. Wonderful." Ruth sat across from Caitlyn, appearing disoriented as she adjusted her blazer.

Caitlyn squirmed, now feeling guilty on top of everything else. Given the contentious relationship between Ruth and the faculty, Caitlyn imagined Ruth already felt self-conscious at these events. Her assistant's presence had made her even more uncomfortable.

I only wanted to hear the talk.

"Thank you all for coming." Will rubbed his palms together. "It's a small group today, but that means we'll have time for all of your questions." He nodded at Ruth. "It's an honor to have you here, Dr. Holloway. And your assistant, Chloe."

Ruth's gaze flicked to Caitlyn for a split second, then she looked back at Will. "I'm so glad I could make it."

Caitlyn contorted her lips into what she hoped was a smile.

"So!" Will threaded his fingers and stretched out his arms. "I'm going to present some analysis of the latest National Election Survey, in particular how views on how racial inequality relate to voting patterns…"

As Will explained his project, Ruth eyed Caitlyn with obvious suspicion. *She knows I don't belong here.* Did Ruth think she had some ulterior motive for attending? Or perhaps she wondered if "Chloe" had misrepresented herself as—well, the type of person who would never voluntarily attend an academic presentation.

Caitlyn supposed it was a blessing that the truth was so outrageous. Whatever Ruth thought was going on, she was unlikely to fathom that she was sitting across from a completely different person.

Anyway, an employee attending events on campus should be a good thing. What could Ruth do—scold her for taking an interest?

Seized with an urge to stress-eat, Caitlyn bit into the cookie. Maybe she'd have two after all.

As Will droned on about his research, Ruth fixed her gaze on the screen. She nodded here and there to show interest, but her mind was preoccupied with a completely different question.

What the hell was Chloe doing there?

In her two months of employment, Chloe had seemed utterly disinterested in the college beyond her assigned duties. From the first day, she'd presented herself as only there for a paycheck. Yet there she was, staying late to attend an academic lecture.

On top of that, Chloe looked different. Her face was fresh and open, almost a different shape, and there was something else... *Ah.* The plastic eyelashes were gone. Chloe must have removed them after work. Ruth wished she would leave them off more often so her bright, hazel eyes could stand on their own.

Snap out of it. Ruth admonished herself for contemplating Chloe's appearance when she had more pressing concerns. Who was this woman who paid attention to percentage calculations and stayed late to learn about voting rates? Where had she been for two months?

Whatever was going on, Chloe's presence raised all sorts of unnerving possibilities. Ruth had thought Chloe didn't have any friends on the faculty—except for the poetry professor, Miguel, who hung out at her desk sometimes. But when Ruth overheard snippets of their conversations as she walked past, they were usually discussing *The Bachelor* or some inane pop culture nonsense, not anything related to the college.

How did Chloe know Joe? Did she talk to Joe about Ruth? What if she was a spy, leaking Ruth's private conversations to the faculty?

Ruth recognized that her thoughts were becoming paranoid. Yet Chloe herself had acted guilty when Ruth appeared. And that line that she was there for the food? *Please.* Kimberly's store-bought cookies weren't worth staying on campus after work.

Will seemed to be meandering toward the end of his presentation. "So, for the next phase of the project, I'd like to see if similar patterns hold in congressional elections. Carmen Vaughn at the University of Maryland has done some interesting work on how voters think about candidate demographics, so that may be another factor to consider in future studies."

He flipped to the final slide, which read: *Questions?* Wiping his brow, he grinned at his tiny audience. "I'd be happy to answer your questions or to hear any feedback you may have."

Everyone turned to Ruth. Were they deferring to her out of respect? Or just curious to see if she'd manage an intelligent response? Fortunately, she had a sense of the project despite her multiple trains of thought.

Ruth cleared her throat. "Thank you for a great presentation. I especially found it fascinating that as the parties became more polarized, white Democrats adopted more liberal views on race—apparently in response to cues from elites. I wondered if your research suggests this has translated into meaningful action."

"That's a great question," Will said. "For the most part, no. But at the same time, what we think of as traditional political activism—joining local organizations and lobbying representatives for change—has been declining across the board in favor of time spent on the Internet and social media. So I suppose it depends on whether you consider a tweet to be meaningful action."

Ruth smiled. "I'd have to say no."

The others chuckled, apparently satisfied with her response.

Ted raised his hand and launched into a lengthy recitation of his political opinions. Clearly, the actual question, if there was one, wouldn't come for some time.

As he rambled on, Ruth wondered if Chloe would join the discussion. She snuck a glance across the table.

Chloe sat with her hands in her lap, gaze darting between Ruth and the faculty as if she were an unprepared student afraid she'd be called on in class.

Sure enough, Chloe remained silent throughout the discussion until Kimberly turned to her with motherly concern. "You've been quiet, Chloe. What do you think?"

"Oh, I don't know." Chloe fluttered her bare lashes. "I only came to listen."

"You're a young person. Why do you think so many in your generation have embraced views that are—what do the kids call it? Woke? Do you think it will last?"

"Um, let me think." Chloe smoothed her napkin. "I'm twenty-nine, so I'm not that young. But previous generations grew up under a less coherent party system, when racial views weren't as strongly associated with party identity. So I think it's possible that young people will maintain their views as they age, now that they're committed to a party ID—since a party tends to be stable throughout life." She laughed nervously. "But, like, what do I know?"

Ruth's jaw dropped. Where did that come from? She never would have guessed Chloe thought about politics, let alone had insightful thoughts to share.

"What I mean is that, um…" Chloe studied her hands. "Never mind. That's it."

They all stared at Chloe.

"That's a great comment," Joe said.

"Thanks." Chloe took a huge bite of her cookie.

When the talk broke up, Joe turned to Chloe with a warm smile. "I hope you'll join us next time."

"Yeah, maybe. If I have time." She shifted awkwardly, then looked at Kimberly. "Thanks for the cookies."

"You should take the rest!" Kimberly gestured at the half-full container.

"Oh, thanks, but I'm good." Chloe started to leave.

"I insist. I can't take these home, or I'll eat them! And Lord knows I don't need the calories." Kimberly slid the carton toward Chloe.

"Okay, thanks." Chloe grabbed the cookies with a grim expression and hurried toward the door.

Ruth wanted to go after her, but the entire point of attending events like this was to network with faculty. She couldn't leave without a proper goodbye.

"Thanks again for coming," Joe said. "You're always welcome at our events, and Chloe too."

"It's a wonderful series. I'm quite busy, as you can imagine—but I'll come as often as I can. If you'll excuse me, I should be getting home."

"Someone waiting for you?" Ted asked.

Ruth tensed at the transparent personal question. *None of your damn business.* She bit back her real reaction and said firmly, "Good night."

When she finally escaped to the hallway, Chloe was long gone.

Chapter 7

THE NEXT MORNING, CAITLYN STEPPED into the office, battling her nerves. She had borrowed her entire outfit from Chloe—a white blouse, plus a tight, pink skirt with a ruffled trim and a slit up the side. Her false eyelashes were back in place, itchy as ever, and her lips were sticky with bold magenta lipstick. If she'd appeared out of character the previous evening, the look would assure Ruth that her assistant was the same Chloe she'd always known—she hoped.

Ruth's door was ajar. Should she stop in and say something?

Good morning. You might be wondering why I attended an academic lecture for the first time in my entire life...

Yeah, right. Concocting some bullshit explanation would only amplify Ruth's suspicions. Instead, she'd busy herself with assistant duties until Ruth forgot the whole thing. Perhaps their paths wouldn't cross for hours, and Ruth would get distracted.

Caitlyn walked softly to the desk and set her purse on the floor without a sound. But when she sat, the adjustable chair sank beneath her, and she yelped.

She got up and used the lever to pump the chair to its usual height, then sat again and faced the desk phone. The orange lights flickered madly, and the digital envelope indicated four new messages already. Sighing, she reached for the receiver.

"Chloe?"

Caitlyn jumped and dropped the receiver back in its cradle. "Yes?"

Ruth poked her head out of her office. "Could you come in here for a moment, please?"

"Sure." Caitlyn's heart thumped as she rose to her feet. *Calm down. This could be about anything.* Forcing herself to take deep breaths, she entered the office and closed the door behind her.

Ruth sat at her conference table, wearing a sleek, charcoal blazer despite the warm temperature. "Please close the door and have a seat. I'd like to talk to you."

Caitlyn's palms sweated as she lowered herself into a chair across from Ruth. The closed door only made her more nervous. What was this about?

Ruth looked her right in the eyes. "I was surprised to see you at the colloquium last evening."

Oh God. Caitlyn felt like a student hauled into the president's office to explain some delinquent behavior. "I'm sorry if I wasn't supposed to go."

"Nonsense," Ruth snapped. "All staff are encouraged to attend events at the college. You know that."

"Oh, okay. Sorry." Caitlyn squirmed.

"Stop apologizing. I just wanted to know what inspired you to attend. How did you hear about it?"

"I saw a flier at Kravings, and I thought the topic sounded interesting." The defensive edge in her voice surprised her. Then, for reasons beyond her immediate understanding, she opened her mouth again. "Are you implying that I'm not smart enough to go to a social science talk?"

Ruth's fair complexion turned red and blotchy. "Of course not. I'm an educator. I don't even believe in *not smart enough.* I was merely surprised because you've never mentioned an interest in the topic."

"Well, you don't know me very well." What was she doing? Why did she care what Ruth thought of her—or, rather, of Chloe?

"I suppose you're right." Ruth's cheeks cooled to a rosy pink. "That's my fault. In fact, I've been meaning to check in with you."

"Oh." That sounded ominous. "Um, about what?"

Ruth shifted in her chair. "I wondered how you've been finding the job."

"It's fine." Where was this going?

"You and I haven't had a chance to talk since you started—what was it, two months ago?"

"That's about right." Caitlyn didn't actually know Chloe's start date, but she figured the real Chloe could have easily forgotten.

"I should have asked earlier, but is there anything I should know as your supervisor?"

"L–like what?"

"Do you have any questions or concerns?"

"Uh, let me think for a second." What would Chloe say? Caitlyn thought back to how Chloe had described the job—and Ruth. *Bitchy. Kind of awful.* She certainly wouldn't relay that feedback to Ruth. Besides, it wasn't accurate. While her first impression of Ruth had been terrible, Caitlyn had realized it was wrong. She would never agree with everything Ruth did as president, but she no longer saw her as a hack on a power trip. Ruth genuinely wanted to help her students.

As a supervisor, Ruth was distant and hands-off. She didn't give much feedback, perhaps because she was always rushing to the next meeting. But her treatment of Caitlyn had been professional, not patronizing as Chloe had described it.

"I'm doing well," Caitlyn said. "Answering the phone can get tedious, but that's the job. I appreciate that you invite me to take notes in meetings sometimes because it gives me a chance to learn more about the college."

"Good." Ruth paused. "To be honest, you haven't seemed interested in the college—well, until the past few days."

Right. Chloe probably spent those same meetings scrolling through Instagram, pausing to type an occasional half-formed note. "I'm sorry if it seems that way. I guess I've had a lot on my mind."

"Yes, I noticed that you've been jumpy lately." Ruth furrowed her brow. "Ever since Monday, actually. I hope everything is okay."

Oops. Caitlyn hadn't been as inconspicuous as she'd hoped.

"I want you to know that if you need accommodations, you can talk to me—if you like."

Accommodations? Was Ruth making a subtle reference to the medication Caitlyn had dropped at her feet? Caitlyn was afraid to ask, but she was touched that Ruth had framed the issue as one of accommodation, rather than treating Caitlyn's anxiety as a problem.

"Of course, you're under no obligation to share anything personal with me," Ruth added quickly. "I just want you to know that, well, I'm here."

The depths of the concern in Ruth's eyes startled Caitlyn. "I appreciate that. Truly. I don't need anything right now, but it's good to know that I can come to you if that changes."

"Well. Good." Ruth clapped her hands. "If there's nothing else, I'll let you get back to your desk."

"Okay, thanks." Caitlyn started toward the door, the tension draining from her limbs.

"Chloe?" Ruth called after her, an odd note in her voice.

Caitlyn stiffened and held her breath as she turned around. "Yes?"

"I'm worried I gave you the impression that I disapproved of you attending the colloquium. That's not the case at all. The faculty were delighted to have you, and they were impressed with your contribution to the discussion—as was I. You are welcome at any event on this campus. I want to make that absolutely clear."

"Thank you. That's good to know."

Interesting. Chloe was right, in a sense, that Ruth didn't know her well. But she was wrong that it was because Ruth didn't care.

Caitlyn returned to her desk and found a new email notification on her phone. She tapped the icon. A response to her post on the Harvard alumni board! Someone named Jonathan Tharp had sent her a private message:

Hi, Caitlyn, I work for the deputy COO in the office of Federal Student Aid. Your sister can reach me at...

He provided his email address and office phone. Harvard had come through.

Grinning ear-to-ear, Caitlyn navigated to Chloe's work email to send Ruth the information. Then she stopped. Ruth didn't know Chloe had a twin—so how could she explain it?

She opened a draft window and slowly typed her message, backspacing and tweaking her wording until she settled on an explanation.

Hi, Jonathan,

My older sister sent me your contact information. Thank you so much for responding to her request. Here at Pulaski College, we have a promising student who has been blocked from receiving financial aid due to unique circumstances in his home country, and we're hoping you can direct us to someone in your organization who can help. I'm CC'ing my boss, Ruth Holloway, who will send more information.

Sincerely,

Chloe Taylor

There. She'd managed to avoid mentioning Harvard or her real name. And Caitlyn had been born first, so technically, the email wasn't a lie.

Well, except for the signature.

The clock had barely moved a millimeter since Caitlyn last checked. She had hoped the new contact at the Department of Education might make the day more interesting, but instead, she was trapped in a long, monotonous afternoon. While Ruth had responded to thank "Chloe" for Jonathan's contact information, Caitlyn had no idea if they'd communicated. In fact, she'd barely seen Ruth, who had been in meetings for most of the afternoon.

The doors to the suite swung open, and a man with a grumpy expression marched in. His thinning, brown hair and prominent jowls triggered Caitlyn's memory.

Steve Stubbons. Caitlyn recognized him from the photos Chloe had shown her. Steve was a professor of something she couldn't recall and the president of the faculty council.

"She ready?" Steve asked.

Would it kill you to say hello? Or tell me what you're talking about? "One moment, please." Caitlyn checked Ruth's calendar. There was a meeting with Steve called *Scheduling concerns.*

"I'll let her know you're here." Caitlyn picked up her phone and dialed Ruth's extension.

"Yes?" Ruth sounded tired.

"Hi. Steve Stubbons is here."

There was a pause. "Please tell him I'll be a few minutes." Her voice was tight.

"Sure thing." Caitlyn hung up. "She's not quite ready."

"Figures." Steve sat on the edge of a chair, hunching forward to rest his elbows on his thighs. After about a minute, he stood and paced the waiting area, muttering under his breath.

While she pretended to focus on her computer screen, Caitlyn watched out of the corner of her eye. Something about Steve gave her the creeps. He appeared angry about a meeting that hadn't even started.

After a couple of minutes, Ruth emerged. "Hello, Dr. Stubbons."

He puffed out his lower lip. "You're late."

Caitlyn glanced at her phone. It was one whole minute past the hour.

Ruth narrowed her eyes. "Good afternoon to you too."

Steve stalked past Caitlyn's desk into the office.

Before she followed, Ruth shot Caitlyn a grim look. Then she entered the office and closed the door behind her.

Ick. Caitlyn tried to recall what Chloe had said about Steve. Not much, just that he was likely to appear in the office from time to time. There had been no mention of the hostility coming off him in waves or the fact that Ruth appeared to dread spending time with him.

Soon, raised voices sounded through the wall. Caitlyn couldn't make out most of the words, but the contempt in Steve's voice was palpable.

Ruth argued with him. Her tone was firm, but she kept her volume in check—to Caitlyn's frustration. She wanted to know what Ruth was saying.

Steve's voice grew louder as he scolded Ruth. Something about "into the ground" and "fucked it up." He sounded like an abusive parent.

Caitlyn clenched her fingers until her nails dug into her palms. *Who does he think he is?* He had no right to yell at Ruth. Whatever his complaint, nothing justified this behavior.

I should go in there. She could make up some reason—a phone call, a question. Any excuse to get between Steve and Ruth. As the argument escalated, the urge to intervene became overwhelming.

Where were these protective instincts coming from? Ruth was an adult and the president of the college, more than capable of looking after herself.

Caitlyn started to get up, then sat back down. *Just stay out of it. Ruth doesn't need you to save her.*

"Your days are numbered," Steve said. Every word was loud and clear.

That's it. Caitlyn jumped up. *I'm going in there.*

"I don't respond to threats," Ruth snapped. She crossed her arms, refusing to get up from the conference table despite Steve's efforts to goad her into a standing confrontation.

Steve loomed over Ruth's chair and jabbed the air with his finger. "It's not a threat. I'm telling you what will happen."

The door burst open, causing them both to jump.

Chloe walked in. "Excuse me."

Steve whirled around.

"I'm so sorry to interrupt," Chloe said, "but someone is on the phone from the governor's office. He said it's urgent."

Ruth pushed a strand of hair out of her eyes. Her pulse was racing from the argument, and now she had to speak to the governor? "Oh—okay. I'd better take it, then." Security threats swirled in her mind. Terrorism? A tornado?

Steve turned back to Ruth with flared nostrils. "Are you kicking me out?"

"I need you to wait outside while I take this call." Ruth stood. "It could be confidential."

Chloe held the door for Steve, who trudged back into the lobby.

Ruth took deep breaths, attempting to compose herself as she reached her desk and picked up the phone. "Ruth Holloway." A dial tone sounded in her ear. She looked down, and none of the call lights were on.

The door clicked shut, but Chloe was still in the office.

"Nobody's on the line." Had the governor given up on her already? It had only been a minute.

"I know. Nobody called." Chloe shifted from one foot to the other with a guilty expression.

"Excuse me?"

"I just thought—well, I thought someone should interrupt. He was screaming at you."

Ruth stared in disbelief. Chloe had come to *rescue* her? "I can take care of myself."

"Oh, I know." Chloe wrung her hands. "I know you can. It was an impulsive decision, I guess. I'm sorry if I overreacted." Beneath the fake eyelashes, her eyes shone with concern.

Chloe was worried about me. A warm feeling spread through Ruth's chest. "Perhaps it was for the best. I can't say I'm sorry for a break from the spittle flying in my face." She took a long sip from her water bottle.

"Would you like me to get rid of him?" Chloe gestured toward the lobby.

The thought of being done with Steve for the day was too appealing to resist. "Yes, tell him we'll have to reschedule. And then please come back in here for a minute." Ruth sank into her chair at the conference table.

Chloe opened the door and poked her head out. "Dr. Holloway must attend to a pressing matter, so she won't be able to finish your meeting. Please send any further thoughts over email." Without waiting for a response, she pushed the door closed.

Imagining Steve's reaction to the cold dismissal brought Ruth cheer. "Have a seat." She gestured at the chair to her left.

Chloe walked over and sat gingerly in her tight, pink skirt, which parted along the side to reveal a stretch of her tan thigh.

She's so lovely. The thought bubbled up unbidden, and Ruth shook her head to banish it. *God, I need to get a grip.* The stress was getting to her.

Chloe shifted and tugged on the fabric. The outfit clung to her like a costume. While Chloe's wardrobe had once seemed appropriate for her personality—if not for the office—Ruth had come to see a different side of her in recent days, one that suggested the flashy clothes were part of an act. A fun persona to hide her serious, self-conscious side from the world.

"I'm sorry if I overstepped." Chloe smoothed the skirt.

"It's okay. Steve can be…"

"An asshole?"

The blunt language took Ruth by surprise. "While that's not what I was going to say, it is apt."

"He's horrible." Chloe scrunched her face in disgust. "I couldn't believe how he spoke to you."

"Really? You're still surprised? I know you've heard Steve pitch tantrums in here before."

"That's what I meant," Chloe said quickly. "It seemed worse than the other times. I heard him say your days are numbered."

"Yes, he did use that cliché. But he wasn't threatening my life, just my job. He said he'd have the faculty vote 'no confidence' in me and that the board would fire me after that." Ruth's blood pressure climbed again.

Chloe's chin rose sharply. "Why would they vote no confidence?"

Ruth rolled her eyes. "Oh, take your pick. I'm spying on them because I've asked them to take attendance. I canceled summer classes with fewer than five students enrolled. I won't make a bunch of new full-time hires that we can't afford. And in this case, he's angry that I won't approve him teaching overload in the fall."

"Overload?" Chloe looked perplexed.

"It's when faculty teach extra courses—more than their contracts require—and get paid an obscene rate for it. But we don't have the budget. If I approved everything the faculty want, Pulaski would go bankrupt. Hell, we might go bankrupt anyway."

Chloe's eyes widened. "I know enrollment is down, but is it that bad?"

"Yes—and it's not just us. A lot of liberal-arts colleges are struggling. We don't have a Rolodex of wealthy donors like universities with business schools, and we can only raise tuition so much without compromising access—or saddling the students with debt they could never repay. That's why I work so hard on recruitment and keeping students in school. Our survival depends on it. But people like Steve won't face reality. He thinks throwing more money at instruction will solve everything." The recitation of the college's problems, combined with the heat, was suffocating. Ruth shrugged out of her blazer.

Chloe frowned at her lap, appearing deep in thought. "It's one thing to… I mean, even if he thinks instruction should be prioritized—which I can understand—he shouldn't get to come in here and bully you like that. You're the president. You're his boss."

A dry laugh escaped Ruth's throat. "That's not how he sees it. Steve Stubbons has tenure, not to mention faculty support. There's nothing I can do to him—not really. Meanwhile, if the faculty vote no confidence, there's a good chance the board will decide I'm not worth the headache." It was strange to confide in Chloe the day after Ruth had freaked out upon finding her sharing cookies with faculty at the colloquium. But whatever her relationships with other faculty, Chloe's actions had proved that she had little regard for Steve.

"I suppose I can see why he feels invulnerable," Chloe said, "but nobody should have to deal with behavior like that. Are you sure you can't file a complaint or something?"

"Yes, I'm sure." Ruth could only imagine the hell Steve would raise if she involved Human Resources.

"Well, it's up to you. But maybe next time you meet with him, I can stay in the room. You can say that you want me to take notes. Or I could interrupt every few minutes, and we could have a signal if you want me to invent another fake emergency."

Ruth's heart swelled at the offer. *She really cares.* "That's kind of you, Chloe. I'll keep that in mind."

Chloe gave her a shy smile. "I guess I should get back to my desk."

"Right. And I've got emails to answer—including one from Jonathan Tharp, by the way." After the kerfuffle with Steve, she'd almost forgotten to thank Chloe in person. "I sent him the details about Amari's case, and he promised to look into it, personally."

Chloe's face lit up. "Oh wow. That's amazing."

"Yes, we got lucky with him. How did your sister know Jonathan anyway?"

The change in Chloe's posture was stark and immediate. She sat up straight, shoulders pushed up, and curled her fingers into her palms. "They went to the same university."

Ruth should have let it go, given Chloe's obvious discomfort, but curiosity won out. "What university?"

"Harvard." Chloe's cheeks flushed.

"Oh?" Ruth couldn't hide her surprise. "Well, please be sure to thank her for me."

"I will." Chloe slid off the chair and hustled to the door, perhaps hoping to flee before Ruth could ask any follow-up questions.

"Thanks again," Ruth called out as Chloe left.

Ruth stared at the open door, trying to make sense of the conversation. Chloe obviously hated to talk about her older sister, but why? Did the sister's achievements make her feel insecure? It was another piece that didn't fit the puzzle—a puzzle that was beginning to preoccupy Ruth.

For weeks, Ruth had barely noticed Chloe. Now that she'd started paying attention, each day brought new clues that there was far more to Chloe than she'd realized. Beneath the surface, she was thoughtful and interested in the college.

Most surprising of all, Chloe had stepped in to help her, and she'd seemed to genuinely care about Ruth's challenges as president. It was tempting to see Chloe as a new ally, but Ruth couldn't afford to let her guard down—not when she still didn't understand the enigmatic woman who sat outside her office, apparently looking out for her.

After work, Caitlyn walked along the footpath that wound through the small campus. The sun was high, and the air was humid, like a sticky hug.

Behind the student services building, she happened upon an abstract sculpture fountain. Two copper chutes coiled around each other like water slides and came together near the bottom, where a gentle stream poured into the pool below. Caitlyn sat on a concrete bench in front of it.

As she listened to the soft gurgling, she tried to make sense of the incident in Ruth's office. Clearly, the power dynamics at the college were different from what she had first assumed. Ruth had a doctorate and a college presidency, and yet she didn't feel empowered to hold Steve Stubbons accountable for his abusive behavior.

If the board didn't have Ruth's back, nobody did. How could she govern an institution when she lacked job security, and everyone knew it?

While Caitlyn didn't agree with Ruth's attitude toward faculty, she was beginning to understand it. Ruth felt personally responsible for keeping the college solvent, and to her, that meant wise spending and working to retain students. Meanwhile, the faculty wanted investment in their programs and total autonomy; no wonder they acted like enemies.

But did it have to be this way? Surely, the faculty had an interest in boosting enrollment and retention. After all, a financial crisis would impact everyone. Why couldn't faculty and administration work together on solutions?

Caitlyn decided there was plenty of blame to go around. Ruth should have secured buy-in for her initiatives. If she didn't treat the faculty like partners, she couldn't expect cooperation. Academics were notoriously stubborn—Caitlyn had seen it in graduate school countless times. To get anything done, they had to be coddled and nudged along.

Then again, perhaps faculty like Steve made it impossible. He obviously loathed Ruth, and he was the leader of the faculty council. Maybe Ruth was doomed to have an adversarial relationship with faculty as long as he was there.

Caitlyn's phone rang in her purse. She was surprised to see Chloe's name on the screen. "Hi, what's up?"

"How's it going?" Chloe sounded perky. "Is work still okay?"

Caitlyn glanced around to ensure no one was listening. "Yes. I admit I haven't been perfect, but no one has guessed that I'm…well, not you."

"Great. I'm so glad it's going well."

"How is Nick?"

A dreamy sigh filled Caitlyn's ear. "He's wonderful. I think he's my soul mate."

That's what she'd said about Jacqueline too. Caitlyn prayed Chloe wasn't rushing into something before she really knew him. "Tell me about him. What's he like?"

"So, first of all, he's hilarious. He makes me laugh all the time. And he's so considerate. Like, he goes out of his way to make sure I'm comfortable."

"All of that sounds good." Caitlyn hoped it wasn't an act. Anyone could be considerate for a few days.

"Anyway." Chloe paused. "He asked me to stay a bit longer."

The phone nearly slipped from Caitlyn's grasp. "What do you mean? How long?"

"Um, we didn't put an end date on it. But we want more time together, and he said I can stay as long as I want."

Oh no. "What about your job?" Had Caitlyn really done this for nothing?

"I'm letting it go. It was so sweet of you to cover for me, but I can't ask you to work there forever."

"I don't mind staying longer." The words escaped Caitlyn's lips before she could think them through. What was she saying?

"Seriously? I thought you'd be miserable working for Ruth."

"Well…" Caitlyn tried to make sense of her feelings. "Actually, I'm not. She can be difficult, but I'm beginning to understand her."

"I'm glad it hasn't been horrible. But I really don't think I'll be back. Nick and I agreed that I could take a break from work for a while, until I find something I'm passionate about doing."

A break from work? Caitlyn cringed at the thought of Chloe becoming financially dependent on Nick. "Are you sure that's a good idea? I know you're getting along, but you've only spent a few days together."

"I'm sure. I know it's fast, but I feel really good about him. So if you don't mind, I'd like you to do one last thing for me. I'd appreciate it."

Oh no. "What is it?"

"It's nothing bad. I just need you to tell Ruth that I'm resigning," Chloe said breezily. "You can wait till the end of the day if you want to get paid for it. Oh, and bring home my makeup. I left some good shit in my desk."

Caitlyn tensed as she imagined telling Ruth she was quitting with zero notice. "Are you sure that's a good idea? Maybe you could send an email over the weekend."

"Wait! Are you afraid of her?"

"Of course not. I just don't want her to pressure me to stay."

"Oh, I doubt that will happen. Ruth doesn't think very highly of me. She'll probably be delighted."

"Yeah." Maybe that had been Ruth's opinion last week, but Caitlyn had already started to change it. Another thought occurred to her. "Have you told Mom that you're staying with Nick?"

"Not yet. I'll tell her soon. We're going to FaceTime tomorrow so Mom can meet Nick. I want to get through that first. Then I'll tell her."

God, Mom is going to flip. "Well, it's your decision."

"Yep, it is." Chloe's tone was light but firm. "Anyway, I'd better go. But I can't thank you enough for holding my job for me when I thought I'd be back. I owe you one. And I'll send you the money as soon as I get paid, okay? Love you, sis."

Caitlyn swallowed. "Love you too."

The line went dead.

Caitlyn sat with her phone in her lap, staring at the fountain. One of the coils had a small dent that sent a steady stream of droplets off course—an imperfection or perhaps the artist had done it on purpose. As she watched the water, she tried to tease out why she felt so down.

For one thing, she would miss Chloe. They weren't as close as they had been as kids, but the summer could have been an opportunity to spend more time together—one that might not come again, depending on where Caitlyn ended up next year.

It was more than that, though. She was also sad for Ruth, who would lose her assistant without notice. Despite Caitlyn's mixed feelings about Ruth's leadership, she didn't want to blindside her. Plus it had only been a few hours since the incident with Steve. Afterward, she and Ruth had shared a moment of genuine connection. Caitlyn had even offered to be an ally in future meetings—and now she'd be quitting the very next day. She didn't want Ruth to think her support had been fake, and the idea that Ruth might think otherwise made her feel awful.

On top of everything, Caitlyn felt sad for herself. Her four days at Pulaski had provided a rare window into leadership at a liberal-arts college, and she was sorry to see it end.

The only upside was that she'd finally have time to deal with her actual career. Aside from acquiring library books, she hadn't made much progress. Meanwhile, the job market wasn't going to get any easier. She needed to stop worrying about Chloe's job and get her head in the game.

Chapter 8

It was Caitlyn's last day of work in a position that wasn't even hers, but she still didn't want to get caught slacking—her authority-pleasing tendencies were too deeply ingrained. So she waited until Ruth stepped out before she phoned Gary.

"Ah, the lovely Chloe," Gary said in sing-song. "How may I be of service?"

Yuck. Caitlyn wouldn't miss that voice. "Hey, could you cover the phone for a while?"

"Sneaking out already? Is this a coffee break or a social call?"

"Gotta go." She hung up, then silently answered his question. *It's a goodbye.*

Miguel's office door was ajar with the light on. Caitlyn nudged it open and found him hunched over his laptop, forehead creased in concentration. She knocked on the doorframe. "Hey."

He looked up and broke into a grin. "Hi, Chloe!" The sparkle in his eyes confirmed he knew her actual identity.

Rolling her eyes, Caitlyn stepped inside and shut the door. "Yes, it's me, Chloe, the worst executive assistant in the history of Pulaski."

"Oh, come on. Chloe isn't the worst ever." Miguel's tone was playful, but an earnest note reminded her that Chloe was his friend.

"Hey, I love my sister. I'm not trying to disparage her. But come on—she left town and sent her twin in her place."

"Okay, fair enough." Miguel laughed. "That's pretty bad. But you're a good double, so it's not like she abandoned the job."

"Yes, well, I'm retiring. That's why I stopped by. You probably know already, but Chloe asked me to quit at the end of the day."

He looked stricken. "She did?"

Oops. Chloe hadn't told him. "Yeah, sorry. She called me yesterday and told me she's staying in Boulder to spend more time with Nick."

"Shit. How long?"

"Indefinitely. I'm not happy about it, but I can't make her come back. If you want to try to change her mind, you have my blessing." Caitlyn kept her voice casual, but part of her hoped Miguel would try.

"Damn. I'm going to miss her. I'll miss both of you."

"I'll miss you too. You've been a good friend—to both of us."

Miguel opened his desk drawer. "Since it's your last day, I'd like to give you something." He held out a slim book with a goofy grin.

"What's this?" Caitlyn stepped forward.

"My poetry." A slight blush appeared on his cheeks. "You don't have to read it, you know, if you don't want to."

"Are you kidding? Of course I'll read it." Caitlyn accepted the book. The cover said, *Sun Song* over an abstract swirl of yellow and gray. She flipped past the title page and saw the dedication: *For Preston.* "Thank you so much."

"You're welcome. So, are you going to tell Dr. Holloway in person?" His grimace suggested he could guess how Ruth would react to the news.

"Yeah. I'm not looking forward to it, but it's the right thing to do. I'll tell her at the end of the day." Caitlyn's gut twisted. *It's going to be awful.*

"Oof." Miguel winced. "The board meeting is today, so she's going to be in a terrible mood."

"Why? Does she hate board meetings?"

"I'd imagine. People use them as a forum for their various complaints, and Ruth has to sit there and listen, which can't be fun. But today…it's going to be a bad one."

Caitlyn's pulse quickened at the thought of Ruth dealing with a bunch of hostile comments. "Why will it be bad?"

"I shouldn't say anything." He covered his mouth as though the gossip were fighting to escape.

"C'mon, what? I won't blab. Who could I even tell?"

"Okay, okay." Miguel took a deep breath. "You didn't hear this from me, but the faculty council president is planning to *obliterate* her in his remarks today."

Faculty council… "Wait, do you mean Steve Stubbons?" The name tasted vile in her mouth.

"Actually, yeah." He cocked his head. "You've met him?"

"Unfortunately. He threw a tantrum in Ruth's office yesterday." Just thinking about it made Caitlyn queasy. "But what do you mean, he's going to obliterate her? How do you know this?"

"There was a meeting last night. I'm not on the council, but the meetings are open to everyone, so I went—just for something to do, really. Anyway, Steve came in ranting about how Dr. Holloway denied his overload request. He said it was time to embarrass her in public so she stops taking us for granted."

"Shit. Do you know what he's planning to say?"

"Yup. He made charts about our enrollment, showing that it's declined on her watch. He's blaming her for canceling courses, saying that she's punishing faculty she doesn't like and driving away students in the process."

"Ruth said something about canceled courses too."

"Yeah, she implemented a new rule. A class needs a minimum of five students, otherwise it gets canceled—unless there are special circumstances, like it's an upper-level course required for a major."

Caitlyn tried to remember the smallest class she'd had as an undergrad. "Five doesn't seem like a lot."

"No, but sometimes Steve has trouble getting enough students because—well, because they think he's an ass. Anyway, he's going to give a speech about how it's all Ruth's fault that enrollment is down. Then he's going to say that faculty will consider a no-confidence vote in the fall. Of course, the main person considering it is Steve." Miguel rolled his eyes. "But saying those words will get press attention."

Caitlyn felt nauseous. "Does she know about this?"

"No. Someone from faculty always speaks at these meetings, but she won't know what he's going to say."

Unless someone tells her. "When is the board meeting?"

"It's at one o'clock. Why? Do you want to go?"

"No. Maybe." Caitlyn's brain buzzed with ideas and arguments that Ruth could use—if she knew what was coming. "What if I warned Ruth? I wouldn't mention you. I'd just give her a heads-up and help her prepare a response."

Miguel's eyebrows flew up. "Seriously? You want to help her? I thought you were on team faculty."

"In some ways, yes. But I hate the way Steve talks to Ruth. It's one thing to disagree on policy, but ambushing her is slimy, and it's obviously personal. I mean, do you really believe Ruth is personally responsible for enrollment trends?"

"Of course not—we had the same problems before she arrived, and she's been trying her best."

"Then please, let me tell her." Caitlyn's heart pounded. She was desperate for him to say yes, especially since she wasn't sure she could keep it from Ruth either way.

"Oh gosh. I don't know. There were about twenty people there last night, so they wouldn't be able to prove it was me. But if anyone found out I leaked…" He mimed a knife slicing his throat. "Steve would make my life hell."

"I swear, I won't tell Ruth who told me. I just want her to be ready to talk about enrollment and canceled courses. That's all." She gripped the book tightly. "I already feel bad about quitting—not to mention that I've been fooling her all week. Please let me help her. It's the least I can do for her on my last day."

Miguel rubbed his forehead. "Okay, okay. You can warn her."

"Really? Are you sure?" Caitlyn felt obligated to ask since she'd pressured him into it, but she prayed he wouldn't take it back.

"You can't tell anyone how you know." Miguel locked his gaze on her. "Promise me."

"I won't tell a soul. I swear." Caitlyn's heart raced with the energy of a new purpose. "I should go—I need to find Ruth. If I don't see you before the end of the day, thanks for everything."

"Good luck." Apprehension hovered in his gaze.

"Bye!" Caitlyn rushed out of Miguel's office and pounded down the steps to the exit. A warm breeze whipped through her hair as she power-walked back to the administrative building.

She arrived at the suite out of breath and marched straight into Ruth's office.

It was empty.

Shit. Caitlyn returned to her desk and plopped into her chair with so much force that it rolled backward. She scooted forward and quickly typed in Chloe's password.

Ruth had added an off-campus meeting to her calendar, scheduled to last until noon. Even if she stopped back at the office before the board meeting, there wouldn't be enough time for Ruth to prepare a meaningful response to Steve's presentation.

Unless I help her.

It wasn't Caitlyn's place to get involved. As Ruth's assistant, she should stick to answering the phone. On top of that, she wasn't really Ruth's assistant. But what was the harm in exploring some data?

Caitlyn jumped out of her chair. She roamed up and down the halls, surreptitiously scanning name plates until she found it: *Maggie Simone.*

An *xkcd* comic adorned the door, which was propped open with a rubber stopper. Inside, Maggie sat with her elbow on the desk and her chin resting on her fist.

"Hi, Maggie? Are you busy?"

Maggie's head jerked up. "Uh, kind of. Why?"

"Sorry, but Ruth—Dr. Holloway—needs some data right away. She had to leave campus for a meeting, so she asked me to convey her request."

Maggie's eyes narrowed. "Dr. Holloway asked *you?*"

"Well, yes. I work for her." Another lie.

Sighing, Maggie gestured to the extra chair behind her desk. "Okay. You can have a seat."

"Thanks!" Caitlyn sat and gave Maggie a wide smile. "So, the first thing she needs is total enrollment by term for the past five years."

"She already has that. I give that to her every term."

But I don't have it. "Hmm. She asked for that data specifically. Maybe she misplaced what you sent earlier."

"Are you sure? It looks like you didn't take notes." Maggie shot a pointed glance at Caitlyn's empty hands.

"Oh. Well, I happen to have a photographic memory." She shrugged. "It's a blessing and a curse." It seemed like something someone with a photographic memory might say.

"Fine." Maggie typed something. "That's it?"

"I'm afraid not. She also needs the list of courses we ran last term, the capacity of each course, and the number of students enrolled."

"Uh, okay." Maggie grudgingly scribbled on a sticky note.

"So can you run those queries and send me the data? I'm sure Ruth can figure out what she needs."

"Ruth? I doubt it. There are different codes, like…" Maggie made a frustrated gesture. "It's complicated, and Dr. Holloway isn't a data person."

"Yeah, I don't know about all that—but Ruth told me to get the data, and I think we'd better do what she said. You have my email, right?"

Maggie glowered. "Obviously."

"Thanks so much." Caitlyn rose to her feet. "I'll let Ruth know you're working on it."

Yet another lie—but it was for a good cause.

Ruth took a massive bite of her sandwich, then pushed open the door with bread hanging from her face. Mouth too full to speak, she waved at Chloe as she walked toward her office.

Chloe got up and scampered after her, toting her laptop.

Ruth swallowed and wiped her mouth. "What's wrong?"

"I need to talk to you about something."

"Can it wait?" Ruth yanked off her comfortable flats. "I've got a board meeting in half an hour, and I wanted to head over early."

"That's what I need to talk to you about. Steve Stubbons is planning to sandbag you with a big presentation about enrollment."

"Wait. What?" Ruth froze, her foot hovering over a pointy high heel. She looked up. "Who told you this?"

Chloe's face was drawn with worry. "Steve talked about it at the faculty council meeting last night. I can't say who told me, but I heard it directly from someone who was there."

Now Chloe had sources on faculty council? Feeling off-balance in more ways than one, Ruth sank into a chair at the conference table. "Sit. Tell me what you heard."

Chloe sat next to Ruth and placed her laptop on the table. "Steve made a whole presentation about the enrollment decline. He's going to blame it on you—saying it's all because of canceled courses and denied overload requests. Then he's going to say faculty are considering a no-confidence vote."

"I see." Ruth balled her hands into fists. *God, what an asshole.* He'd probably get fawning press coverage too, as a brave faculty member fighting for academics, when he was really a bully who only cared about himself. *But Chloe sees the truth.* "Thank you for telling me. Unfortunately, he can say whatever he likes. But at least it won't be a surprise."

"Do you have any thoughts on how you might respond?" Chloe asked.

"Yeah, sure. I'll hit all my usual notes—the recruitment initiatives, retention, everything we're doing to turn it around." Ruth had the talking points memorized.

"That sounds good. But I thought you might want some data." Chloe's voice wobbled. "So, um, Maggie and I worked on some slides."

"Slides?" Ruth repeated the word without understanding.

Chloe opened her laptop and angled it toward Ruth. "We thought maybe you could use this."

On the screen, a line graph showed the enrollment declines at Pulaski plotted against the overall trend at other Illinois colleges and universities. Pulaski tracked closely with the statewide trend, except in the previous year when it had actually fared a bit better. "Maggie did this?" Ruth stared at Chloe. "I don't understand."

"Yeah, Maggie ran a few queries, and I think she got the rest of the data from the Illinois Board of Higher Education." She fidgeted as she watched Ruth anxiously.

"But the formatting—it looks professional." Usually, Maggie made amateurish charts in Microsoft Office with all of the default colors, fonts, and grid lines. The chart before Ruth was clean with neat labels, like something from a journal or a book. Ruth doubted Maggie was capable, but who could have done it?

Chloe averted her gaze. "Well, I helped with that part—making it look pretty."

"But how? This doesn't look like PowerPoint."

"It's just some free software. Don't worry—I didn't download anything shady. Here, we also looked at course capacity versus enrollment." Chloe hastily flipped to another chart, as though hoping to distract Ruth from her questions.

It worked. Ruth gaped at the slide titled *Average course utilization by term*. It had the same clean formatting and labels, but this time with blue columns showing the value per term.

"See, utilization has declined over time." Chloe pointed to the screen. "You're allowing smaller classes to run, even though it costs more money."

"These numbers came from Maggie too?" Ruth had never seen anything like it at Pulaski.

"Uh-huh." Still avoiding eye contact, Chloe tapped the keyboard again. "We also made a list of the smallest classes that ran last term and the number of students. I don't know the reasoning behind all of these courses, but you certainly haven't been stingy."

Ruth stared at the slide. Steve would lose his mind if she came prepared with a rebuttal like this, but could she trust the information? Chloe was obviously exaggerating Maggie's role in the presentation, but then who had done the rest? It couldn't be Chloe's work...could it?

It was almost one o'clock. Ruth didn't have time to figure it out. "How certain are you that these numbers are right? I can't present this to the board unless I'm sure that it's accurate."

"Well, look at the numbers. You should be familiar with at least some of the data, even if you haven't seen it presented exactly like this. Does it match your expectations or not?"

Ruth scanned the list of small classes on the screen. She remembered each one since she had granted special permission to run them. "May I?" She gestured at the keyboard.

"Of course."

Toggling back to the previous slide, Ruth thought about how the schedule had changed since she'd been at Pulaski.

"We double-checked everything." Chloe met her eyes. "You can trust me."

For some reason, Ruth did trust her—despite her evasive answers about the origin of the presentation. Ruth's gut told her Chloe was on her side. "Okay. I need to get moving. Could you print these out for me?"

"Already done. The printout is on my desk." Chloe pulled a flash drive out of her pocket and set it on the table. "I also put the presentation on here, in case you're allowed to use the projector."

"Of course I am. You came with me last month when I presented on the budget. Don't you remember?"

"Oh, that's right." Chloe tugged on her hair. "I forgot."

Now Chloe was back to acting spacey? *God, whatever. I need to move.* Ruth plucked the flash drive from the table. "Will I recognize the file name?"

"It's the only file on the drive. Here, I'll get the printed version." Chloe jumped up.

Ruth watched Chloe scurry out of the office. *She thought of everything.*

Chloe returned seconds later with a stack of paper. "I made two copies in case you want to share." Her eyes sparkled. "Like, maybe you could share them with Steve."

Ruth cackled as she slid the charts into her bag. "Perhaps I will." She stepped into the abominable high heels and started toward the door.

"Good luck," Chloe said.

Ruth leveled a serious gaze at Chloe. "When the meeting is over, we're going to talk about where this really came from. But for now…thank you."

Chapter 9

RUTH PURSED HER LIPS AND nodded along as Zachary presented the budget report. The tedious recitation gave her a chance to ruminate.

She didn't believe for one second that Maggie was behind the presentation. Maggie might have helped with access to the data, but the sleek visualizations were beyond her capabilities. Could the mysterious faculty member who had tipped Chloe off have helped? At first she'd assumed the leak was Chloe's friend Miguel Fumero, but poets weren't known for their data visualization skills. Perhaps one of the social science faculty was involved?

It was possible, but Ruth's instincts told her otherwise. Chloe's nervous body language, combined with her earnest assurance that the numbers were legitimate, strongly implied she was responsible. But where had she learned those skills? And why was she suddenly invested in Ruth's presidency, after weeks of sporadic attendance and indifferent performance?

Meanwhile, Steve Stubbons smirked at her from the front row of the section reserved for faculty—a section that was nearly empty since most faculty considered themselves to be on summer break. It brought Ruth cheer to know that one of Steve's faculty friends had leaked his plan to Chloe. Perhaps some of them were catching on to his act.

At last, the trustees reached the standing agenda item called *Faculty Update*. If Steve was going to speak, this would be the time.

Sure enough, Steve stood and whispered something to the board's secretary, Ramona, who operated the laptop and projector.

Soon, a table appeared on the screen, showing Pulaski's enrollment over the past five years.

Ruth sucked in a breath. *Chloe was right.*

Some of the observers murmured to each other, and Zachary shot Ruth a dirty look. He probably thought she should have shut Steve down ahead of time—as if she had that kind of power over faculty. It was an unlikely miracle that Ruth was even prepared to respond.

"Good afternoon." Steve surveyed the sparse audience. "We are days away from beginning a summer term with the lowest enrollment in four years. This trend is of grave concern to the faculty, and we have done all we can to reverse it." He shot a pointed glare at Ruth. "Unfortunately, our college leadership has contributed to the decline."

From there, Steve launched into a tirade about course cancelations, arguing that every canceled class drove students away from the college. The cancelations had deprived students of intimate seminars. Worst of all, faculty were forced to teach tedious general education courses instead of their preferred topics.

As he blathered on, Ruth watched the faces of the board members. They were all frowning, except for Brian Skylar, who appeared absorbed in his phone. Zachary's jaw churned as though chewing an invisible wad of gum.

Steve flipped to a garish PowerPoint slide titled *Failed Strategy*, Steve accused Ruth of hacking away at instruction so she could divert funds to extracurriculars and the much-maligned career center. "Faculty have attempted to address the enrollment crisis with Dr. Holloway, but she refuses to listen. If we don't see instruction prioritized, the faculty will consider a vote of no confidence." He paused as though the audience needed time to absorb his dramatic announcement, then leaned into the microphone. "Thank you."

Typically, Zachary responded to the faculty update with a few remarks. As he reached for the microphone in front of him, Ruth clicked her microphone on. "May I respond?"

"Please." Zachary sat back.

Ruth flashed a warm smile at Ramona. "Could you please pull up the slides I gave you?"

"Yes, ma'am." Ramona tapped the laptop, and Steve's presentation disappeared from the screen.

While she waited, Ruth couldn't resist a quick glance at Steve.

His eyes were wide. He hadn't expected Ruth to have a response ready—let alone slides.

When Chloe's first slide appeared on the screen, Ruth turned to address the board. "It's true that our enrollment has declined in recent years, largely due to external economic and political factors. However, please note that colleges throughout Illinois experienced the same decline—and in fact, since I arrived two years ago, Pulaski has fared better than the statewide average."

Zachary's mouth quirked into something resembling a smile.

Ruth turned to Ramona. "Next slide, please? Thank you. We cancel courses that don't have enough students, as long as equivalent courses are available. But as you can see, the average utilization rate has declined each year that I've been president. In other words, classes are smaller than ever. This means that each year, we spend *more* money on instruction per pupil than we did the previous year."

Ruth nodded at Ramona, and the final slide appeared. "Finally, these are the smallest classes we ran last year. They all had five students or fewer. I share Dr. Stubbons's concerns about enrollment, but the idea that it's a consequence of cuts to instruction couldn't be further from the truth."

When she finished, Ruth turned to Steve, noting with satisfaction his red face and bugged-out eyes. "Dr. Stubbons, I hope you will correct any erroneous statements you may have made to the faculty council. Furthermore, I'd ask any faculty who are concerned about low enrollment to make sure they participate in my retention initiatives—such as recording attendance in GradesFirst." She turned back to Zachary with a sweet smile. "Thank you for the time."

Zachary broke into a grin, then quickly suppressed it. He cleared his throat. "Thank you, Dr. Holloway, for that clarification. I believe this should put any concerns about the class schedule to rest. Will you make the slides available so we can include them in the board report?"

"I'd be delighted."

"Good. I believe our next agenda item concerns the cafeteria contract."

Ruth sat back, basking in her victory. Zachary was pleased. Steve was livid. It couldn't have gone better.

Now it was time to figure out what the hell was going on.

Caitlyn saw the whole thing. She watched the live video feed at her desk, letting the phone ring and ring.

Her shoulders tensed when Steve began his little speech. It was exactly as hostile as she'd anticipated, not to mention unfair. He'd obviously never dug into the data beyond the fact that enrollment was down—and the formatting was hideous. *Nice slide, jackass.*

Then Ruth, serene as a summer breeze, asked if she could respond. She spoke with her shoulders back and her chin raised, waving her elegant fingers as she enunciated her points. Her performance was poised and professional. Only the spark in her eyes betrayed her delight at the opportunity to demolish Steve's presentation.

God, this is hot. Caitlyn fanned herself as she gazed at the screen. She couldn't help it—smart women kicking ass were her kryptonite.

When Ruth finished, Caitlyn bounced in her chair, incapable of sitting still. She had made a real impact on the discussion and possibly on Ruth's presidency. The thought that her analysis had helped Ruth made her giddy.

As the meeting wrapped up, however, Caitlyn's excitement faded. Soon, Ruth would return to the office, and Caitlyn would have to answer questions about the origin of the slides.

For a moment, Caitlyn allowed herself to fantasize about taking credit. *It was me. I crunched the numbers and made the slides. I'm actually trained in quantitative research. I have a PhD...*

Warmth spread through her as she imagined Ruth's eyes gleaming with gratitude. *You did this for me?*

Shaking her head, Caitlyn banished the daydream. Telling the truth was impossible. She wouldn't put Chloe at risk by even hinting at what they'd done. Not to mention, Caitlyn was the one wearing a badge with a false name. She could be arrested, and then she could impress everyone on her prison cell block with her fancy degree.

She would stick to her story: Maggie had done most of the work. Hopefully, Ruth wouldn't get a chance to talk to Maggie until next week, when Caitlyn was long gone.

The harder question was how to break the news that "Chloe" wouldn't be back on Monday—or ever again. Every time Caitlyn imagined the conversation, she felt queasy. She didn't want to let Ruth down, and she didn't want to leave.

Ruth swept through the doors with flushed cheeks and beads of sweat on her forehead. "It's too hot for this damn suit."

"Oh, yeah. I bet." Caitlyn held her breath as Ruth neared the desk.

Ruth walked right past her. A moment later, she returned with her feet clad only in stockings. "I'm going to freshen up. Then we'll talk."

"Okay." Caitlyn's mouth had gone dry. She took a swig of her water and waited.

Ruth was most likely using the private restroom connected to the back of her office; she'd return any second.

Should I go in? Or wait to be summoned? Caitlyn hated ambiguous instructions, the bane of any perfect student. After a minute, she got up and tentatively approached Ruth's office. She hovered just beyond the door until Ruth reappeared.

"Come in, come in." Ruth gestured at the chair beside her desk. "Have a seat." She'd ditched the blazer, revealing a sleeveless cream top that clung to her breasts. While she appeared more comfortable, her skin glowed with a lingering heat.

Caitlyn tried to appear calm as she sat down, but she couldn't stop fidgeting. Finally, she clamped her right hand with her left in an effort to be still.

Ruth sat next to her, angling her desk chair so they faced each other. She crossed her legs and pushed her bangs out of her face. "So."

Was that Caitlyn's cue to explain? "Um. I watched the board meeting on the video feed. You did a great job." It came out in an oddly high pitch.

"Yes. Thanks to you—and *Maggie*." Ruth gave her a pointed expression.

"Um, yeah." Caitlyn squirmed and averted her eyes. "We were happy to help."

"Look at me," Ruth said sharply. "Who made the slides?"

Caitlyn reluctantly met her gaze. "What do you mean? I already told you." She was blinking too much, a combination of nerves and the damn fake eyelashes, but she couldn't seem to stop.

Ruth tilted her head. "So if I call Maggie right now, she'll tell me the same thing?"

Oh shit. Caitlyn swallowed. "Uh-huh."

"Good. Let's give her a call, shall we?" Ruth watched Caitlyn closely. "In fact, I'll ask her to stop by so I can thank her in person."

It was a trick. Caitlyn held her breath, determined not to cave.

Ruth picked up the phone and tapped the speaker button, filling the office with the sound of a dial tone. "Let's see, what is Maggie's extension?" She opened a drawer and pulled out a piece of paper. "Ah. Here."

Caitlyn felt like a criminal sweating under bright lights while an unflappable detective threatened to call her bluff.

Beep… Boop…

"Okay, okay!" She held up her hands. "Don't call her. I'll tell you the truth."

"I'm listening." Ruth crossed her arms.

Caitlyn took a moment to catch her breath, while her brain scrambled for a way out. She couldn't deny what she'd done, but maybe she could downplay it. "When I heard what Steve was planning, I went to see Maggie. I asked her for some data, and I did a couple of basic calculations and made the slides."

"Okay." Ruth sat back, appearing relieved that she had an answer, but nowhere near satisfied. "Where did you learn how to do this?"

"Nowhere. I mean, I took a math class in college, and I'm pretty good with Excel." She shifted and scratched her arm. "Anyway, I just aggregated the data and calculated some percentages. It's not advanced econometrics or anything."

"No." Ruth squinted. "You did more than that. You asked the right questions, and you knew which data to request. Then you presented the information in a way that refuted Steve's claims—and if I have the correct timeline, you did it in a couple of hours. That's more than knowing how to use Excel."

Warmth rose in Caitlyn's cheeks at the compliment. But she had to focus. "You're right. I like to learn on my own—searching the web, reading articles and tutorials, things like that."

"You studied data analysis and graphing software in your free time? Why?"

Fuck. Why would Chloe study those topics outside of school?

Caitlyn decided the safest strategy was to stick to Chloe's actual biography. "Well, you already know that I stopped after my associate's degree. Originally, the plan was to transfer to a four-year college and get my bachelor's degree. But I had this girlfriend, Jacqueline. She was a musician."

Ruth's head jerked up at the word *girlfriend*, but she quickly adopted a neutral expression.

Welp, I came out to Ruth. Or Chloe did. Caitlyn pushed her instinctive anxiety aside; Ruth was far too intelligent to be a homophobe, and besides, Chloe wouldn't be back. "Anyway, Jacqueline convinced me to travel with her band. I was on the road with her for almost a year. When she dumped me, I was broke and had loads of credit card debt, so I had to work—and with every year that went by, it seemed less likely that going back to college was something I would ever do." An unexpected sadness came over her. While Chloe had never cared much for academics, she would have loved the four-year college experience. It was a shame that she'd never gone.

"I see." Ruth's expression remained skeptical.

"But even though I didn't have an institutional affiliation, I didn't let it stop me from learning. I mean, the Internet exists. And I'm smart enough." Caitlyn looked past Ruth out the windows, where a lone student walked on the cobblestone path with a stack of books in his arms. "All I ever wanted was to belong to a community of scholars that wanted me. But if that wasn't possible, I could still read and learn."

"Well, that's admirable. But why didn't you say anything before?"

Caitlyn looked back at Ruth. "What do you mean?"

Ruth scratched the back of her neck. "Why didn't you tell me you had an interest in data?"

"Because I'm your assistant. You didn't hire me to analyze data, so why would I bring it up?"

"No." Ruth wagged her finger. "Come on, it's more than that. Until recently, you've acted like—well, you know what I mean. Not terribly interested."

Thanks, Chloe. Caitlyn fumbled for an explanation. "That's true, but... um...it's a defense mechanism. Sometimes, I'm insecure about not having more of a formal education, so I sort of put on an act." Her voice came out high-pitched and hesitant.

"Hmm." Disapproval darkened Ruth's eyes. "Don't downplay your intelligence ever again. Especially not with me."

"Okay. I promise I won't." *Because I'm quitting my job, and you'll never see me again.* Caitlyn had to tell Ruth somehow, but the words didn't come.

Ruth slapped her thighs with both hands. "Well then. Now that I know what you can do, I'm not going to let those skills go to waste. I'd like you to work with me on our retention strategy. We're trying something new this year, and I need to know if it's effective. Maggie will get you the data you need."

Caitlyn imagined having a wealth of student data to slice and study in different ways. It was a sociologist's dream, and she had to say no. *Why is Ruth making this harder?* "That sounds amazing. But the thing is—"

"Don't give me excuses. I know you can do it, and I need your help. You bailed me out today, but I have to do something about enrollment. I need hard data on the attendance initiative so I can show the whiners that it works."

Whiners meant faculty. There was that attitude again. This was Caitlyn's last chance to say something, and she decided not to waste it. "Look, presenting data isn't going to get the faculty on your side. If you want them to support your initiatives, you need to include them in the planning. Otherwise, you'll always be the out-of-touch administrator encroaching on their turf."

Ruth blinked at her. "Where is this coming from? I didn't think you were on their side."

"There are no sides! That's what I'm saying. Sure, you have a few jerks like Steve, but you also have professors who care. They'd be willing to help if you approached them in the right way."

"And what is the right way?" There was an edge to Ruth's tone, but her gaze was curious.

"You need to bring them in at the beginning. Ask for their opinions. Instead of ordering them to take attendance, tell them the problem and come up with a solution together. You'll get buy-in if they feel like they were part of the process. Plus you'll be a lot more popular if faculty know you respect their experience—and their expertise."

For a moment, Ruth didn't speak, and Caitlyn worried she'd said too much.

"I never thought my assistant would tell me how to run my college," Ruth said finally.

Caitlyn flinched. "I'm sorry—"

"I especially never thought she'd be right." Ruth regarded Caitlyn with something like wonder.

"Oh." Caitlyn offered a shy smile.

"The question is what to do about it." Ruth picked up her iPhone and tapped the screen. "I'd like you to schedule a meeting on Monday for the two of us. Right now, I've got a hold on my calendar until eleven. You can schedule it for nine or ten, whichever you prefer."

"I…" *I won't be here because I'm resigning.*

"I need to map out a strategy for faculty engagement on the retention issue, and I'd like you to help. There's no need to prepare anything in advance. We can brainstorm together and go from there. I want you to be a thought partner with me on this."

Partner. Ruth—the president of an entire college—wanted Caitlyn to work with her as an equal. Caitlyn had a wild urge to give Ruth a hug.

"But…" Caitlyn whispered. It was excruciating. Ruth's proposal was like a dream, and she had to quit instead. But she didn't have a choice, did she?

Ruth looked up from her phone. "Don't be scared. I know this is outside of your normal duties, but I need you. You seem to have insight into how the faculty think, but you're not faculty yourself—and you're not one of the administrators who constantly sucks up to them. You're someone I can trust. You proved that today. So, can I count on you?"

I'm moving away.

I found another job.

She meant to say it. She really did. But what came out of her mouth was, "Yes. You can count on me. I'll be there."

———

Caitlyn found her mom curled up on the couch, knees pulled up to her chest. *Her anxiety is bad today.* For the hundredth time, Caitlyn wished her mom would see a psychiatrist, but it would be pointless to bring it up again.

"Hi." Caitlyn squeezed her mom's shoulder and sat on the other end of the couch. "Did you talk to Chloe and Nick?"

"Chloe told me she's staying in Colorado." Her mom didn't look up. "She said you already knew."

Caitlyn winced. That explained it. "Yes, but only since yesterday. She said she wanted to tell you herself."

At last, her mom raised her head. Worry lines creased her forehead and the skin around her eyes. "I'm concerned."

"I know. Did you see Nick? What did you think?"

"He seemed nice, I guess. It's hard to say. They told me he's going to pay for everything. I guess he's not concerned that she's leaving her job after less than two months."

"Um, about that." Caitlyn shifted to the side and pulled her legs onto the couch. "Chloe asked me to resign at the end of the day, but I didn't. They're expecting me—well, Chloe—at work on Monday."

"What?" Her mom sat up. "You're going back next week?"

"Maybe?" It came out in a squeak. "Yes. I said I would."

Her mom's eyes brightened. "Oh, this is good. If you hold on for another week, Chloe will have more time to think. Who knows, by this time next week, she could be on her way home. Whatever she's saying now, it's much better for her to be employed."

"Uh-huh. Right." Except the longer Caitlyn spent working with Ruth, the harder it would be for Chloe to take her place. *What a mess.* How had she gotten in so deep in only a week?

"So, are you going to tell Chloe that you haven't quit yet?"

"Yeah." Caitlyn let out a long sigh. "I can't exactly hide it. She'll notice when she keeps getting paid. In fact, I'd better call her before she posts photos of Colorado on Instagram. I'll do it right now."

"Good idea. And maybe—I know we can't push too hard, but maybe you can talk to her about coming back."

"Okay." Caitlyn got up and walked toward the stairs.

"Caitlyn?"

"Yeah?" She turned around.

Her mother gave her a grateful smile. "I appreciate you doing this for your sister. And for me. I know it's a lot of work and not what you wanted to be doing this summer. But it means a lot to me."

Caitlyn managed a lopsided smile before she turned around, hoping her mom didn't detect the guilt in her eyes. She didn't want to explain that she wasn't staying for Chloe, but for Ruth—and for herself.

Caitlyn decided a conversation like this should be face-to-face or at least the closest substitute. She settled on her bed with her laptop and held her breath as she tapped the video icon.

After a few seconds, Chloe appeared in a kitchen, wearing a sleeveless top with hoop earrings and her hair in a messy bun. Her cheeks were rosy, and her smile was carefree. "Hey! We're making dinner, but I can talk for a minute. What's up?"

"We? Is Nick with you?"

"Hi, Caitlyn," a male voice said. The picture blurred, and Nick appeared, chopping zucchini on the counter. He set down the knife and approached the camera. "Wow. You look like Chloe."

That's what identical means. "I guess I'll take that as a compliment. What are you making?"

"Flat bread with pesto and vegetables." He gestured proudly at the pile of chopped vegetables behind him. "My personal recipe."

"Sounds great." Caitlyn tried to assess the man who had inspired Chloe to leave her job and family behind, but she couldn't glean much.

Chloe turned the camera back to herself. "Nick is an amazing cook. Plus he's a vegetarian, so everything's healthy." She raised a glass of red wine to her glossy lips, completing the picture of a leisurely summer evening.

"That's good." Caitlyn couldn't help the pang of jealousy as she watched from her childhood bedroom. It had been ages since Caitlyn had been on a grown-up date with anyone. With her future in limbo, she had no idea when dating would even be a realistic possibility.

"So, how did it go with Ruth?" Chloe asked. "Was she pissed? I bet she was."

"Um, about that…" Caitlyn tensed, preparing for her sister to flip.

"What?"

Just say it. "I didn't quit."

Chloe giggled. "You couldn't face her, huh? I know she can be scary. Don't worry—I can send her an email from here."

"No. I'm saying I don't want to quit."

"Wait, what?" Chloe's smile collapsed. She turned her head, looking past her phone. "I'm going to the living room."

The camera captured a short hallway and then a navy-blue couch. Chloe plopped down and held her phone in front of her face. "What do you mean, you don't want to quit?"

"Um." Caitlyn's voice cracked. She swallowed, but her mouth and throat were dry. "Your job is actually interesting. I'm learning a lot about how a college administration functions, and Ruth—well, we're getting along better than I expected. So if you don't mind, I'd like to take your place a little longer."

Chloe looked baffled. "You...what? Did Mom put you up to this? I know she wants me to come home, but she can't expect you to—"

"No. This is coming from me. I really want to stay for a little while longer."

"Wow. I never imagined you'd like it there." Chloe's forehead creased. "I don't know what to say. You did me a big favor by taking my place, especially after you went through a hard time with the job market. If you're getting something out of it, of course I want to support you. It just complicates things for me. Like, I can't post any pictures of me and Nick on Instagram because I'm not supposed to be in Colorado."

Caitlyn had expected an argument. Instead, Chloe was already entertaining the idea—for Caitlyn's sake, not her own. *She's a good sister.*

Guilt gnawed at Caitlyn. She'd spent the past few hours thinking of herself, trying to figure out how to persuade Chloe to allow her to stay so she could impress Ruth. She should have been thinking about Chloe too.

Wait, that's it. Maybe the arrangement could benefit them both. "How about this? We can split your salary. You keep half of your net pay and send me the rest. That way, you'll still have an income in Colorado, and I can keep helping Mom with expenses."

Chloe perked up. "Really? You'd do that for me?"

"Of course! It's a good deal for both of us. You deserve some of the pay since it's your job, after all." *Plus you won't be financially dependent on Nick.* Even if Chloe didn't come back to Linvale, helping her maintain some independence was a worthy cause.

"Well, okay. If you really don't mind, we can keep up the twin switch a little longer."

"Thank you." Caitlyn exhaled as some of the stress left her body. "I appreciate it."

Chloe shook her head. "I can't believe you're thanking me for the chance to work at my crappy job. I guess you're more interested in higher education than I am."

Caitlyn leaned back against the headboard. "Honestly, it's a fascinating place. I could do a sociological study of how faculty function as a collective, and the incentives—"

"Stop! This is getting too nerdy." Chloe laughed. "So, how long are you thinking of staying there anyway? Another week, or...?"

"Let's just see how it goes. For both of us." Of course, she couldn't hang out in Chloe's job indefinitely. But it was only June.

"Okay. Well, the extra income will be nice. And Miguel will be happy too."

"Oh yeah?"

"He likes you. He lit up my phone about quitting, but he also said he would miss talking to you."

"I like him too. Actually, most of your coworkers are nice. But what's the deal with Gary Baker? When you told me about him, you didn't mention his creepy crush on you."

"Oh, him." Chloe made a grossed-out face. "Soon after I started, I realized he's more agreeable when I'm nice to him. Unfortunately, he gets... excited." She pointed to her mouth in a gagging motion.

"Well, as the new you, I seem to have inherited his affections. How nice were you, exactly? And is really worth it to avoid listening to a few voice messages?"

Chloe shrugged. "Maybe not. Just ignore him, I guess." She sat up with a cheery smile. "Well, I'd better get back to helping Nick."

How convenient. "Okay. Have a nice dinner. I love you."

"I love you too."

Caitlyn ended the call and flopped backward onto the mattress.

Relief coursed through her as she stared at the ceiling. Pulaski gave her a real, if temporary, sense of purpose, and she was grateful she hadn't already lost it. Most importantly, she wouldn't be forced to let Ruth down—at least not yet.

Chapter 10

I NEED CAFFEINE. RUTH HAD only been at the office for ten minutes, but already she regretted her halfhearted resolution to cut back. As she scrolled through the usual onslaught of Monday morning emails, her thoughts were sluggish and uninspired.

A soft tapping sound interrupted her stupor—either a weak knock or her imagination. Could it be Chloe? They had a meeting, but it wasn't scheduled for another thirty minutes.

"Come in!"

The door opened, and Chloe and took a tentative step into the office, wearing a loose magenta dress with sandals, her hair secured in a low ponytail. Her face looked soft and open.

Ruth spotted the reason. *No false eyelashes today.* She realized she was staring and tore her gaze away. "Good morning."

"Sorry to interrupt." The sandals squeaked as Chloe shifted from one foot to the other. "I know you said not to prepare anything for our meeting, but I was wondering if there are any documents I should print for reference—such as the standard faculty contract or the course schedule. Or anything else that might help."

Once again, Ruth marveled at the change in Chloe. A few weeks ago, she hadn't even looked up from her phone when Ruth passed by the desk. Now she hovered and asked for extra work. "This is more of a brainstorming session, so we shouldn't need reference materials. But I wouldn't mind an iced latte." She opened her wallet and retrieved a few bills. "It's already hot in here. Would you mind taking a quick walk and getting something for both of us?"

"Oh gosh. You don't have to pay for mine." Chloe clasped her hands behind her back and bit her lip. "In fact, it's my turn to pay."

"Nonsense. I'm not such an awful boss that I'd let my employee buy me lattes." Ruth held out the cash with a firm nod. "Consider it a tip for the errand."

Chloe accepted the money with a sheepish smile. "Okay. Thanks." She scurried out and closed the door behind her.

Ruth smiled to herself as she returned to her email. Knowing that caffeine and Chloe were on the way, she already felt more energized.

Twenty minutes later, Chloe returned with Ruth's iced latte.

"Thank God." The ice cubes sloshed gently in the cup, and beads of condensation slithered down the sides. Ruth lifted the straw to her lips and sucked in a generous sip. "Ah. Heaven."

Spots of pink had appeared on Chloe's cheeks. She took a teetering step back. "Well. I guess I'll wait at my desk."

Ruth chuckled. "Okay, okay. I can tell you're ready to go. Let's start." She pushed back her chair and stood.

Chloe brightened. "I'll grab my computer." She returned a moment later with her laptop and an iced latte of her own.

"No whipped milkshake today?"

"Oh. Um." Chloe glanced at her drink. "I got tired of those."

"There's no need to be nervous." Ruth winked. "This might even be fun."

That earned a smile. Chloe walked over to the table and started to sit.

"Actually, you can sit over there, in front of the board." Ruth gestured to the white board that hung on the far wall.

"Oh, okay." Chloe quickly resettled.

Ruth set her drink on the table but remained standing. She uncapped a dry-erase marker and began to scribble on the board. "We have two related problems—low enrollment of new students and low retention of existing students. We've made progress on recruitment, thanks to a new director and increased outreach at the high schools. But retention hasn't budged. As you pointed out on Friday, we need a strategy that includes faculty from the beginning. So what are our first steps?"

Chloe rested her elbows on the table. "I know it's a cliché in academia, but I think we need to form a committee."

"Oh God, another committee." Ruth let out a long-suffering sigh. "We already have so many. But I suppose you're right. We need to engage the faculty consistently and in person."

"You can call it a working group if that makes you feel better. Or a task force."

Ruth grinned. "An action team?"

"A project crew," Chloe countered.

"Mission club."

Chloe tapped her chin. "A goal gang?"

Ruth chuckled. "That's the one. But only between us. We'll call it a working group in public."

"Fair enough." Chloe's eyes sparkled.

It was refreshing to joke with someone at work besides Piper. Ruth had to watch her words around most administrators and faculty since anything could be taken out of context and used against her. But Chloe had proved her loyalty last week, and that meant Ruth could relax a little.

"So how do we pick the faculty? I don't want—well, you know." Ruth took a sip of her drink.

"Steve Stubbons and his asshole friends?"

Ruth stifled a spit-take. "You said it. Not me."

"Why don't we ask for volunteers? We might get a few spies or people who want to complain, but I bet there are people out there who want to help. They just don't get asked."

"Hmm." Ruth raised the marker, then lowered it. "Steve Stubbons will expect to be consulted."

"Fuck Steve Stubbons." Chloe clapped her hand to her mouth. "Sorry."

Struggling for composure, Ruth wondered how she'd missed this side of Chloe. She shouldn't approve of cursing directed at a faculty member, but she couldn't help liking it. "Again, I said nothing."

"Noted." Chloe lowered her hand. "But seriously, why don't you send a mass email? Most faculty aren't on the council. I don't think they'd appreciate missing out on an opportunity because Steve Stubbons anointed himself the keeper of goal gangs." She spoke in a mock authoritative voice and rolled her eyes.

Ruth finally lost it laughing. "Okay. It's official." She wiped her brow. "We'll send a mass email to faculty. Who else needs to be there?"

"Student services, for sure."

"Definitely." Ruth added it to the board. "And financial aid."

"For a retention strategy?" Chloe tilted her head. "I assumed they would focus on new students."

"True, but some of our students lose their eligibility for aid. Or they encounter new hardships, and they don't realize all of their options."

"Interesting." Chloe tapped her keyboard. "I'll do some reading."

"And, of course, the vice president." Ruth kept her tone neutral in case Chloe didn't share her negative opinion of Alice Stewart.

"Absolutely," Chloe said. "Alice needs to be there."

So, they do get along. Good to know.

"If we put her on the work group, she can't complain about the results," Chloe added. "I'm pretty sure I read that in *The Art of War*."

Or not. "Excellent point. Anyone else?"

"Hmm." Chloe drummed the table with her fingertips. "Maybe we should keep it small. We don't know how many faculty will come, and God knows it's hard to keep even a handful of academics on track for an hour."

"Very true, although I must say, it's sad that you've picked up on that after only a couple of months."

Chloe's head jerked up.

"What?" Ruth asked. "What's wrong?"

"Nothing." Chloe shook her head, causing her bangs to swish back and forth. "I just wondered when we should have the first meeting. A lot of faculty aren't around in the summer, and—this is just a guess—I wonder if they consider summer off-limits for committee work."

"Oh yes. Breaks are sacred. I used to feel the same way when I was faculty. Of course, now that I only get two weeks off per year, I find it rather difficult to sympathize."

"Well, they need time for research." Chloe spoke with a defensive edge.

There it was again, Chloe's inexplicable sympathy with the faculty perspective. Was it all Miguel's influence? "Sure. Some of them do fieldwork or write articles." She added under her breath, "The ones who aren't deadwood anyway."

"Does that mean we have to wait until fall?" Chloe looked crestfallen.

She's so eager. This must mean a lot to her. Ruth supposed Chloe was desperate for challenging work. "Don't worry. We don't have to wait. We're not forcing anyone to attend over the summer."

"Oh, good." Chloe relaxed.

"But we also don't want to meet too soon, before we're prepared. Let's aim for the end of July. That will give us a head start, so we don't spend the whole fall semester starting a committee. Often by midterm, it's too late for some of these students who have fallen behind."

Chloe nodded. "That's why you started the attendance initiative."

"Yes. But I don't know if it will be successful."

"Right. You mentioned that." Chloe typed something on her laptop. "I'd like to do some research. Today is the first day of the term, so data should be coming in."

"What do you have in mind?"

"Well, this is the first time it's mandatory for faculty to record attendance, right? But you don't expect everyone to participate, so maybe we can look at course outcomes for faculty who use the system versus those who don't—controlling for other factors, like whether it's an upper-level course."

Ruth wrote *attendance study* on the whiteboard. "It's a good idea, but I can tell you right now that faculty won't like it. You said I need to earn their buy-in. Calling out the delinquents will only make them more defiant in the future."

Chloe frowned. "Good point. Maybe I can look at trends over time." She typed a few more words. "I'll figure something out."

"That would be wonderful." Ruth loved the idea of a formal study showing the results of her initiative. She could already picture the professional slides that Chloe would produce. "Maggie can show you how to export the data. I'll send an email so she knows the request came from me. You can present some data to the group."

"Maybe." Chloe's determined expression dissolved, and she began to fidget with her fingers.

"Don't be scared," Ruth said. "If you're capable of producing impressive slides, you've got to learn how to present them too. This will be important for your career."

"Okay." Chloe still appeared uneasy but didn't argue. "When exactly will the first meeting be? I know you said the end of July, but do you have a more specific date?"

"I'll look at my calendar and pick something later today. Would you like to draft the email invitation? Then I'll make some edits and send it out." Ruth could have drafted it herself, but she wanted to find out if writing was one of Chloe's secret skills.

"Sure, I can write a draft." If Chloe was intimidated, it didn't show.

"Good. I think that's all for today. Once we have RSVPs, we'll huddle to make an agenda."

Chloe closed her laptop and stood but made no further move to leave.

"Something else?"

"I was just wondering when you're going to contact Maggie about the data. Like, will it be today or...?"

Ruth regarded her with amusement. "Excited to start?"

Chloe blushed. "Kind of. Yeah. I mean, of course I'll still answer the phone and everything."

"I had no doubt."

"But this is more fun."

"Well, I'd hate to delay your fun. I'll email Maggie right now."

"Thanks!" Chloe broke into a wide smile before she hurried out.

She's so cute.

Ruth blinked. Where did that come from? *Must be exhaustion.* She shook her head and took a long sip of her iced latte.

Caitlyn poked her head into Miguel's office. "Hi."

"C... Chloe?" Miguel squinted at her.

She glanced around the hallway, then shook her head.

Caitlyn? he mouthed. "What are you doing here?"

"So, a lot has happened since we last spoke." Caitlyn stepped inside and closed the door behind her. "Can I sit down?"

Miguel gestured impatiently at a chair. "What is it? Tell me."

"First of all, the board meeting. How much have you heard?"

"Oh my God." He dropped his head into his hands, then peeked through his fingers. "Steve is so pissed that Holloway was ready for him. He's on a witch hunt to find out who leaked."

"Oh shit. Does he suspect you?"

He sat back up, shaking his head. "Thankfully, no. I'm new, and I'm not the type to get involved in politics. Right now, his top suspect is Jenn Christiansen, which makes no sense. Jenn clashes with Dr. Holloway as much as anyone—she has zero interest in helping the administration."

"So why does he suspect her?"

"Because Jenn and Steve hate each other. And because, well—"

"She's a woman," Caitlyn said bluntly.

"Yeah." Miguel grimaced. "Steve thinks women are more prone to gossip."

"Of course he does." *Sexist jerk.*

"Anyway, I'm sure you and I have been seen together on campus, but I doubt he's observant enough to make the connection. Why would you care about any of this stuff? He certainly won't suspect you of making those PowerPoint slides." Miguel paused. "Those were amazing, by the way. I watched the video later. I can't believe you did all of that in a few hours."

Caitlyn shrugged. "I'm an assistant with many talents."

"What did Ruth say? She must have been floored."

The memory of Ruth's reaction made Caitlyn warm. "She was surprised, obviously—and glad to be prepared for the meeting. But her gratitude went beyond the work I did. More than anything, she seemed happy someone was looking out for her."

"I'm sure. I'd imagine she feels isolated most of the time."

"I think she does. After the meeting, we talked. At the time, I thought I would never see her again, so I was frank. I told her what I think about her talking down to faculty when she should be consulting them from the start. And she actually *agreed* with me. She asked me to work with her on a retention strategy—one that will involve the faculty from the beginning."

"Whoa." He covered his mouth. "Holy shit."

"Yeah, and I get to look at data too. I couldn't say no. How could I resign after an offer like that?"

"Uh. Well." Miguel appeared at a loss.

"I know, I know. This isn't really my job. But I want to help Ruth as much as I can. Chloe said I can work here a little while longer. She'll stay off the radar in Colorado while I work here, and I'll split the income with her." Hearing the words out loud, Caitlyn realized how it must sound. Absurd. Reckless. At best, a waste of time. No wonder Miguel wasn't enthused.

"How long are you going to do this?" he asked.

"I don't know." She fussed with a loose thread on her dress. "It's hard to explain, but I'm not ready to leave. Ruth and I met this morning, and it was really cool. The president of a college asked for my opinion. And I love working with her. She can be fun, like…" She searched for the word.

"Fun, eh?" He crossed his arms and leveled a knowing gaze at her.

Heat rose in Caitlyn's cheeks. "Okay, she's smart and hot. I'm only human. But I'm in it for the intellectual…you know."

"Stimulation?" he said dryly.

"Something like that. But also…she believes in me, you know? I sent my academic work to sociology departments all over the country, and nobody was interested. Meanwhile, Ruth doesn't even know I have credentials, but she still wants my input."

"Well, I don't think it's a good idea. Okay, that's an understatement. But I'm here for you. Let me know how I can help."

"Actually, you can—and it will help you too. We're going to send out an invitation for a retention working group. I'd love for you to join. It will count as service to the college." She searched his face for a sign of interest.

Miguel rubbed his chin. "I have to admit, it sounds perfect for my tenure file. I just hope it doesn't conflict with my class."

"Send me your schedule, and I'll make sure it doesn't."

"Really? You have that kind of power?"

Caitlyn wasn't sure, but she owed Miguel. "I update Ruth's calendar—plus I could always pretend I have some personal conflict with your class time. Whatever it takes, I will make sure you can come."

"Well, in that case, you can count on me to attend."

Caitlyn exhaled in relief. *He's in.* "Thanks. I'm really glad." She rose to her feet. "Anyway, I'd better get started on that email."

"Okay. Just…" He held back whatever he'd been about to say. "Just be careful, okay? With all of this."

"Sure, I will. See you later." As she left his office, doubt wormed through her. Was she underestimating the risk?

Her pulse spiked as she imagined herself in handcuffs and an orange jumpsuit, desperately wishing she'd quit after the first week instead of pushing her luck.

That won't happen. No one had questioned her identity in the first week, when she'd had to fake her way through the days. Now she knew names and faces and where to buy lunch. As long as Chloe stayed in Colorado, no one would see Caitlyn as anyone else.

Ruth's stomach gurgled. *Food. I need food.*

She had managed to ignore the hunger pangs when her last meeting ran past one o'clock, but now her body begged for sustenance.

She swiveled in her desk chair and kicked off her shoes, then turned back to her computer. Perhaps wading through the latest batch of emails would distract her while she waited for Piper to arrive with lunch. One caught her attention:

Draft invitation to faculty.

Chloe had already written something?

As she double-clicked the message, Ruth hoped Chloe had produced something usable. The invitation to collaborate on a leadership strategy should have assured Chloe of Ruth's high opinion of her. Yet when they'd met that morning, Ruth had sensed a hunger for praise that surprised her. She'd been around long enough to know it came from insecurity, having seen that look in countless faces, including her own in the mirror. Chloe wanted to help, but she also wanted Ruth to recognize what she could do. Ruth didn't want to ruin their new working relationship by telling Chloe her draft wasn't any good.

Then again, Chloe couldn't know how to approach faculty with a request. Perhaps she wouldn't take Ruth's edits personally.

Ruth's eyes widened as she skimmed through the draft. When she reached the end, she started at the beginning and read slowly.

Chloe started with a warm opening, followed by a paragraph on the importance of retention. Then she slathered on the flattery, praising the faculty's unique insight and skills that would be vital for tackling the problem. The message concluded with an announcement of the new work group and a call to action. *Perfect*. On top of the spot-on messaging, Chloe's spelling and grammar were impeccable.

A rapid knock signaled the arrival of Piper, who shoved the door open without waiting for a response. "Ready for lunch?"

"God, yes." Ruth pushed her bare feet against the floor to wheel back from her desk.

They sat together at the table. Piper passed Ruth a grilled vegetable panini—her favorite—along with a can of La Croix. Then she unwrapped her Italian sub.

"You're my hero." Ruth sank her teeth into the crispy sandwich. The injection of carbohydrates calmed her hunger, and she felt her whole body relax. "God, that's delicious. I was so hungry." She dove back in.

Piper allowed her to demolish half of her sandwich in silence before she spoke. "So. How did it go with Chloe?"

Ruth wiped her mouth. "It went well. Seriously. I know you're skeptical of this, but she's smart."

"She'd have to be smart to pull off what she did for you on Friday—if it was really her work."

"Oh, come on. Who else would produce a data presentation for me and allow *Chloe Taylor* to take the credit?" Ruth took a swig of her drink. "Besides, you're the one who told me to talk to her more."

"I meant about her *assistant* job. This is very strange. All of a sudden, Chloe makes data presentations?"

"It's not just that." Ruth reached backward to grab her phone from her desk, then pulled Chloe's email up on her mobile app. "You work in public relations. What do you think?" She slid the phone over to Piper.

Piper raised her reading glasses from the cord around her neck to her eyes. Twin reflections of the screen appeared on the lenses as she read through Chloe's email. After a minute, she removed the glasses and looked up at Ruth. "Chloe wrote this? By herself?"

"Yes. I asked her to write a draft, and she sent this a few hours later." Ruth held her breath, hoping Piper would agree with her assessment. She thought the draft was objectively well-written, but she couldn't rule out bias given her gratitude for Chloe's heroics the previous Friday.

"It's good," Piper said. "I'm trying to remember her education. She has a two-year degree?"

"Yes, from LCC. From what she has told me, she's insecure about not having a bachelor's degree. But I plan to revisit that conversation soon."

"Hmm." Piper took another bite of her sub. "She's eligible for tuition benefits."

"Exactly." Ruth drummed her fingers on the table. "I'd like her to start earning credits while she works for me, and then we can talk about her enrolling as a full-time student. Perhaps I can create a work-study position for her."

Piper set her sub down. "Is this all because of what happened on Friday?"

"No. It's more than that. When I talk to her—I mean, really talk—she has a lot of insight. Somehow, in only a few months, she figured out how the college works and in particular how the faculty think. Not to mention the flaws in my leadership style."

"Flaws?" Piper scoffed. "Now you're taking leadership advice from Chloe?"

"I suppose I am." As much as Ruth valued Piper's loyalty, she wondered if confiding in just one person had stunted her growth as a president. Piper encouraged Ruth to fight for her vision and steamroll the opposition. It was the sort of advice best friends gave. *Fuck them. You're in charge.* But perhaps it wasn't the best strategy for effecting change. Ruth raked her fingers through her hair. "Look, I've tried it my way. It's not working. Maybe if I can make the faculty feel included, make them think my initiatives were their idea—"

"Ah." Piper gave her a knowing nod. "You're not talking about *actually* listening to them."

"Well, look. If someone has a good idea, of course I'm open to that. But if they come to me with the same old shit—more full-time hires, more research funding, smaller class sizes, unicorns for the quad—I can't seriously entertain those suggestions. But maybe if I nod and smile for a while, they'll be more open to the actual strategy."

"We'll see." Piper kept her tone neutral. There was no judgment, but certainly no optimism either.

Ruth started on the second half of her sandwich, deep in thought.

Perhaps Piper was right to be cautious. Still, Ruth was committed to the project. If she and Chloe could accomplish something together, she owed it to both of them—and the college—to try.

Chapter 11

CAITLYN KNOCKED ON MAGGIE'S DOOR. "Hi. It's Chloe."

"It's open," Maggie called through the door.

As Caitlyn stepped into the office, she tried to calm down. When she'd ambushed Maggie with a flimsy lie, she hadn't counted on ever seeing her again. Now she worried she was in for an unpleasant conversation.

Maggie typed on her desktop computer as though Caitlyn weren't there. Her frown cut a crease across her forehead while her gaze bored into the screen.

"Thanks for meeting with me," Caitlyn said.

Maggie glanced up from her computer. "You don't need to thank me. Dr. Holloway told me to meet with you."

Shit. She hates me. It was bad enough that she'd corrected Maggie about percentages in front of Ruth. Her involvement in research threatened Maggie even more. *I'd hate me too.* However, Caitlyn was determined to turn things around. "I appreciate you making time so quickly. I know you've got a lot on your plate."

"Well, yes." Maggie lifted her chin. "I am the director of research."

"Absolutely." Caitlyn sat in the extra chair. "I'm looking forward to learning from you."

"You don't have to lie." Maggie crossed her arms. "Dr. Holloway told me to give you a bunch of data so you can study it by yourself."

"Actually, I was hoping we could work together. From what I hear, you know the source systems better than anyone. Then maybe we can work together on some analysis."

Maggie studied her warily. "What is your analysis background exactly?"

Uh-oh. Caitlyn twitched and broke eye contact, hoping Maggie wouldn't notice her discomfort. "I took math in college, but I've been studying on my own ever since." Caitlyn worried the lie would only make Maggie feel worse, so she added, "Well, it's not like I'm totally self-taught. I took a bunch of courses online." Before Maggie could ask for names, she added quickly, "What about you?"

Maggie looked down at her keyboard. "I studied database systems in college, and I got a job here in IT. When the old director left, I was the only one who knew how to write queries, so I got promoted. But I don't really do research. I just run reports."

"That's important too," Caitlyn said gently.

"I guess. But sometimes, I feel like an impostor. Then you showed up and made Ruth a presentation that she likes better than anything I've ever done." She pressed her lips together and looked away.

The unexpected vulnerability pierced Caitlyn's heart. "Hey." She waited for Maggie to meet her eyes. "You're not an impostor. You got this job because you have a valuable skill that helps the college. I meant what I said about us learning from each other. If you teach me about the data, I'll show you how I made those charts—and how you can make similar ones."

Maggie looked uncertain, but then she nodded. "Okay."

"Today, you can teach me about the different systems. Then we can schedule time to work together on the analysis. Sound good?"

"Yeah. It does." Maggie offered a shy smile. "I guess I'll start by showing you the class scheduling system."

"That sounds perfect." Caitlyn was genuinely excited to teach her a few things. In grad school, she had enjoyed helping undergrads with research. Perhaps this would be similar.

She hid a smile as she realized that in less than two weeks at Chloe's job, she was already involved in research and teaching data analysis.

You can take the girl out of academia, but you can't take academia out of the girl.

"Uh-huh… I understand, but Dr. Holloway isn't available." Caitlyn doodled on a sticky note as she tried to get a persistent vendor off the phone.

Ruth would never grant time to a random salesperson pitching *revolutionary* student engagement software. Yet he refused to accept anything less than an audience with the president.

"Our clients include Mars Hill University and Tri-State Bible College," he said brightly. "I'd love to tell Dr. Holloway about some of their results…"

Caitlyn's phone buzzed on the desk. She tapped the screen. It was an email from her advisor, responding to the draft of her new cover letter.

Damn, that was fast. Usually, Andrew took weeks or even months to send feedback, which was why she'd sent him the cover letter well before fall. Maybe her job market flameout had inspired him to give her more attention.

Meanwhile, the vendor blathered on about performance metrics, not even pausing to breathe.

Caitlyn swung her legs back and forth, desperate for him to shut up so she could focus on the email. "I understand, but Dr. Holloway doesn't have time for a meeting. I'm happy to take a message, or I could, um…" Her voice faded as she read Andrew's email.

Looks good. —AK

That was his feedback? All of it? Caitlyn scrolled in search of an attachment but found none.

"I'm actually going to be in Chicago next week," the vendor said. "It would be no trouble at all to drive to Linvale."

"I'm sorry. There's an emergency. Goodbye." Caitlyn hung up and turned her full attention to her phone.

Looks good? The words were a slap in the face. A good cover letter was essential, and Caitlyn had hacked hers apart and rewritten it. This was his only comment?

Caitlyn fought tears as she turned back to her computer. She stared at the spreadsheet, but the numbers blurred.

The desk phone rang.

"Fuck off." She pushed the button to silence the ringer with far more force than necessary.

The sound of the doors being pushed open interrupted her brooding.

Miguel walked into the suite. "Hey there. I just came to say hi." His smile wilted as he approached the desk. "What's wrong?"

"Nothing. It's just..." *He's an academic. He'll understand.* "I sent my advisor a new cover letter, and he blew me off. See?" She tapped her phone and held it up.

Miguel's eyes widened. "That's his entire response?"

"Yup. That's what I get after trying to please this guy for seven years."

"Wow." Miguel pulled up a chair and sat next to her. "Do you think he's blowing you off because you already graduated? Because that would be gross. All of my classmates' advisors stuck with them until they got a job or quit."

His words were validating, but also depressing. "Sadly, this is nothing new."

"Does he hate you for some reason?"

"Actually, no. Andrew is perfectly nice to me. He wants me to succeed, at least in theory. God knows he was happy to brag when I got published in a top journal. But he hardly ever made time for me."

The phone rang again. Caitlyn sat up straight and checked the caller ID. External number. She silenced the ringer. "They can leave a message."

"I'm really sorry about your advisor. You didn't deserve to be treated that way. Were your other committee members any better?"

"Actually, yeah. They tried to help me. Unfortunately, they aren't big names. One of them—oops." Caitlyn clamped her mouth shut as Ruth stepped into the suite.

"Hello, Dr. Fumero." Ruth walked up to the desk with her blazer slung over her arm, holding a stack of papers in front of her shimmery silver blouse. "Chloe, I just met with the chair of the assessment committee. He gave me these slides on learning outcomes in the sciences. I thought you might find it interesting."

Caitlyn accepted the stack of printed slides. "Oh, cool. Thanks." She breathed in the scent of lavender, trying not to visibly react to its effect on her.

Ruth nodded, strode into her office, but didn't close the door.

Miguel glanced at it and shrugged. "Well, I suppose I should leave you to it."

"Yeah, thanks for the talk."

Miguel winked as he got up to leave.

Alone in the office, Caitlyn flipped through the deck from Ruth. It was littered with pixelated pie graphs, tables, and bullet points. Teasing out the methods would take some time, and she doubted she'd be impressed.

Still, it was kind of Ruth to share them with her. Most bosses wouldn't bother to support their assistant's supposed extracurricular interest in research. Perhaps this was a sign that they were moving past their awkward encounter from the previous week.

It was ironic. Academia had no place for her and perhaps never would—but Ruth believed in her despite thinking she didn't have any credentials. No wonder she was reluctant to leave a place where someone saw value in her.

———

Caitlyn paced the copy room as the printer churned out her slides. She'd opted for the color printer, wanting to make the best possible impression.

When the printer finished, Caitlyn gingerly retrieved the stack of warm paper and paged through the deck. She broke into a satisfied smile at the sight of her work in print. In a week, she and Maggie had sliced Pulaski's retention data in every possible way.

The next step was to set up a meeting with Ruth to go over the results. But did she have to wait? Caitlyn was dying to show Ruth what she could produce with more than a couple of hours. Maybe she could steal a few seconds to give Ruth a preview.

Caitlyn returned to the suite, but Ruth's door was closed. *Damn it.* She sat at her desk and pulled up Ruth's calendar. Meetings and conference calls cluttered the rest of the week, and Ruth had placed holds between most of them—her strategy to ensure she'd have time to eat and to do actual work. Ruth was in the middle of one of those holds, most likely having lunch with the door closed.

Ruth wouldn't mind a quick interruption, right?

Since they'd begun working on strategy, Ruth had been noticeably warmer. When she passed through the suite, she greeted Caitlyn with a nod that conveyed a shared purpose—a sense of being on the same team.

Deciding their new alliance gave her implied privileges, Caitlyn approached the door and rested her ear against the wood.

Nothing.

She knocked, but there was no response. Had Ruth slipped out the back?

Caitlyn inched the door open and peeked inside.

The office was empty and dark with the blinds closed.

Oh well. Caitlyn decided to leave the slides on the desk and hope Ruth saw them in time to comment before she rushed off to her next meeting. She started toward the desk.

When the back door opened behind her, Caitlyn jumped and whirled around.

Ruth walked into the office, wearing pants, a bra, and nothing else.

Caitlyn gasped, frozen in place.

At the same time, Ruth jumped and flung her arms over her chest in an X—but not before Caitlyn glimpsed full breasts encased in a sheer balconette bra. As Ruth covered herself, Caitlyn's gaze drifted down to her soft belly and wider hips.

"Chloe!" Ruth's sharp voice broke the spell.

"Sorry!" Caitlyn turned away, shielding her eyes as though she'd seen something horrific instead of a gorgeous body. "I thought—I didn't think you were here. I'll go now." She ran out and yanked the door shut behind her.

Caitlyn sank into her chair. The papers spilled to her feet, then slid in different directions on the carpeted floor.

I can't believe that just happened. She had seen almost every part of Ruth's boobs: The rosy nipples had shown through the tulle, while the generous swell strained the lace trim and cast shadows on delicate cleavage. Even the brown spot above the left one—a large freckle or a tiny mole—was burned into her memory. Warmth curled in her belly as she dwelled on every curve.

In some corner of her brain, Caitlyn knew she should be unhappy about what had transpired. After all, she spent her days trying to please Ruth, and now she'd gone and upset her. She would remember to be unhappy about it soon—as soon as she snapped out of the stupor inflicted by the sight of Ruth without her top.

The door opened, and Ruth emerged, wearing a dark purple blouse Caitlyn hadn't seen before. Pink stained her cheeks, and her hair flopped in four different directions, but she didn't look angry—just shocked.

"I'm sorry," Caitlyn said again.

Ruth tugged the hem of her blouse. "I spilled balsamic vinaigrette on my shirt. Then I went to change in my restroom, but—"

"I knocked." Caitlyn squirmed. "There was no response."

They both startled as the glass doors opened.

Ted, the mail carrier, pushed his cart into the lobby. "Good afternoon, ladies."

"Good afternoon," Ruth echoed, sounding dazed.

They waited in silence. The air was thick with tension and the shared knowledge that it would be inappropriate to discuss the incident in front of someone else.

Nice timing, Ted. Caitlyn remembered her intrusion and chastised herself for the flagrant projection.

Ruth returned her gaze to Caitlyn, then seemed to notice the papers on the floor. "What's that?"

"Oh." She had forgotten. "That's why I came in. I was going to bring it to you."

Ruth tapped one of the pages with the tip of her matte black shoe. "You made this?"

"Y-yes." Caitlyn forced herself to meet Ruth's gaze, craning her neck to ensure everything below Ruth's chin remained outside her field of vision. "Um, Maggie and I looked at…" Her mind was as empty as a ghost town, the wind blowing tumbleweeds past a vintage sign that said *I Saw Ruth's Boobs*. "We looked at…" Her cheeks burned. At last, a word popped into her head. "Variables," she whispered.

This was a disaster. Violating Ruth's privacy was bad enough. Now Caitlyn had overreacted in front of Ruth, becoming too rattled to form sentences.

What was Ruth thinking? Probably something like, *My queer assistant ogled my boobs and came unglued. She must have a massive crush on me.*

Caitlyn's face grew even hotter. She couldn't let Ruth think "Chloe" was mooning over her. If Ruth suspected such a thing, it would be the end of their working relationship.

Ruth glanced at Ted, who leisurely sorted through envelopes. She combed her fingers through her hair, somehow mussing it even more. "Just come in." She inclined her head toward the door.

"Okay. As soon as I—um." Caitlyn awkwardly crouched to retrieve the papers from under her desk.

Ruth walked back into her office, leaving the door wide open.

Caitlyn gathered the papers and scrambled to her feet. She had to prove the incident didn't mean anything. *Game face.* She straightened her spine and practiced an indifferent expression. *Boobs? What boobs?* "Be right there!"

Ruth attempted to steady her breathing. She checked the notifications on her phone without reading any of them. All she could see was Chloe staring at her half-naked body.

Ultimately, Chloe had done what most people would do; she'd averted her gaze, apologized, and rushed out. It was a typical reaction to an embarrassing mishap—*except* for how long it had taken her to react.

For several charged seconds, Chloe hadn't moved. She'd stared at Ruth's breasts with parted lips and wide eyes, as though Ruth's forty-two-year-old, out-of-shape body were a sight to behold.

Chloe liked women. She had once mentioned an ex-girlfriend in passing, then kept on talking while the revelation implanted in Ruth's brain and erased assumptions she didn't remember making. Any lingering doubt had been obliterated by that potent stare.

An unwelcome but undeniable burst of arousal coursed through her and pulsed between her thighs. She squeezed her legs together, willing it to disappear. *Not now. Christ. And not ever with Chloe.* Ruth wiped beads of sweat from her forehead. Her new shirt was thin, but the office was like a sauna.

Chloe walked in, clutching the papers. "I'm so sorry again. I never meant— Ah, just a second." She backtracked and closed the door behind her. "I didn't mean to walk in on you like that."

"Of course." Ruth tugged on the bottom of her shirt.

Chloe fanned herself with the papers. "They still haven't fixed your air conditioning, huh?" Her cheeks were a rosy pink.

"Have a seat." Ruth waved at the conference table.

As Ruth settled at the far end, Chloe sat two chairs away and began to smooth and organize the papers.

"Let me see." Ruth held out her hand.

Avoiding Ruth's gaze, Chloe pushed the stack halfway across the table.

Ruth was forced to scoot closer to retrieve it. She couldn't help noticing the flushed skin at the base of Chloe's neck. *Focus*, Ruth scolded herself. *For the love of God.* She studied the charts, which covered student demographics, retention patterns, and trends over time.

Damn, she's good. After the presentation for the board meeting, Ruth shouldn't have been surprised. But this was her assistant who had a spotty, unimpressive resume. Chloe had only been hired due to a shallow applicant pool, and yet she was capable of this.

"This"—she shook the pages, ensuring there would be no doubt that she meant the charts—"is excellent."

"Thank you." Chloe blushed hard, a deep red climbing up her cheeks. "Maggie helped too. We've been working together."

"I see," Ruth said dryly. "I hope Maggie is taking advantage of the opportunity to learn." She wasn't sure why Chloe always downplayed her skills, but she wouldn't get away with it anymore.

Chloe's sheepish smile indicated she knew she'd been caught. "Well, I've been learning from her too. Anyway, I know this is your lunch break, but maybe we can talk about other hypotheses later this week. Then I can work on a model predicting the likelihood of dropping out." She winced. "Sorry, I'm babbling."

"A model?"

Chloe pulled on a strand of her hair. "Well, I read about how to do it. Maybe that's too ambitious."

"Nonsense. Nothing is too ambitious if you're willing to learn. Why don't you give it a try, and then we'll look at it together? I studied linear models in grad school. I can help you if you get stuck."

"Really?" Chloe sat up straighter. "You don't mind helping?"

"Of course not. I am an educator, after all." Ruth heard the defensive tone and reminded herself that it was unnecessary. Some faculty saw her as an administrator rather than a teacher, but Chloe had never questioned her experience. "It's not that I have endless time for such things, of course, but I'll make time for this. You're worth it."

Chloe's expression collapsed as her nerves seemed to melt into a softer emotion. "Thank you." Her voice cracked, and she looked as if she might cry. "That means a lot to me."

Behind them, the computer chimed—an Outlook Calendar notification, signaling a meeting in five minutes.

Ruth opened her mouth to excuse herself, but the words didn't come. She was lost in long lashes and hazel eyes flecked with green and gold. *How did I ever find Chloe? And why did it take me so long to notice her?*

"Well." A quiver in Ruth's voice betrayed her feelings. "I have…" What was the word? "Meeting."

"Oh. Oh!" The spell broke, and Chloe looked away. "Of course. I'll get out of your hair. I mean your office. Thanks. I mean, bye."

As Chloe rushed from the room, Ruth remained at the table, hands folded in her lap. *What am I doing?* She shouldn't gaze into Chloe's eyes—especially not moments after Chloe had seen her half-naked.

Chloe was objectively beautiful, but completely off-limits. If Chloe had a crush, that was flattering—but nothing Ruth could ever encourage. Chloe needed a mentor, someone to prod her to finish her bachelor's degree and ultimately get a much better job. No matter how savvy she might seem at times, they weren't equals in any sense.

The presidency was a lonely job. Technically, every single person at the college worked for her—and that meant she had to maintain boundaries with everyone.

She hadn't realized how *alone* she would feel with so few allies at the college or even on the board. For a long time, Piper had been her only confidant. Now that she had a connection with Chloe, she was tempted to let her in—but it was too dangerous.

Ruth resolved to dial back the friendly relationship she'd inadvertently developed with Chloe. From now on, she would be polite but professional at all times. If the distance made her job even more lonely, well, that was the price of being the boss. She couldn't let Chloe get the wrong idea.

Or the right one, a voice in her brain piped up.

Oh, shut up. There might be an infinitesimal kernel of truth to the idea that she was attracted to Chloe, but it hardly mattered. Her professional obligations came first.

Outlook chimed again. It was time to go.

Ruth dug in her desk for some chocolate—the one comfort she could have without complications.

***

Caitlyn sank into her chair and blew out a breath. *What the hell just happened?*

In any other context, she would be confident in the answer. But this was Ruth. Chloe's boss. The college president. It seemed impossible, but Ruth's gaze had been charged with meaning.

Questions poured into her brain. Was Ruth single? Did she like women? Did she realize they'd shared a potent moment, and was she freaking out too?

There was only one person Caitlyn could ask. She jumped up and power-walked to the English department.

Miguel sat at the small table in his office, studying stack of papers with a can of Diet Coke in his hand. He startled at Caitlyn's urgent knock.

"Is Ruth queer?" Caitlyn had planned to segue into the topic, but screw it—she was too antsy.

"Whoa. Hang on a second." Miguel jumped up and pushed his office door closed.

"Oh yeah. Good idea." Unable to sit still, Caitlyn rapped her foot on the chair leg in a string of quick beats.

Miguel returned to his seat. "The short answer is…probably."

Caitlyn's heart thumped. *He knows something.* "What's the long answer?"

"Well, as far as I know, Dr. Holloway doesn't talk about her personal life at work—and as you can imagine, no one dares to ask."

"Yeah." Caitlyn cringed at the thought of a faculty member raising the subject.

Miguel leaned in. "However, I have a friend in Chicago government, and he told me Holloway used to date the mayor's director of legislative affairs, a woman named Emily."

Caitlyn tingled at the confirmation. *Ruth dates women.* Not that it mattered, of course. Nothing could ever happen between them. Still, against reason, it felt important to know.

Miguel slurped his soda. "Anyway, I don't know how Dr. Holloway identifies herself, but to the extent that I have a gaydar for women, she certainly pings it. Right?"

"Yes, there's a certain vibe. Do you think she's in the closet here?"

He frowned. "I don't see why she would be. It's a lefty liberal-arts college. If anything, she'd get more respect from faculty if they knew—with the exception of a few ancient grumps, I guess."

"Yeah, it was the same in grad school. Very accepting, to the point where you almost had more cred if you identified as queer. Ruth probably just likes her privacy."

"So." Miguel squinted. "Why did you want to know?"

Caitlyn shifted and crossed her arms. She should have known asking the question would trigger an interrogation. "No reason."

"Oh, come on. I know what lesbians like. Short hair, authority." He gave her a teasing grin.

"I'm bi, remember?" Caitlyn stalled.

"Okay, what do you like?"

"Fine. I also like short hair and authority," Caitlyn grumbled. "But I wondered because…" She sighed. Miguel already knew her biggest secret. Surely she could trust him with this. "There was a tiny incident."

"You kissed?" His hand flew to his mouth.

"No! God, no. I accidentally walked in while Ruth was changing her shirt, and I kind of froze. Not for long, but I think Ruth knew—she sort of caught me staring." Her pulse raced all over again as she recalled the scene with perfect clarity.

Miguel's eyes bulged. "You saw her topless?"

"In a bra," Caitlyn said quickly. "Pants and a bra. But then later, when we were looking at data, we… It's hard to explain, but we looked into each other's eyes."

"Wait, are you saying Ruth hit on you? Or was flirting with you?"

"No, nothing like that." Caitlyn searched for the words. "It was like she saw *me*. Caitlyn. I mean, not literally. She still thinks I'm Chloe. But it was like she could see into my head. She knew I was looking at her *like that*. And her guard slipped for a second, and I swear there was something there."

"Oh my God." His eyes grew even wider. "But you can't— You're supposed to be Chloe!"

"I know, I know." Caitlyn groaned. "Don't worry, I'm not going to do anything. I only wanted to know for sure that I didn't imagine the, um, tension." *Shit, shit, shit.* She was supposed to be keeping a low profile, and instead she'd gone and developed a silly crush on Chloe's boss. For one million reasons, she couldn't let a moment like that happen again.

"I hate to ask this," Miguel said carefully. "But do you think she would ever hit on you?"

"No." Caitlyn didn't have to think about it. "Ruth is ethical. She would never put me, or any subordinate, in that situation."

"I think you're right. She wouldn't proposition an employee." Miguel brightened. "Then again, you're not really her assistant. Technically, you don't even work here!"

"Har har." Suddenly eager to change the subject, she asked, "How is your class going?"

"Oh come on. This is so much more interesting."

"Please?" Caitlyn already felt exposed. She needed time to process her feelings in private.

Miguel relented with a put-upon sigh. "Okay. We're starting with eighteenth century poems…"

As Miguel talked, Caitlyn half-listened while she ruminated on her depressing situation. She'd grown so comfortable at Pulaski, sometimes she forgot she was an impostor. Her job was to stay off Ruth's radar, not get attached.

Besides, whether she worked there or not, nothing would ever happen. Caitlyn's entire identity was a lie, and that meant she had already blown her chance for a real connection with Ruth. She'd have to settle for helping Ruth as much as she could before it all had to end.

Chapter 12

DETERMINED NOT TO BE EARLY or late, Caitlyn knocked on Ruth's door the second her phone displayed three o'clock.

"Come in," came the faint response.

Caitlyn sucked in her stomach to calm the flutters. She had barely seen Ruth since the incident, aside from tight nods when Ruth strode past her desk. After two long days of fretting that she'd made Ruth uncomfortable, Caitlyn had resorted to a Microsoft Outlook calendar invitation to talk with her.

She cracked the door. "Um, is this still a good time?"

"Yes, it's fine." Ruth sat at her desk, looking stern in a blazer and blouse that buttoned up to her collarbone despite the warm, stuffy air in her office. "Remind me what this is about?"

Caitlyn crept forward. "You said we could talk about a predictive model?"

In reality, Caitlyn had scheduled the meeting because she couldn't stop obsessing about what had happened and whether Ruth was avoiding her. Since Ruth had offered to help, it was a useful pretense.

"Ah. Right. Have a seat." The studied indifference in Ruth's gaze was too exaggerated to be anything but a performance; it meant the opposite. She was uneasy.

Caitlyn deflated at the confirmation of her fears. *This is my fault.* She'd lost herself in Ruth's creamy curves, her slow reaction revealing too much, and now Ruth was avoiding her. It was the last thing she wanted.

She trudged to the conference table and sat with her laptop, hoping her sadness didn't show on her face.

Ruth started toward a chair on the other side of the table, then wavered. "I suppose I'll need to see the screen." She pulled out the chair next to Caitlyn and sat. But instead of wheeling up to the table, she kept several feet between them.

The distance felt like miles. Would they ever joke over lattes again?

"What have you got?" Ruth crossed her arms.

Right. The model. In reality, Caitlyn had studied models in graduate school. On top of that, Maggie had given her a good sense of the data available—and Caitlyn knew the futility of attempting to model something as complex as retention with only the information the college happened to collect already.

Oh well. Here goes. Caitlyn pulled up a spreadsheet. "So, this is a list of the variables we have in our data systems. Basic demographics, courses taken and grades, high school name, and financial aid data."

Ruth peered at the screen. "I see. What sort of model are you thinking about?"

"Well, I read that when you have a binary outcome—like returning to school or not—a logit model could be good."

"You've done your homework." Ruth looked begrudgingly impressed.

You have no idea. "Just some Internet research."

"Yes, a logit would be acceptable."

"Great. What are my next steps?"

"Hmm." Ruth drummed her fingers on her chin. "You should decide which variables to include, based on your theory. Then you'll need software to run the model and perform some tests. For example, you can look at the R-squared value."

Pseudo R-squared, Caitlyn corrected silently.

"Actually, it's called something else for a logit. I learned this over a decade ago, but I think it's called Pseudo R-squared. You can also look at the residuals, and... Let's see." Ruth squinted. "Make sure they're normally distributed."

Nope. That's OLS regression. Caitlyn didn't blame her for forgetting the difference. Ruth had been an administrator for years, and she had no reason to have these details memorized. "Thanks. I'll do some reading."

"Yes. Good." Ruth pressed her lips into a line.

Caitlyn wasn't getting anywhere on her real goal or even her fake goal. Maybe she could steer the conversation away from math concepts. "So, the first work group meeting is coming up. How are you feeling about it?"

"Fine." Ruth's face was a wall.

Caitlyn stared. "That's it? You feel...fine?"

Tension cracked between them. "Two math faculty confirmed that they're coming," Ruth said at last.

"That's great." It came out high-pitched and perky.

"We'll see." Ruth studied her fingernails.

Gathering her courage, Caitlyn decided to be direct. "I'm sorry again for what happened the other day. I don't want you to feel awkward or self-conscious around me."

Ruth's posture stiffened. "I don't feel awkward."

Sure, everything is normal and chill.

Caitlyn waited, but Ruth remained silent as a statue. Defeated, she closed her laptop. "Well, I know you're busy. I'll let you get back to work."

Ruth exhaled audibly and pushed back her chair.

As Ruth returned to her desk, Caitlyn tucked her laptop under her arm and headed for the door. Her mood couldn't sink any lower.

"Chloe?" Ruth's voice stopped her.

Caitlyn turned around.

"Set up another meeting once you've settled on your variables. In the meantime, I'll do some reading and refresh my memory on logit models." Ruth's tone contained a trace of an apology.

Caitlyn latched on and held it close, the one sign that the ice might thaw. "Thanks. I really appreciate it." She walked out and closed the door behind her.

Not awkward at all.

Two days later, Ruth and Chloe had a scheduled meeting. There was a knock on the doorframe at the exact moment the calendar notification popped up on Ruth's computer.

Chloe stood in the doorway, clutching her laptop with both hands. She shifted between her feet. "Um, hi. It's two o'clock."

"Indeed it is. Please come in." Ruth stood too quickly, then gripped the desk to steady herself. She still felt guilty about her cold demeanor a few days ago; this time, she was determined to strike the right balance with Chloe—friendly, but professional. There was no reason they'd have to forgo the warm working relationship that obviously meant something to both of them.

Chloe's sandals clicked as she walked over to the conference table. She sat in a prim pose and smoothed her skirt before opening her laptop.

Ruth averted her gaze, determined to look at anything but Chloe's legs. *Professional.*

"So, I'm not sure if we should talk about this at the work group—I'll leave it up to you—but I have the results from your early-alert initiative."

"Oh!" Ruth dropped into the chair next to Chloe and leaned in to peer at the screen. If the summer pilot went well, she could make a strong case for fall. But if not… "Just tell me, is it good news?"

"Yes." Chloe tapped the screen, revealing one of her stylish graphs. She pointed to a taller column at the end. "We're up seventeen percent for retaining students in the term, meaning they're still enrolled in at least one class."

"Whoa. How many faculty participated in the alert system?"

"One second." Chloe paged through a few slides before landing on one with a graph divided into red and green bars. "Eighty-six percent recorded attendance—and their retention rates were twelve percent higher than the ones who refused."

"Fantastic." A text box caught Ruth's eye. "You even list the names. Oh, they would not be happy about this." She resisted—just barely—the urge to cackle.

"This is just for us." Chloe shot Ruth a warning look. "Remember, we don't want to antagonize the faculty."

"Sure, sure." Ruth waved her hand. "Did you find anything else in the data?"

"Actually, yes." Chloe pointed at the chart. "Every full-time faculty member recorded attendance except for Steve and someone named Randolph Hayes."

"Randy. Of course." Ruth rubbed her temples. "He's a business professor who has been here since the dawn of time. A lost cause, as far as computers go."

"Got it." Chloe gestured to the other bar. "But look, only half of the adjunct faculty submitted reports. And they were more likely to lose students."

"Okay." Ruth waited for Chloe to get to the point.

Chloe shifted in her chair to face Ruth fully. "I've heard you mock the idea of hiring full-time faculty when adjuncts can do the same job for a fraction of the cost. So I thought you should know what the evidence shows."

Ruth opened her mouth to deny it, then recalled a certain day in her office, almost two months ago. She'd been talking to Jack about the budget, and Chloe's eyes had flashed with unexpected rage. "I believe I remember the relevant conversation. I take it you disagreed with what you heard."

"Honestly, yes." Chloe held her gaze. "I know you have a tight budget, but I didn't think any academic would prefer adjunct labor. These are people with PhDs making poverty wages."

Ruth's cheeks grew hot. Her words had been careless, but at the time she hadn't known Chloe was *really* listening. "I didn't mean—look, I'd love to reduce the number of courses taught by adjuncts, but we can't afford luxuries. We're broke and dipping into our reserves to stay solvent. So I can't give the faculty what they want. I can't even do what *I* want."

"I understand." Chloe relaxed her posture at last. "Now that I've gotten to know you, I see how hard you work for the college. And I know it's not easy to balance resource constraints with the mission, especially with the board and the faculty pulling you in different directions. It was just hard to hear you be so flippant."

"You're right. I shouldn't speak that way, not even behind closed doors. I know the adjuncts are underpaid, and I don't take any pleasure in their circumstances. I regret that my words implied otherwise. It's just…"

"What?" Chloe asked gently, the hard edge gone from her gaze.

"Ever since I got here, most of the faculty have treated me as the enemy—the bitch administrator out to destroy everything they hold dear. Not all of them, certainly. But dealing with it every day for two years gets to me. So, sometimes, to blow off steam, I'd mock their demands in front of someone like Jack or Piper. I already know the board's position on adjunct pay, but if I could do something about it, I would. It's the same with the budget and hiring. So, sometimes I make thoughtless comments. But that's not who I am. And I'm going to try not to do it anymore."

Ruth took a deep breath and exhaled slowly to calm down. She was never vulnerable at work; she'd learned long ago that emotion was a liability, especially for women. But this was important. She couldn't let Chloe think the worst of her.

Chloe smiled. "Thank you. I have a close friend who had trouble getting an academic job, and when you spoke that way—well, I guess I thought of her. But I'm glad your real feelings are more sympathetic."

"I understand." Ruth empathized with Chloe's friend more than she realized. Should she explain her struggle to find another job after New Mexico? Perhaps then Chloe would understand that she meant what she said. She'd suffered, too, from the indignities of the academic job market.

No. It's too personal. Ruth had resolved to be professional. She settled on another point. "If we can increase enrollment and turn retention around, perhaps we can revisit adjunct pay—or even the ratio of full-time to part-time instructors."

"Really?" Chloe's hopeful smile touched Ruth's heart.

I don't want to let her down. "I can only promise to try. Maybe you can even put together some more data like this to help make the case."

"I'd love that."

"Good. We'll talk about it after we get through the first goal gang summit."

Chloe laughed.

Okay. We're still on good terms. Ruth decided not to think too much about why that felt so important to her.

Chapter 13

RUTH SHIFTED IN HER CHAIR as a fresh wave of nausea coursed through her. *Fuck.*

Jack shot her a questioning look. He knew she detested meetings with wealthy donors, but today she probably looked as if she might vomit on the conference table.

Attempting to appear normal, Ruth returned a weak smile. Then she turned her gaze to Zachary and silently cursed him for her current predicament.

Okay, she could blame Zachary for texting late at night, but it wasn't *technically* his fault that he'd texted right after Ruth's phone alarm reminded her to take her nightly antidepressant.

Still, perhaps if Zachary were capable of reading a student complaint without coming unglued and sending apoplectic texts at all hours, Ruth would have remembered the damn pill—and if his tantrum hadn't still been on her mind the next morning, perhaps she would have realized it then, instead of hours into her work day when she finally thought to question why she felt unwell.

Now the onslaught of withdrawal symptoms was underway, and Ruth had back-to-back meetings all afternoon—meetings she couldn't ditch unless she had an open head wound, and perhaps not even then.

She needed her pill. But how could she get it?

There was one person at Pulaski who had been to her home—Piper—but in an unlucky coincidence, Piper was spending the day in Chicago with her daughter.

What about Chloe? Ruth clenched her fingers under the table. A few weeks ago, Ruth never would have considered asking Chloe for this kind of help, for good reason. It would require tremendous trust to send Chloe to her home unsupervised.

Ruth didn't think Chloe was the type to snoop. She wouldn't rifle through drawers, searching for secrets. But in the space of a quick walk through the house, Chloe's analytical brain would catalog the contents of Ruth's living room and draw all sorts of conclusions about Ruth as a person.

Most importantly—even if she could make peace with all of that—could Ruth trust Chloe with the information that she took psychiatric medication?

If word got out, Ruth would have plenty of defenders. Academics tended to be liberal; most supported mental health care. Still, it was inevitable that some people would see her differently—and those people might include members of the board.

Yet Chloe had proved her loyalty when she'd helped Ruth with the board meeting. They'd worked well together in recent weeks. And Ruth had seen Chloe's bottle of antidepressants for herself. Surely, Chloe understood the importance of discretion.

A soft hiss escaped her lips as she struggled to remain still. There was no choice. She had to take her pill as soon as possible—and with Piper out of town, Chloe was the only person she would even consider asking.

Keeping her attentive smile fixed on her face, she transferred her phone from the table to her lap and tapped out a text message.

———

Caitlyn was absorbed in a spreadsheet when her phone chirped. It was a message from Chloe:

Text from Ruth.

She snatched her phone. This was the first time Ruth had sent "Chloe" a text message since the switch. Caitlyn's gut told her something was wrong.

A few seconds later, Chloe sent a screenshot of a message:

Please come to rm 204 in Li Hall ASAP. I'll step out of the room when you arrive.

Caitlyn texted back:

Tell her I'm on my way.

Chloe responded with a thumbs-up emoji, followed by another message:

How are you?

Good. We'll catch up later, okay?

Caitlyn wasn't about to dawdle when Ruth needed her ASAP. She shoved her phone into her pocket and set off for Li Hall, a cube-shaped building on the east side of campus. The thought that Ruth needed her for something—perhaps something important—filled her with a heady sense of purpose. She walked quickly despite the sweltering heat and broke a sweat within a minute.

When she arrived, she accosted the first security officer she found. "Excuse me. I'm looking for room 204."

The officer flicked a skeptical gaze to her ID badge, and Caitlyn had a sudden fear that she'd encountered the only person on campus who could tell her and Chloe apart. Then he pointed to the ceiling. "Second floor, right above our heads. It's the fancy conference room."

"Thanks!" Caitlyn hurried up the stairs. When she emerged on the second floor, panting for breath, room 204 was right in front of her. The door was closed, but a small window allowed her to peek inside.

Ruth sat at a green marble conference table. Jack was there too, along with the board chair and a few men in suits that she didn't recognize. One of the men was speaking while the others nodded along.

As she listened, Ruth planted her elbows on the table and rested her chin in her hands. Her lips were frozen in a tight half-smile.

Is she okay? Caitlyn couldn't recall seeing Ruth slouch in a meeting.

Ruth's gaze traveled to the door and caught Caitlyn's eyes. Immediately, she straightened and said something to the group, then pushed her chair back and strode to the door. She pushed it shut behind her and walked down the hall a few paces.

Caitlyn followed, sensing Ruth wanted to speak privately. Her chest swelled at the implication. *Ruth trusts me.*

The hallway was vacant except for a lone custodian about twenty yards away.

"Thank you for coming." Ruth let out a shaky breath. "Phew. Sorry." The air was chilly—a stark contrast to Ruth's office—but her creamy cheeks were blotched with pink.

"Are you all right?" Caitlyn whispered.

"I'm afraid not." Ruth shifted between her feet. "I need to ask you to do something, and I hope it won't make you uncomfortable—"

"Anything." Caitlyn looked into Ruth's eyes, and the vulnerability she saw there pierced her heart. Whatever Ruth needed, she would deliver.

"I take a pill every night. Last night, I forgot. Unfortunately, this is a pill I can't skip. So I need… What I'm asking…" She took a deep breath and blew it out slowly. "Would you drive to my house and bring me the bottle?"

Empathy overwhelmed Caitlyn as she processed the reason for Ruth's discomfort. Something was physically wrong. Ruth could be in pain or worse. Whatever it was, Caitlyn wouldn't rest until she made it better. "Of course. I can leave right away."

"My keys are in my purse in the top drawer of my desk. The gold one opens the front door—that's the only one you need. I'll text you the address."

No texts. Caitlyn didn't want to wait for Chloe to check her phone when Ruth needed help right away. "I've got my phone right here. Could you type it in?" She opened her Notes app, then pulled up a blank page.

"Okay." Ruth accepted the phone and began to type. Her fingernails were short with translucent, pearly gloss—a good match for the understated elegance of her sleek pants and turquoise blouse.

Caitlyn averted her eyes, admonishing herself. Ruth needed help and comfort, not inappropriate staring.

Ruth passed the phone back. "The bottle is in my upstairs bathroom next to the sink. There are two bottles, but I typed the name of the one I need."

Caitlyn read the screen. *Desvenlafaxine.* She recognized the name instantly. It was one of the antidepressants she'd tried when she first sought treatment for anxiety, before her psychiatrist had switched her to sertraline.

Poor Ruth. Caitlyn had experienced antidepressant withdrawal a handful of times, and she'd found it impossible to function. Ruth's situation was worse—she had to be the president, a role that required poise at all times.

Trying not to let on that she recognized the medication, Caitlyn pocketed her phone. "Will you still be here when I get back?"

"No. My next meeting is in my office. Just interrupt me when you're back, and I'll step out."

"Got it. I'll leave right now."

"Thank you." Ruth's gaze was pained.

"Hang in there," Caitlyn said softly.

Ruth gave her a grim nod before going back inside the room.

As soon as the door closed, Caitlyn took off down the hallway in a sprint.

Caitlyn burst into Ruth's office and closed the door behind her. She could only imagine what people would think if they caught her digging through Ruth's purse.

As usual, Ruth's desk was pristine. The gleaming mahogany surface held only Ruth's computer, a fountain pen, and a cube of sticky notes. When Caitlyn opened the hefty top drawer, however, she found it stuffed with a chaotic assortment of snacks, office supplies, and personal items.

Whoa. Caitlyn had never seen Ruth eat candy, but the drawer contained a sizable stash of Caramello bars. *Is this her secret weakness?* In addition to the bars, there were a few mini bags of chips, a box of tampons, and lavender-scented deodorant.

Behind those items, Ruth's purse had been stashed in a second compartment. It was a plum-colored satchel purse with chunky handles and a magnetic clasp.

Caitlyn pulled it open and dug past a tube of lipstick, a compact mirror, a small hairbrush, and another Caramello bar until she found a ring of keys. The gold house key gleamed under the fluorescent lights as she power-walked to the exit.

Traffic was light, and Caitlyn sped through town with little regard for the speed limit. The first red light gave her time to contemplate what she'd learned. Ruth took antidepressants. Most likely, she suffered from depression, anxiety, or both.

Caitlyn knew mental health issues were often invisible, but she couldn't help feeling surprised. Ruth had always presented herself as icy cool and confident, in contrast to Caitlyn, who was a jumble of nerves and insecurities. It was hard to imagine Ruth struggling. Then she thought back to Ruth's confession about how hostile faculty members made her feel and how she hid behind sarcasm and flip remarks. *She's afraid to show weakness.* It made Caitlyn even more determined to come through.

Google Maps led Caitlyn to a suburban neighborhood with homes that looked about mid-twentieth century. Each lot was a perfect square. Three turns later, she arrived at a modest house with gunmetal-gray siding. She parked in the driveway and hustled to the door with Ruth's keys bouncing against her thigh.

Caitlyn's heartbeat accelerated as she slid the key into the lock. Holding her breath, she pushed open the door and stepped into Ruth's house.

The living room was cozy, with a plush, gray sofa, a television, and bookshelves lining the walls. On the sofa, a fuzzy blanket had been left unfolded with a hardback book on top of it: *Caste* by Isabel Wilkerson.

Ruth reads sociology! She imagined lounging on the couch with Ruth, sharing the blanket, each with a lofty book and a mug of tea.

Focus. Forbidden daydreams could wait. Ruth needed her.

Caitlyn took the stairs two at a time and searched around for the master bedroom. She wandered into the first open door and found herself standing in front of Ruth's bed.

Warmth flowed through her at the sight of the intricate patchwork quilt. The bed was made, technically, but it looked as if Ruth had spent about two seconds yanking the quilt toward the pillows before abandoning the task.

Two framed photos adorned the dresser. One showed an older couple in front of a Christmas tree. Ruth's parents? In the second, Ruth posed in her graduation gown. Caitlyn's feet moved her closer before she could stop herself.

In the photo, Ruth's eyes were bright, and her grin was infectious. Her hair fell to her shoulders, and she looked younger, although Caitlyn wouldn't have guessed she had aged more than ten years since then.

Caitlyn wanted to know everything about the woman in the picture. What had grad school been like for her? Was she one of those students who seemed to excel at everything while hiding the personal costs? Perhaps, like Caitlyn, she'd started taking medication during her program.

Medication. *That's why I'm here.*

Caitlyn moved past the bed and stepped into Ruth's spacious bathroom. She scanned the sparse collection of products cluttering the counter and spotted two bottles of pills between the toothbrush holder and lavender hand soap. The one facing front said *desvenlafaxine.*

Caitlyn grabbed it and exited the bathroom, then hurried down the stairs to the front door. *Hold on, Ruth. I'm coming.*

Ruth was miserable. The pain started in her brain and radiated through her body, while her stomach sloshed and her skin crawled. Her pill was seventeen hours late, and the withdrawal had only gotten worse.

She wanted to curl up in bed, where she'd be free to fidget and squirm and groan. Instead, she had to sit through an interminable meeting about Pulaski's partnership with a Chicago-based software firm that sponsored scholarships.

The CEO, a shrewd older woman named Marilyn, kept shooting questioning glances at her. She seemed to sense that Ruth wasn't fully present, although she hadn't said anything.

Marilyn's deputy, a thirty-something tech bro, remained oblivious—as did Zachary, who wasn't even supposed to be in the meeting. He had hung around after the donor engagement to bless an unrelated discussion with his extemporaneous thoughts.

Normally, Ruth cringed at Zachary's tendency to dominate conversations regardless of his familiarity with the subject, but today she was grateful for his incessant chatter. As he bloviated on about the future of software, as imagined by a man who hadn't worked a single day in the industry, Ruth watched the clock on the wall tick at an agonizing pace.

Her office door opened a few inches, and Chloe stuck her head through the crack.

Their eyes met, and Chloe gave her a thumbs-up sign.

Thank God. "Please excuse me for a moment." Ignoring Zachary's puzzled expression, Ruth lurched from her seat and reached the door with a few quick strides. She closed the door behind her and leaned against it.

"I got it." Chloe held out the medication.

"Thank you so much for this." Ruth exhaled as she accepted the pills and popped off the top.

"Would you like some water?" Chloe held out a bottle. "I keep a case in my car, so it's a little warm—"

Ruth grabbed the bottle, twisted the top off, and let the cap fall to the floor. She washed the pill down, then took a few more gulps of the tepid water. Just knowing the pill was in her system caused her shoulders to loosen. "I'll pay you back for the water. And the gas."

"Don't worry about that. I won't accept money." Chloe's earnest gaze said she meant it.

"Okay. Thanks." Ruth wondered if Chloe knew what she was experiencing. Had she recognized the medication? If not, had she Googled it?

"Seriously, it was nothing. Oh, and I have your keys." Chloe reached into her pocket and held them out.

Ruth closed her fist around the keys. "It wasn't nothing. You've done me a big favor—one well outside your job description—and I appreciate it."

"Okay." Chloe offered a small smile.

"Well." Ruth stuffed the keys in her pants pocket. "I'd better get back."

"I'll be here if you need anything. Anything at all."

Ruth regarded her assistant with wonder. She didn't trust easily, but she knew in her bones that Chloe cared about her. "I'll be okay. But thank you."

She took another sip of water and a few deep breaths. The next thirty minutes would be agony, but then she'd be free—and thanks to Chloe, she already felt better.

After the meeting, Zachary stuck around to pontificate on various topics until Ruth pointedly offered to walk him to his car. At last, he got the hint and sauntered out, thankfully declining the offer.

Alone at last, Ruth kicked off her shoes and sank to the floor behind her desk, leaning against the wall. "Fuck," she whispered, massaging her temples. Her nausea had receded, thanks to Chloe—but her insides ached, and she was still jittery.

When the door opened, her head jerked up. *Shit.* She didn't want Zachary to see her on the floor in a heap.

"Ruth?" Chloe's voice was soft.

Relief washed through her. *Chloe*. Someone she trusted. "I'm here."

Chloe crept around the desk, face etched with worry. "Are you okay?" She knelt on the floor a few feet away.

"I will be." Her voice came out scratchy. Ruth cleared her throat. "What are you still doing here?"

"Um." Chloe blushed and looked down at the floor. Her bangs fell into her face, obscuring her eyes. "I didn't want to leave before your meeting ended—in case you needed anything."

"That's very kind of you." Ruth hugged her knees. "I suppose you figured out what I'm taking?"

Chloe hesitantly met Ruth's gaze. "I know what it is. But I didn't Google it—I swear. I took desvenlafaxine for a short time, so I recognized the name. It gave me insomnia, and then I switched to sertraline. I think maybe you saw the bottle a few weeks ago."

A stab of guilt reminded Ruth that she hadn't said anything to reassure Chloe at the time. She hoped Chloe hadn't spent these weeks worrying Ruth would judge her. "I'm sorry. I never meant to invade your privacy—"

"It's okay." Chloe looked sheepish. "I dropped it right in front of you."

"Yes. Well." Ruth wrung her hands. "If you've ever missed a dose, you have some sense of what I've been dealing with today."

"Absolutely." Chloe settled on the floor. "The withdrawal is awful. My whole body feels nervous and sick, and I hurt everywhere. That's why I keep a bottle in my purse."

"I used to keep a few pills here in my desk." Ruth gestured at the drawer containing her personal items. "But then I ran out and never replenished them." It occurred to her that Chloe had seen the entire contents of the drawer, and the inside of her purse...not to mention her house and bedroom. Warmth crept up her neck at the thought of Chloe in her private spaces. She hoped she hadn't left panties on the floor—and that if she had, they weren't granny panties.

"You should pack a few pills tonight, in case this ever happens again."

"Good idea." Ruth winced as pain shot through her head. "Sorry. Brain zap." She crossed and uncrossed her legs, unable to get comfortable.

Scooting next to her, Chloe took her hand.

Ruth blinked at her.

Chloe looked down at their joined hands. "Oh gosh. I'm sorry."

As Chloe started to withdraw her hand, Ruth tightened her grip. "No, it—it helps."

They sat in silence for a moment. Chloe's smaller hand was warm with a gentle but secure grip. The contact steadied Ruth.

Chloe turned her head to meet Ruth's gaze. "I hope you know this about me already, but I won't tell anyone your private medical information. I promise."

"I appreciate it." Ruth squeezed Chloe's hand. "I'm not ashamed to take medication, but I'm sure you know it carries a certain stigma."

"Oh, for sure. I think that's why I waited so long to get help with my anxiety. I was having panic attacks and missing class, but somehow I didn't think it was bad enough to warrant professional help. So I tried to suck it up until—well, until I couldn't anymore."

So, Chloe took the medication for anxiety, not depression. Her fidgeting and skittish behavior made more sense. Ruth wondered if her struggles had contributed to Chloe not continuing with school, despite her obvious interest in academics. "Was this in college?" Ruth asked gently.

"No. I mean, yes." She glanced away. "It was during college." Chloe sat with her head bowed and a slight slump in her shoulders, still holding Ruth's hand.

"I'm sorry. I didn't mean to make you uncomfortable." Ruth paused. "I hope you know by now that I'd never judge you or anyone for taking medication. Perhaps it goes without saying since I'm also on an SSRI, but...I wanted to say it."

Chloe gave her a grateful smile. "I really appreciate it."

Should Ruth share in return? She trusted so few people with her mental health history that hiding was a reflex. Chloe wouldn't blab or react with scorn, but would she see Ruth differently?

Ruth looked down at their linked hands, and then up at Chloe's serious mouth and clear eyes beneath natural lashes. If opening up made Chloe feel less alone, it would be worth the risk. She took a deep breath. "I have depression. That's why I take desvenlafaxine."

Chloe listened with an open gaze—questioning, but not pushing.

"I went through a bad time in college, but it wasn't until grad school that avoiding medication became…untenable." Ruth ran her free hand up and down her shin as she spoke.

"I've heard that lot of people struggle with mental health during PhD programs."

"That's an understatement. Grad school is hell on mental health—not to mention physical and emotional health. My depression gets triggered by stress, and in grad school the stress was unrelenting." Her muscles tensed as she remembered. "I had a very harsh advisor. Nothing was ever good enough for him, and he wasn't shy about letting me know when I failed to meet his standards."

"Oh, that sounds awful." Chloe looked genuinely devastated for her. "Was he your chair?"

"Yes, he was." Somewhere in her jumbled brain, Ruth noted Chloe's easy invocation of the shorthand for *dissertation committee chair.*

"You probably had to work with him, huh? Because of your topic?"

"That's right." Another surprise. Most people thought grad students could simply switch advisors, but apparently, Chloe was well-read enough to know better. "I had classmates who talked about their advisors rubber-stamping whatever they wrote, but mine made me re-do my papers again and again. In my second year, I shut down. I spent days in bed, not dealing with anything. The work piled up, but I couldn't bring myself to care. I gained twenty pounds, and my doctor referred me to a psychiatrist."

"I'm so sorry." Chloe tightened her grip on Ruth's hand. "Is that when you started taking medication?"

"Mm-hmm. It wasn't the only intervention—I went to therapy, and I learned how to be more proactive in looking after my mental health. But the medication made a tremendous difference."

"I feel the same way. I mean, I've never had clinical depression—just straight-up anxiety. At the time, I didn't even know they prescribed anti-depressants for anxiety, but sertraline changed my life. I'm still anxious, of course, but it's not overwhelming anymore. The medication keeps me healthy enough to avoid succumbing completely."

"Exactly." Ruth marveled at the similarities in their stories.

Chloe ran her thumb back and forth over the back of Ruth's hand, sending goose bumps up Ruth's arm.

"How are you feeling?" Chloe asked.

"Better." It was true. Perhaps the medication was kicking in at last, or maybe it was Chloe's touch and understanding helping Ruth to decompress. Whatever the reason, the worst was over. *I'm okay.*

"Do you need a ride home?" Chloe asked.

It was tempting. Ruth could relax in the passenger seat while she waited out the remaining symptoms. A ride would also mean more time with Chloe, prolonging the connection they'd formed that afternoon.

Then she played it out. Chloe would insist on picking her up the next morning, and Ruth didn't want to inconvenience her more than she already had. Chloe was still her assistant—and Ruth remembered all too well how Chloe had looked at her when she stepped out of the bathroom topless. The boundary between them had blurred, and Ruth had to be careful.

"I'm okay," Ruth said. "Truly. I should let you get home." She pulled her hand back but then instantly missed the contact.

"Okay. If you're sure." After wavering for a few seconds, Chloe pushed herself up. "It was nice to talk."

"Yes, it was." Ruth looked up at her.

They stared for a moment too long. This time Ruth wasn't half-naked, but she felt no less exposed, and those hazel eyes were just as potent as they'd been on that day. Chloe looked at her as if she were a vision—not a rumpled academic slouching on the floor.

When Ruth looked at Chloe, she didn't see an employee. She saw a friend—and a beautiful, caring woman. It was hard to believe Ruth had once strode past Chloe's desk with barely a glance in her direction. Now she couldn't stop noticing her thoughtful eyes and sweet smile.

Finally, Chloe tore her gaze away. She left and closed the door with a soft click.

Ruth rested her head against the wall. *God.* What was happening between them?

———

Caitlyn's phone chipped in the passenger seat. She pulled into the driveway and turned off the car—safety first—before checking the message.

It was from Chloe:

Ummmm explain this?

There was a screenshot of a text from Ruth:

Thank you again for today. I am sure you know I loathe being vulnerable at work. You were there for me without judgment, and your kindness got me through the afternoon. I won't forget it.

"Shit," Caitlyn whispered. Now Chloe knew something had happened.
She longed to respond with her own sentiments—to thank Ruth for her trust and to provide reassurance. But she couldn't send the message through Chloe, compromising Ruth's privacy. Caitlyn typed back:

I helped Ruth with something today. No big deal. Don't worry about it.

Chloe's response came right away.

What did you help her with?

Caitlyn should have known her sister wouldn't be satisfied. She would have to be more direct.

I can't say because it's personal. I promised I wouldn't tell anyone.

Seriously? She thought she was telling ME.

While technically Chloe was correct, the relationship Caitlyn had with Ruth was fundamentally different. Ruth never would have opened up to the real Chloe about something so personal. Caitlyn typed back,

I'm sorry. I can't.

Chloe sent a frowny emoji. *WTF am I supposed to write back?*
Sighing, Caitlyn started to type a response.

I'm here for you. She deleted it, typed a new version, and then repeated this process until she settled, unhappily, on something both Ruth and Chloe could read.

Thank you. I'm glad I could help.

Maybe in a couple of weeks, she could give Ruth her "new" phone number. If she stayed that long. Of course, at some point, she'd have to get back to her real life and the academic job market.

Who was she kidding? Caitlyn had no intention of leaving in such a short time. Lying to Ruth was bad enough—she couldn't abandon her. After all, they were just starting the retention initiative. *Ruth needs me.* And some part of her needed Ruth too. Caitlyn would stay until she absolutely had to go.

Chapter 14

"ANYTHING ELSE WE SHOULD DISCUSS?" Jack tapped his pen on the table in a rapid patter.

Ruth set down her notepad. "I think that's enough budget for a Friday afternoon. I'll see you tonight at trivia."

"Shit." Jack leaned back in his chair. "That's tonight?"

"Yes. It's the first Friday of the month."

"Damn—you're right. Well, I can't come anyway."

"Oh, come on." Ruth smacked the table. "Ah. Sorry." She drew her hand back and curled her fingers. "It's just that we need you on geography. Beverly already dropped out. If you don't come, it will just be me and Piper."

"My daughter has a swim meet." Jack had the decency to look apologetic. "I'll be there next month."

"The faculty will crush us. Again." Ruth could already picture their smug faces.

"Sorry." Jack stood and pushed in his chair. "Hey, it's the middle of summer. Maybe they'll have attendance problems too."

"No. They enjoy beating us too much." Ruth realized she sounded excessively bitter. "Not that winning matters, of course. I only go to support the scholarship."

"Uh-huh. Sure." Jack clearly wasn't fooled. He'd seen Ruth play enough times to know better.

Ruth sighed. "Good luck to your daughter."

"Thanks. Good luck tonight." He walked out.

Luck won't be enough. Ruth needed more players. She squinted at the wall that separated her office from the front lobby.

Chloe had come through for her yesterday, and they'd shared a moment of genuine connection. Still, the text message Chloe had sent afterwards gave Ruth pause.

I'm glad I could help.

It was polite but distant, with no reciprocation of the sentiment Ruth had conveyed. If they'd been dating, Ruth would have interpreted the message as a sign to back off. Even though they weren't dating, of course—a ridiculous notion—it had given Ruth a sour feeling.

Would an invitation to trivia make Chloe uncomfortable? While the event was for college scholarships, it was held at a bar after work—not exactly a professional setting. Still, how intimate could it be with Piper in attendance? If anything, Chloe might feel a bit like the third wheel since she and Piper were such good friends.

With a determined nod, Ruth pushed to her feet and walked out to the lobby.

Chloe sat hunched over her keyboard, squinting at the monitor. The screen displayed a pivot table in Microsoft Excel. Even on a Friday afternoon, Chloe was working.

"Chloe?"

Chloe jumped. "Oh! Sorry. I was...absorbed."

"Anything interesting?"

"Maybe." Chloe's eyes sparkled. "I'm not sure yet."

Ruth lost herself in Chloe's eager gaze before she remembered her purpose. "Are you free tonight?"

"I..." Chloe sucked in a breath. "Yes?"

Shit. Ruth tensed as she realized how it sounded. "No! Uh, I mean, there's a monthly fundraiser at Flannigan's for the first-generation scholarship fund. It's a trivia game, with teams of up to six people. We have a team of administrators who play, but we're down to just me and Piper for tonight. Of course, there's no pressure to come, but—"

"I'd love to come." Chloe sat up straight and clasped her hands. "Should I bring cash?"

"I'll cover the donation. All we need is your knowledge of pop culture. I know you keep up with all of that celebrity news—between you and Piper, we'll win that round for sure." While Chloe had been more interested in spreadsheets in recent weeks, Ruth had caught her browsing entertainment websites on multiple occasions when she'd first started. Chloe could be their secret weapon.

Chloe's smile faded. "Oh. I don't really know that much. I mean, I hope I don't disappoint you."

"Nonsense. It's for a good cause. Of course, I'd love to beat the faculty, but with only three people we're just hoping for a respectable performance."

"We play the faculty?"

"Well, yes. Other people play too—it's open to anyone—but some faculty go every month. Sometimes they have enough people for two teams. They're big supporters of the scholarship program." *And they love to gloat when they win.*

"Hmm. That makes it even more interesting. What time?"

"Six o'clock. Parking is tight, so we usually ride over together in my car. Then I'll drop you and Piper back here when we're done."

"Okay." Chloe beamed, and Ruth knew she'd made the right decision.

Satisfied, Ruth walked back into her office and retrieved her phone from the conference table.

There was a new text from Piper:

Madeline isn't feeling well. I'm going to have to skip trivia tonight.

Ruth clutched her phone to her chest. "Oh no." Without Piper, she would be there with Chloe...alone...at a bar.

Should she rescind the invitation?

No. She couldn't turn around and cancel just because Piper couldn't come; that would give Chloe the idea that Ruth didn't want to spend time with her—or worse, that Ruth was afraid to spend time alone with her.

Nothing inappropriate had happened between them. Nothing ever would. Therefore, there was no reason she couldn't attend with Chloe.

So why was her heart thumping against her ribcage, her pulse so loud she could hear it in her ears?

———————

Caitlyn speed-scrolled through the Entertainment Weekly website, frantically attempting to absorb a decade's worth of pop culture knowledge in less than an hour. Two actors were rumored to be dating. Was that important? Caitlyn had never heard of them.

Chloe would be fantastic at pop culture trivia. She always knew the latest celebrity gossip. Unfortunately, Ruth seemed to know this about Chloe.

Of course, Caitlyn wouldn't get in trouble if she didn't know enough pop culture trivia. Ruth wouldn't be angry, and she certainly wouldn't suspect a false identity just because Caitlyn couldn't name a few celebrities. Still, the trivia game was a competition against faculty. She didn't want to let Ruth down.

At five-thirty, Ruth emerged from her office with her purse slung over her shoulder. "Ready?"

Caitlyn nodded and reached for her purse. "Will Piper meet us by the car, or...?"

Ruth stiffened. "Actually, Piper won't be able to make it. Something came up at the last minute."

Caitlyn's heart thumped. "So our team is just...the two of us?"

"If you're uncomfortable with that—"

"Of course not." Caitlyn stood and pushed in her chair. *You're the one who looks nervous.* "I was just thinking with only two people, our chances of winning won't be as good."

"Oh, we'll lose, for sure." Ruth walked to the doors and held one open for Caitlyn. "The faculty have a natural advantage since they all have different specialties. Politics, history, biology—they've even got a sports guy. They've always got more players—not that any of that stops them from rubbing in their victories."

Caitlyn walked through the door and waited while Ruth locked the suite for the night. "Maybe we'll surprise them tonight. You never know." She wasn't optimistic—the few facts she'd gleaned from cramming entertainment news were jumbled in her brain. Still, her steps were light and she couldn't help smiling. This was her first chance to spend time with Ruth outside of work. Sure, the event was related to the college, but there would be no meeting agenda—and no one else at their table.

Ruth, however, didn't seem to share Caitlyn's giddy anticipation. As they walked to the parking garage, Ruth's steps were swift, and she didn't bother to make small talk. Was Ruth actually worried about their performance at pub trivia? Or was her tense demeanor because it was just the two of them?

In the garage, Ruth led Caitlyn to a black Prius parked in front of a large metal sign that said *RESERVED FOR PRESIDENT*. She flushed and made a fluttery gesture at the sign. "That was already here when they hired me."

How adorable that Ruth, who oozed authority in meetings, was self-conscious about a designated parking space—something any man would expect. "Hey, you deserve it." Caitlyn walked over to the passenger side. "We can't have the college president circling the parking deck when there's important business waiting."

Ruth's mouth quirked. "Indeed."

Caitlyn settled in the passenger seat. The car was clean except for a cardboard coffee cup in one cup holder and a crumpled Caramello wrapper in the other. The air in the vehicle smelled like Ruth—lavender, with a hint of something sweet.

Ruth was quiet on the short drive to the bar, appearing to concentrate on the road despite the absence of traffic.

As they pulled into the parking lot, Caitlyn decided she might as well broach the likely subject of Ruth's discomfort. "Do you think people will wonder why I'm here?" *Why we're here together?*

"You're an administrator. You belong on the team." Ruth nodded firmly and unbuckled her seatbelt. "Let's go in."

The pub was dark with yellow lanterns hanging from the ceiling and a candle flickering on every table. A full bar lined one of the walls, while Celtic artwork hung on the other. Most of the tables were full.

A wave caught Caitlyn's eye. It was Joe from the sociology department. There were five other people at the table, two she recognized—Jenn Christiansen and Dan Toscano—and three she couldn't place.

Ruth gave a quick wave back and then made her way to an open table. It was small with two chairs and a candle in the center.

Like a date. As she slid into the rickety metal chair, Caitlyn fantasized that Ruth had chosen to be there with her, and only her, instead of stumbling into the situation because Piper had canceled.

A waitress with a high blonde ponytail appeared at the table. "Hi there, what can I get you?"

"A Diet Coke and—" Ruth looked at Caitlyn. "Do you like soft pretzels?"

Caitlyn imagined them sharing food from a little basket. "Sounds great. And I'll have a ginger ale."

Ruth unsnapped her slim wallet and pulled out three twenty dollar bills. "We'd like to play trivia. Please donate the change."

"Sure thing." The waitress retrieved a slip of paper from her apron and set it on the table. "I'll put those drink orders in."

"You know," Ruth said as the waitress departed, "you can order alcohol. I don't mind. I'm drinking soda because I'm driving."

"Oh, that's okay." Caitlyn hesitated, then reminded herself that it was safe to explain. Ruth took similar medication. "Alcohol hits me hard because of Zoloft. For me, having one drink is like someone else having three."

"I understand." Ruth nodded. "That's one of the reasons I don't drink when I'm driving—a low tolerance. I'm not sure if it's my medication or if I'm just getting older, but either way I won't risk it."

"That's smart. Besides, we need to stay sharp to beat the faculty."

Ruth flicked a glance at the crowded faculty table. "Don't get your hopes up."

The host announced the first round: sports trivia.

"Oh no." Caitlyn grimaced. "I don't know anything about sports. Do you?"

"A bit, but it won't matter. The faculty have Dan, who is like a walking sports almanac. They always win."

The first question concerned a new signing on the Chicago Bears football team. Ruth picked up the pen and wrote down a name on their answer sheet in elegant blue print.

"Wow. That's impressive."

Ruth shrugged. "I watch football."

Caitlyn pictured Ruth on the edge of her couch, watching a tackle and perhaps shouting at the screen. It was an amusing image.

As the round went on, Ruth answered three additional questions with confidence. They both drew blanks on the rest.

The waitress collected their answer sheet, and a few minutes later, the host announced the scores. Ruth and Caitlyn got four points, another team got five, another got seven—and then the host announced the winner: *Facul-tee-birds.*

The faculty table burst into applause, and a waitress carried a table of shots to their table.

Ruth's mouth twitched as she caught Caitlyn's gaze, a subtle gesture of annoyance that only Caitlyn could detect. But amusement danced in Ruth's eyes, indicating she didn't take the game too seriously.

"What's our team name?" Caitlyn asked. She hadn't noticed what Ruth had written on their answer sheet.

"Oh, I just write Pulaski administration."

"But that's so boring. You're supposed to think of a pun—or something dirty."

Ruth chuckled. "Maybe next time."

Caitlyn tingled at the suggestion that there would be a next time. Would Ruth make her a permanent member of the team? She hadn't chosen an exact end date for her stint as Chloe, but surely there'd be no harm in staying an extra month. Especially if there was a chance of repeating an evening out with Ruth.

When the host announced the entertainment category, Ruth winked at Caitlyn. "Your time to shine."

Oh Lord. She hoped that by some miracle, the celebrity news she'd studied a few hours earlier would make up for a lifetime of indifference.

"Question one," the host said. "Jennifer Aniston has a new man in her life. What is his name?"

Ruth looked at her expectantly.

"Um." Caitlyn had no clue. "I'm sorry."

"There's no need to be sorry." Ruth chuckled. "I certainly don't know the answer."

"I know she's not with Brad Pitt anymore. I guess I lost track after that."

"Question two. Beyoncé was just announced as the headline act for what major event?"

Shit. Chloe loved Beyoncé. She'd know the answer for sure. "Um, the Super Bowl?" Caitlyn lowered her voice to a whisper—not that overhearing her guess was likely to help the other teams.

Ruth leaned in. "I doubt it. She already headlined a few years ago, when Baltimore played San Francisco." As they huddled closer together, the candlelight threw a warm glow on Ruth's lips and cheeks.

Caitlyn grinned. "You really do like sports. Let's make an educated guess. Lollapalooza? Maybe they asked the question because it's in Chicago."

"Why not?" Ruth wrote down *Lollapalooza.*

The next questions covered television shows, more celebrity news, and the Emmy award nominations. Caitlyn didn't know any of the answers. "I guess we tanked that round," she said as the waitress collected their answers.

"Perhaps we should be proud that we did so poorly. It means we devote our attention to more intellectual pursuits."

"Like football?" Caitlyn teased.

Ruth laughed. "Okay, maybe not." They smiled at each other.

The faculty didn't win either. A table behind them received a tray of shots.

When the hosts announced the next round, history, Ruth rolled her eyes. "They've got a history professor." She jerked her thumb at the faculty. "They always win this one."

Hmmm. I like history. Caitlyn rubbed her palms together. "We'll see."

"Question one. Who was the first African American Supreme Court Justice?"

Thurgood Marshall, Ruth mouthed.

Caitlyn nodded in agreement, and Ruth wrote the answer.

"Who is the author of *The Protestant Ethic and the Spirit of Capitalism?*"

Caitlyn grinned. A sociology question.

Ruth frowned. "It sounds so familiar. Um."

Caitlyn grabbed the pen and paper and wrote *Max Weber.*

"That's—that's actually correct." Ruth stared at Caitlyn as though she'd never seen her before.

"How many US presidents were assassinated in office?"

Caitlyn began to count on her fingers. "Lincoln and Kennedy," she whispered.

"Garfield," Ruth added. "Three?"

"I think…" Caitlyn searched her memory. "McKinley." She wrote *4* on the answer sheet.

"Ah, right. I forgot about him." Ruth peered at her. "You know your history."

They took turns writing down answers to the rest of the questions. When the waitress came around to collect their answer sheet, they had filled in all ten.

"I think we got them all right," Caitlyn said happily.

Ruth drummed the table. "Maybe. I'm only 90 percent sure about that one question—about India."

"No, you were right. Rajendra Prasad." Caitlyn hadn't said anything at the time, but she had also known the answer Ruth wrote on their sheet.

After a few moments, the host turned on the mic. "The winner is… Pulaski administration!"

Caitlyn squealed. *We beat the history professor.*

Ruth acknowledged the victory with more poise—she smiled at Caitlyn and then stole a quick glance at the faculty table.

Several of the professors looked extremely put out. "What did we miss?" one of them asked.

"They probably forgot McKinley," Caitlyn whispered.

Ruth chuckled.

The waitress brought a tray of shots to the table, their prize for winning the round.

"Remember your advice to be nicer to faculty?" Ruth gestured at them with a sly smile.

"Yes…" What was Ruth up to?

"Why don't we offer these shots to our friends?"

Caitlyn laughed. "I love it."

They each picked up two and walked over to the faculty.

"We thought we'd share the spoils of victory," Ruth said.

"Well done," Dan said with grudging respect.

"Have a great night." Ruth turned to walk back to the table.

Caitlyn gave them a fluttery wave before she turned to follow. It was the most fun she'd had in ages.

Outside, the sky was dark, and the air was warm. Ruth slid into her car beside Chloe. "I'll turn on the air conditioning."

Chloe nodded. "Thanks." Her cheeks were flushed. "That was really fun."

"Thanks for coming. I couldn't have done it without you." They'd won the history and current events rounds, while tying the faculty on music, earning a few grumpy stares. Ruth had enjoyed their moments of glory a little too much, partly because she and Chloe had done it together. Even after work, they were on the same team—a fearsome pair and worthy competition.

Not that winning at trivia mattered, of course. It was just for fun—and the scholarship program. Work was another story. She needed allies with the future of the college at stake, not to mention her own career. Chloe was a true partner and friend.

My employee, she corrected herself. They clicked so well that it was easy to forget, but they weren't equals.

As they turned onto the main road, the moon appeared before them. "Whoa." Even partly obscured by trees, it was magnificent: huge and full, with an ethereal orange glow.

"Oh wow." Chloe sat up straight. "It's one of those supermoons."

"That's amazing. I've never seen one so big." Ruth shifted her gaze back and forth from the moon to the road, entranced by the sight but mindful that she was operating a motor vehicle. She turned the car into the parking garage. "What floor are you on?"

"The third." Chloe turned to her. "But I bet the moon looks cool from the very top of the garage," she said with hope in her voice.

"Let's find out." Ruth navigated the twisty path to the top floor, an open-air lot ringed by tall metal guardrails.

"Oh, look!" Chloe's voice came out in a gasp.

The moon hovered before them, unobstructed and whole.

"Gorgeous." Ruth stopped the car across two empty parking spaces.

"Do you mind if I get out? I'd like to get a picture."

"Go ahead."

Chloe unbuckled her seatbelt and slipped from the vehicle.

Ruth rested her thumb on the red button of her seatbelt, hesitating. There was no reason not to follow—so why did her heart thump as though it were dangerous? Shaking off the unwelcome feeling, Ruth unsnapped the seatbelt and threw open the door.

A few paces ahead, Chloe's hair bounced lightly behind her as she reached the guardrail at the edge of the lot. She held up her phone to snap a photo.

Ruth walked up beside her. "Did you get a good shot?"

Chloe inspected the result and giggled. "No. It's terrible. See?"

Ruth moved closer to peer at the screen. The moon appeared as an orange dot in the center of an otherwise black photo. "Not quite Ansel Adams," she said dryly.

Chloe laughed harder and dropped her phone to her side, brushing Ruth's arm. "Oh well. At least we get to see it." She stepped even closer to the guardrail.

With Chloe's focus on the sky, Ruth was drawn instead to Chloe's profile, which seemed to glow in the soft orange moonlight. Every inch of her was art—full cheeks, high cheekbones, defined chin. The slight slope of her nose. Her eyes gleamed at the sight before her, while her lips parted in wonder. A breeze ruffled her hair, sending a few strands askew.

"It's really something," Chloe said, brushing an errant whisp from her eyes.

"Beautiful," Ruth said without thinking. When Chloe turned, Ruth was openly staring at her, the moon nowhere in her field of vision. *Shit.* Ruth's pulse sped, but she couldn't look away.

Chloe watched Ruth closely, a question burning in her eyes.

Ruth wrenched her gaze away from Chloe and fixed it on the moon. What was she doing? She had no business speaking like that to her assistant, especially not alone together at night. And Chloe's silent reply said she knew it had nothing to do with the wonders of astronomy.

Chloe could file a Title IX complaint for that stare.

"I'm..." Chloe paused.

The only sounds were the cicadas and the rumbling of an engine far below them.

Ruth's stomach flopped like a fish on sand. *What?*

"I'm really glad you invited me tonight." Her warm voice suggested a Title IX complaint would not be forthcoming.

Ruth struggled to get a grip. "Yes. Me too." It came out scratchy. She cleared her throat. "After all, you're part of the administration, so you belong on the team. Perhaps you can join us next time, when Piper and the others come too."

"Right." Chloe exhaled, and her whole body seemed to deflate.

Guilt twisted within Ruth. She hadn't meant to put Chloe in her place, but that was obviously Chloe's interpretation. When their gazes met again, a hard wall stood between them.

It's for the best. "Come on," Ruth said gently. "I'll drive you to your car."

Chloe nodded and followed a few paces behind her. The sound of her slow, sullen footsteps broke Ruth's heart.

***

Caitlyn sat alone in her car, fingers trembling in her lap. This time there was no ambiguity, no plausible excuse for the intensity of Ruth's stare.

Ruth likes me. Not as an assistant, a colleague, or even a friend. She had called Caitlyn *beautiful,* the soft word slipping from her lips as though Ruth were talking to herself. The shocked look that followed confirmed the sentiment was genuine, a private thought Ruth hadn't meant to express.

For a few reckless seconds, Caitlyn's heart had filled with warmth and joy—until Ruth's strained demeanor brought her back to reality. While Ruth clearly struggled with the employer/employee conflict, a personal relationship was impossible for more reasons than Ruth could ever fathom.

"Fuck." Caitlyn winced and rubbed her eyes. Why did it have to be so hard?

When Caitlyn had first impersonated Chloe, she had imagined the worst-case scenario: security, handcuffs, the end of her career. Instead, the universe had devised a more sinister punishment—bringing Ruth into Caitlyn's life and tormenting her with the knowledge that a true connection between them was impossible, thanks to her lies.

Chapter 15

RUTH'S PULSE SPIKED ON CUE as she approached her office. She'd had the whole weekend to recover from the charged moment on the parking deck, but she still hadn't fully calmed down. Passing the assistant's desk shouldn't come with a whirl of conflicting emotions, and yet—*Ugh, him again?*

Gary Baker was loitering in front of Chloe's desk again, causing a bitter taste in Ruth's mouth.

"You should really watch it." Gary leaned in. "It's the smartest show out there."

Chloe sat with arms crossed. "I totally would, but I don't have a Hulu account." She leaned her head back, putting a few more inches between her and Gary, who was practically breathing in her face.

"Ah, never fear. I'll gladly share my password." Gary glanced up, and his friendly smile vanished.

"Good afternoon." Ruth didn't know what she'd ever done to Gary, aside from refusing to tolerate incoherent phone messages. Alice must have turned him against her.

"Welcome back," Chloe said. In contrast to Gary, she straightened and smiled. Then she seemed to catch herself and tightened her expression, clasping her hands in her lap.

Ruth dipped her chin as she passed the desk, wishing a single nod could convey everything she couldn't say—that she'd cherished Friday night, but a personal relationship between them, even platonic, couldn't happen. That she hoped their warm working relationship could continue, somehow, within the boundaries she couldn't afford to discard.

Of course, it was grossly inadequate.

Sighing to herself, Ruth sat at her desk and began to scroll through the barrage of emails. Soon, her eyes glazed, and she instead listened to the conversation wafting in from the outer room.

Gary continued his awkward flirting. Chloe's disinterest was obvious, but she stopped short of telling him to scram, so he kept on talking.

Didn't he have work to do, or at least his own phone to cover?

Seized with an impulse to interrupt, Ruth rose from her chair and marched back out. "Chloe!"

Chloe turned her head. "Sorry. Did you need something?"

Good question. Ruth's neck grew hot as she drew a blank. "The... Yes. Please contact Eugenia Philips, and tell her the HVAC in my office is either broken or set to heat, and that *this time* instead of sending her grunty and incompetent lackey, I would prefer—" She took a breath. "Actually, just call her and tell her to stop by at her earliest convenience. Thank you." She spun around and walked back into her office.

"I guess I'll let you make your phone call." Gary's morose voice drifted behind her.

His palpable disappointment brought Ruth cheer. *Leave Chloe alone.* She huffed and pulled on her collar. Ulterior motive aside, her request was legitimate. The office was stifling.

Satisfied that Gary was on his way out, Ruth returned to her email with renewed focus. One message in particular caught her eye. She read quickly, then slowly to be sure she hadn't misunderstood. "Chloe! Get in here!"

Chloe rushed in, hair whipping behind her. "What? What's wrong?"

Ruth pushed her chair back and stood. "I heard back from Jonathan. They're approving Amari's financial aid."

"Oh!" Chloe broke into a wide smile. "I'm so happy." Despite having no connection to the student, she was glowing. "Does he know?"

"Not yet. I found out ten seconds ago." Ruth wanted to clap or dance or *something*. She stepped out from behind the desk, her blood buzzing with the rush of victory. "We did it—thanks to you." A rush of gratitude swept through her.

Laughing, Chloe moved closer. "This is amazing. He's going to get thousands of dollars because of us." She bounced on the balls of her feet. "I can't believe it."

Ruth didn't know how it happened or who closed the gap, but suddenly, they were in each other's arms.

Chloe's firm breasts pressed against Ruth's chest, and her hands locked behind Ruth's back.

Ruth hugged back, inhaling the scent of coffee and dessert—some soap or shampoo that smelled like food. Chloe's heartbeat pounded against her, fast and hard.

"Ahem." Eugenia's harsh voice interrupted them.

Chloe gasped as they broke apart. "Sorry! We were celebrating."

Ruth stepped back. Her cheeks flamed.

Eugenia regarded them with narrowed eyes. "I see what you mean—it is hot in here."

Caitlyn managed to refrain from scratching her arms, but she tapped her foot, bounced her knees, and swiveled her chair back and forth.

We hugged. First that look on Friday night, and then we hugged...

Ruth's door was closed, but the muffled sounds of Ruth arguing with Eugenia drifted out. The conversation would probably continue for some time, and then Ruth would be in meetings. Would they ever talk about it?

Caitlyn imagined Ruth sitting her down for a stern talk about how nothing could happen between them.

No kidding. If Ruth knew the truth, she would never speak to Caitlyn again. Ruth would regret every kind word, every gesture, and—of course—the hug they'd just shared. Caitlyn bowed her head, feeling like scum.

Maybe if Caitlyn kept the focus on work, they could avoid an excruciating and ultimately pointless conversation. Work was all she could do for Ruth anyway in her short stint as Chloe—and she would put her guilt and longing aside to do her very best. She owed Ruth that much.

Chapter 16

RUTH HAD LED COUNTLESS MEETINGS at Pulaski, but this one was different. The retention working group was her initiative, and she'd gone around the faculty council to invite people directly. She would hate to see poor attendance—especially in front of Chloe.

Not that Chloe's opinion mattered, of course. This was about enrollment.

Holding her breath, Ruth pushed through the door.

Phew. Almost every seat was filled. In addition to the administrators she'd invited—who had little choice but to come, several faculty were there. Joe from sociology sat with Kimberly from political science and Miguel Fumero. Across from them, Lena Batalli and Kyle Marks from math were huddled together, whispering. Ruth nearly fell over when her gaze landed on the woman next to Kyle: Jenn Christiansen from philosophy.

This should be interesting.

Chloe stood at the podium, fiddling with the buttons that controlled the projector. She wore a maroon blazer with her black dress, and her hair was pinned up in a neat bun. Her eye makeup was subtle, yet striking. Chloe's style had evolved over the summer, and Ruth couldn't help but appreciate the result—from a distance, of course.

When Chloe noticed Ruth, she ran over as fast as her three-inch heels would allow. "Hi! Everything is ready."

Ruth nodded. "I had no doubt."

"It's a good turnout, right?"

"Very good. Especially for summer." Ruth suppressed a comment about the faculty's dedication to their summer vacation. After all, they did come.

"I agree." Chloe smiled. "So, I'll wait until you call on us?"

"Yes, I'll call on you *two*." Ruth's lips twitched as she withheld another comment. Chloe had been determined to include Maggie as a co-presenter, insisting that she had done half the work. Ruth suspected this was an exaggeration, but no matter—it would be good for Maggie's self-esteem. "You're going to do great." She lifted her hand to touch Chloe's shoulder, then jerked it back down.

As Chloe walked away, Ruth curled the fingers that had almost betrayed her. *Get a grip, Holloway.* The last thing she needed was to start touching Chloe in front of everyone. Or to touch her at all.

Ruth sat at the head of the table and waited for conversations to quiet. "I'm happy to see so many faculty here, especially during summer. I'm very appreciative."

Chloe gave her an encouraging smile.

"We are here because we need a comprehensive strategy to boost retention at Pulaski, and we can't wait until fall to start. I've been working on this problem since I arrived, but I invited faculty to the table because administration cannot solve this problem alone. You know the students best, and I need your insight to fully understand this problem."

Ruth paused to sip her water and glanced around for their reaction.

Several of the faculty nodded.

That was a good sign, so Ruth continued, "I also need your expertise. I want to implement solutions that work, and I'll need your help to evaluate the results. To get us started, Chloe and Maggie will present some preliminary data."

Several people turned to look at Chloe, who offered a shy smile in return. *They have no clue what she can do.*

"After the data presentation, we'll map some of the causes and brainstorm solutions as a group." Ruth turned to Chloe. "If you're ready?"

Chloe's chair screeched against the floor as she jumped up. "Yes, we're ready. Thank you." She motioned for Maggie to join her.

They stood at the front of the room. Maggie removed her hands from her pockets, then shoved them in again.

Chloe, however, looked comfortable at the front of the room. She tapped the laptop, and the screen filled with one of her gorgeous charts. "So, this is the average year-to-year retention at Pulaski."

Jenn had the decency to look impressed. "Wow! That's a nice visualization."

Miguel grinned. He had probably come to support Chloe—and perhaps Ruth too, since he was her top suspect for leaking Steve's plans for the board meeting.

Chloe advanced to the next slide. "Next, Maggie will review some student demographics." She stood back and gave Maggie an encouraging nod.

"Okay. Thanks. So this slide looks at age and gender..." Maggie appeared nervous at first, making excessive hand motions as she spoke. As she continued, however, her confidence grew.

When Maggie finished, Chloe resumed control of the laptop. As she paged through her charts and tables, the audience watched with wide eyes and raised brows.

At one point, Beverly caught Ruth's eye and mouthed, *She made this?*

Ruth merely curved her lips in response. Inside, though, she swelled with pride. Chloe was poised, professional, and in command of the room. *Not bad for an office assistant.*

The faculty interrupted with numerous questions, and Chloe fielded each one with ease. When Lena asked about first-generation students—information Chloe hadn't prepared—she spoke about possible ways to study the topic, then smoothly promised to look into it. If Ruth didn't know better, she'd think Chloe was a seasoned lecturer who had presented data countless times.

Chloe dedicated several minutes to the results of Ruth's early-alert initiative, dwelling indulgently on each slide showing the positive results. While she kept her tone neutral, the joy in her eyes left no doubt that she loved every second of proving that Ruth had been right.

She's on my side. Ruth relished having an ally who was both brilliant and loyal. Chloe was special—and Ruth had discovered her first.

Finally, Chloe reached the last slide. "That's all we have for now. I appreciate your attention and the great questions."

There was a moment of stunned silence.

"So!" Joe cracked his knuckles. "How much is Ruth paying you? Because it's not enough."

Everyone laughed.

Chloe averted her eyes. "I'm paid enough."

"What's your background, Chloe?" Kimberly asked. "Where did you learn how to do this?"

"Oh gosh. I don't want to take up time with my life story." Chloe slipped out from behind the podium and returned to her seat, flanked by Maggie, who seemed just as eager to be out of the spotlight.

Ruth realized Chloe must feel embarrassed that she didn't have much formal education. She cleared her throat. "I'm fortunate to have an assistant with many talents. But we should use this time to talk about retention." She stood and walked over to the dry-erase board on the wall. "Let's start by making a list of the reasons students drop out."

Uncapping the blue marker, Ruth prepared for a waste of time. She had already reviewed the relevant research and mapped out the problem on her own—which she was more than qualified to do given her PhD in education. However, Chloe had insisted this part was necessary. *Faculty need to feel like you value their opinion.* So, fine—they'd go through the exercise.

"Poor academic performance," Joe said.

Obviously. "Great." Ruth wrote it on the board.

Kimberly raised her hand. "Financial reasons. I've had students who can't afford to come back. Some of them end up working to support their families, and they say it's temporary—but it doesn't turn out that way."

Ruth had already considered this one too, but she nodded and wrote *financial hardship* on another section of the whiteboard. "Good one. Thanks."

"Sometimes it's personal reasons," Joe said. "Pregnancy, mental health, substance abuse."

"Yup. The worst is when the girls drop out for some loser boyfriend," Jenn added.

As she wrote *personal* on the board, Ruth recalled Chloe's explanation of her stalled education. Some heinous *girlfriend* was responsible for Chloe squandering her academic potential. Well, Ruth would get her back on track. Somehow.

Turning back to the room, Ruth waited for someone else to speak. She'd expected the pool of insight to be shallow, but had they hit the bottom already?

"So," Chloe said, "we've got three big categories, but maybe we should drill down a bit further. Like, for the first one. Why do some students struggle with academics?"

"Poor preparation," Kyle said immediately. "In math, we have students who are in over their heads from day one."

Ruth frowned. "But we have a placement test. No one should be unprepared."

"Yes, but it's optional," Lena said. "Some of us think it should be mandatory, but even that won't solve everything. Honestly, we have students who need at least two semesters of high school math before they're ready for the lower-level course. I don't know how they passed math in high school."

Was it really that bad? Pulaski admitted most students regardless of SAT scores, but the students should at least be college-ready. "What about the peer tutoring program? Doesn't that help the students who are behind?"

"Some," Lena said. "If we can get them to go. It's not easy."

The other faculty nodded.

As Ruth scribbled on the board, her thoughts ran in several directions at once. Should the placement test be mandatory? How could they help students who placed below college-level math? And why weren't students going to tutoring?

"We need to have a longer conversation about math." Ruth turned to Chloe and Maggie. "I'd also like to see data on this. Do we know which students go to tutoring? And how often they go?"

Chloe gave Maggie an encouraging nod.

"Yes, we have some data," Maggie said. "We can look into it."

"What else?" Ruth asked.

"The ones who struggle stop coming to class," Jenn said. "I can't help them if they don't show up."

Joe nodded. "Attendance is an issue. No question."

If only we had some way to monitor attendance. Ruth swallowed the comment, remembering Chloe's advice. This wasn't the time to push her initiative. The goal was for the faculty to propose solutions.

Instead, Ruth simply wrote *attendance* on the board. "Now there's something to think about. What else?"

Over the next forty minutes, Ruth filled the white board with all of the different reasons students struggled. She knew several of the problems already, but the faculty also surprised her with new insights.

When she asked for possible solutions, she received some of the unrealistic proposals she'd expected: grants to pay students' personal bills, a mental health center—nice ideas for an alternate universe where the college wasn't struggling to remain solvent. But they also had ideas for how faculty could help for free: mentoring groups and working more closely with the tutoring program. When the meeting came to a close, Ruth had an entire list of ideas to ponder.

"That was great," Joe said as he passed Ruth on the way to the door.

Kimberly walked up behind him. "I'm so glad you reached out to faculty. We'll be at the next meeting too."

Jenn passed by Ruth without a word, but her chin dipped in acknowledgment.

No smart remark? Amazing. Ruth couldn't have asked for a better response, particularly from a curmudgeon like Jenn. The first meeting was a resounding success.

Soon, Ruth was alone in the room with Chloe.

Chloe switched off the projector. "I thought that went pretty well. What do you think?"

"Your presentation was excellent. And the meeting was...revelatory. I should have done this two years ago." Ruth tilted her head. "Well, two years ago I didn't have you."

Chloe blushed. "I'm glad I could help."

"Schedule another meeting for the two of us. We'll talk about our next steps—and I want to talk about your next steps too."

"My next steps?" Chloe blinked rapidly. "What does that mean?"

"We'll talk about it at the meeting." Ruth didn't want to spook Chloe, but they were due for a serious talk.

"Okay. I'll try not to be scared." The high pitch of her voice suggested she'd already failed.

"Nonsense. You've done well, and I'm very pleased." Ruth collected her belongings. "Send me a meeting invite, and we'll talk more then."

The conversation wouldn't be easy, but it was the right thing to do. In a couple of months, Chloe had become indispensable—and every day made it more obvious that a clerical job was all wrong for her.

Ruth would have loved to keep Chloe at her side forever, but she owed Chloe more than that—and she couldn't let her own interests get in the way of Chloe's future.

Hey, can we FaceTime tonight?

The text from Chloe arrived as Caitlyn walked to the parking garage. A wave of dread crashed through her, washing away her good mood. Chloe wouldn't propose a video call unless she had something serious to say.

While she couldn't rule anything out when it came to Chloe, Caitlyn guessed it was one of two possibilities. Either she was getting married, or she was coming home.

Caitlyn wouldn't be able to focus on anything else until they talked. She texted back:

I'm on my way home from work. Can we talk in about 20 minutes?

Sure. Call whenever you're ready.

Caitlyn sped home, accelerating to rocket through yellow lights as they turned red.

After a brief hello to her mom, she climbed the stairs to her bedroom. Her sense of dread intensified with every step. She closed the door, sat on the bed with her laptop, and started the call.

Chloe appeared on the sofa in a spaghetti-strap top with wavy hair and heavy makeup. The smears of mascara on her cheeks said the news wasn't good.

"What's wrong?"

"Hi." Chloe sniffled. "Nick and I are over."

The sight of Chloe in pain broke Caitlyn's heart. It always would, no matter the reason. "What happened?"

"We had a horrible fight. He said he feels suffocated with me here all the time. He wanted to go back to long distance, but I told him I don't want to go backward in our relationship. I said that if he makes me leave, I'll consider it the end." Chloe wiped her nose with the back of her hand. "Anyway. He said that I should leave."

"I'm so sorry. But if he won't even try to work it out, he doesn't deserve you." *Also, fuck him.* Caitlyn wished she could smack him for making Chloe cry.

"I bought a plane ticket for tomorrow afternoon. Then I can start back to work on Friday." She gave Caitlyn a tearful smile. "I'm so thankful that you kept covering for me—almost like you knew this would happen. I owe you, like, one hundred favors."

Caitlyn's vision blurred. Chloe wanted to come back to work?

"You'll have to catch me up on everything that happened," Chloe said, "and especially that weird text from Ruth."

Oh God. "Wait. It's not that simple."

Chloe sniffled. "What do you mean?"

"You can't just come back. My role—your role—has changed since you left."

"What are you talking about?"

"I…" Caitlyn braced herself. "I've been helping Ruth with data and strategy. She found out that I'm good at research, so I've been running numbers and exploring some of her hypotheses. And, um, we started a working group to collaborate with faculty on solutions."

Chloe's bloodshot eyes widened. "What the hell?"

"I know it sounds bad. I never meant to get involved in research while I was pretending to be you, but Ruth needed my help. Maggie has an IT background. She isn't really a researcher." Caitlyn paused. "Well, I've been teaching her basic research design, but we still have a lot to cover."

"You've been teaching Maggie how to do research?" Chloe's voice rose. "You're supposed to be me! How the fuck did you explain that?"

Caitlyn's heart beat faster. "Um, I told Ruth that I've—well, that you have been studying independently ever since LCC. She thinks you took some online classes, um, and learned on your own."

Chloe dropped her head into her hands. "Jesus Christ."

"I didn't think you'd come back! You said you were staying in Colorado, and I thought we agreed that I would work there for a few more weeks, and then I'd move on, and it would all be over." Caitlyn's voice broke on the word *over*. She wasn't ready for it to end.

Chloe looked up. "So that's why you wanted to stay? You wanted to keep doing *research* for Ruth Holloway?"

There was no point in lying to her twin. "Yes."

"God!" Chloe rubbed her forehead with her fists. "This is so typical."

"Huh? What part of this is typical?"

"You and your need to be better than everyone! You couldn't stand being *just the assistant*—you had to show off your fancy education. And now I'm getting screwed out of my job because I'm not ridiculously overqualified." Chloe's face crumpled as more tears escaped.

"What? I don't need to be better than everyone."

"Oh please." Chloe's eyes flashed with anger and hurt. "You've always been obsessed with perfect grades and honors and awards. You always had to be better than me—ever since they put you in the gifted program."

"You're still bitter about the gifted program?" Caitlyn was incredulous. "That was twenty years ago."

"I'm not bitter." Chloe shook her head as she blinked her tears away. "Actually, I think that gifted program was the worst thing that ever happened to you. You got so much praise for being smart—from Mom, our teachers, and everybody—and now it's like you can't live without it."

"That's not true." Caitlyn flinched. The words stung, but that didn't mean Chloe was right. She didn't need praise—did she? "You don't understand the pressure I've been under—the expectation that I'll succeed at everything like it's nothing. I mean, no wonder I have an anxiety disorder."

Fresh tears rolled down Chloe's cheeks. "Well, I'm sorry you had to excel at literally everything. Poor you. I can't believe you're talking to me like this when I just lost my boyfriend."

"I'm losing someone too!" Caitlyn covered her mouth as though she could stuff the words back in.

"What? What are you talking about?" Chloe's eyes bulged. "Wait. You mean Ruth? You're in love with Ruth?"

"No. God. Of course not." Caitlyn's pulse raced. "I'm not in love with her. But we've gotten to know each other."

"You're friends with my boss? Like, you two hang out?"

"Well, no. I'm—we have a good relationship, and I'm going to miss her."

Chloe stared through the screen, her face streaked with makeup and tears. "I'm sorry you got attached to Ruth. But this is *my* job. Not yours. I'm coming back to Linvale, and I'm going back to work."

What could she say? Caitlyn had no claim to the job or Pulaski or Ruth. As much as she liked to pretend she had a place at the college, it wasn't real. She just happened to look like the woman Ruth had actually hired. "You're really coming back."

"Yeah." Chloe hung her head, breaking eye contact. "I guess I'll see you tomorrow." Before Caitlyn could speak, she hung up.

"Shit." Tears leaked from Caitlyn's eyes. A few hours ago, she'd been on a high from her presentation. Now she was facing her last day at Pulaski.

Caitlyn wasn't in love with Ruth. Of course not. It was just that her whole chest ached at the thought of losing her.

Yet losing Ruth was inevitable. Whether Chloe came back or not, Caitlyn couldn't impersonate her forever. There was only one way this could end, and it was with Caitlyn walking out of Ruth Holloway's life forever.

Caitlyn closed her laptop and flopped back onto the bed. *It's over. It's over, and after tomorrow, I'll never see her again.*

Chapter 17

RUTH CHECKED HER EMAIL AND immediately broke into a smile.

Alice had emailed to cancel their 9 a.m. meeting, citing a migraine. Few things improved Ruth's mood like a reprieve from an hour with Alice. Best of all, she'd be able to use the hour for something important—a serious conversation with Chloe.

However, Chloe wouldn't be in the office for another twenty minutes or so.

Tapping her fingers on the desk, Ruth considered picking up espresso drinks for both of them. *Just normal boss behavior.* After all, Chloe had done an outstanding job at the work group meeting. Ruth's impulse to treat her was simply a professional gesture of appreciation.

She strolled from her office to Kravings and ordered two iced lattes. When she returned to the office, Chloe was at her desk.

Chloe's turquoise blouse was professional, but she looked less put-together than usual. Her hair fell in limp strands, still damp as though she'd just come from the shower. While the false eyelashes were thankfully absent, she'd painted her lash lines with thick, black eyeliner. The makeup couldn't hide her fatigue.

"Good morning." Ruth held up the drinks. "Do you have time for a chat?"

"Sure." It came out in a croak. Chloe cleared her throat. "Is one of these for me?"

Ruth held out the drink, feeling pleased with herself. "I know you usually order those blended concoctions, but I remembered you got an iced latte last time, so that's what I got you. I hope I guessed right."

"Oh, thank you." Chloe accepted the drink and took a long sip. "Mmm. That's good. I didn't sleep well, so I really needed this." She seemed to catch herself. "Um, but I might go back to my usual drink in the future." There was an odd note of sadness in her voice, as though she'd be forced to give up lattes.

Ruth almost asked, but decided she must have imagined it. No health plan would advise trading lattes for glorified milkshakes.

They moved to the conference table in Ruth's office. Ruth sat across from Chloe, then sucked in a breath. Chloe's blouse had dipped down as she sat, revealing the tops of her purple bra cups and an eyeful of cleavage. Ruth forced her gaze upward.

Not fast enough. Chloe blushed and pulled her blouse up.

Ruth's cheeks warmed. *Focus.* This was important. "I want to talk about your future."

Chloe's eyes widened. "My—what do you mean?"

"You had me fooled for a few weeks, I admit. Your carefree slacker act was quite convincing. But now we both know you are overqualified for your job. You may not have credentials, but you have skills—not to mention an instinct for leadership. I can't allow you to continue as my assistant when you're capable of much more."

Chloe blanched. "Oh. That's okay. I don't mind. I like being an assistant."

"Nonsense. I've seen the spark in your eyes when you work on data and strategy. You can't tell me you have the same passion for answering my phone."

"Well, no. But I think… Actually, I'd like to cut back on those other projects." Chloe twitched and twisted her hands. "I should focus on my regular job."

Why does she look terrified? "Calm down. I'm not firing you. I've thought of two options, but trust me, I plan to keep you here."

"Options?" Chloe squeaked.

"Number one, a promotion. Maggie is already the director of research, but I can create a new position for you. Data strategist, perhaps. Something like that. We can look at some postings to get ideas."

Ruth waited but saw none of the enthusiasm she had expected.

Instead, Chloe shrank in her chair, looking as if she might cry.

What was wrong with her? Was Chloe afraid of failure? Or afraid of success? Whatever the reason for her distress, Ruth resolved to overcome it.

"What's the other option?" Chloe whispered.

"You can enroll here at Pulaski. I'm sure I can finagle a tuition waiver for you, along with a part-time work-study position here in administration. I'm aware of your skills because I've seen them for myself—but when you're ready to move on, you won't get far without a four-year degree. This is an opportunity to finish what you started at LCC."

"Oh gosh." Chloe stared miserably at her lap. "I don't know what to say."

"Look at me."

Chloe slowly lifted her chin and met Ruth's gaze with eyes full of pain.

"I don't know what happened in your past that made you feel you don't deserve to be here, but I can tell you with full authority that it's not true. You are good enough. You're more than good enough. So I need you to tell me what you want."

Tears welled in Chloe's eyes. "I just want to be your assistant. I like working for you, and, um…I don't want to leave."

She looked so broken that something else occurred to Ruth. "Is this about me?" Her chest grew so tight, her lungs felt strangled. "You want to continue as my assistant…because of me?"

Chloe wrapped her arms around her body. "I…I think everything should go back to normal. I think that's what I need."

"What…what does normal mean?" Ruth searched Chloe's gaze, desperate to see into her head. Did Chloe want to return to the days when Ruth barely acknowledged her? Ruth had thought their connection was mutual, but maybe she'd been wrong. *Oh no, what if I made her uncomfortable?*

"I'm sorry." Chloe shot a desperate glance at the door. "Could I take some time to think about it?"

Anxious as she was for answers, Ruth couldn't force her to talk. Or to stay. "Well. Of course."

"Okay, thanks." Chloe scrambled to her feet and fled the office.

Ruth stared after her with her mouth hanging open. They'd grown closer in recent weeks, but Ruth never imagined Chloe would be in tears at the thought of leaving her job as Ruth's assistant.

Shit. Ruth rubbed her forehead with her palms. If Chloe was prepared to turn down opportunities simply to continue spending her days at Ruth's side, Ruth had screwed up even more than she'd feared. And she had no idea how to fix it.

———————

Caitlyn wandered around the campus until she found herself at the fountain. The water pressure was weaker than it had been in the past; an anemic trickle flowed down the sculpture and dripped into the pool below.

She sank onto the bench and slumped in defeat. How had it all gone so wrong?

Caitlyn had prepared for a day of silent, secret goodbyes. She'd resolved to be inconspicuous, only to ruin it when tears fell freely after their meeting. Her phone camera confirmed the damage: puffy eyelids and runny mascara. She'd wanted to look nice the last time Ruth saw her—the real her—and now even that was a lost cause.

What would Ruth think when the real Chloe showed up on Friday, behaving as though her memories of the past two months had been erased?

Chloe didn't care about Ruth. She wouldn't lift a finger beyond her assigned duties, and she certainly wouldn't have Ruth's back. Caitlyn supposed Chloe would have agreed to drive to Ruth's house to retrieve her pills—Chloe had a generous heart and didn't mind helping someone in trouble—but she wouldn't have stayed to make sure Ruth was okay. She certainly wouldn't want to help with the retention initiative.

After a few days, Ruth would conclude that Caitlyn had lost interest in their working relationship, and there would be no explanation for the change.

Pain sliced through Caitlyn when she imagined how Ruth would feel—all because of Caitlyn's foolish decision to build a relationship with her under a false identity.

She should have known better. She *did* know better, but she'd gotten caught up in the fantasy of some other life, where she had purpose and friendship with Ruth—and now she'd have neither, only guilt.

I could tell her the truth. Some rebellious part of her brain finally surfaced the thought she had suppressed for weeks. For once, she allowed herself to play out the possibility in her mind.

Ruth wouldn't take it well—obviously. No one would, but Ruth was primed for an apoplectic reaction. She was private and slow to trust. She'd be horrified to learn she had let her guard down in front of someone who'd been lying about almost everything.

Caitlyn would beg her to listen. *Hear me out. Please.* But nothing she said would make it okay.

Perhaps Ruth would decide against alerting the authorities if only to spare herself the attention. But would she ever forgive Caitlyn? Would she even speak to her again?

Caitlyn already knew the answer.

Not that it mattered. She couldn't risk exposure, not with her entire career in limbo. Plus, there was no way to explain without implicating Chloe. If she ruined Chloe's future as well as her own, she'd never forgive herself.

The truth wasn't an option.

Caitlyn watched the water for a long time. When she was sure Ruth's next meeting had started, she trudged back to the office.

Her iced latte was on her desk, now sitting in a puddle of condensation. Ruth must have placed it there for her. She took a long slurp and sank into the chair.

The lights on her phone were blinking; three new messages had arrived since she'd last checked.

She picked up the receiver with a defeated sigh. There was nothing to do except slog through the day.

A cloud of déjà vu followed Caitlyn as she trudged up to the English department to say goodbye to Miguel for the second time. She found him at the desk, pondering his laptop screen with a deep frown creasing his forehead, squeezing a tri-colored Koosh ball in his fist.

"What's wrong?" Caitlyn asked.

Miguel startled and dropped the ball. "Oh—nothing." He closed the laptop. "What's up?"

Caitlyn closed the door behind her and sat across from him. "Have you talked to Chloe?"

He winced. "Yes. I heard what happened. She's a wreck."

Guilt stabbed at her stomach. Chloe's emotional state was primarily due to the breakup, but their fight couldn't have helped. "Did she tell you, um...?"

"I know about the fight." Miguel bit his lip. "She just needed someone to talk to, you know? Someone who knows the situation."

"No, it's okay. I get it. I've been feeling isolated too because we can't tell anyone what's going on. Well, except for our mom, but she has enough anxiety—which leaves you. Sorry you're stuck hearing about all our twin drama."

"Are you kidding? I don't mind at all. It has been fun to be the only one at Pulaski who knows the secret."

"Well, I'm sure Chloe told you the great twin switch experiment is coming to an end. She wants her job back."

Miguel's smile fell. "Yeah. That's what she said."

"What do you think?"

"Honestly, I'm worried. Ruth isn't an idiot. She didn't notice the switch because she hardly paid attention to Chloe. But it's safe to say that has changed." He shot her a meaningful look.

Caitlyn stiffened. "Right. Because I'm helping with enrollment."

Miguel scoffed. "Come on, it's not just that. I saw the way she looked at you when you presented that data."

"What do you mean?" Caitlyn squirmed.

"She looked proud, but also...enraptured. Ruth is taken with you. Anyone can see it—if they're looking. Honestly, I have no idea how she will react when you turn into the real Chloe."

"God. I really fucked up." The weight on her chest was suffocating. "I never should have done this."

"Maybe." He offered a small smile. "Anyway, I'm glad that I met you."

"Me too. We should keep in touch. Maybe after things go back to normal for a while, we can hang out."

"Sure." Uncertainty flickered in his eyes. "If I'm still here."

"What do you mean? You're leaving?"

"Maybe." Miguel picked at the Koosh ball, twisting the plastic hairs between his fingers. "I've been looking at jobs in Vancouver. Non-academic jobs." He whispered the words as though they were sinful.

"Oh wow. Have you applied?"

"No, I haven't gotten that far. But I miss Preston. His lawyer isn't getting anywhere, and I don't see how we can stay married if there's no plan to ever be in the same country." He dropped the ball, which plopped onto the desk and quivered. "I don't know. I'll probably stay. It would be foolish to give up a tenure-track job, right?" He searched Caitlyn's gaze. "What would you do?"

"I have no idea. You're in an impossible situation." Caitlyn shook her head. "I'm sorry. I wish I could help."

"It helps to talk about it," Miguel said. "You've been a good friend. Both you and Chloe. Whatever happens, we'll keep in touch, okay?"

"Absolutely." Caitlyn rose and walked to the door. She paused with her hand on the knob, then turned around. "I can't tell you what to do," she said softly. "No one can. But I read your poems. They're all about love."

Miguel's eyes widened. "Thank you."

She nodded. "Take care."

Caitlyn didn't see Ruth for the rest of the afternoon. When five o'clock arrived, she was still in a meeting on the other side of campus.

Perhaps it was for the best. If there was some lie Caitlyn could tell that would explain away Chloe's future behavior, it escaped her. There was no way to make it better and no way to say a proper goodbye. She packed up the few items she'd kept on the desk, leaving Chloe's makeup behind, and walked out the door for the last time.

The drive home passed in a blur. When Caitlyn pulled into the driveway, she couldn't remember any of it. She dragged herself out of the car and went inside.

Chloe sat at the kitchen table, wearing yoga pants and a sweatshirt. She looked up from a bowl of ice cream with red-rimmed eyes. "Hi." Her makeup didn't hide the circles beneath her eyes, either because they were too dark to conceal or because she hadn't bothered. Even Chloe's hair was disheveled, a clear sign of distress.

Any lingering resentment dissolved as Caitlyn approached her twin. "I'm so sorry." She laid her hand on Chloe's shoulder.

Sniffling, Chloe pushed to her feet. "Thanks." She fell into Caitlyn's arms, and they embraced.

Caitlyn squeezed Chloe hard, wishing she could take all the pain away.

When they broke apart, Chloe sat back down, and Caitlyn settled in the chair next to her. "I'm truly sorry about the breakup. I know you really liked Nick, and I can see how much it's hurting you. I should have been more sympathetic instead of thinking about myself. I was a jerk. I'm really sorry."

"Thanks." Chloe's lower lip trembled. "I'm sorry too. I shouldn't have said those things about you. I'm sure you were trying to help Ruth. Really, it was nice of you. I just don't know how I'm going to explain why I'm suddenly incompetent."

The word grated on Caitlyn. She hated when Chloe put herself down, and this time she felt directly responsible. "You're not incompetent. And... you weren't wrong."

"What do you mean?"

"Well, I didn't think of it as showing off at the time. But I admit it was hard for me to be at a college, surrounded by professors, after not getting a job. And it didn't help to be treated like...well, like an assistant. I know that makes me sound stuck-up."

"No, it makes sense." Chloe's gaze was free of judgment. "I know the job search has been hard for you. I didn't even think about how working at Pulaski might make you feel."

"Yeah. Grad school really fucked me up." She slouched in the chair and looked down at her hands. "I probably shouldn't have agreed to cover for you in the first place, but when I did, I should have kept my head down instead of trying to impress Ruth. Anyway, she was only impressed because she thought I was self-taught. If Ruth knew my real background, she wouldn't be surprised that I can calculate percentages and make graphs."

"It's still cool that you can do that stuff. I mean, I'm sure you did much more for Ruth than I ever could. You're an impressive person. Anyone can see it." Chloe gave her a shy smile.

Caitlyn looked up at her exhausted, heartbroken sister, still generous and kind to her despite the mess she had created. "What you said about the gifted program and—um, everything..."

"Oh gosh, just forget it. I was upset."

"But you weren't entirely wrong." Caitlyn took a deep breath. "I got labeled early on—the good student, the responsible twin."

"The one Mom didn't have to worry about," Chloe said ruefully.

"Exactly. I made it part of my identity, and doing well in school made me feel validated. So I just kept going in college and grad school until—well, until last month." Caitlyn realized it was her first time out of school since toddlerhood. No wonder she'd been lost.

"And with you getting all the A's and awards, I needed my own identity," Chloe said. "So I became the twin who liked fun and parties and adventures—and I guess I also decided academics weren't for me."

"But they could be," Caitlyn said. "You're smart and creative and curious about the world. You're just as capable as anyone, and if I ever made you feel otherwise, I'm really sorry."

"Thank you." Chloe's eyes turned shiny. "It wasn't always easy to be the, um, less accomplished twin. But I'm proud of you."

"Thanks. That really means a lot to me."

Chloe swirled her spoon in the ice cream. "So you really connected with Ruth, huh?"

"We did. Probably because we're both academics, and we have other things in common too." Should she tell Chloe about Ruth's antidepressants? She supposed Chloe would need to know everything—well, almost everything. Ruth was unlikely to bring up the day Caitlyn saw her without a top. "I'll need to catch you up on what you missed. I already told Ruth I don't want to work on any more research projects, but you should at least be aware of them."

"Okay. But what if she asks me to analyze data? I won't be able to do it."

"I suppose you'll have to refuse. Tell her you want to focus on your assistant duties. I doubt she can fire you for that, and if she does—well, you'll be no worse off than you would have been if you'd quit in the first place."

"It's worth a try." Chloe slurped a spoonful of ice cream. "I think I'm going to take a nap soon. Can we go over everything later tonight?"

"Sure. In the meantime, I'll look over my notes to make sure I didn't forget anything."

"Notes?" Chloe grinned. "Always the perfect student." This time, she said it with affection.

"Can't help it." Across the room, Caitlyn's phone chimed. She got up and retrieved it from her purse. "It's a text from Miguel."

Chloe laughed. "It's cute that you're friends now too. We should all hang out."

Caitlyn swiped to read the message.

Have you seen this???

There was a link to a newspaper article. Caitlyn's heart sank as she read the headline.

"What?" Chloe asked. "What's wrong? Did someone die?"

Ruth sat frozen in her office chair, staring through her computer screen with an unfocused gaze.

A knock sounded.

Piper stood in the doorway. "Hi." She stepped in and closed the door behind her.

"I just saw it." The article was still open on her computer screen: *Some Pulaski faculty unhappy with leadership.*

Piper pushed a chair over and sat down. "Steve Stubbons is behind this."

"No doubt. The reporter quoted him at length." Ruth read aloud: "Ever since Ruth Holloway took over, everything is about numbers and efficiency. Faculty feel she cares more about money than students, and that mentality can kill an institution, unfortunately."

"Ridiculous." Piper huffed. "What a crock."

"At least he thinks it's unfortunate." Ruth skimmed farther down. "'It's hard when you're dealing with a career administrator rather than an academic,' Stubbons said. Dr. Holloway served as an assistant professor at the University of New Mexico for seven years. She left after the university declined to grant her tenure."

It was an old wound, but reading the words made it sting all over again. Ruth looked up at Piper. "Steve must have told them. I've never talked about New Mexico to the press."

Piper grimaced. "I'm sorry. He's an ass."

"Oh, but it's not just Steve. Kimberly said faculty are 'demoralized' over the early-alert system." Ruth scowled at the screen. "She came to the retention work group meeting. She thanked me on the way out. Did she think I wouldn't see this?"

"It's disgusting. I never imagined Kimberly would be so two-faced."

"Some of them smile at me, but in the end they stick together," Ruth said quietly. "I'm not sure why I expected anything different."

"The reporter wanted to write a hit piece. He barely used what I gave him, and most of it is at the end—just a perfunctory paragraph so he can say he included both sides."

Ruth frowned. "Maybe I should have spoken to him about some of the good things I've done. The grant for the music department, for example."

"Why didn't you?" Piper asked gently.

Ruth sat back and flicked her fingers at the screen. "I didn't want to dignify a bunch of baseless whining with an official response. But now it looks like the whole college hates me."

"Hey, I don't hate you." Piper reached out and squeezed her arm.

And Chloe doesn't. Until the article, Ruth had spent most of the day puzzling over Chloe's erratic behavior at their morning meeting. Now she found herself wondering how Chloe would react to the article. When would she hear about it? What would she say?

"It's after six." Piper patted her knee. "You should go home. There's nothing you can do about it today."

Ruth nodded. "I suppose I can answer Zachary's irate phone call just as easily from home."

"Answer it, then turn off your ringer and relax. I can feel your tension headache from here."

"Okay." Ruth shut off her computer monitor. "You're right. I need a break."

Caitlyn scrolled up and down the article on her phone. The parts about Pulaski were bad enough, but she kept returning to the same quote: *...declined to grant her tenure.*

The thought of this happening to Ruth made Caitlyn's heart ache. Aside from never getting a tenure-track job in the first place, a tenure denial was Caitlyn's worst nightmare. She couldn't imagine spending years with a group of colleagues only to have them vote her out of the department.

It's their loss. Caitlyn couldn't imagine having Ruth as a colleague and then letting her go.

Had Ruth's history made it harder to sympathize with the faculty at Pulaski? After all, they had something she had failed to achieve, and all they did was complain. Caitlyn had struggled with jealousy when she first started working there—she wouldn't blame Ruth for having similar feelings.

"Yeah, that's pretty bad." Chloe held up her own phone, where she'd apparently found the article.

"Did you ever hear anyone talk about her tenure denial? Was it common knowledge?"

Chloe shrugged. "It's news to me, but I didn't talk to the faculty that much, except for Miguel. He never said anything."

"Poor Ruth." Caitlyn slumped. "She must be so upset."

"I guess she'll be in a bad mood tomorrow. But on the bright side, maybe she'll be too busy to notice her assistant's IQ dropped fifty points."

"Stop it. You're not stupid." Then Caitlyn processed the rest of what Chloe had said.

Chloe was wrong. Ruth wouldn't ignore her because of the article. If anything, it would be the opposite. Based on the relationship they'd built over the summer, Ruth would seek her out for support. And thanks to the terrible timing, Ruth would get the real Chloe.

Caitlyn tried to imagine how Chloe would respond when Ruth confided in her about the article. Probably something like, *That sucks.* She wouldn't be a jerk, but she would be distant—like an assistant—making Ruth feel rejected.

Ruth might even believe Chloe's cold behavior was a reaction to the article. The thought made Caitlyn sick. She couldn't allow Ruth to think "Chloe" had pulled away from her over a despicable smear job. She looked up at Chloe.

"What?" Chloe asked.

"Can I please be you for one more day? Just for tomorrow? Ruth must be feeling awful, and I want to be there for her."

Chloe wrinkled her brow. "What do you mean, *be there for her?* You want to, like, give her a hug?"

The memory of their one and only embrace made her ache. Her whole body wanted to hold Ruth and make it okay—but touching Ruth would cross boundaries that would be critical when Chloe took Caitlyn's place. "I only want to talk to her about it and about where she can go from here. I've been helping her with faculty relations, so I know all of the context."

"Um, I don't know." Chloe looked away.

"It would mean a lot to me. Then you could start fresh on Monday, when you're rested from your trip—and we'd have the whole weekend to catch you up. Please?"

"Okay." Chloe threw up her hands in surrender. "You can go. As long as this is truly the last time."

"Absolutely. After tomorrow, the gig is all yours." Caitlyn got up and walked to the fridge in search of a soda. She was still livid about the article, but she had a new bounce in her steps. *I get to see Ruth again.*

Chapter 18

CAITLYN RUSHED DOWN THE HALLWAY to the president's suite, her strides as long as her high heels would allow. When she reached the door, she grabbed the handle and yanked, only to find it locked. As she fumbled for her keys, she peered through the glass. Ruth's door was ajar, but the lights were off.

What's going on? Ruth was always there before nine, and she didn't have a planned day off. Caitlyn knew this for sure, having personally scheduled some of the meetings on Ruth's calendar. Was she staying home because of the article?

A horrible thought occurred to her. Ruth hadn't been fired, had she? Would the board boot a president over one newspaper article?

Once inside the suite, Caitlyn sat at the desk she had thought she'd vacated for good. She shook the mouse to clear the screen saver, punched in Chloe's password, and pulled up her email.

There was a message from Ruth, sent an hour ago:

Chloe,
I'm taking a personal day. Please inform anyone who calls that I'm unavailable.
RH

Caitlyn sat back and caught her breath. Okay. This was good. Ruth still had access to her Pulaski email address, and that meant she hadn't been fired.

But I won't get to see her.

"Fuck." Caitlyn pushed the mouse away. She'd begged Chloe for one more day, and now she had to spend it answering the phone and responding to emails. Couldn't one damn thing go right?

She had to see Ruth. Maybe she could persuade Chloe to let her come on Monday. The alternative—that she'd never see Ruth again—was unacceptable.

But I can't wait till Monday. Ruth would stew all weekend without hearing from her. Caitlyn kicked the bottom desk drawer. "Damn it."

She couldn't even send Ruth a text because Chloe had the only phone number Ruth would recognize. Caitlyn couldn't claim she'd changed her number only to "change it back" three days later. The desk phone was an option, but she'd have to get Ruth's cell phone number from Chloe. Would Ruth even answer a call from the college?

An errant thought crept into her consciousness. *I know where Ruth lives.* She still had Ruth's home address in her phone; it would be easy to drive there again.

It was a terrible idea. Ruth could be day-drinking in her underwear for all Caitlyn knew. It would be inappropriate—a boundary violation.

Then again, what was the worst that could happen?

Assuming Ruth wouldn't fire her for the intrusion—and Caitlyn was certain she wouldn't—the worst possible outcome was that Ruth would be angry...*with Chloe.* Not with Caitlyn, who would wake up Monday morning unemployed in every sense of the word. Chloe didn't care about Ruth's opinion anyway—any residual annoyance wouldn't bother her.

The phone on the desk rang. Caitlyn glanced at the caller ID. It was an external number, which could mean any number of unpleasant possibilities: an unhappy student or parent, a reporter hoping to bypass Piper, a vendor making cold calls. *Fuck them all.*

Caitlyn fired off an email to Gary, asking him to cover the phone, then logged out of the computer and shoved her keys into her purse. If Ruth wasn't coming to campus, Caitlyn would go to her.

Ruth flipped from MSNBC to CNN, then back again. Daytime cable news was inferior even to the networks' tedious primetime offerings. Not having a nine-to-five job—or in Ruth's case, playing hooky because she couldn't stand another second—did not mean one lacked the capacity to comprehend more than cliché talking points regurgitated by Z-list hacks.

How do they have time for all this chatter? Is there no actual news?

A knock came from the front door.

Ruth turned her head and scowled. A surprise visitor? *Unacceptable.* No one she wanted to see would show up without contacting her first.

It was probably a solicitor or some other odious pest. Sighing, she settled back into the cushions.

She tensed as another thought occurred to her. Had a reporter come to her home, seeking comment about the *Tribune* article?

Ruth had nothing to say to the press, but she found herself itching to know for sure. She turned off the TV, tiptoed to the window, and slid a single slat out of place so she could peer at her front porch undetected.

Chloe stood on her doorstep in a long skirt, a burgundy blouse, and high heels. She shifted between her feet as she waited.

Ruth pulled back from the window. What was Chloe doing there? She could have texted or called if there was an emergency.

Chloe must have seen the article by now. Had she come to offer support? The possibility filled Ruth with a swirl of affection and alarm.

She started toward the door, then glanced down at her outfit: sweatpants and a gray T-shirt that said *The Art Institute of Chicago* across the chest. No bra. Should she run upstairs and get one?

Hell, Chloe had already seen her wearing less. Ruth straightened and opened the door.

Chloe's head jerked up. "Hi."

"What are you doing here?"

Chloe scanned Ruth's outfit, then quickly returned her gaze to Ruth's face. "I'm sorry to bother you on your day off, but…well, I saw the article in the *Tribune*, and I wanted to make sure you were okay."

"Of course I'm okay." It came out in a bark, causing Chloe to flinch.

"I guess this was a mistake." Chloe's eyes were big and vulnerable like a wounded kitten.

How could she turn Chloe away when she looked at her like that? "Fine. Come on in."

"Are you sure?"

Ruth stepped back. "Yes."

"I like your house," Chloe said as she walked in. "I mean, of course I already saw it when I was here the one time. I didn't look around or anything, but out of the corner of my eye, I couldn't help noticing that it was nice."

"Thank you." Ruth's gaze drifted over her living room.

A blanket lay crumpled on the couch, and a dirty plate and mug adorned the coffee table—visible evidence that she'd spent the morning moping in front of the television.

"Let's sit down." Ruth hastily folded the blanket and sat stiffly beside it on the couch.

Chloe sat on the love seat, facing her.

"I appreciate the thought, but you really didn't need to check on me. The article was discouraging, but I'm fine. I know you're aware that I have a history of depression, but I assure you, I'm not—everyone takes personal days, even people who take psychiatric medication."

"Oh God." Chloe's eyes widened. "I wasn't worried because of your medication. I just thought you might want to talk about it with someone who supports you." She lowered her gaze, then looked up shyly through her long lashes. "I know I'd want to talk about it."

Ruth's shoulders loosened at Chloe's words. *She cares about me.* She pulled her legs up to the couch and curled them underneath her. "All right. Let's talk."

Caitlyn did her best not to react to the unexpected sight of Ruth's natural beauty. Her hair was soft without products, and her face was free of even the minimal makeup she wore to work. Without a bra, the loose T-shirt showed her teardrop-shaped breasts.

She had never seen Ruth look so informal. Yet despite the casual attire, Ruth didn't seem comfortable. With gray circles beneath her eyes and her forehead creased from overthinking, she looked tired and tense.

Feeling overdressed in her blouse and skirt, Caitlyn wished she could change into pajamas and curl up on the sofa as they talked like friends.

Instead, her posture was straight and compact—legs together, her hands firmly in her lap. "So, did you know the article was coming?"

Ruth nodded wearily. "I didn't know the details, but the reporter asked for a comment. Piper talked to him a few days before the article came out."

"Yeah, I saw Piper's statement." *Her very short statement.* Caitlyn knew Piper was on Ruth's side, but the article made it sound as though she hadn't said much in Ruth's defense.

"That's not Piper's fault." Ruth seemed to read her thoughts. "She told him all about our efforts and our accomplishments, but he didn't use most of the information. I suppose it didn't fit the narrative he'd already constructed."

"I thought it was incredibly biased, like he wanted to make you look bad. It isn't right." Her blood pressure rose all over again as she thought of the hack reporter who had done this to Ruth. How dare he impugn her motivations when all she ever tried to do was good?

"Steve wanted this to happen, and he succeeded. He probably fed the reporter everything and got his friends to speak on the record too." Ruth raked her fingers through her hair. "A faculty in revolt makes juicy copy. We can respond with our talking points, but I can't tell a reporter that Steve is a vindictive, misogynist ass who is pissed that I don't let him do whatever he wants."

Caitlyn curled her lips in disgust. "I wish I could slap his smarmy face."

"Well, your presentation helped me to shoot down his ridiculous arguments at a board meeting." The corner of Ruth's mouth twitched. "That's even better."

"I guess. But it didn't stop him from smearing you in the paper." Caitlyn wondered if she should bring up the section where he had essentially called her a failure as an academic. Tenure denial was a sensitive subject, but Caitlyn longed to know more. Her own rejection from academia was still raw, and she hated the thought of Ruth going through something similar in the past—or enduring a public reminder from faculty seeking to undermine her.

This is my last chance to ask. Caitlyn took a deep breath. "Um, the article said you didn't get tenure at the University of Mexico."

Ruth sat up straight, pain piercing her eyes. "Yes. That's true."

"Was that publicly known before the article?" Caitlyn asked gently. "Or did Steve find out and tell the *Tribune*?"

"It's not a secret." Her voice was even and stiff. "The committee asked what happened when I interviewed for this position. Some opposed my hiring on the grounds that I had 'failed' as an academic and therefore was unqualified to lead an academic institution. From what I understand, Steve was one of those people."

Caitlyn ached at the thought of Ruth forced to explain it over and over for the rest of her professional life. "I'm so sorry. That's really unfair."

"Yes. Well. In a sense, he was right. I didn't get tenure. I'll have that mark on my career forever, and some will always judge me for it." Her voice was gruff, but vulnerability shone in her eyes.

"Anyone who holds it against you is an asshole." It came out louder than Caitlyn had intended, but she couldn't stand to see Ruth hurting. "Things like the academic job market, tenure, whether research gets published—it's all subjective. These decisions come down to the whims of a handful of people who have their own biases and agendas, and anyone who reads more into it doesn't understand."

Ruth gave her an odd look, one Caitlyn had seen several times at Pulaski. It meant she had said or done something Ruth didn't expect. "That's right," Ruth said slowly. "Most people don't understand the subjective nature of the process. Yet somehow, you do. You always seem to understand." Her voice softened to a whisper. "How do you know so much about everything?"

Shit. "Not everything."

"Well, you're lucky you haven't been through anything like this." Ruth stared past Caitlyn with unfocused eyes. "My department only had six senior faculty at the time. I knew the chair didn't like me. He didn't like my politics or that I dared to have my own opinion even as a lowly assistant professor. Still, he led me to believe my tenure would be approved. All six of them told me, in so many words, that I'd be okay."

"Oh no. They *lied* to you?" Caitlyn's stomach dropped. She'd heard stories of departments blindsiding faculty on academic blogs, but she'd never met anyone who had been the victim of such reprehensible behavior. "I can't believe it."

"I think a couple of them were just cowards." Ruth's voice sounded far away. "They were afraid to tell me the truth, that I didn't have the votes and never would. As for the others…" Her gaze darkened. "To this day, I believe they wanted to sandbag me. They were nice to my face, implying it was a done deal—and then they voted against me."

"That's awful." Caitlyn clenched her fingers into fists. "God. I can't imagine working with people for years and then facing a vote like that. It must have felt so personal." Her heart throbbed as she imagined Ruth going through it. Did she have friends back then? Or had she coped alone? Caitlyn wished that somehow she could have been there to hold her close and tell her it would be okay. Hell, she wished she could do it now.

"Yes, it did feel personal, especially the way they conspired to keep it from me. If I had known what was coming, I could have tried to address their reservations, or I could have applied to other positions before my tenure clock was up. They made sure I wouldn't do either one." Ruth let out a long, defeated sigh. "Afterward, my depression..." Her mouth moved without words, and she waved her hand. "Let's just say it was a rough time."

"Fuck. I'm so sorry." Caitlyn felt sick. How could anyone harm Ruth when she did nothing but work her ass off?

"It taught me an important lesson." Ruth's voice hardened. "You can't trust anyone."

Caitlyn longed to say, *You can trust me.* But it wasn't true. The inescapable reality made her sick. "Is that why you...?" She hesitated. "Never mind."

"What?" Ruth cocked her head. "Just say it."

"Well, you can be sort of guarded at work. You've obviously had conflicts with some of the faculty, but I've hardly seen you relax around anyone—except students, and only when no one is watching. You also have a tendency to take on projects yourself rather than collaborate. So, I wondered if your past experience makes you less likely to trust the faculty and, um, people in general." Caitlyn squirmed as she worried she'd gone too far.

"I'm right not to trust them." Ruth's eyes flashed. "If you need evidence, read the *Tribune*. Kimberly came to our work group and smiled at me—then she told the reporter I'm a bad leader. You can't trust anyone in academia. Whatever they say, they don't have your back."

Caitlyn wanted to disagree, but what could she say? Ruth had been betrayed—by her old colleagues and now by the faculty who sided with Steve. "I hate that it's like this for you. You work so hard and get nothing but shit for it. It's not fair. I wish I could do something."

Ruth's aggressive posture collapsed. "You know the truth, and you're here for me. That does help. It means a lot."

And I'm leaving. Caitlyn fought tears. She desperately wanted to wrap her arms around Ruth, to express the affection that threatened to spill out of her any second. Her whole body hurt from how badly she wanted to close the distance between them.

Fuck it. They had already hugged once. A second time wouldn't jeopardize Chloe any more than Caitlyn's previous behavior already had. And right now, in this moment, Ruth needed her. Pushing her reservations aside, she got up and sat next to Ruth on the couch.

Ruth's eyes widened, but she didn't move away. "What...?" The word was barely audible.

Caitlyn looked into Ruth's eyes. "You're a great president. You're smart and strong, and you give your best to the college every day. Anyone who can't see that doesn't deserve you." Their knees touched, the slight contact sending a shiver down Caitlyn's back. "But I see it."

Ruth's pupils dilated as she held Caitlyn's gaze, not speaking or making a sound, and Caitlyn could see it, clear as those stunning blue eyes. She wanted this too.

Caitlyn closed the gap and moved in for an embrace.

At the same time, Ruth turned her head to the side, where her mouth collided with Caitlyn's. She pulled back with a gasp—and then crushed their lips together as she sank into Caitlyn's arms.

The kiss overwhelmed Caitlyn's senses and short-circuited her brain. Ruth tasted like coffee and cinnamon, mixed with the heady aroma of lavender that Caitlyn knew by heart. She couldn't think and couldn't stop.

Abruptly, Ruth pulled back. "Oh no." Her whole body went rigid. "I can't—I shouldn't have done that." She scooted back, putting as much space between them as the couch would allow.

Caitlyn watched in a daze. Her lips and her limbs were bereft at the loss of Ruth moving against her, melting into her.

"Chloe, I'm your boss." Ruth's voice shook. "We can't do this."

The name broke through. *She thinks she kissed Chloe.* Caitlyn's heart rate jumped as adrenaline shot through her body. *Oh God. Oh fuck. What have I done?*

"It's unethical. An abuse of power." Ruth covered her mouth. "I can't believe I did that. I've never crossed that line with an employee. Never."

As she watched Ruth berate herself, a terrifying realization washed over Caitlyn. *I crossed a line.* Not just a line—a Rubicon. Somewhere along the way, she had passed the point where switching back was an option.

Caitlyn's chest heaved as she struggled to breathe. She was fucked. Completely fucked. It was one thing to fool a teacher, an acquaintance, or a boss who had barely noticed her assistant up until then. But she and Chloe had never managed to fool the people who truly knew them.

Ruth *knew* her. They had connected intellectually, emotionally, and as people with more in common than Ruth could fathom. They'd tasted each other's mouths.

If Chloe came to the office on Monday morning, Ruth would sense right away that something was very wrong. Even if Chloe had the exact same analytical skills as Caitlyn, it wouldn't matter. Ruth would know. And even if they could somehow switch back without Ruth catching on, Caitlyn couldn't bear to do it. If she kept lying and allowed Ruth to think "Chloe" no longer gave a damn about her outside of a paycheck—if she denied Ruth the chance to make sense of what was happening—Caitlyn would become one more person who had betrayed Ruth. She couldn't live with herself.

It was too late. She'd embarked on a collision course with the truth, and there was no stopping the train.

"I'm sorry." Ruth rubbed her own arms with both hands. "Nothing can ever happen between us while you're my assistant. I take full responsibility, and I—"

"I'm not your assistant." Caitlyn's voice broke.

"Of course." Ruth met her gaze with eyes full of anguish. "You're much more than that. But what matters is that I'm your boss."

"No, I mean I'm not..." She swallowed. "I'm not Chloe."

Ruth frowned. "What do you mean?"

Time seemed to slow as Caitlyn prepared herself to speak. "My name is Caitlyn Taylor. I'm Chloe's identical twin, and I've been coming to work in her place since June."

"Come on. Be serious." *Chloe's twin?* It was preposterous. Yet even as Ruth spoke, some part of her brain recognized the truth—not in the literal words, but in the idea that she'd been deceived. All summer, she'd been trying to understand the parts of Chloe that didn't add up or make sense. There was something she had missed, something important. She sucked in her breath as she struggled to make it make sense.

"I need to show you something." With shaky hands, Chloe reached for her purse and pulled out her phone. After a few swipes, she turned it toward Ruth. "This is me and Chloe at Christmas."

It was a photo of Chloe—except there were two of them. Sisters. Twins. Ruth recoiled. "What the hell?"

"I'm sorry." She trembled. "I'm so sorry for deceiving you."

"You're not Chloe?" It came out shrill, almost hysterical. "Who the fuck are you?"

"Caitlyn." She shrunk backward. "Caitlyn Taylor."

"But what...how?" Ruth sputtered, desperate to make sense of the person who had worked so hard for her all summer, who surprised her each day with keen insights and effortless intelligence. The woman who knew Ruth's secret vulnerabilities and, instead of running, had embraced her and kissed her like—*God.* How could it all be a lie?

The room tilted and blurred, and she had an urge to bend over and puke. But she forced herself to focus, to get answers before she kicked *Caitlyn* out of her house. "You said your name, but who *are* you? How did you know so much about the college? And data? How did you know about me?"

Caitlyn's face was deathly pale. "I'm a sociologist."

Ruth fixated on the suffix. Caitlyn wasn't a social science major or someone with an interest in education. She was a sociolog*ist*—a professional researcher, probably a PhD. "You're an academic?"

She nodded miserably. "Yes." Her voice was a hoarse whisper.

Jesus Christ. No wonder Caitlyn could analyze data as if it was nothing. Her supposed flashes of brilliance were child's play for someone with her expertise. How could she have been so stupid?

Caitlyn squirmed and scratched her arms. "I'm so sorry. It was only supposed to be for a week, but one thing led to another, and I really liked working for you. I wanted to help you as much as I could."

She wanted *to help*? Hot fury coursed through Ruth's veins. How dare she frame her con job as some sort of magnanimous act? "You lied to me."

"I know." Caitlyn's eyes filled with tears. "I know, and I feel terrible about it. But the things I've said are true—aside from my name and my background, I've been as genuine with you as I could be."

"Fuck." Ruth got up from the couch and began to pace. "You accessed college computer systems, email, student data. I told you my private medical information."

"I've never told anyone about your medication," Caitlyn said, growing frantic. "I swear. Not even Chloe. I'd never betray your confidence, Ruth. I care about you."

The words ripped through Ruth like a chainsaw. Caitlyn had pretended to care, but none of it was real. She was a fraud.

Ruth faced her. "Why? Why did you pretend to be Chloe? And for that matter, where the hell is Chloe?"

"Chloe went to Colorado to be with her boyfriend, and she asked me to hold on to her job until she got back. Well, she's back now. They broke up." Caitlyn lowered her head. "She got back yesterday."

"And you were going to—what? Switch back?" Ruth's mouth hung open. After everything they'd been through together, Caitlyn was going to send *her twin* back to work? As if Ruth wouldn't know the difference?

Caitlyn hunched forward, curling into herself. "Um. Well. Chloe wanted to come back on Monday. But I should have known it wouldn't work, not after the time we've spent together. And after the—the kiss—I couldn't lie anymore."

God, the kiss. Ruth would never forget the taste of her mouth, the feel of her breasts, the scent of her hair. Now it all made her nauseous. "I trusted you," she choked out. "What you did is a crime. I could call the police."

Caitlyn looked up, a new glimmer of fear in her eyes. "Are you going to report us?"

Images flashed through Ruth's mind. Caitlyn in handcuffs. Reporters. Press. The faculty whispering, *How could Ruth not notice?* "I don't know. I need time to think."

A tear slid down Caitlyn's cheek. "Okay."

Ruth pressed her fingers into her temples. "You need to leave. I can't look at you anymore."

With her head bowed, Caitlyn collected her purse and rose to her feet. She swayed and gripped the coffee table to stay upright. "Ruth, I'm so sorry. I'd give anything to make it right. Anything in this world."

"You *betrayed* me. You can never make it right. Ever." Ruth jabbed the air with her finger. "Just go. Get out of my house."

With her shoulders slumped, Caitlyn stumbled toward the door.

Ruth realized it wasn't enough. "Wait. One more thing."

Caitlyn turned around, eyes red and face contorted in pain.

"You're fired. You, Chloe, both of you. I haven't decided how to handle this with HR, but you will *not* come to work again."

"Okay," Caitlyn said in a strangled whisper. She opened the door, slipped out, and closed it behind her.

Ruth collapsed on the couch. Her heartbeat throbbed in her ears, and the focused rage she'd channeled to evict Caitlyn dissolved into a haze of hurt, confusion, and shame.

I trusted her. I cared for her.

I kissed her.

Her emotions overwhelmed her and made it hard to think. She didn't know what to do next. So, she didn't do anything. She curled up on the couch, touched her fingers to her lips, and closed her eyes.

Caitlyn sobbed the whole way home. She couldn't stop. Tears streamed down her face, mixing with snot and spit and makeup. Her gasps filled the car as she drove, swiping at her eyes to clear her vision. Somehow, she managed to stay on the road.

When she pulled into the driveway, she was still crying. She pulled a tissue from her purse and dabbed her face, but she didn't bother to conceal her tears as she walked to the house. There was no way to hide what had happened from Chloe—or from their mother.

She pushed through the door, kicked off her high heels, and dropped her purse at her feet. Then she ripped off her Pulaski badge and let it fall to the floor.

Chloe was in the kitchen, washing a dish in the sink. "You're home?" She turned her head. "Oh my God. What happened?"

"Ruth knows." Another sob seized Caitlyn as she sank onto a kitchen chair.

"How?" Chloe gasped. "How does she know?"

Caitlyn wiped her nose. "It never would have worked. She knows me too well. We're more than boss and employee—or at least we were."

"What? You're babbling. What do you mean?" Chloe's eyes were huge.

"We kissed." Fresh tears spilled over.

"What?" Chloe dragged a kitchen chair back and collapsed into it. "What the fuck?"

"Not at the office." As if that made a difference. "Ruth took the day off, and I went to her house. We were talking about the article and some other things, and it just happened. And I knew I didn't have a choice anymore. I was so foolish to think this could work, that I could get to know her like this and she'd go on thinking we're the same person. It was always doomed."

"You kissed Ruth? And you told her the truth? What were you thinking? Do you know how much trouble we'll be in now? Oh my God. What is she going to do about it?" The questions came fast until Chloe finally paused to breathe.

"We're fired. That's all I know right now. She said she needs time to think." Caitlyn grabbed a napkin from the table and blotted her face. "She's furious, obviously. But I don't think she'll report us."

"How do you know? You think she won't turn us in because—because she's in love with you?" The words came out in a gasp.

The word *love* kicked Caitlyn in the gut. She and Ruth had spent two months together, and she'd been lying the entire time—they couldn't be in love. Yet her feelings went beyond the crush she'd developed once she'd first looked past Ruth's frosty façade. And she wasn't alone—the emotion in their kiss had come from both sides. But whatever Ruth had felt for her an hour ago, it no longer mattered.

"I guess I hope that some tiny part of her still cares for me." It came out sounding pitiful. She cleared her throat. "But that's not why. She won't report us, because she would be implicated too. The fact that this happened on her watch, a few yards from her desk—it would look very bad for her too."

"Okay." Chloe started to calm down. "That's a good point. Ruth would hate that kind of scrutiny. She hates when people judge her or, like, when there's bad press."

Caitlyn winced as she thought of the article. *God, she has to deal with this and the media all at once.* "Yes, she does."

Footsteps sounded in the hallway.

Oh no. This would be worse than telling Chloe.

Their mom walked in, hefting a grocery bag, and glanced between them. "What's wrong?"

"Ruth knows," Chloe said bluntly. "Caitlyn kissed her. And then she told her that she's not really me. And now I've lost my job."

Their mom's jaw dropped. "You *kissed* Chloe's boss?"

Caitlyn sagged. "Yes."

Her mom's breathing accelerated, a sign of rising anxiety that Caitlyn had seen countless times. "And you told her that you're not Chloe? Why would you do that?" She fumbled to hold on to the grocery bag, then bent over and let it drop to the floor.

"Because I didn't have a choice. Look, Mom, if I dressed up like Chloe, would it fool you? Even for a second?"

"Of course not. But you're my daughters. I know you better than anyone. You said Ruth didn't even notice when you turned up in Chloe's place. If you hadn't told her, Chloe could have gone back on Monday. It would have been fine!"

Caitlyn shook her head. It was too late for anything to be fine. "Ruth knows me too. We've spent a lot of time together, and…and we became close." She turned to Chloe. "I'm really sorry I put us at risk by telling Ruth. But please trust me. There's no way we could have switched back."

"Wait. What do you mean you've grown close?" Her mom's pitch rose to a shrill. "You never told me that. Have you kissed her before?"

"No. This was the first time." Caitlyn looked down at the table.

"Why couldn't you just keep your head down? Stay out of sight, answer the phone. Hold the job for Chloe. Why couldn't you do that?"

The disappointment in her mom's voice was excruciating. *I let her down. Again.*

Chloe met Caitlyn's gaze, and she seemed to understand, without words, exactly how miserable Caitlyn felt. "Don't be too hard on her, Mom. I'm upset too, but if Caitlyn hadn't stepped in, I would have lost my job weeks ago."

"How much trouble are you in? Will she tell the police?" Her mom's anxiety seemed to be escalating as she processed the situation.

"I really don't think she'll tell anyone," Caitlyn said.

"How do you know? What did she say exactly? Can you call her and find out for sure?" Their mom started to hyperventilate.

Caitlyn couldn't deal with it anymore. "Look, I don't know anything for sure. Ruth is angry. She needs time. I can't call and bug her to make a decision." She pushed her chair back and stood. "And I need to be alone."

Without giving them time to respond, Caitlyn ran up the stairs to her bedroom and locked the door behind her. She collapsed on the bed and threw her arms around a pillow. "I'm sorry, Ruth," she whispered into the pillowcase. "I'm so, so sorry."

Ruth's phone buzzed beside her on the couch. *Piper.* She shoved it away and returned to her laptop—and the Google search results for Caitlyn Taylor.

Apparently, Caitlyn had received her PhD in sociology from Washington University in St. Louis. She had a profile on the *Job Candidates* page, featuring a professional headshot and her curriculum vitae. The profile listed her dissertation title: *Divorce rates among parents of multiples: The role of state support.*

Ruth's heart squeezed as she read the title. Had Chloe and Caitlyn's parents divorced? And if so, did Caitlyn believe having twins was the reason?

Never mind. She cursed her impulse to feel compassion for Caitlyn, whose family history wasn't her concern.

Returning to her search, Ruth found a Twitter account with the same headshot. There was little original content, just retweets of news articles about academia and her research interests. Ruth guessed it had been sanitized for the job market.

There was no evidence that Caitlyn had found a job. Was that why she had time to spend the summer impersonating Chloe?

Ruth tried to recall Caitlyn's words about academia. *It comes down to a small group of people with their own biases and agendas.* Perhaps she'd been speaking from personal experience.

Before the revelation, Ruth had often been amazed at how well Caitlyn seemed to understand her. Now she knew why. They were both women in academia. They'd both dealt with rejection and mental health issues. Caitlyn hadn't been sympathizing as an outsider—she could relate.

Somehow, learning how much they had in common made it all worse. It would be one thing if Caitlyn were a con artist who'd been hustling Ruth the whole time, picking up on her weaknesses and exploiting them. In that case, Ruth could feel simple, uncomplicated rage. But Caitlyn had formed a genuine connection with her, all while lying about something so fundamental that she had to know Ruth would be devastated if she ever learned the truth. It was cruel.

Now she had to decide what to do about it.

Caitlyn had broken the law. She had worked under a false identity, accessed confidential information—including student records, which were meant to have special protections. If Ruth reported the switch to the authorities, Caitlyn would face real consequences. Arrest, maybe even jail. Her academic career would be over.

But what would happen to Ruth? Nothing good. There would be hard questions about how she'd failed to notice that a completely different person had replaced her assistant. The board would investigate, and it would spill into the press eventually.

They would all blame Ruth, and she would deserve it.

Ruth hadn't paid attention to Chloe—the real Chloe. She had decided Chloe was a nonstarter and had proceeded to interact with her as little as possible. No wonder she hadn't noticed when Caitlyn appeared in her place.

She should have made an effort to get to know Chloe, to find out her goals, and to help her to improve. The fact that she hadn't was her failure as a supervisor. Then she had ignored or rationalized all of the signs that something was amiss.

I didn't want to see the truth. Ruth had been so relieved to find an ally and collaborator, she hadn't followed her instincts.

She clicked back to Caitlyn's profile. Caitlyn's eyes were bright and hopeful in the photo. Ruth had seen that same light when they'd worked together to help the college.

"Damn it." She closed her laptop. Caitlyn deserved consequences, and perhaps Ruth did too. But she couldn't put the college through an avoidable scandal. There was only one decision to make.

She reached for her phone and tapped out a text:

Hello Chloe. I assume you can share this message with Caitlyn. There is a small park at the intersection of Miller Road and Devlin Avenue. You and your sister will meet me there tomorrow at 2 p.m. Bring your badge, your keys, and anything else in your possession that belongs to the college.

After pressing send, she lay back on the couch and waited, clutching the phone to her chest. A few minutes later, it buzzed.

We will both be there. Also, I want you to know that I am very sorry. This is from Chloe.

Ruth rolled her eyes. "Save it."

Chapter 19

RUTH SPOTTED THEM FROM A distance. Two brunettes sat side-by-side at one of the plastic picnic tables behind the playground. Both wore summer dresses, one with exposed shoulders, the other more conservative. The park was deserted, as she'd predicted; it was attached to a school that had closed several years earlier.

As she approached the table, Ruth observed their heart-shaped faces, their slim noses and high brow lines. Mirror images. As she got closer, however, she could see the slight differences: their posture, for one, and something in their faces she couldn't pinpoint.

By the time she reached the table, she was certain that Chloe was the one in the revealing pink dress, slouching and looking nervous, while Caitlyn was the one sitting up straight, eyes puffy and full of torment.

"Hmm." Ruth sat on the bench across from them. "You really do look alike. There are subtle differences in the shapes of your faces—just subtle enough, I suppose."

Caitlyn squirmed under Ruth's scrutiny but didn't speak.

Silence stretched until Chloe opened her mouth. "I am *so* sorry for leaving. I just really needed time off to see my boyfriend in Colorado—well, he's my ex-boyfriend now—and I didn't have any vacation days left. I knew Caitlyn would do a good job because she's so responsible and good at everything, so I thought it would be fine. But it was wrong to send her to work without telling you."

"Wrong?" Ruth swept an unforgiving gaze between them. "*Wrong* doesn't even begin to cover what you both have done. I didn't hire Caitlyn Taylor. She never had a background check, never signed a single form with her real name. She waltzed in off the street, a complete stranger, and trespassed in my office. She accessed confidential data. You could go to prison for this."

Chloe turned pale, while Caitlyn bowed her head.

Ruth wasn't done. "Have you ever heard of something called FERPA? You put the entire college at risk. If this got out, every single student in *Caitlyn's* retention spreadsheets could sue Pulaski for allowing an unaffiliated individual to view their student records."

"I'm really, really sorry," Chloe said again.

Caitlyn still hadn't spoken. She stared intently at the table, her mouth a brittle line.

"You both deserve to experience the full consequences of your actions." Ruth paused to watch their reactions.

Chloe's eyes were wide and fearful, but Caitlyn's expression remained unchanged.

Ruth sighed. "But I won't let the college suffer if I can help it. However, before I decide on a course of action, I need you to tell me everyone who knows that you took Chloe's place. Every single person."

"Miguel knows," Caitlyn whispered. "He's the only one at the college."

"You told a *faculty* member?" The words came out in a dangerous growl. Ruth had wondered about Miguel, but she'd convinced herself Caitlyn wouldn't be that reckless.

"Um," Chloe said in a squeaky voice, "I'm the one who told him. But he's my best friend at work. He would never tell anyone—I swear."

Ruth clenched her jaw. "Who else?"

"Our mom," Caitlyn said. "But you don't have to worry about her. She's terrified that we'll get in trouble. That's it, right?" She turned to Chloe.

"Well, almost." Chloe chewed her lip. "Nick knows."

"Nick?" Ruth asked. "Who the hell is Nick?"

"My ex-boyfriend. The one I stayed with in Colorado. But I had to tell him. I had to explain why he couldn't tag me on Facebook or Instagram or anything."

"Did you..." Ruth attempted to calm herself. "Did your relationship end on bad terms?"

Chloe's face crumpled. "You could say that. He dumped me."

"But he's not angry with you," Caitlyn said. "Right?"

"No," Chloe said. "He feels bad. Today he sent me a text with the crying emoji—the one people use for real crying, not the fake crying one. He would never do anything to hurt me. I mean, except for breaking up with me."

Ruth rubbed the bridge of her nose. "So aside from Miguel, your mother, and Chloe's ex-boyfriend, does anyone else know?"

"No," they said at the same time.

"Okay. Here's what we're going to do. Chloe, you're going to resign, effective immediately. Don't give an explanation. Just quit. I want this via email by the end of the day. Do you understand?"

They both nodded.

"Did you bring your badge and your keys?"

Chloe pulled the items out of her purse and set them on the table.

Ruth snatched them. "Do you have any other items belonging to Pulaski?"

"Yes," Caitlyn said quietly. "Some library books." She reached for a canvas bag at her feet and pulled out a stack of five books.

Ruth caught the words *Sociology* and *Family* on one of the spines. She'd wondered if Caitlyn had availed herself of college resources for her sociology research. Apparently, she had. "Did you leave anything in the desk that could identify you as Caitlyn? Any personal documents?"

"No," Caitlyn said. "Never."

"Fine. Human resources will mail your belongings to the address on file. You will not set foot on campus ever again—either of you—and you will not tell a soul what you've done. Chloe worked for me until Friday, and then she quit. That's the story, and all three of us will stick to it. Do you understand?"

"Yes," they said in unison.

Was this some annoying twin thing?

"If you're lucky," Ruth said, "no one will look into it further, and you won't get the punishment you deserve. If someone finds out..." She shook her head. What could she say? They'd all be fucked.

"I'll take the blame," Caitlyn said. "If they somehow figure it out, I'll say I never told you anything. You thought I was Chloe the whole time."

"If they find out, it won't matter." Ruth glared at her. "I trusted you, and that's on me. I should have seen what you really are."

Caitlyn flinched backward as though she'd been slapped, then dropped her gaze to the table.

"Caitlyn is a really good person," Chloe said. "She never would have done this if I hadn't asked, and she ended up really liking you. So if you have romantic feelings for her—"

"Chloe!" Caitlyn swatted her arm.

"I'm just saying, Caitlyn really cares about you." Chloe seemed unable to stop babbling. "That's why she wanted to stay even after I told her to quit."

"Excuse me?" Ruth wondered if she'd misheard.

Caitlyn cringed. "Oh God."

"What I mean…" Chloe's gaze darted back and forth between them. "After I spent some time with Nick, I decided to stay in Colorado. So I told Caitlyn she could go ahead and quit my job. But she asked to stay for a few more weeks."

Ruth's breath came out in a hiss. "When was this?"

Chloe looked over at Caitlyn, who regarded her with murderous eyes. "It was after the first week," she said in a tiny voice.

"The first week?" Ruth was practically shouting. "After one week, you weren't even helping your sister anymore? You stayed there, lying to my face every day, for what? For fun?"

"Because I wanted to help you," Caitlyn said desperately. "You were facing all these problems by yourself, and I wanted to support you."

"Bullshit," Ruth snapped. "You lied to me. From the second you showed up until yesterday, you were lying. That's not support. It's betrayal."

"I'm sorry." Caitlyn's voice cracked.

Ruth met her watery eyes with a cold stare. "So am I." She stood and collected the badge, keys, and books. "Send the resignation tonight. And then we're through."

She marched to her car without looking back.

Ruth stopped by Human Resources first thing Monday morning. She found the HR director, Keith Reeves, slurping coffee at his desk. "Excuse me." Then she remembered to add, "Good morning."

"Dr. Holloway! Good morning." His chair screeched as he sat up straight and put his cup down. "Have a seat."

Why does he look so nervous? Then she remembered—the article. Perhaps he thought she wanted to punish or fire those responsible. *If only.*

Ruth remained standing. "This won't take long. I wanted to let you know Chloe Taylor resigned over the weekend, effective immediately. She'll need her access revoked, her account disabled, and so on."

"Ah, really? I'm sorry to hear that. You liked her, right?"

The words were like a corkscrew twisting into Ruth's heart. *I liked her too much.* "Her performance was...uneven."

"Oh really? I didn't interact with her much, but she seemed like a sweet girl."

"Well, she's gone, so it doesn't matter," Ruth said firmly. "I'll forward her resignation when I reach my desk. Please handle it right away and then post her position. I'll borrow an admin for the time being, but I need a new assistant." The work wasn't urgent, but Ruth couldn't stand to walk by an empty desk day after day. Not after everything that had happened.

"Understood. I'll post it today." He picked up a pen and scribbled something on a sticky note.

"Thank you." Ruth turned and walked out, giving tight nods to the staff she passed on the way. She wondered how many had read the article. Probably all of them. After all, it had been out for several days now.

When she turned the corner to the hallway that led to her office, Jenn Christiansen and Kimberly were loitering out front.

What the hell do they want?

Kimberly should have had the sense to stay out of sight after speaking to that reporter, and Jenn should have known that Ruth would be in no mood for one of her complaints.

"Did we have an appointment?" Ruth knew perfectly well that they didn't.

"No," Jenn said. "We were hoping to catch you before your day got busy."

Kimberly smoothed her dress and offered an anxious smile.

Ruth unlocked the doors to the suite, tensing as her gaze fell on the vacant assistant's desk. "Fine. I can give you a couple of minutes." In reality, she didn't have a meeting until ten, but they didn't need to know that.

Jenn and Kimberly settled at the conference table while Ruth stashed her purse in her desk drawer.

Ruth gazed longingly at the Caramello bars, then shoved the drawer shut. She sat at the head of the table. "Well?"

Kimberly twisted the wedding ring on her finger. "I'll go first. I wanted to tell you I had no idea how my quote would be used. Steve said it was for a story about trends in higher education, and the reporter took it out of context. I would never intentionally participate in a negative story about you. Never." Her nerves were clearly not an act; she looked ready to faint.

"That's good to know." Ruth tempered her tone.

Jenn stuck out her jaw. "The article was the biggest load of crap I've ever seen. That's what I came to say."

Ruth's head jerked. Since when was Jenn on her side?

"Some of us are writing a letter in response," Jenn added. "We're going to submit it as an editorial."

"A letter?" Ruth couldn't hide her surprise.

"Yes. A good one. Steve shouldn't get away with this—and someone needs to call out that hack reporter for his shady tactics." Jenn crossed her arms.

Kimberly's head bobbed. "We already started drafting it. We talk about everything you're doing for enrollment, and we make it clear that you have our full support. My whole department is going to sign."

"I'm..." Ruth was lost for words. "Thank you."

"I don't always agree with you," Jenn said. "But that's how it's supposed to be. You push us to worry about money and metrics so the place doesn't get shut down, and we push back to make sure we stay true to our mission. That's good for the college."

"I didn't know you saw it that way." Jenn certainly hadn't behaved as though she valued Ruth's perspective.

Jenn barked out a laugh. "Well, I have to be a pain in the ass. I'm a stubborn old academic. It's what I do. But I know better than to chase out a perfectly good president because I don't always get my way." She turned serious. "Look, you haven't always listened to faculty or even included us. But I can see that you're starting to change. I especially see it in the enrollment work group you started. If you keep doing things like that, we'll get along well enough."

"Fair enough. I'm glad you appreciate the work group." *Caitlyn's work group.* Ruth never would have started the group without her. Despite her anger, she had to admit that Caitlyn had helped her—and not just with analytics. Caitlyn had encouraged her to treat faculty as partners, and now she had several coming to her defense.

"We should get out of your hair." Jenn pushed to her feet. "I know you're busy."

Kimberly still looked worried. "Yes, we'll let you go. I'm just so sorry for talking to that awful reporter. You have my support—I promise."

"I appreciate that." Ruth remained seated at the conference table as they filed out the door.

Jenn popped her head back in. "Hey, when does Chloe get in?"

Ruth stiffened. "Actually, Chloe resigned over the weekend."

"You're kidding!" Jenn stepped back into the office. "I can't believe it!"

Kimberly walked up behind her. "Wait. Did you say Chloe resigned?"

"Yes." Ruth did her best to sound calm.

"Why?" Kimberly asked. "She was wonderful—so much more than an assistant. Oh, is that why she left? Did she find a better job?"

"Unfortunately, I can't discuss personnel matters." Ruth realized she'd implied there was a story. "Not that there's much to discuss. The bottom line is that she won't be back."

"Well, that stinks!" Jenn said. "I bet you'll miss her."

"Such a shame," Kimberly agreed.

They left again, and the doors to the suite hissed shut behind them.

Ruth continued to sit at the conference table, staring blankly at the wall.

The worst part was that she did miss Caitlyn. She'd spent the weekend fuming about the lies, but now that she was alone in her office, the reality sank in. She would never see Caitlyn again.

She closed her eyes. *Damn you for doing this to me.*

Ruth spent her morning in a stupor, barely saying a word in her first two meetings. Her next meeting was with Piper, to discuss their official response to the *Tribune* article.

Truthfully, Ruth no longer cared. Ever since she'd learned the truth about Caitlyn, Steve's hit job seemed less important. But she couldn't explain that to Piper.

"Knock knock." Piper pushed through the door, bearing her notepad and a paper plate with a cupcake on top.

"What's that for?" Ruth asked.

Piper set the plate on the conference table. "I thought you could use something sweet." Her gaze fell on the crumpled Caramello wrapper on Ruth's desk. "Oh, I'm too late."

Ruth got up from her desk and sat at the table. "I'll take it. Today, there isn't enough chocolate in the world." She plucked the cupcake from the plate and peeled off the wrapper, salivating at the whipped chocolate icing with sprinkles.

"Chloe's off today?" Piper asked.

Biting into the cupcake to buy time, Ruth mentally rehearsed her explanation. As much as she wanted to confide in Piper, it was too risky. "Chloe quit over the weekend."

"What?" Piper's eyes widened. "Why?"

"I don't know. There was no explanation—she just sent me an email with her resignation, effective immediately." Ruth hated that Caitlyn's lies now compelled her to lie to Piper, but too many people knew about the switch already.

"Well, did you call her?"

"No, there's no point. If she doesn't want to be here, I'm not going to beg her to come back." Ruth prayed Piper would drop it.

"But you loved working with her. You talked about giving her a promotion." Piper searched Ruth's gaze, then narrowed her eyes. "What aren't you telling me?"

"Piper..." For a moment, she let the mask fall. "I don't want to talk about it, okay?"

"Are you sure?" A deep frown creased Piper's face.

Ruth nodded miserably.

"Well, whatever happened, I'm sorry."

"Me too." Ruth stuffed the rest of the cupcake into her mouth.

Piper stared for another moment, then seemed to give up. She flipped open her notepad. "Well, as for the *Tribune*, I don't think we should respond to the article directly. I went back and forth all weekend, but I believe it's the best move. We can't push back on the quotes from faculty, and arguing over data will draw more attention to Steve's narrative."

"Actually, some of the faculty are going to respond."

"Oh?" Piper quirked an eyebrow.

"Jenn and Kimberly came to see me this morning. They're working on a letter to the editor in my defense."

"You're kidding." Piper's glasses slid down her nose as her mouth dropped open.

"Kimberly insists her quote was out of context, and as for Jenn…" Ruth shrugged. "Apparently, she doesn't hate me."

Piper broke into a genuine smile. "Maybe there's some hope for this place after all."

"Maybe." Ruth stared at the crumbs on her plate. "You know, it was my fault that things got as bad as they did with the faculty."

"What do you mean?"

"I should have included them more. Whether I wanted their input or not, it was bad politics to shut them out. And actually, when I gave them a chance, they made some decent points." Ruth looked up. "I think unconsciously, I thought they would be like my old colleagues in New Mexico—selfish, conniving backstabbers. When I saw the article, I thought I'd been right all along. But now…"

"Some of them are decent." Piper's mouth quirked. "I suppose."

"Yeah." *Caitlyn was right.* As an academic herself, Caitlyn had diagnosed Ruth's leadership failures right away. Her advice hadn't been revolutionary—faculty had asked for shared governance from the start—but Ruth hadn't taken it seriously until it came from someone who seemed to be on her side.

Caitlyn had helped her career. *But she also broke my heart.* Ruth tensed as the thought echoed through her mind. Heartbreak implied love or something like it—but she didn't love Caitlyn. How could she when Caitlyn had lied? No, she'd been duped into forming a slight attachment, but certainly not love.

She wrapped her arms around herself and rubbed her elbows in a soothing motion.

"What's wrong?" Piper asked. "What are you thinking?"

"Nothing." Ruth shook her head. Maybe she'd tell Piper someday when it was far behind her, when it didn't hurt so much.

Chapter 20

"Have you heard anything?" Caitlyn's mom asked quietly.

Chloe flinched and looked down at her half-eaten plate of spaghetti, while Caitlyn tightened her grip on her fork.

Their mom knew the question was unwelcome, but Caitlyn had been applying for jobs for three months—ever since she'd left Pulaski. Her mom's impatience was understandable.

Caitlyn resigned herself to having the conversation again. "No. I don't have any job market news. I've gotten a couple of rejections, but most schools haven't contacted me at all." She paused, battling her annoyance. "Look, if I get an interview, I'll tell you. Asking me over and over stresses me out."

Her mom huffed and straightened in her chair. "Well, I was just wondering. You never talk about it, so how am I supposed to know how it's going?"

Caitlyn's blood pressure increased with her mom's stress. As usual, she absorbed her mom's anxiety despite her efforts to remain detached. "There's literally nothing to tell. I can't tell you how it's going if I haven't heard anything." Of course, that wasn't entirely true. Eventually, the absence of news would become an answer. There was no single moment of definitive rejection on the academic job market. Instead, the odds grew bleaker as the weather turned colder. The chill of mid-November was a bad sign, and they all knew it.

After dinner, it was Caitlyn's turn to clean up. Her mom wandered off to the living room, and Chloe squeezed Caitlyn's shoulder before heading upstairs.

Caitlyn stood alone at the sink, washing the dishes. She swirled a salad bowl in the murky dishwater, scrubbed it with the sponge, and ran the tap to rinse it. When she pushed the faucet, it didn't quite reach the off position. She lifted her hand but found herself transfixed by the thin trickle of water. It reminded her of the fountain at Pulaski, when the water pressure was low.

For a moment, she stared in silence. The only sounds were the faucet and the faint crackling of the soap suds. Then she gasped as her eyes filled with tears.

My academic career is over.

The tears overflowed and spilled down her cheeks. Caitlyn let out a sob, then bent over and covered her face with her wet hands. "Oh God," she whispered. "Oh my God."

She shuddered as cascading emotions overwhelmed her. Shame, sadness, and a twisted sense of relief as years of worry gave way to grief. She had never wanted to be untethered from the academy, with nothing but time and squandered potential. But as academia closed the door for the second year in a row, this awful freedom was hers.

The next day, Caitlyn unsnapped her guitar case and pulled out the instrument for the first time in over a year. It was badly out of tune, but all the parts were intact. She carefully tuned each string, using an app on her phone for reference. At last, her strum produced a harmonious chord.

She scooted back and reclined on a pillow, her slouching posture the opposite of what she'd been taught. Then she began to pick out "You Were Meant for Me" by Jewel. She missed a few notes, but after some practice, it came back to her. Once she'd run through the guitar part a few times, she began to sing the sad lyrics she still remembered from her childhood.

Partway through the warbling chorus, Chloe burst through the door. "Jesus."

Caitlyn stopped playing. "What?"

"Your middle-school breakup song?" Chloe crossed her arms. "This is sad. Really, really sad." She narrowed her eyes. "Wait, are you singing about Ruth? Or the academic job market?"

"I don't know." Caitlyn set the guitar down. "Just singing."

"Miguel's having a bad day, and he wants to try a new pie place that opened near his apartment. We're meeting there tonight. We didn't invite you because you always say no, but you should come with us. Seriously. You need to get out of the house."

Did she? Caitlyn was indifferent to whether she stayed in her bedroom or left, but the thought of numbing her sadness with pie had undeniable appeal. "When are you going? I have virtual tutoring at six—some prep school kid flunking statistics."

"We're not meeting until eight."

"Hmm." Tutoring would only take an hour. "Okay, I'll come."

"Really?" Chloe brightened. "Well, good. I'm glad. I guess I'll leave you to your music until then."

Instead of resuming the song, Caitlyn rested her head on the pillow, thinking. When she told Miguel about the job market, he'd probably ask what she planned to do next. She had no answer. All she knew was that she couldn't spend year after year trying to break into the profession, living with constant uncertainty as her odds diminished further with each new cycle.

Caitlyn thought of the job Ruth had proposed before it had all fallen apart. *Data strategist.* Did jobs like that exist elsewhere? Surely all colleges needed, at minimum, someone like Maggie who could produce reports— but perhaps there were more interesting gigs too? She picked her phone up and held it above her face as she tapped out search words on Google. *Jobs + college + data + strategy.*

The page filled with results. Data analytics, data strategy, data-driven initiatives. Her advisor would view taking any one of those jobs as a failure. But at this point, she had already failed. There was no harm in looking.

The pie shop was located in an old warehouse with towering ceilings, a cement floor, and an expansive dining area. Behind the counter, chalk-drawn menus advertised sweet and savory pie slices, and a glass case held an eclectic collection of whole pies. Some had crust, while others were topped with whipped cream, meringue, or a layer of fruit.

"I like it here," Caitlyn said as she scanned the room for Miguel.

"There he is." Chloe pointed to the back of the room.

Miguel sat at a circular table with empty chairs on either side of him. When he spotted them, he jumped up. "My twins!" He held out his arms to embrace them both.

"It's so good to see you!" Chloe squealed as they accepted the hug.

"Okay, don't tell me who is who. I want to guess." Miguel stood back and made a show of examining them.

Caitlyn glanced at Chloe's sparkly eye shadow and curly hair, an obvious contrast with her straight hair and light makeup. There was no way he could guess wrong.

He pointed to Chloe. "You're obviously Caitlyn." Then he cracked up. "Kidding!"

"Very funny." Caitlyn took off her coat.

Miguel gestured at the counter. "So can we get some pie? I waited for you, but I've been watching everyone else eat, and it's torture."

"Sure. Our stuff can save our seats." Caitlyn draped her coat over one of the chairs, and Chloe did the same.

They joined the line and ordered one at a time. Caitlyn ordered the chocolate s'more pie, while Chloe ordered strawberry and Miguel opted for coconut cream. After paying the cashier, they moved to the side to wait for their slices.

"So," Chloe said to Miguel, "we talked about this on the way over. If anyone from Pulaski sees us all together, I'm going to be Chloe."

"If you say so." Miguel shrugged. "But I have to say, Caitlyn looks more like Chloe at this point. Er—you know what I mean."

"That's why Caitlyn will fake a British accent." Chloe grinned. "She can be my long-lost sister who grew up overseas."

"Uh-huh. So how have you been?" Caitlyn asked. "Chloe said you had a rough day?"

Miguel's face fell. "Yeah. Preston's lawyer told him we're out of options, you know, to come to the United States."

"I'm sorry," Caitlyn said.

"Shit," Chloe said. "That sucks."

"It's not a surprise, since we haven't gotten anywhere." Miguel's mouth twisted bitterly. "But hearing the words—it's just hard."

"It's awful," Caitlyn said. "I wish there was something I could do."

"You're doing it right now," Miguel said. "Keeping me company while I stuff my face with pie. Really, I just need to think about something else for a while. Preston and I talked about it all afternoon, and I'm worn out."

"Miguel, Caitlyn, and Chloe!" A woman deposited three plates on the counter, each with a generous slice of pie.

"Oh wow." Caitlyn salivated at the sight of her chocolate pie with marsh-mallow fluff meringue and graham cracker crust. "I think this is exactly what I needed."

They settled at the table. The pie was so good, they spent several minutes eating in silence. When she'd finished half of the indulgent dessert, Caitlyn gulped her water and took a breath. "How is everything else going? Um, how is work?" Her pulse ticked up as she anticipated learning something—any-thing—about how Ruth was doing.

"Actually, it's going really well," Miguel said. "Thanks to you. Yesterday, Ruth had the first enrollment work group meeting with everyone back on campus. So many faculty signed up, she had to move it to a bigger room."

Caitlyn's gut twisted. The initiative they'd started together was working. She was happy for Ruth, but it killed her that she was missing it. "That's good to hear."

"Maggie presented some data," he said. "She did well, but not like you. I bet Ruth misses you."

Yeah, right. "Ruth hates me. She never wants to see me again."

"Well, she shouldn't hate you. Your work group was a great idea. She's more popular than ever. You may have saved her presidency."

Caitlyn hoped it was true. Of course, she wished Ruth success, but more than that, she wanted Ruth to look back on their time together with some-thing besides regret. "Well, that's good. Good for her." She paused. "So, I didn't get a job."

"Oh no," Miguel said. "You've heard from everywhere?"

"Not officially, but it's almost Thanksgiving. Most schools contact candidates in September, maybe October if they're running late. If I were a finalist, I would have heard by now." She spoke in monotone, no longer able to get worked up about it.

"I'm so sorry." Miguel looked crushed. "I've been trying not to ask you for updates, but I've been thinking about you. I'd hoped you were just being secretive."

"No. There's no secret job. I struck out again. I mean, technically there will be more postings in the spring for temporary contracts—but I don't know how much more of this I can take. I've been doing online tutoring to make some money in the meantime, but now I think I'm going to apply for a real job."

"Real?" Miguel couldn't hide his surprise. "You mean a non-academic job?"

"Yeah. I think... I think I want to do what I did for Ruth—analyze data and help with strategy. I searched online, and there are a lot of jobs like that—even some in the area."

"Wait, are you serious?" Chloe asked.

"Why not? I'm qualified. It would be like what I did for Ruth—not that I can put that on my résumé."

"Wow." Miguel blinked. "Last time we talked, you were committed to the academic path."

"I know, but it's not working out. Why should I keep torturing myself year after year, just for the chance that one day it might happen? I turned thirty last month. When do I get to start my life?" The words came out as if she were begging Miguel for permission—but she wasn't. It was her choice.

"Hey, I agree with you," Miguel said. "I mean, I studied poetry. Most of my classmates didn't get academic jobs."

"Do you know what some of these jobs pay? Eighty, ninety thousand dollars."

"Damn!" Chloe rubbed her thumb and fingers together in the "money" gesture.

"Whoa." Miguel sat back. "That is considerably more than I make."

"Exactly. And why shouldn't I have a job like that?" Caitlyn stabbed her pie with her fork. "In grad school, they taught us that anything less than an academic job meant failure. But this is my life. Do I really need to be a professor to be happy, or am I just desperate to prove that I'm good enough?"

"You've always felt pressure to succeed," Chloe said quietly. "I mean, you always tried so much harder than I did in school."

"You're right." Caitlyn picked up water glass but didn't take a sip. "My whole life, I've chased trophies—grades, degrees, prestige—for bullshit emotional reasons. I mean, I've had therapy. It's not some mystery. Dad left, and Mom fell apart, and I never got over it. And somehow, I thought that if I accomplished all these things, I would finally have the love and approval I always wanted. But you know what? It never worked. Dad is still gone, my advisor doesn't care about me, and Ruth won't talk to me. But now I have these credentials. I have a fucking PhD. And maybe it won't make anyone proud, but I'm going to use it to do something that matters. And I'm going to make ninety-thousand dollars doing it." She set her water down hard, causing the liquid to slosh against the sides.

Chloe applauded, causing a few other patrons to turn their heads. "Oops." She dropped her hands into her lap. "Sorry. I'm just really proud of you."

"Thanks." A lump formed in her throat. Whatever happened, she had Chloe—and herself. And glorious, decadent pie. She would be okay.

Chapter 21

RUTH WOVE THROUGH THE CROWD like a fish swimming upstream. Most conference attendees were headed to the hotel ballroom for a panel on accreditation, but she needed a break.

She considered leaving the hotel entirely, but Chicago was chilly in March, and she'd checked her coat. So, she joined the line at the café in the hotel lobby, which sold bottled drinks and prepackaged sandwiches—the kind where the condiments were already smushed all over the bread whether you wanted them or not. Uninspired by the options, Ruth bought a shrink-wrapped chocolate chip cookie and a Diet Coke.

Of course, every seat was taken. But perhaps she could catch someone about to leave. Ruth scanned the tables...and locked gazes with Caitlyn.

Ruth fumbled her drink and barely caught it. She had spent months with heightened awareness of everyone around her in public, wondering if the next face she saw in the grocery store would belong to Caitlyn. But this was the last place she had expected them to meet.

Caitlyn sat alone at a two-person table with a bottle of water and one of those four-dollar fruit cups in front of her, along with her purse and phone. She wore a badge around her neck, indicating she was registered for the same conference. But why?

Ruth should have turned and marched in the other direction, but she stayed frozen in place. Her heartbeat throbbed in her ears as she tried to decide what to do.

Licking her lip, Caitlyn slid her belongings closer and made room on the other side of the table. The look she gave Ruth was sad yet hopeful, as if her eyes were saying *please.*

I have to know what she's doing here. Ruth moved forward until she stood next to the table. Her heart pounded as they stared at each other.

"Hi," Caitlyn whispered. Aside from her nervous expression, she looked pretty and poised in her baby pink blazer over a white blouse that flattered her curves. Her hair was longer, with subtle highlights, and her makeup was a work of art: taupe eye shadow in a subtle gradient with curled lashes. The look reminded Ruth of the day Caitlyn had presented at the first retention work group meeting, speaking as though she'd explained data countless times. Which, of course, she had.

A man started down the narrow path that Ruth was blocking. "Excuse me."

Ruth pulled out the other chair and sat at the table. "I see you're here as yourself." She gestured to the badge that said *CAITLYN TAYLOR* in bold letters. Then she read the smaller print beneath the name: *Linvale Community College.* "LCC? You're a professor there?"

"No." Caitlyn fiddled with her plastic spoon. "A researcher. I analyze data and work with the president on strategy."

The words were like a jackknife to her gut. "The same work you were doing for me." It came out as an accusation, as though Caitlyn had no right to provide her skills to some other president.

"I couldn't tell them I had experience, of course. But I managed to do okay in the interview." Caitlyn's lips curved into a hesitant smile.

"Well." Ruth strained to keep her composure. Sitting two feet away from Caitlyn, Ruth found it hard to breathe.

"How's Pulaski?" Caitlyn asked.

"Not bad. Enrollment is stable for the first time in four years. We've had fewer withdrawals and fewer students in debt." Part of Ruth hated to admit that Caitlyn's strategies had been working, but another part wanted Caitlyn to be proud of herself—and proud of Ruth.

"That's wonderful!" Caitlyn broke into a wide smile. "Oh, Ruth. I'm so happy for you."

The heartfelt joy touched Ruth. She couldn't help it. *But Caitlyn lied to me.* Ruth struggled to tame her turbulent emotions. "I should get back to the conference."

Caitlyn's face fell. "But it's past the hour. All of the sessions have started already."

"I'm going to take a walk." Ruth stuffed the cookie and soda into her purse.

"Couldn't we talk for a bit?" Caitlyn's voice faltered. "I feel awful about the way things ended, and I—I miss you."

The words pierced Ruth's heart. She missed their connection—the one they'd had before she knew the truth. But she couldn't drop her guard again, not with someone who had told her so many lies. "No. I have to go." She slid out of the chair and stood.

"Wait." Caitlyn reached into her purse and frantically dug through the contents. "Please, wait one minute." She retrieved a business card and a pen. "Let me give you my cell phone number. If you never want to see me again, I'll accept it. But I want you to have it in case you ever want to talk." She scribbled on the card and held it out.

Against all reason, Ruth accepted the card and dropped it into her purse. *I'll throw it away later.* "Goodbye, Caitlyn."

Ruth hurried toward the exit. The glass doors whisked open, and she stepped outside into the chilly air. Wind whipped through her hair, and she shivered in her thin blazer. Still, she kept going.

She followed the sidewalk until she reached the Chicago River. Catching her breath, she stood on the bridge and stared down at the murky water.

Caitlyn misses me. How absurd that it meant anything to her, that her insides melted when she heard those words in her head. They'd only spent two months together, and Caitlyn had lied the entire time. Any residual attachment was muscle memory. Her heart hadn't caught up to her brain.

Ruth pulled out the card and read it for the first time. The front of the card said *Caitlyn Taylor, PhD. Data analyst* and listed Caitlyn's work email and phone number. She flipped it over and read the personal number Caitlyn had scrawled on the back. The area code wasn't local, but it looked familiar. Perhaps it was from St. Louis, where Caitlyn had gone to school.

Pinching the card between her fingers, she imagined tossing it into the river. She'd watch it float on the surface until the card stock soaked through.

The ink would blur as it sank and disintegrated into nothing. Then Ruth could go back to her life that did not include either one of the Taylor sisters.

She held it over the water, closed her eyes…and didn't let go.

It's wrong to litter. That was why she held on. Never mind the trash can three yards to her left.

She folded the card and slid it into her purse. Then she hugged herself and rubbed her arms, somehow feeling even colder.

"Hmm?" Ruth looked up at Piper.

"I said, what's wrong?"

"Oh, nothing." She jammed her fork into her salad, causing dressing to splatter her office table. "Just lost in thought. Sorry, what were we talking about?"

"I asked about the conference. How was it?"

"Oh. It was fine."

"Ruth." Piper's tone was tough, but her gaze was gentle. "I've known you for fifteen years. I know you're not okay. If you don't want to talk about it, that's fine—we could eat quietly, or I could go—but I'm here for you. Just don't lie to me."

"I'm sorry." Ruth had resolved long ago not to tell another soul what Caitlyn and Chloe had done, but months had passed without anyone becoming suspicious, and she longed to talk to her friend. "Something happened a few months ago, and I couldn't tell anybody. I want to talk about it, but I need you to promise you won't repeat it."

"Okay." Piper nodded.

"I'm really serious. You might feel angry, or—or you might feel some obligation to the institution to come forward. But whatever your reaction, I need you to take this to your grave."

Piper's glasses magnified her intense eyes. "I promise."

"It's about 'Chloe.' The real reason she left." Ruth hesitated. Once she spoke the words, there was no turning back.

Piper studied her. "Did something happen between you two? Something romantic?"

Ruth dropped her fork. "What? Why would you think that?" She hadn't even planned to tell Piper about the kiss.

"I suppose it's the way you used to talk about her—and the way she used to look at you, with so much admiration and concern. I suspected she had a crush at the very least." Piper spoke carefully, withholding judgment. "When she left abruptly and you wouldn't talk about it—well, I admit I wondered."

Piper was right. Caitlyn had looked at her that way, with care that had seemed genuine, and the feeling had been mutual. That's what made it hurt so much. "Look, this is bigger than that. Chloe has an identical twin sister named Caitlyn. At the beginning of June, Chloe went to Colorado, and Caitlyn took her place."

"What?" Piper leaned forward, her forearms landing on the table next to her lunch. "Are you serious? Chloe wasn't Chloe?"

"That's right."

Piper's mouth dropped open. "Oh my God." Her eyes shifted back and forth, and Ruth could see her mind scrambling to piece it all together. "So much about Chloe didn't make sense. One day, she was an assistant, and then suddenly she was a data expert and a faculty relations advisor—out of nowhere—because she was *literally* at different person. I can't believe it."

"I know it's a lot to take in."

"How did you find out? *When* did you find out?"

Ruth should have known there would be more questions. "It was the day after the article came out. I took a mental health day, and Caitlyn came to see me at my house."

"Hold up." Piper held up both hands, palms out. "She went to your house? Why? How did she know where you lived?"

"I had sent her there once on an errand—an emergency—while I was on campus. This was the first time she came over when I was home. We talked, and she…" *Fuck it.* Piper suspected anyway. "We kissed." Her lips burned at the memory of their clumsy kiss, half-accidental yet scalding hot. She'd never forget it.

Piper gasped. "Oh my God."

"After it happened, she told me the truth. She told me her name was Caitlyn and that she'd been impersonating her twin since the beginning of June. I kicked her out, of course, and then over the weekend, I fired her. Well, I fired Chloe. You know what I mean."

"Why did she do it?" Piper asked.

"Apparently, it was only supposed to be for a week so that Chloe could get time off to visit her boyfriend. Then Chloe decided to stay in Colorado, and Caitlyn kept coming in. She said it was because she wanted to help me, you know, because she cared so much." Ruth wanted to say it was bullshit—Caitlyn had never cared for her—but in her heart she knew otherwise. Caitlyn did care, and that made it all so much harder.

"Wow." Piper took off her glasses and rubbed her eyes. "This is a lot to process. Why are you telling me now?"

"Because I saw her this weekend. She got a job as a researcher at LCC, and I saw her at the conference. She said she missed me, and she gave me her phone number." The card was tucked in her purse, secure in a side pouch with a zipper.

Piper was silent for a minute. "Do you miss her?"

Ruth paused. "Of course. I mean, I miss the person I thought I knew—before I found out she was lying." She gathered lettuce on her fork and lifted it to her mouth, but she'd lost her appetite.

"Well. Are you going to call her?" Piper's tone was studiously neutral.

Ruth set the fork down without eating. "You think I should?"

"I don't know. I'm still wrapping my head around everything you told me. But you seemed to connect with her in more ways than one. And she doesn't work here anymore." Piper laughed dryly. "I suppose she never did."

"We did connect." Ruth remembered the day Caitlyn came to her rescue after she had forgotten her pill. It had meant so much to her. "But she was lying to me."

"It sounds like she lied so that she could stay. Because she wanted to keep working with you—and to spend time with you."

"Perhaps." Ruth didn't know what to think of Caitlyn's motives anymore.

"You have a lonely job. You've told me many times. And the hours are so long, I'm not sure when you'd have time to make friends or to meet someone special."

Ruth blushed, regretting that she'd confessed the kiss.

"I'm saying, maybe it wouldn't be the worst thing to spend time with someone who appreciates what you have to deal with here, without actually being part of it. Whether it's romantic or a friendship."

"How could I trust her after what she did?" Ruth asked softly. It wasn't rhetorical. She really wanted to know.

Piper shrugged. "Well, she told you herself. That's something. And I imagine she wanted to tell you for a long time before that."

She doesn't understand. "I don't want to be betrayed again."

"Of course you don't. But no one can promise that. There's a risk of getting hurt in any relationship, any connection with another human being. But if it happens, you will survive. You have before."

"I saved the phone number." Ruth watched for signs of surprise but saw none. "I was going to throw it out, but…I didn't."

Piper gave her a knowing smile. "Maybe you should at least have a conversation. Get some closure, if nothing else."

"Yeah." Ruth picked up her fork again and stared into her sad little salad. She wished she had ordered something greasy, perhaps with a side of dessert. "I'll think about it."

Caitlyn walked into the living room with a root beer. "I heard a text. Is that your phone or mine?"

Chloe didn't look up from her ice cream. "Yours. I don't leave my sound on like an old person."

Caitlyn searched around for her phone, expecting to be disappointed as usual. *It's not Ruth. Don't get your hopes up.* It was probably a robo-text from the Democratic party or some other form of spam.

She located her phone on the couch, under a throw pillow, and tapped the screen.

Hi. This is Ruth. Can we talk?

"Oh my God." Her hand flew to her mouth.

"What?" Chloe mumbled around a spoonful of ice cream. "What's wrong?"

"Ruth texted me. She wants to talk." Caitlyn's pulse raced, her breathing fast and shallow as the possibilities swirled in her mind. Had something happened involving her stint at Pulaski? Or did Ruth *want* to talk?

"Holy shit." Chloe sat up straight. "Do you think we're in trouble? Or do you think she really wants to talk?"

"I don't know. I'm going up to my room."

"No fair!"

Caitlyn bounded up the stairs, clutching her phone. She closed the door behind her and sank onto the bed. What did *talk* mean? Should she text back? Or did Ruth want her to call?

Screw it. The message was ambiguous enough that she felt justified in tapping the call icon. As it rang, she attempted to steady her breathing, with zero luck.

"Hello." Ruth's voice was quiet.

Caitlyn's heart thumped at the sound of Ruth's voice. "Hi. It's Caitlyn. I got your text." She was glad Ruth couldn't see her fidgeting.

The line was silent, a slight hum of static the only indication that Ruth hadn't hung up.

"Is everything okay?" Caitlyn asked. "I mean, did something happen? Or did you want to talk about something specific? Or did you want to talk…to me?" *Jesus. Stop babbling.*

"Nothing happened." Ruth paused. "I've just been thinking."

"Oh?" Caitlyn resisted the urge to fill the silence with nervous blather. If she wanted to know Ruth's thoughts, she'd have to let her speak.

"I was hoping we might talk in person. Somewhere far from campus."

Yes! Yes! Yes! "I would love that. Did you have somewhere in mind?"

"Are you familiar with Anderson Park?" Ruth's tone remained somewhat formal, as though she were scheduling an interview.

"Sure." It was a popular picnic destination outside of town. "But it has been cold all week. Would indoors be better?" Caitlyn didn't want to risk Ruth cutting their outing short due to unfriendly weather.

"It's supposed to be sixty-five degrees on Saturday."

"That's awesome. I mean, I guess it's not great because of global warming. It's more like a silver lining—one I would happily trade to refreeze the ice caps, of course—"

"Caitlyn." A slight smile crept into Ruth's voice, washing over Caitlyn like summer rain.

"Sorry. I'm rambling."

"Let's meet at the entrance by the parking lot—say, Saturday at two?"

"Perfect." *Just a few days.*

"I'll see you then." The call ended.

Caitlyn flopped back on the bed, dizzy with joy.

Chapter 22

CAITLYN UNZIPPED HER JACKET AS she approached the entrance of the park. The air was cool and temperate with only a light breeze ruffling her hair. On the inside, though, her stomach churned, and her heart pounded in anticipation of seeing Ruth again.

She sat on a bench near the entrance and crossed her legs. For ten minutes, she checked her phone and then put it back, only to pull it out again, over and over.

At last, Ruth appeared on the other side of the parking lot. She wore casual slacks and a snug sweatshirt with *University of Pennsylvania* embroidered on the lapel. Her hair was soft and free of visible product, the way Caitlyn liked it. She looked comfortable, although as she got closer Caitlyn could see the tension in her face.

She's nervous too. Caitlyn offered a shy wave.

Ruth stopped in front of her. "Hi."

"Hi." Caitlyn stood. "It's really good to see you."

Ruth nodded but didn't smile. She seemed guarded, as if she wanted to be friendly but was holding back.

It took a lot for her to come here today. Caitlyn prayed Ruth wouldn't regret it.

"There's a coffee bar inside the field house," Ruth said. "I thought we could get drinks."

"Sounds great." There was no roadmap for their situation, no established ritual for reconciliation after two people connected only to discover one was impersonating her twin. They had to make it up. *First, order coffee.*

Caitlyn followed Ruth to the field house, where they joined the short line for the coffee bar.

"So what do you really drink? Did you even like whipped drinks?" Ruth asked the question without malice, but with an unmistakable edge.

A fresh wave of guilt tumbled through Caitlyn. "They're okay. But I usually drink lattes or plain coffee with milk."

"Hmm." When Ruth reached the counter, she ordered two lattes.

Caitlyn pulled cash out of her purse, but Ruth brushed it away. "I've got this."

"Thanks." She wanted to say, *I'll get the next one*, but it would have been presumptuous. Ruth hadn't promised an ongoing relationship of any kind, just a talk.

They walked outside with their lattes and scanned the park. Ruth pointed to a cluster of vacant picnic tables. "We could sit over there."

"Sure." Caitlyn shivered at the memory of the last conversation they'd had at a picnic table. This one couldn't be any worse.

Fallen leaves cluttered the table. Ruth brushed them away, and they sat across from each other with their lattes. The park was silent except for the faint swirl of voices in the distance and the rustle of wind through the trees. There was nothing left to do but talk.

Ruth looked her over. "Calm down."

"Hmm? Oh." Caitlyn realized she'd been scratching her arms through her jacket. "Sorry. I'm nervous."

"So it's you, not Chloe, who has anxiety?"

"Yes." How could Ruth think Caitlyn would lie about something so fundamental to their connection? *Because I'm a liar.* All she could do was tell the truth. "Everything I said about my mental health was true. When I dropped that bottle of medication, it had my real name on the label—that's why I was so scared that you saw it."

"I see." Ruth took a slow, deliberate sip of her latte. "I'd think that impersonating your twin would cause you a great deal of anxiety. Surely you knew what the consequences would be if you were caught."

"Yes." Caitlyn squirmed at the visceral memory of her first moments at Pulaski. "Honestly, I was a wreck."

"So why?" Ruth's eyes cut into her like lasers. "You told me you did it so Chloe could keep her job—a job she cared so little about that she missed work constantly and then skipped town. There has to be more to it. Why was it worth the risk?"

"It's hard to explain, but I'll try." Caitlyn wrapped her hands around her latte, absorbing the warmth with her palms. "Chloe has a rough history when it comes to romance. She falls hard and fast, and when it all blows up, our mom has to pick up the pieces. We were both worried about her giving up her income for some guy she'd only met online. Chloe came up with this crazy idea for me to take her place, and, of course, I refused at first. Until eventually, I gave in."

Ruth rubbed her chin with her thumb. "I suppose it makes sense. You didn't want your twin to be in a vulnerable situation. But I still don't know how she talked you into it. Aside from this twin switch madness, you strike me as a responsible person. Not one to take foolish risks."

"I'm not, but..." Caitlyn twisted a strand of hair around her finger, trying to decide how much to reveal. She didn't want to explain her entire life story and scarred psyche, but Ruth deserved a full explanation. "My dad left when I was eight, and we all took it hard. Especially my mom."

Ruth's expression softened. "After you told me your real name, I looked up your profile from grad school. You studied the impact of twins on divorce rates?"

Startled, Caitlyn straightened on the hard bench. *Ruth looked me up?* "Yes. I didn't tell many people in grad school that I had a twin, because I didn't want them to make assumptions about why I chose my topic."

"It's none of my business," Ruth said carefully, "but it sounds like you may have blamed yourself."

Caitlyn bent forward and hugged her stomach. "I don't blame myself or Chloe. I mean, that's the first thing they tell you in therapy. *Your parents' divorce isn't your fault.* We couldn't help being twins or that we were a handful from a young age. But my parents were under a lot of stress before the split—financial and otherwise."

"Plenty of parents of twins stay together, and parents of singletons divorce all the time. You can't know for sure that it was the reason."

"I know. But when we were kids, it was harder to understand. Chloe and I coped in different ways. She acted out, getting into various scrapes and minor trouble. And I started doing well in school—really well. Every time I got an A, it was like I was worth something. My teachers praised me, and my mom was proud. I lived for that feeling, but it never lasted. Ten seconds later, I'd be worried about the next assignment. And when I didn't do well on something, I took it hard. I felt worthless. What I'm saying is that I grew up with a very strong drive to please authority figures. My teachers, my bosses. My advisor. And my mom." Caitlyn released a heavy sigh. "Then I struck out on the job market, and I had to move back home."

"You felt like you let her down?" Ruth asked gently.

"Yeah, I did. Chloe was already living at home again, and after all of that school, I ended up in the same situation. When my mom asked me to help Chloe, it pushed me over the edge, and I said yes." She searched Ruth's gaze for a reaction, hoping to see some glimmer of understanding.

Vulnerability flickered in Ruth's eyes. "I admit it makes me feel better to know that you didn't fool me for fun—or the paycheck."

"No! God, no." Caitlyn shook her head so hard, her neck cracked. "It wasn't about the money at all. I was in a very low place."

"You're a stats person. I'm sure you've seen the data. The job market is abysmal right now. Many talented scholars never find a full-time position."

"I know. But for seven years, I had this one goal—a tenure-track position. When it didn't happen, I couldn't cope. I felt like a failure."

Ruth reached across the table, then snapped her hand back.

Did she almost touch my hand? The prospect made Caitlyn's insides mushy.

"Academia makes you feel that way. I can't pretend I don't relate." Ruth rubbed her elbows. "I think I already told you I went through a terrible depression after New Mexico. Eventually, I applied to other positions, but I never found another job as faculty. However, I wound up in a career that is just as rewarding."

"You're the one who showed me that it's possible," Caitlyn said shyly. "After I left Pulaski, I applied to academic jobs all over the country. For the second year in a row, no one called. But this time it was different. Because of you."

"Me?" Ruth looked skeptical.

"Yes. It was your example, plus the work that I did for you. Working in administration made me realize I can still be a researcher and a teacher in my own way—and I can make a difference in the real world at the same time. My skills can translate to policy work, advocacy, program evaluation. I just had to get over myself to see it."

"Well." Ruth's lips curved. "I'm glad. Does this mean you like your job in administration?"

"I really do." Caitlyn brightened at the chance to talk about it. "In grad school, I used to have to beg people to share data with me for my research, and they usually said no. Now I have all this student data at my fingertips, and people use my research to make actual decisions. It's very cool."

"What kind of decisions? I'd love to know more—if it's not confidential."

"Not at all." Caitlyn laughed. "Community colleges are very open about research and strategy, probably because we're all public institutions with a shared mission. Plus any document I create can be requested under the Freedom of Information Act. We truly have no secrets. Well, not many."

Ruth cringed. "Thank God we're private. Some of my emails…"

"Can be a bit blunt." Caitlyn smiled. "I remember."

"Hmm. I suppose you do." Ruth seemed to tense at the reminder of Caitlyn's deception, but then she allowed an amused little smile. "So if it's not secret, what are you working on?"

"We have a huge number of students who need remediation before they're ready for college-level math and English. A lot of them drop out, and most never come back. We're experimenting with accelerated programs to get them into college-level classes faster."

"Oh really? Like what?"

"We have a pilot program where some students enroll in the college-level course along with an additional course that fills in the gaps. I'm analyzing data to compare their performance with students who take the traditional route."

"You already sound like an education professional." Ruth gave her an approving nod.

It made Caitlyn warm. *We're like colleagues.* Not peers, exactly, but not boss and employee either. They were two professional women, working in the same field, who could become friends.

"What have you found so far?" Ruth asked.

Caitlyn sat up a little straighter. "Well, this is the first semester, so I don't have final grades yet. But midterm retention rates are up compared to last year—and compared to the traditional remediation courses."

"That's great. I'm happy for you. Truly."

Feeling encouraged, Caitlyn decided to ask what she really wanted to know. "Why did you want to meet up today?"

Ruth dropped her head, staring at her cup. At last, she looked up. "I wanted to learn more about why you did what you did. But also...I wanted to see you again."

Caitlyn's heart swelled. "I'm really glad." She hesitated, afraid to ask but desperate to know. "Did you mean for this to be a one-time thing, to get closure? Or do you think we could do it again?"

"When I called you, I wasn't sure." Ruth bit her lip. "But I think I'd like to do it again."

Caitlyn broke into a broad smile. "I would really like that."

"But I have a condition." Ruth leveled a stern gaze. "Never lie to me again."

"I promise." Caitlyn looked into Ruth's eyes, wanting her to see that she meant it. "Lying to you made me feel sick. I shouldn't have put myself in that situation in the first place, but now that it's over, I'll never do anything like that again. I swear."

Ruth blew out a slow breath. "I know you mean that. But it might take me some time to trust it."

"That's completely fair." Caitlyn kept her expression serious, but excitement fluttered through her as she realized *some time* implied that they would continue to stay in touch.

"I had wondered what you'd be like when you weren't pretending to be Chloe. If your clothes or appearance would be different." Ruth peered at her. "I don't see much of a change."

"No. Despite the lie, I was genuine with you—as genuine as I could be. I wear a bit less makeup than Chloe, and my clothes aren't quite as fashionable. But I had already made that shift at Pulaski."

"That's true. You have your own style, and you didn't act much like Chloe. I knew from the start that something had changed about you. I just never imagined you were someone else."

Caitlyn slumped as a fresh wave of shame washed over her.

"I'm sorry. I don't mean to dwell on it." Ruth swished her hand back and forth as though shooing the unpleasantness away. "Let's change the subject."

"Okay. Um, could I ask a question about you?"

"Sure."

"I know you're from Vermont, but otherwise, I don't know much about you outside of work. I was wondering about your family. Do you have brothers or sisters?"

"No. I'm an only child. I don't know what it's like to have a sibling, let alone an identical twin. Growing up, I spent a lot of time with my parents outdoors—hiking, skiing, ice fishing. They still live there, and they're in much better shape than I am despite being thirty years older."

"But you like to be outdoors?"

"Oh yes. I don't get much time to enjoy nature these days, but I love to be outside. That's why I suggested the park. I couldn't resist a cool spring day."

"Maybe we could go hiking sometime." The words spilled out, and Caitlyn panicked. *Too much. Too soon.*

Ruth's eyes brightened. "I'd like that."

"Cool." Caitlyn fought the urge to grin. She didn't hike much—well, ever—but she'd happily scale mountains if it meant spending more time with Ruth. "I have another question. You don't have to answer."

"Okay." Ruth looked wary.

"Are you gay? Or queer?"

Ruth narrowed her eyes. "I thought certain events—involving the two of us—had made that clear."

Heat rushed to Caitlyn's cheeks. "Well. Yes. But I also heard a rumor that you had a girlfriend in Chicago."

"Really? I didn't know faculty were aware." Ruth didn't look upset, merely curious.

"Not faculty in general. Miguel has a friend who was involved in Chicago politics."

"Ah." Ruth took a long sip of her latte. "Yes, I'm gay. It's not a secret—just none of their business."

"Got it. I'm bi. So is Chloe, actually. When I said I ran off with a woman instead of continuing with school, that was her. But we've both been into women since high school."

"I see." A slight blush colored Ruth's cheeks.

They sat in silence, not making eye contact.

Suddenly, a football landed in the center of the table with a *thunk* and then bounced.

"Whoa!" Caitlyn jumped. Her cup wobbled but stayed upright.

Ruth leaned away from the impact but managed to keep her composure.

"Sorry!" a man shouted from across the field. "My bad, my bad." He started toward them, his blond hair flapping as he jogged.

With total calm, Ruth scooped up the football, rose to her feet, and sent it sailing toward him in a gorgeous arc.

The man caught it easily. "Hey, thanks!"

Ruth primly took her seat as though nothing had happened.

That was so hot. "Where did you learn to do that?"

"I played flag football in Chicago."

"Seriously?" Caitlyn tried to picture Ruth on a football field with dirt on her face and numbers on her back.

"Mmm-hmm. Quarterback. Why do you look so surprised? I wasn't always an overworked college president with little time for exercise."

"I'm impressed." Still flush from the unexpected display of skill, Caitlyn gathered her courage. "When you said before that we could spend time together, does that include…? Did you mean as friends, or…?"

Ruth's silence seemed to stretch for an eternity. "Let's see how things go."

"Okay. Sure." Caitlyn's heart swelled. *She didn't say no.*

Ruth could feel herself getting sucked in. She had planned to spend the afternoon figuring out where Chloe ended and Caitlyn began so that she could make an informed decision about future contact. But as the afternoon passed, she found herself slipping back into the rhythm they'd had when they had worked together. She smiled more easily and even laughed some.

After tossing their empty latte cups into a trash can, they took a walk along the perimeter of the park. As usual, trees were slow to bloom in Illinois, but a smattering of spring flowers dotted the grass. The fresh air felt good on her face.

"Do you have any plans for spring break?" Caitlyn asked.

"I'm flying home to Vermont."

"Oh." Caitlyn looked disappointed. "Just you and your parents?"

She wanted to spend time together. The thought sparked dueling bursts of fear and pleasure. "I'll visit my parents and my Aunt Millicent—the other spinster in the family."

"Do they really think of you as a spinster?"

Ruth laughed. "Unfortunately, yes. My parents met at the University of Vermont when they were nineteen. They can't really fathom my being single at forty-two." She glanced over, unsure if Caitlyn had already known her exact age or if she would be surprised.

Caitlyn appeared unfazed. "Yep, it's similar in my family. My mom and dad were high school sweethearts and married by twenty-one. Meanwhile, Chloe and I are still single at thirty."

A twelve-year difference. Could Ruth really date someone so much younger? *This isn't a date,* she hastily reminded herself. She had a perfect memory of their kiss, and Caitlyn's presence still made her body warm—but that didn't mean dating was a good idea.

"My parents' marriage obviously didn't work out, so my mom never wanted us to rush. The opposite, really. She always told us to wait for the right person."

"Good advice. Does she mind that you and Chloe date women?"

"Not at all. My mom is really liberal. She says we're lucky because we have more choices." Caitlyn chuckled. "Of course, being bi doesn't mean you can choose who you're into. It just happens—sometimes when you least expect it."

The implication was obvious. Feeling flustered, Ruth unzipped her sweatshirt to get some air. Perhaps changing the topic would give her a chance to catch her breath. "Speaking of Chloe, how is she doing?"

"Better. She got a job answering the phone for an apartment company. Residents call when they need a plumber or an appliance breaks. Things like that."

"Well. Good for her." Ruth couldn't help but have a negative opinion of Chloe after what she'd done—but she had brought Caitlyn into Ruth's life, and that was something. "Does she like it?"

"Actually, yeah. She gets to hear about drama, which she loves—like when a resident locked out her boyfriend after he cheated on her. They ended up calling on two different lines, each one pleading their case."

Ruth snorted. "Sounds like the reality shows she was always talking about at her desk."

"Exactly." Caitlyn paused. "Chloe still feels bad about, you know…"

"Good." It came out too fast. "I mean, I'm glad she has been reflecting."

After completing the full circle around the park, they approached the entrance.

Ruth was torn between wanting to extend their time together and wanting space to process.

"I guess I should head back," Caitlyn said.

"Sure. Me too." Ruth shuffled her feet while Caitlyn clasped and unclasped her hands.

"So, maybe we can hang out again sometime?" Caitlyn's eyes were round and hopeful. A breeze blew past them as she waited, and a dry leaf lodged itself in Caitlyn's hair.

Ruth reached forward and gently picked out the leaf, enjoying Caitlyn's confusion. She held the leaf up to show her before letting it fall. Then she gave Caitlyn's shoulder a soft squeeze. "I'd like that."

Caitlyn's smile lit up her face. "I'll text you."

As Ruth walked back to her car, she rubbed her thumb and fingers together. It had felt good to touch Caitlyn, even in a brief, ambiguous way, after so many months apart.

What am I doing? A few weeks ago, she never would have imagined giving Caitlyn another chance. Yet there she was, doing it. And she wanted to do it again.

Chapter 23

CAITLYN SET DOWN HER FORK. "I'm thinking of getting an apartment."
Her mom looked up from her dinner. "Oh?"

"An apartment here?" Chloe asked. "I didn't think you were ready to commit to Linvale. I mean, I know you like your job, but I guess I thought you might still want to be a professor someday."

The words hurt, but not as much as before. The pang was more like a memory. "No, I'm done with that. I would have liked to be a professor, and it sucks that it didn't work out. But I *am* happy."

"That's great," her mom said. "How long do you think you'll work at LCC?"

"I don't know. But my job pays well, and I'm learning a lot. I'm not in any hurry to leave." *Especially not when I might have a reason to stay.*

Caitlyn knew she was getting miles ahead of herself, but she kept daydreaming about what might happen with Ruth. And if she was going to date an older woman with *President* in her job title, she needed more than her childhood bedroom.

"March isn't the best time to look for apartments," her mom said. "Usually, there are more vacancies in the summer when the students move out."

"Yeah, I know. But I've been browsing Craigslist, and there are a few units available."

Chloe twirled her fork thoughtfully. "What's the rush?" Then a smile spread across her face. "Oh."

"What?" her mom asked.

"She needs her own place to impress Ruth." Chloe giggled. "And so they can have privacy."

Their mom furrowed her brow. "Is that the reason?"

Caitlyn shot Chloe a glare, but she shouldn't have been surprised—occasional mind reading came with the territory of having a twin. "Okay, it might be part of the reason."

"I see." Her mom took a wary sip of water. "I admit I'm still processing the fact that you're dating the woman who fired your sister."

"Mom, Chloe left town and sent me in her place. Anyone would have fired her—literally anyone. And we're not dating. We're...seeing where it goes. Besides, that's not the only reason."

"Okay, what else?" Chloe asked.

"It's just... I was so poor in grad school, you know? I lived in a studio, while my friends from college were buying homes. Now I can finally afford a real apartment, and I don't want to wait anymore. I'm ready to be an adult."

"That makes total sense," Chloe said. "I'm glad we'll still get to see each other."

"Of course. We'll hang out all the time. We need to make up for all those years we lived in different cities."

"I can't tell you how happy it makes me to have both of my daughters here in town. And you both have jobs." Her mom beamed. "I'm proud of you two."

This isn't failure. It's not a consolation prize. Caitlyn had lost the specific career she had once imagined, but she had gained just as much by letting it go.

After dinner, Caitlyn washed the dishes. As she dried her hands, her phone buzzed on the counter. It was a text from Ruth.

I have a craving for my favorite restaurant in Chicago. Would you like to go on Saturday?

Caitlyn clutched the phone to her chest, grinning so hard it hurt.

Ruth didn't care for makeup. Sure, she wore a dusting of eye shadow and a dab of lip gloss to work, but only because of the sexist view that professional women weren't "polished" unless they painted their faces. Outside of work, her face was always bare.

So why was she in her bathroom, smearing long-expired foundation on her forehead?

She had hoped it would blur away bumps and fill in the fine lines between her eyes. Instead, the application seemed to enhance her flaws while giving her skin a faintly orange hue—reminding her why she never wore foundation in the first place.

Her phone chirped with a text from Caitlyn:

I'm outside.

Ruth bent over the sink and scrubbed her forehead clean. Her actual skin would have to do.

She smoothed her hair as she ran downstairs. Then she steadied herself, took a breath, and opened the front door.

Caitlyn stood before her in a fitted gray jacket with opaque purple tights and boots up to her knees. Her hair fell in waves that brushed her shoulders, and her makeup was flawless: smoky eyes with natural lashes and rosy lips. "Hi. I'm a little early, but I didn't want to risk being late." Her smile was shy, but her eyes glittered.

Ruth caught herself gawking and shook her head. "Hello. Come on in."

A fruity fragrance filled the entryway as Caitlyn stepped inside, causing Ruth's skin to tingle. She unbuttoned her coat and shrugged it off, revealing a black cocktail dress. "I was afraid I had overdressed, but you look really nice."

"Oh, it's not much—but thank you." Ruth was glad she had discarded her plain blouse in favor of the one with silver pinstripes. They were well-matched. "I'm actually ready to leave. We'll take my car?"

"Sounds great." Caitlyn put her coat back on, short, pink fingernails catching the light as she redid the buttons.

Ruth pulled her cream-colored drape coat from the closet and led the way to her garage. As she unlocked her Prius, she realized she had forgotten to check that it was clean.

Fortunately, there wasn't much in the passenger seat—just an umbrella. Caitlyn moved it to the floor and settled into the seat. "I like your car."

"Thank you." They sat in silence as Ruth backed out of the garage. "So is anything new? Well, I suppose it has only been a week." She had a sudden fear that they wouldn't be able to make conversation all the way to Chicago. Did it mean something if they couldn't?

"Actually, yes." Caitlyn perked up. "I'm moving."

"What?" Ruth's stomach dropped. "Moving away?"

"Oh no, I'm staying in town. But I'm moving out of my mom's house. I got an apartment by work."

"Oh." Ruth let out her breath, startled by her own dramatic reaction. "Well. That's great. What's it like?"

"It's really nice. It has two bedrooms and in-unit laundry for only eight hundred per month. In St. Louis, you'd pay twice as much for the same square footage."

Ruth hoped it wasn't located above a shady strip club or some other unsavory situation that explained the low rent. Still, the important thing was that Caitlyn had committed to the area, at least for the duration of a lease. "So you're planning to stay at your job?"

"Yes, for now. I really like it."

"I'm glad." Ruth turned out of her neighborhood onto the main road. "Working on anything interesting?"

"A lot of things. Now that I've been there for a few months, more people know who I am, so they're coming to me with requests. I'm working on projects with student services, Financial Aid, and even the physics department."

"Physics?" Ruth thought of the grumbly physics faculty at Pulaski. "They want to work with administration?"

"Actually, yes!" Caitlyn laughed, most likely guessing Ruth's thoughts. "Our physics faculty are fun. They're launching a new tutoring program, and they want me to help them see if it's effective or not."

"Hmm." Ruth considered the research question. "You're the social scientist, but isn't there an issue with selection bias?"

"Oh yes. Selection is a huge problem, but that's what makes it so much fun. It's a challenge. How do you study a program when the students who attend are systematically different from those who don't—in both directions? They struggle more than the top students, but they're also more motivated than the students who don't go to class at all."

Ruth loved the joy in Caitlyn's voice. "So, do you have any ideas?"

"I have too many ideas. I still haven't decided on an approach, but one thing I've been looking into is called random encouragement. We can't limit access to tutoring, obviously, but we can randomly assign students to receive extra marketing."

"Interesting." Ruth considered Pulaski's student supports. "I wonder if we could do something like that for our advising program. What are your outcome measures? Grades?"

"Yes. But also attendance and course completion."

They talked about research strategies in education for most of the drive. Ruth relished the intellectual conversation with someone who shared her interests but wasn't an employee. They were on equal footing, each with plenty of ideas to contribute.

After talking throughout the ninety-minute drive, they arrived at the restaurant, a French bistro in Bucktown, Chicago.

Ruth locked the car. "We should be right on time for our reservation."

Together, they strolled to the entrance, elbows brushing against each other on the narrow sidewalk.

Ruth pulled on the door handle, but it didn't budge. Then she noticed the neon yellow sign that said *LICENSE SUSPENDED*.

"What the hell?" Ruth jiggled the handle back and forth. "They're closed?"

"Oh no." Caitlyn moved closer to read the fine print.

Ruth huffed. "I can't believe this. I had a reservation."

Caitlyn peered at the sign. "I guess no one told the Department of Business Affairs and Consumer Protection."

"Unbelievable. You'd think they would have the courtesy to call." Her jacket felt hot and constricting as she grew more flustered; she tugged the buttons apart and let it hang open.

Caitlyn, however, seemed to take it in stride. "I wonder what happened. Maybe they were caught serving liquor to minors. Or they could owe a bunch of taxes. Hmm, it could also be something big like money laundering."

How mortifying. So much for impressing Caitlyn with her knowledge of fine dining. "I'm sorry. What a disaster."

"Hey, it's okay. We'll figure something out. Do you have a second-favorite restaurant in Chicago?"

"I know a few other places, but I can't imagine we'd get a table on Saturday night. All the good restaurants are booked by now." Ruth pulled her phone out of her coat pocket. She'd heard of apps that booked reservations, but she'd never downloaded any of them.

"I might know a place. How do you feel about Middle Eastern food?"

Ruth lowered her phone. "I'm in favor of it."

"There's a place called Taste of Lebanon in Edgewater. It's not fancy, but the food is outstanding. And since most people get takeout, it's never crowded, not even on the weekend." Caitlyn pulled out her phone. "If that sounds okay, I could look up the address."

Ruth hadn't envisioned a takeout joint. But confronted with Caitlyn's eager eyes, she couldn't say no. Besides, what she wanted more than anything was to spend time with Caitlyn. The venue didn't matter. She took a loud, deep breath. "Okay. Let's do it."

They returned to the car, and Ruth plugged the address into her GPS. Thirty minutes later, they paid for parking at a meter in front of the restaurant.

As soon as they walked in the door, a spicy aroma swirled around them. The restaurant was casual but clean, with several open tables as Caitlyn had promised.

"We order up there." Caitlyn pointed to the counter, where a cashier stood below a giant banner listing the menu options. "Everything is good, but the lentil soup is famous."

"Then I'll have to try some." It wasn't the dining experience she'd imagined, but Ruth had to admit the food smelled incredible.

They both ordered shawarma wraps and lentil soup. Caitlyn pulled out her credit card before Ruth could stop her.

"I can pay. After all, I asked you—to come." Ruth had almost said *asked you out*. While the evening was like a date in every way, she hadn't officially acknowledged it as one, and she wasn't ready to say it out loud.

"You can pay next time." Caitlyn threw a flirtatious smile at Ruth, then seemed to catch herself. "Anyway, we used your gas to get here," she said quickly. "So it's about even."

When the food was ready, they settled at a table with their trays.

Ruth tasted the soup. *Oh my God.* A warm mix of lentils, lemon, and comforting spices filled her mouth. "This might be the best lentil soup I've ever had." She dabbed her mouth with a napkin. "How did you find out about this place?"

Caitlyn dipped a triangle of pita in her soup. "I had a good friend who lived in this area, so I visited a lot in high school and college—mostly on summer breaks." She bit into the bread with a contented sigh. "She introduced me to all her favorite spots."

Ruth wondered if *good friend* was code for a significant other. It wasn't her business, but the irrational slither of jealousy she felt was another sign that this wasn't a platonic outing.

"So what were you like as a teenager?" Caitlyn asked.

"Awkward." Ruth made a face. "I was still figuring out my sexuality, so I was self-conscious around boys and girls. I knew I wasn't ultra-feminine, but I had no idea how to dress. I looked like a roadie for a grunge band."

"Well, you look nice now." Caitlyn ran an appreciative gaze down Ruth's blouse. "I mean, I like your style. It's simple and flattering."

Their eyes met, and heat crept up Ruth's neck. "Thank you."

The drive home started with plenty of chatter, but they grew quiet as the streets became familiar. Ruth sensed they were both preoccupied with similar questions. How would the night end? Where was this going?

Ruth pulled into her driveway and cut the engine. "So."

Caitlyn unbuckled her seatbelt but made no move to exit the car. Instead, she searched Ruth's face with a gaze that looked dark in the shadows.

Warmth pooled in Ruth's belly. She took slow breaths, attempting to get ahold of her body's reaction. Meanwhile, the unspoken questions lingered between them.

They'd behaved as though they were on a date, with countless moments confirming their mutual interest. Whatever was happening, something great or a looming disaster, it wasn't friendship. Ruth decided to put them both out of their misery. "We both have a tendency to overthink...and to worry."

"It's true," Caitlyn said sheepishly.

Ruth unbuckled her seatbelt and shifted to face Caitlyn. "I think it might help both of us to be direct."

Anxiety flashed across Caitlyn's face, but she steadied herself and held Ruth's gaze. "Okay."

"I enjoy spending time with you, and I'd like to do it again. As more than friends." Ruth held her breath.

The tension in Caitlyn's face dissolved into elation. "I would *love* that." As she moved closer, the light from the porch lamp caught her face, and she glowed. Her lips gleamed from the shimmery lipstick she'd reapplied in the car, and Ruth watched, mesmerized, as her smile softened into a sensuous pout.

I want to taste those lips. She leaned in to capture them.

Caitlyn collapsed against her, wrapping an arm around Ruth's back as their mouths smashed together in a hungry kiss.

The lipstick smeared between them as Ruth's tongue brushed teeth and probed deeper. Caitlyn tasted like spices and sweetness and heat, and Ruth's whole body pulsed in response.

Caitlyn groaned, a tortured sound from low in her throat, and pulled Ruth closer. Her breasts pushed into Ruth's chest.

Ruth lost all sense of time as she plundered Caitlyn's hot, wet mouth. When a thought broke through, like *it's getting late*, she shoved it aside. Desire coursed through her like a drug, and she never wanted to come down from the high.

In the end, Caitlyn pulled back first, breathless and radiant in the lamplight. "I feel so happy."

"Me too." Ruth's insides quivered. The temperature in the car had climbed several degrees. If Ruth invited Caitlyn inside, there was a good chance they'd take things even further—but it was too soon. She wasn't ready.

"Well, I guess I should go?" Caitlyn said uncertainly.

"You're not too tired to drive?"

Caitlyn snuck a glance at Ruth's front door. Then she shook her head firmly. "No. I'm okay. I'll see you again soon?"

"Definitely." It came out raspy.

Caitlyn opened the door and slipped out, closing it behind her.

Ruth stayed in her seat and watched Caitlyn get into her car. Soon, the headlights came on, and Caitlyn slowly drove away.

She touched her finger to her bruised lips. *We kissed. We're dating.* There was no doubt that she wanted this. But at the same time, fear trickled through her. She was falling hard for a woman who had lied to her for months.

Since their reunion, their time together had been perfect. But could she ever trust Caitlyn with her whole heart?

———

"I need another break." Chloe dropped a box on the floor. "You have too many books."

"There's no such thing." Caitlyn wiped the sweat from her brow and surveyed her new apartment. "Besides, I need to fill all this space with something. I don't have much stuff aside from my books and clothes."

"True. Now that you have a job, you'll need to go shopping for some grown-up decorations so you can make it presentable for Ruth. Maybe you can get some candles and lanterns—you know, to set the mood."

"Very funny." Chloe was having entirely too much fun with this. Caitlyn sat on a box and twisted the cap off her water bottle.

Secretly, she had been thinking of Ruth ever since she set eyes on the spacious two-bedroom unit in south Linvale. She wanted to make a good impression with her home, and she wanted Ruth to feel comfortable visiting often.

Unfortunately, she didn't have much stuff, and what she did own screamed *broke grad student*. Her bookshelves were flimsy, and her television was a decade old. But she'd resolved to think of the move as an opportunity. She was starting fresh with a lot of empty space. "A nice couch will help a lot. I hope."

"The new furniture comes tomorrow, right?"

"Yeah. The store gave me a ridiculous delivery window, so I have to spend the whole day waiting. But it will be worth it." The plum-colored couch would be perfect for relaxing with Ruth, perhaps with tea and snacks on her new oval coffee table. She had also splurged on a sturdy queen-sized bed.

Chloe glanced at her phone. Her lock screen was littered with notifications, even though she never went more than ten minutes without checking.

Caitlyn walked over to the kitchen counter, where she had left her own phone. She perked up when she saw a message from Ruth.

It's nice to be hundreds of miles away from Steve Stubbons. How are you?

The message was a good sign. They hadn't talked much about Pulaski on their trip to Chicago or in the text messages they had exchanged since then. It could have been an easy topic for them to discuss since Caitlyn knew the cast of characters from personal experience, but it was also a reminder of Caitlyn's dishonesty.

Ruth seemed to have forgiven her. They wouldn't have kissed if she were still angry, right? Still, Caitlyn wouldn't believe Ruth had made peace with the past until they could talk about it openly without tight lips or tense shoulders. Perhaps this text message was a start.

Instead of pushing her luck, though, Caitlyn responded with a laughing emoji. Then she typed,

How is Vermont?

Raining. But it's good to see my family. How did the move go?

Caitlyn glanced at the pitiful pile of boxes that represented two hours of work, minus several breaks to chat and check phones.

Still in progress.

She hesitated, then added,

Would you like to come over and see it sometime?

The bubbles seemed to last years before Ruth responded,

I'd love to. Next Saturday?

Caitlyn's chest swelled.

It's a date.

She returned to the living room. "It's official. I've got one week to make this place look good. Ready to get back to work?"

"Yes, let's get back to moving you into your new love nest, so you can impress my old boss, who fired me."

Caitlyn rolled her eyes but then turned serious. "Thanks again for your help."

Chloe tossed her hair. "What are twins for?"

Chapter 24

RUTH WAS PLEASED TO DISCOVER that Caitlyn's apartment was located on a calm residential street with ample parking. She found a spot right out front.

As she stepped up to the entrance with a box of gourmet chocolates, her body seemed to buzz. An evening at Caitlyn's home promised to be more intimate than their date in Chicago, and after the steamy kiss they'd shared in Ruth's driveway, it would be hard to resist the temptation to do more. The thought of what *more* might entail made her shiver with anticipation—and nerves.

She located Caitlyn's name on the panel next to the door. After a pause to steady herself, she pushed the button.

"Ruth?" Caitlyn's voice crackled through the speaker. Even with the distortion, Ruth could hear the excitement in her voice.

"Yes—" She cleared her throat. "Yes, it's me."

"Come up to the third floor!"

A loud noise made Ruth jump backward. She yanked the door open in time, however, and climbed two flights of stairs.

"Hi!" Caitlyn stuck her head out the door. Her hair was styled in a high ponytail with thin wisps framing her face. She wore black leggings and a marled gray sweater with a floppy, oversized collar. The sweater hugged her curves all the way to her thighs, creating a look that was casual and sexy all at once.

"Hello." Ruth reached the doorstep. "It's good to see you."

"Come in!" Caitlyn moved to the side. "I can take your coat."

Ruth stepped inside and slipped off her flats. As she removed her coat and sunglasses, she peered past Caitlyn but couldn't see much of the apartment.

Caitlyn opened a narrow door, revealing a hall closet. "This closet is *just* for coats. Fancy, right?"

"I'm impressed." Ruth recalled her first apartment after grad school and how much she had cherished the little things. After Caitlyn hung her coat, Ruth held out the box. "I brought chocolate."

Caitlyn scanned the box with bright eyes. "Ooh, it's from that fancy shop. Thank you so much." She bounced on her heels. "Are you ready to see the apartment?"

Ruth smiled. *She's so cute.* "I can't wait." She followed Caitlyn to the living room.

"So, what do you think?"

"Oh wow." The room was spacious, even with bookshelves lining most of the far wall. The purple couch was spotless, and it matched one of the colors in the abstract painting that hung above it. A tall floor lamp cast soft yellow light over the room. "It looks like one of those perfect rooms in furniture catalogs."

"Almost everything is new," Caitlyn said proudly. "I wanted to upgrade from my grad school days."

"I remember feeling the same way. By the time I graduated, I was twenty-nine and desperate to feel like an adult." Ruth walked over to the bookshelves. "I can tell you're an academic. You have hundreds of books and a tiny television."

"An ex-academic anyway." Caitlyn shrugged.

"Nonsense. You'll always have a PhD. Not getting a tenure-track job doesn't change that—nor does losing one. We're both doctors, no matter what we do for a living."

"Good point." They shared a smile.

It was good to be with someone who understood, not just in theory but viscerally, how it felt to dedicate years to academia only to face a rejection that seemed to obliterate one's career prospects and identity all at once.

They looked into each other's eyes in silence until Caitlyn moved forward and ran her fingertips down the side of Ruth's cheek.

Ruth melted into the touch, and a soft purring sound escaped her lips.

Caitlyn leaned in and kissed her.

The brief contact sent waves of desire through Ruth's body.

Caitlyn stepped back. "The first kiss in my new apartment."

Ruth steadied herself on the counter. "The first of many, I hope."

When Caitlyn had offered to cook, Ruth had expected something like boiled pasta with sauce from a jar—perhaps a projection of her own culinary ineptitude. Caitlyn surprised her with a flavorful stir-fry served over rice from an actual rice cooker, plus a side salad with homemade lemon vinaigrette.

"That was delicious," Ruth said. "I'm not just saying it."

"I'm so glad you liked it." Caitlyn couldn't hide her proud smile. "Shall we sit on the couch?"

"Sure." Ruth picked up her plate and collected her silverware.

"Oh, don't worry about the dishes." Caitlyn waved her off. "I'll get them later."

"Are you sure?"

"Definitely. I'd rather spend this time talking." She led the way to the living room and settled on the couch.

Ruth sank into a plush cushion. "Oh—this couch is comfortable."

"Thanks." Caitlyn grinned. "Chloe and I sat on about fifty of them before I decided."

For a moment, no one spoke. Ruth sat back and crossed her legs. "So where did you learn to cook?"

"YouTube, mostly." Caitlyn shrugged. "I couldn't afford to get takeout every night, so I had to learn or starve."

"You managed better than I did back in grad school. I lived on instant noodles." Ruth still found it odd to talk about grad school with Caitlyn. It was something they had in common, but Caitlyn hadn't been able to talk openly until the secret was out. "What was grad school like for you, other than long and lacking in financial resources?"

"Grad school was hard, I guess in all the usual ways. The workload, the stress. My advisor, Andrew, never made enough time for me. He treated me like an inconvenience rather than part of his job."

"That's appalling," Ruth said. "I can't imagine having the opportunity to work with you and blowing it off. I bet you were one of the best grad students they've ever had."

"I tried to be," Caitlyn said softly. "Maybe my work wasn't great, but no one tried as hard as me. I never missed class, and I passed my qualifying exams with honors. I worked so hard on my dissertation, did everything Andrew wanted—and I was pleasant and appreciative even when I was screaming on the inside. I did literally everything right. But it wasn't good enough."

Ruth made a disgusted sound. "The university should have intervened. Did you talk to the dean?"

Caitlyn blinked. "Um, that wasn't really an option. Technically, Andrew did the minimum for me to graduate, so…"

Ruth forced herself to calm down. Her instinct to defend Caitlyn was overriding her experience and what she knew to be true. "Of course. You're right. Most people don't understand why grad students or new professors can't appeal to authority when they get screwed—but I do understand."

"Yeah." Caitlyn smiled gratefully. "You get it. I just did my best to get through it."

"Is that when your anxiety got bad?" Ruth asked. All she remembered from Caitlyn's original explanation, long ago, was that she'd had anxiety during "school."

Caitlyn nodded. "I've always pushed myself hard at the expense of my health, but grad school was a new level of hell. I really struggled with my confidence, and some of my coping mechanisms weren't very good." She stared at her plate.

"You don't have to talk about it." Ruth's mind ran through possibilities—several of her own classmates had self-destructed in different ways—but she didn't want to ruin a nice evening by pushing.

"No, it's okay. I want to. Um, when things got bad, it was hard for me to sleep without medication. And I used to, um, scratch my arms and legs, sometimes until I was bleeding."

"I'm sorry you went through that." Consumed with an urge to pull her close, Ruth reached out and touched Caitlyn's wrist.

"Thank you." Caitlyn took her hand and squeezed it, confirming the contact was welcome.

Ruth scooted closer and wrapped her arm around Caitlyn's back.

Caitlyn leaned into the embrace. "It was rough, but in my second year, I finally got help. The medication changed my whole life. It's not that I never struggle, but I'm able to work through my stress before it spirals out of control."

"That's wonderful. I feel the same way about my medication. It's not a cure, but it helps a lot. And I'm able to catch myself when I start slipping into the early stages of depression."

"We really are similar." Caitlyn turned her head to meet Ruth's eyes. "When I was at Pulaski, there were so many times I wished I could tell you—not just who I really was, but how much I could relate to you. I hated lying to you every day."

Ruth's muscles tensed.

"I'm sorry. Maybe I shouldn't have brought up the—the switch. I know we're trying to move past all of that."

Forcing her body to relax, Ruth pushed away her discomfort. The deception was over. "It's okay. I know what you mean. Even when I thought you were Chloe, I sensed that you understood me. It didn't make sense back then, but now it does."

They exchanged awkward smiles, and then Caitlyn stood abruptly. "I thought we could try those chocolates." She retrieved the box from the counter and returned to the couch.

"Excellent plan." The break in the tension was a relief.

"It was so thoughtful of you to bring these."

"I was thinking of myself too. I'm a big fan of chocolate," Ruth said with a wry smile.

"I know." Caitlyn's eyes crinkled. "I've seen your stash of Caramello bars." She slid the ribbon off the box and scanned the tray of truffles. "Ooh. They all look amazing."

"Do you have a favorite flavor?"

"I don't think I could choose. But I'm going to start with coconut." Caitlyn held it to her mouth and ran her teeth down the edge, shaving off a sliver of coating.

Ruth's breath caught as she watched. Was Caitlyn doing this on purpose?

Caitlyn gave her a sweet little smile. "I like to savor it." She sank her teeth in farther and let out a long, throaty sigh. "Oh my God. This is incredible. It's so rich and creamy."

Definitely on purpose. Ruth's chest and neck flushed. "That good?"

Moving closer, Caitlyn looked into Ruth's eyes. "Want a taste?"

God, yes. Ruth closed the gap and met Caitlyn's mouth with hers.

Caitlyn dropped her head back and parted her lips, allowing Ruth's tongue to indulge.

Pleasure pooled within Ruth as chocolate mixed with the taste of Caitlyn. She pulled their bodies closer together until Caitlyn's hard nipples nudged her chest. Her nipples ached in response.

They made out on the couch like teenagers, hands roaming the curves of each other's backs and hips. Ruth squeezed her thighs together as arousal throbbed in her center. "I want you." The words poured from her lips in a loaded whisper before she could think them through.

Caitlyn's breath was steamy against Ruth's skin. "You can stay. If you want. I have a brand-new bed."

"Um. I don't know." Ruth longed to say yes, but Caitlyn's invitation brought her back to earth—and what it would mean to strip off her clothes and be completely vulnerable.

She imagined herself naked, nervous, and unable to respond how Caitlyn wanted. Would it be okay? She had tried to move past the months of lies, to not let her issues hold her back from a relationship that had the potential to become something special.

"It just takes a lot for me to, um…" Ruth sucked in a breath and tensed her abs. "I'm sorry. I know I've been the one escalating the, ah, physical aspect tonight. But I'm not ready for more yet—as much as my body says otherwise." Her mouth quirked into a rueful smile.

"Oh my gosh, of course." Caitlyn grasped both of Ruth's hands. "There's no rush, and I would *never* pressure you. Never."

"Thank you." The immediate acceptance and reassurance made Ruth feel safer. "I just need to calm my hormones a bit."

Caitlyn reached for the tray of chocolates. "I know what you need."

Ruth laughed. "The next best thing." She plucked a truffle from the tray and popped it into her mouth whole. The explosion of chocolate and caramel on her tongue didn't sate her craving for Caitlyn, but it would have to do. *For now.*

Two days later, Ruth was at work with the early signs of a headache. An administrative snafu had resulted in a double-booking for the campus auditorium, and neither party was backing down, so the week was off to a trying start.

She was searching her desk drawer for her Advil when a knock sounded. "Come in!" She slammed the drawer closed.

Maggie walked in, bearing her laptop, red curls bouncing with each buoyant step. "Hi!"

Ruth smiled at Maggie's confidence, another positive change Caitlyn had brought to the college. Her thoughts drifted to their last date, but she shoved them away and cleared her throat. "How can I help you?"

"Do you have time for some good news?"

"There's a meteor headed straight for my desk?"

Maggie pouted. "Sorry, I guess it's not a good time."

"Wait." It was wrong to take out her mood on poor Maggie. "Apologies. Please have a seat."

"Okay." Maggie sat at the table and opened her laptop.

Ruth settled beside her. "So what's the news?"

"It's the end-of-term data. Final grades are in." Maggie tapped the mouse pad, and a table appeared on the screen. "I haven't had a chance to make it pretty, but look. Withdrawals and incompletes are way down."

Ruth leaned in to study the data. "Really?"

"Yes. We improved across the board, but look at this." She pointed to the bottom of the table. "Withdrawals dropped ten percent in remedial math—er, I mean ten percentage points."

Ruth's mouth twitched as she recalled the day Caitlyn had taught her senior staff about percentages. "This is excellent news. Thank you for sharing. And thank you for all of your help with the enrollment work group this semester. You've done a great job."

Maggie blushed. "I should thank Chloe. She's the one who taught me how to do the analysis." She paused. "Honestly, we didn't get off to the best start, but now I miss her."

"I miss her too." *After all of three days.* It was strange to speak the truth aloud at work, even in a cryptic way that Maggie wouldn't understand.

"Did you ever hear anything about where she ended up?"

"No. She hasn't kept in touch." *Back to lying.*

"Too bad." Maggie closed her laptop. "Well, I'll let you get back to work. I just wanted to share these results right away."

"I appreciate it. Email those numbers to me when you get a chance."

As Maggie walked out, Ruth remained at the table, resting her chin on her fist as she thought about Caitlyn. Perhaps she needed to talk to someone who knew at least some of the truth already. She got up and walked down the hall to Piper's office.

Piper sat at her desk, absorbed in whatever was on her computer screen. Her thick glasses rested on the knob of her nose.

Ruth knocked on the doorframe. "Hi. Is this a bad time?"

"Not at all." Piper gestured to the small table in the corner of her office. "Have a seat."

"Are you sure? You looked like you were really concentrating on something."

Piper looked guilty. "It was about the…Kardashians."

"Ah." Ruth closed the door and plopped down in one of the chairs. "Well, this is personal, so we're both off-task today."

"Oh good. What's up?" Piper sat across from her.

Ruth decided she might as well say it. "I've been seeing Caitlyn Taylor. Socially."

"Socially as in…romantically?"

"Yes." While Piper had all but encouraged it, Ruth still felt self-conscious. Her pulse accelerated as she waited for a reaction.

Piper's gaze was calm. "Well. Good. How is it going?"

"For the most part, really well. We have a lot in common, but we're different in some ways too. We never run out of things to talk about. The, um, attraction is strong."

"Sounds wonderful. What's the problem?"

Ruth shifted in her chair. "Since we've started spending time together, she has been nothing but open and straightforward—as far as I can tell. But part of me is afraid to trust her with…everything. Meaning, there are certain steps that I want badly, but…" She licked her lips. "Um."

"What do you…?" Piper's eyebrows rose. "*Oh.*"

"No!" Ruth hadn't meant to say this much. Maybe she could backtrack. "I'm not talking about any specific activity or milestone. Just our relationship in general. I can feel myself holding back. I keep ruminating about her deception and wondering what it means for us."

"I see." Piper toyed with the stress ball she kept on the table. "You know, I don't condone what she did here at Pulaski. It was reckless, and she put the whole institution at risk." She paused. "But that girl worked her bottom off to help you. I've never seen anyone shut down Steve Stubbons the way you did at that board meeting, and it was because of Caitlyn. The enrollment work group was a great idea, one that was long overdue—and I've noticed that you've been more accessible to faculty all semester. I'm not saying it's all her influence, but you have to admit, she gave good advice."

"You're right," Ruth said. "I just saw Maggie, and our withdrawal rate has dropped. The faculty are finally working with me instead of against me, and I can already see the results. I feel secure in this position for the first time, and I'm not sure it would have happened without Caitlyn. I just wish it could have happened without the lies."

"I know." Piper patted her arm. "But there's nothing either of you can do to change the past. You can only move forward."

It was an obvious point, but one she needed to hear. "You're right. Whatever I think or feel about it, Caitlyn coming here as Chloe will always be part of our story. It will always be how we met. I need to accept it—and if I can't, our relationship will never work." Her gut clenched at the thought. *That's not an option.*

Piper gave her a rueful smile. "I never thought I'd say this, but I'm rooting for you two."

"Thanks, Piper." She rose to her feet. "I'll let you get back to the Kardashians. I've got a text to send."

Caitlyn knew it looked bad to check her phone in a meeting, but when the screen lit up with a message from Ruth, she couldn't restrain herself.

Hope you're having a good day. I'd love for you to come over on Friday evening.

Warmth spread through her chest, and her limbs tingled with happiness.

As discreetly as possible, she slid the phone to her lap and typed a response:

I'd love to come over. Thank you.

She added a heart emoji and tapped send.

"Caitlyn, could you please present the transfer data?" Dr. Tomlin, the LCC president, asked.

She popped her head up. "Of course." Fortunately, she already had the presentation open on her laptop. She tapped the icon to mirror her screen on the wall-sized monitor.

"This chart shows our transfer metric over time. As you can see, it increased a few years ago and then plateaued." She tapped to change the slide. "And these are our top transfer destinations, sorted by percent."

Dr. Tomlin furrowed his bushy brows. "It makes sense that the University of Illinois is on top. They've done a lot of recruitment here. But we're underperforming with some of these other four-year schools in the area."

"Pulaski should be higher," said Nina Crenshaw, the dean of student services. "They're located twenty minutes from here."

Caitlyn flinched. *Act natural.* She wasn't supposed to have strong feelings about Pulaski College.

"I agree," Dr. Tomlin said. "It should be an appealing option for our students who can't leave the area—especially older students, those with children."

"What's our relationship like with Pulaski?" Nina asked.

"I've met the president, but I don't know her well." Dr. Tomlin paused. "Truthfully, she seemed a bit frosty."

Caitlyn averted her eyes, worried her coworkers could somehow detect that she had weekend plans with the woman under discussion.

"They send recruiters," Nina said, "but the information isn't really tailored for our students. I'm not sure how well they accommodate nontraditional students. Plus they don't accept some of our courses for transfer credit. So I'm not sure they really want our students to apply."

Nina was wrong. *Ruth needs the enrollment.* If there was an opportunity to improve the relationship between LCC and Pulaski, surely she would welcome it.

"Hmm." Dr. Tomlin rapped his fingers on the table. "Perhaps we should reach out to them. We'll think about it. You can go to the next slide."

"I know someone at Pulaski." The words came out before Caitlyn could think better of them.

"Oh?" He lowered his glasses. "Who?"

She could have said a number of names. After all, she had become acquainted with the deans, the director of research, and several faculty members. But most of them had never heard of Caitlyn Taylor, and with everyone staring, she was afraid to involve anyone besides Ruth. "I know the president. Ruth Holloway."

"Wait, really?" Dr. Tomlin didn't hide his surprise. "How do you know the president?"

"Well, my sister used to work with her at Pulaski, and we...became acquainted. She's actually great when you get to know her. Very smart and hard-working. She really cares about students. I also happen to know that enrollment is one of her top priorities."

"I didn't know you had a sister working in higher education," Dr. Tomlin said warmly. "It must run in the family."

"I guess so. Anyway, I could talk to Ruth if you want—and if she's interested, I'm happy to set up a meeting."

"That would be wonderful. Thank you."

Caitlyn hoped she hadn't made a mistake. But on the bright side, they already had something to discuss on Friday night.

After work, Caitlyn drove to her mom's house for dinner. She found Chloe in the living room, sprawled out on the couch and scrolling through her phone. She had already exchanged her work clothes for leggings and a T-shirt.

Chloe looked up. "Look who can't stay away."

"Hey." Caitlyn plopped down on the armchair. "How was work?"

"Not bad. I got a few interesting calls—like, one lady called because she wanted maintenance to remove a spider from her unit. She was hysterical, insisting it was poisonous. Anyway, the guy who went over told me later that it was a harmless house spider, about the size of a penny."

"Oh my." Caitlyn laughed. "Imagine if a bee ever gets in."

"I'll hear about it for sure." Chloe set her phone aside and sat up. "How was your day?"

"It was interesting. I might set up a meeting with my boss and Ruth."

Chloe's mouth fell open. "Really? Are you going to pretend you don't know her?"

"No, I said that we knew each other—but not that I'd worked there, of course. My boss wants to increase the number of students who transfer to four-year colleges, and it seems like we have a missed opportunity with Pulaski."

"Wow. Well, good luck." Chloe's amusement shone in her eyes. "Don't make googly eyes at her in front of your boss."

Caitlyn rolled her eyes. "I don't make googly eyes."

"Oh please. You make them at *your phone* when she texts you."

"Ha ha." Caitlyn turned serious. "So, I have a question for you. When you went to LCC, how serious were you about transferring to a four-year college?"

"Oh." Chloe turned somber. "Well, I don't know. I always meant to finish my degree, but I wasn't eager to actually do it. You know school isn't my thing. Then when Jacqueline asked me to go with her, I told myself school would always be there. I didn't know that it would be hard to go back after a break."

"Do you regret going with Jacqueline?" Caitlyn asked. "Sorry, I guess that's an obvious question." Of course, Chloe regretted giving up college for a failed relationship.

"No, I don't regret it."

"Really? I mean, no judgment but…"

Chloe chuckled. "It's okay. Look, it was a disaster. And after it went bad, I stayed too long. But at least I know, right? I don't have to wonder if she was the love of my life."

"I guess that makes sense," Caitlyn said slowly. "You had to play it out."

"Exactly. I feel the same way about Nick. I mean, at least I tried." Her smile was lopsided.

Once again, Caitlyn regretted that she hadn't been more supportive of Chloe's relationship from the start. "It was brave to go to Colorado. You've always followed your heart, and I admire that."

"Thank you for saying that." Chloe's eyes were shiny.

"I mean it. I've never done anything like that. Part of me has always been jealous of you. I always felt this intense pressure to succeed, and I made so many sacrifices for school. Then I looked at you, and you were free. If I were more like you, maybe I wouldn't have been so anxious and miserable for most of my life."

Chloe smiled. "I don't know about that. You spent a couple of months impersonating me to be near a hot bossy lady that you liked. That was reckless as hell. It might be the biggest risk you've ever taken."

"It's true." Sometimes, Caitlyn still couldn't believe she had done it. "It was a huge risk. I may have gone there for you, but I stayed for me. When you said you weren't coming back, I should have quit and spent the summer preparing for academic jobs, but I wanted to stay and work for Ruth, and I did."

A feeling of peace settled over her as she processed the summer in a new way. For once, she had broken the rules and followed her heart.

Chapter 25

CAITLYN KNOCKED ON RUTH'S DOOR and waited.

And waited.

As she reached for her phone, the door swung open.

Ruth stood before her in an apron with disheveled hair and spots of pink on her cheeks. "Come on in."

Caitlyn grinned. She loved seeing Ruth a little out of sorts—not that she'd ever tell her. "You're cooking?" As Caitlyn stepped into the house, the smell of burned food assaulted her nose.

Ruth grimaced. "I'm trying to make a vegetable quiche. The first attempt is in the trash."

Caitlyn slipped off her shoes. When she looked up, a cloud of smoke wafted toward her from the kitchen. "Um." She pointed.

"It's okay. I disconnected the smoke alarm. I'll start over once it clears." Ruth wiped her forehead. "Can I get you something to drink?"

"Uh, that's okay." Caitlyn smiled. Ruth's ineptitude in the kitchen was adorable. "Maybe we could sit down for a minute? Seems like you could use a break."

"Sure. Let's sit in the living room." Ruth untied her apron and slung it over the back of the couch before she sat.

Caitlyn settled next to her. "So…hi."

"Hi." Ruth cupped her cheek and gave her a kiss that tasted like minty lip balm, warm and cool all at once. "How are you?"

"I'm good. Happy to be here with you." Caitlyn noticed a smear of flour on Ruth's jaw and another on her sky-blue T-shirt. "You're cute when you're flustered."

"I'm sure." Ruth's blush returned. "How was your week?"

"Well, it was interesting." Caitlyn hesitated. *Just tell her.* No more secrets, no more lies by omission. "Your name came up at work, actually."

"Oh?" Ruth tilted her head, looking intrigued but not concerned.

Caitlyn prayed Ruth wouldn't freak out. "We're trying to improve the number of students who transfer to four-year schools, and there was a suggestion that we could collaborate more closely with Pulaski—since you're so close to us."

Ruth frowned. "But we send recruiters to LCC every semester."

"Yes, but our dean mentioned that the presentation isn't always relevant to our students. It sounds like there's also an issue with transfer credit. We might want to explore some new articulation agreements, so our students would have a bigger incentive to transfer to Pulaski."

"Hmm." Ruth tapped her chin. "It's worth discussing. We'd certainly welcome more applications from LCC students."

"I'm glad to hear that because it came up in a meeting, and I sort of… Well, I said that I knew you." She clasped her hands together to stop her fingers from fidgeting.

Ruth straightened. "What did you say exactly?"

"I said that my sister used to work with you, and that's how we became acquainted. That's all I told them. Um, and I volunteered to set up a meeting with you and some of our staff." Caitlyn held her breath.

"I see." Ruth's posture remained stiff.

"I probably should have discussed it with you ahead of time. But I know you're interested in boosting enrollment, and I didn't want to let the opportunity pass." The words tumbled out quickly as she searched Ruth's face for signs of anger.

Ruth took a deep breath. "It's okay. If we continue to see each other— and I hope that we do—we can't hide the fact that we know each other. Your story is as good as any. We'll say Chloe worked for me and left on good terms. You and I met through Chloe, and a few months after she resigned, you and I began to spend time together."

"That's essentially what I said." Caitlyn paused. "I'm sorry we have to lie to everyone else. It's my fault, and I wish I hadn't put you in this position."

Sighing, Ruth leaned back on the couch. "You know, I've been thinking about this. I've been holding back a bit because of the past."

"I'm sorry," Caitlyn said immediately.

"No, that's not—I don't want you to keep apologizing. What I'm saying is that I made peace with it. What you did could have gone very, very wrong for both of us. But it didn't. Instead, you helped me. My presidency is better than ever thanks to what we started together." Ruth reached out and brushed her fingers down Caitlyn's arm, then took her hand. "Most importantly, if you hadn't done it, we wouldn't be sitting here together. So if I said I wished you had never taken Chloe's place, then I'd be wishing for those good things to go away. And that's not what I want." She shook her head. "We got lucky. We got so damn lucky, and I don't want to waste it."

The words filled Caitlyn with joy and relief. "Thank you. I don't deserve your forgiveness, but I'll never take it for granted. I promise." Unable to hold back for another second, Caitlyn launched herself into Ruth's arms.

Ruth sighed into the embrace and pressed her lips to Caitlyn's temple before working her way to Caitlyn's lips. The kisses started sweet and slow, but soon their breathing grew heavy as their tongues tangled and heat rose between them.

Caitlyn melted against Ruth's body, luxuriating in the scent of lavender and the feel of Ruth's mouth.

Suddenly, Ruth pulled her head back. "Let's go upstairs."

"Are you sure? There's no rush. Seriously." Caitlyn took her hand. "I can wait as long as you want—weeks, months, whatever."

"I'm sure." Ruth's eyes were sharp and clear. "I want this. I'm ready. Unless—oh, I forgot about dinner. Are you hungry?"

Caitlyn's heart pounded. "Not even a little."

Ruth lay on the bed and motioned for Caitlyn to join her. "I just remembered—this is your second time in my bedroom." She flashed a smile to let Caitlyn know she spoke without resentment when referring to the "Chloe" days.

Caitlyn's teeth toyed with her lip as she climbed onto the mattress. "I have to admit, I loved seeing your bed. Of course, I didn't snoop through your stuff, but since I had to walk through this room anyway…" She lay next to Ruth. "I looked around. Briefly."

"Well, you did me a tremendous favor that day. You were so kind and supportive."

"Of course." Caitlyn brushed a strand of hair from Ruth's face. "I've been through antidepressant withdrawal too. And even if I hadn't known what you were going through, I've cared for you ever since I got to know you—the real you, not the hard-ass administrator you pretend to be." She nudged Ruth's shoulder playfully.

"Hey, I *am* a hard-ass administrator." Ruth gave Caitlyn her best withering glare.

Caitlyn's eyes widened in mock horror before she dissolved into giggles. "I'm sorry. It doesn't work on me anymore. But don't worry—I won't tell the faculty you have a softer side." She stroked Ruth's arm, and the reassuring motion became a sensual caress.

Ruth sighed as Caitlyn's touch relaxed her and sent waves of warmth to her center. *She accepts me.* Caitlyn knew Ruth's flaws, but she still gazed at Ruth as if she were perfect. The unwavering adoration in Caitlyn's eyes gave Ruth the courage to speak. "I want this, and I'm ready. But I should tell you something first."

"Anything." Caitlyn scooted even closer. "You can tell me anything."

"Okay." Ruth let out an audible breath. "You know I take desvenlafaxine. I don't know if you've heard of this, but I have something called sexual side effects." She risked a glance at Caitlyn, whose expression hadn't changed. "It's not that I can't have an…orgasm. I can, and I do. But sometimes it takes a while, compared to before the meds." Her cheeks burned, and she fought the urge to bury her face in the pillow.

"That's okay." Caitlyn took her hand and gave it a reassuring squeeze. "We have all the time in the world."

"Well. It was an issue with a past partner. She thought I wasn't really into the sex or wasn't attracted to her. And if I get nervous, I can't get there at all. I don't want you to think it means something if I can't—I mean if my body doesn't cooperate. It doesn't mean I don't want you, because I really,

really do." Unexpected tears stung her eyes as she flashed back to her former girlfriend's cruel words.

"Oh, hey." Caitlyn ran her fingertips down the side of Ruth's face. "You don't have to worry about that. Not with me. I had sexual side effects on my medication for the first few months. They faded eventually, but I remember how it felt. Anyway, I would never judge or blame you for something you can't control." She gave Ruth a soft, reverent kiss on the forehead and then on her lips. "Never. I promise."

"Thank you." Ruth thought she might actually cry, but she managed a watery smile instead. "That means a lot to me."

"All I want is to touch you and be close to you. Orgasms are nice, but that's not what I care about." She moved in closer and wrapped an arm around Ruth's back. "All I need to be happy is for you to let me in. If you do that, you'll never disappoint me."

Ruth pulled Caitlyn close. "How did I get so lucky?" She laughed as she realized the answer—Chloe's irresponsible behavior had kicked off a series of events that somehow, against unfathomable odds, had led to this moment.

"I'm the lucky one." Caitlyn ran her hand up and down Ruth's back. "I swear to God." She kissed Ruth's cheek and then moved her soft lips down to Ruth's jaw.

All thoughts of Chloe vanished. Ruth whimpered as the delicate kisses made her tremble.

"Tell me what you like," Caitlyn murmured. "I want to do what you like best—whatever it is. I just want you to feel good." Her voice was husky, yet earnest.

Be honest. There was little point in pretending. "Well. Sometimes penetration hurts without lube. But I like…ah." Ruth glanced away, struck with sudden shyness, but faced Caitlyn again to see only warmth reflected back at her.

"Oral?" Caitlyn asked. When Ruth nodded, Caitlyn's smile turned delighted. "I would love to taste you. We will definitely do that—eventually." Caitlyn pressed their bodies close and placed a wet kiss on Ruth's neck. She sucked the tender skin with practiced delicacy, just light enough to avoid hickeys, followed by a tiny nibble.

Ruth shuddered and squeezed her thighs together. "Your mouth should be illegal. A schedule-one drug."

Caitlyn chuckled against Ruth's skin, then looked up with a questioning gaze. "Do you think we could...?"

"What?" Ruth's hips squirmed. Already, it was hard to keep still.

Caitlyn tugged on Ruth's blouse. "Take this off?"

It was such a simple thing—of course they'd be getting undressed. Yet Caitlyn had checked in to ensure Ruth's comfort before proceeding. The genuine care was touching and also sexy, causing another rush of desire. "Of course." Ruth sat up and stripped off the blouse, then lay flat on her back and shimmied out of her pants, wanting Caitlyn to be sure of her consent.

"Oh wow." Caitlyn took in Ruth's body with hungry eyes. "You're so beautiful."

She means it. Ruth's heart swelled as she basked in Caitlyn's admiration. She thought of her figure as unremarkable—okay for forty-two, but she didn't have much time for fitness. However, Caitlyn's lust-blown pupils couldn't lie.

Caitlyn climbed on top and straddled Ruth's belly, still fully dressed while Ruth was nude except for her panties and bra. The weight of her firm ass pressed down on Ruth's hips, intensifying her arousal.

Damn. That's hot. Ruth shivered at a cool draft on her skin, while her belly filled with warmth.

Caitlyn traced Ruth's black satin bra strap with her index finger. "May I?" When Ruth nodded, she slid her hand behind Ruth to unhook the bra.

The wire and elastic fell away, freeing Ruth's breasts. She groaned and arched her back to push them into Caitlyn's touch. As Caitlyn massaged them with languid ministrations, Ruth nipples grew unbearably hard. "That feels good."

"I'm glad because I love them. And I think they like me too." Caitlyn scooted down and draped her body over Ruth's so that her breasts pushed into Ruth's belly. Then she lowered her mouth to Ruth's breast.

The sensation of Caitlyn's hot, wet tongue circling the areola overloaded Ruth's senses, causing her to flinch. "Oh God."

Caitlyn looked up. "Too much?"

"It's amazing—just intense." A blush heated Ruth's cheeks.

"You're sensitive." Caitlyn beamed as though it were a wonderful thing. "I'll go slow. Let me know if you want me to stop."

When Ruth nodded, Caitlyn kissed the swell of Ruth's breast and then slowly worked her way toward the nipple, pausing every few seconds to simply breathe against Ruth's skin. Her strokes were painfully slow, and the anticipation made Ruth ache.

By the time she reached the hard peak, Ruth was a helpless puddle of desire. "Yes. That's so good. Yes."

Caitlyn tasted and teased the nipple until Ruth's hips rocked up, arching her thigh into Caitlyn's center. "Oh!"

Ruth reveled in the sight of Caitlyn's flushed cheeks and parted lips. Knowing their pleasure was mutual relaxed Ruth further. She lolled her head back and surrendered to Caitlyn's tongue.

Caitlyn anchored herself with both hands and nudged her knee between Ruth's legs, brushing her panties. "Is this okay?"

Sucking in a breath, Ruth pushed against Caitlyn's leg. "God, yes." She pulsed with need.

They thrust against each other in sync, and Ruth caught herself grinning because it felt good—really good—and she wasn't nervous. She was happy.

Caitlyn slid down Ruth's body and kissed her belly. She stroked Ruth's sides and hips with both hands, soothing her, before she let them travel south to the fabric of Ruth's panties, causing her to gasp.

"Okay?" Caitlyn asked.

Ruth nodded. "Mmm. Yes. I'm ready."

When Caitlyn tugged the panties off, Ruth quivered at the cool air on her sensitive skin. Then warm breath and soft lips tickled her curls.

Caitlyn touched her gently with her tongue.

Ruth sucked in a breath. "Oh wow." The sensation sent licks of heat up her body. "That's so good."

With delicate strokes, Caitlyn traced her way toward the center. She circled and grazed Ruth's clit before she tasted the place that made Ruth cry out.

Pleasure flowed through Ruth's body like water. She arched as pressure built within her, then fell back as she came close to the edge without tumbling over.

For a split second, Ruth's old insecurity resurfaced, and she worried Caitlyn would grow tired or frustrated. Then she swatted the thought away.

Caitlyn had promised no pressure to come. *I trust her.* She reached for Caitlyn's strong shoulders and held on.

While Caitlyn's tongue moved like magic, she caressed Ruth's thighs. Instead of speeding up to urge Ruth toward a climax, she kept a languid pace as though they had all day.

Ruth's hips rose and fell as she rode the waves of sensation. When her responses came harder and faster, Caitlyn matched Ruth's rhythm. Ruth lost all track of time until her muscles tensed, and she dug her nails into Caitlyn's shoulders. Then it happened—an orgasm that made her clench and tremble. As she rode out the aftershocks, she felt euphoric, not just from physical release but from happiness.

Ruth panted hard and stared at the ceiling, too spent to speak.

Caitlyn placed tender kisses on her thighs. She slowly kissed her way up Ruth's abdomen and then curled up beside her. "That was so hot. The way you taste, the sounds you make. God, I was in heaven."

Ruth lolled her head to the side to meet her gaze. "You made it good for me. I felt comfortable, even though it was the first time. Do you know how rare that is for me?"

Caitlyn glowed. "That's all I wanted. To be with you and make you feel good."

"You did." Ruth shifted to face her fully. "You always do." Their breasts brushed against each other, sending goose bumps up her bare arms. An unexpected boldness filled her, and she pulled on Caitlyn's shirt. "My turn."

"If you insist." With a giddy grin, Caitlyn sat up and removed her top, revealing round breasts in a pink plunge bra with white lace trim. She rolled her leggings off, leaving only the bra and black panties with lace at the waist.

With her slim belly, model-perfect curves, and smooth hair, Caitlyn could have been posing for a lingerie catalog, but shyness lurked beneath her fluttering eyelashes.

Ruth's heart thumped. Despite Caitlyn's obvious beauty, she had her own insecurities. Ruth looked Caitlyn in the eyes, determined not to hold back. "You're gorgeous."

Caitlyn smiled. "You're sweet."

"And I've got two functioning eyes." Ruth raked her gaze down Caitlyn's body. "You are perfect."

Blushing, Caitlyn reached back and began to fiddle with her bra clasp.

"Let me." When Caitlyn nodded, Ruth leaned forward and unhooked the satiny bra. It fell away, and Ruth sucked in a breath at the sight of Caitlyn's creamy breasts. She watched, transfixed, as Caitlyn pinched the waistband of her panties and slowly worked them down her legs.

Caitlyn faced Ruth on her knees, fully nude. A trace of insecurity lingered in her gaze.

"Beautiful. I can't wait to touch every inch of you," Ruth said, earning a smile. "Lie down." She reached for Caitlyn and guided her backward, then straddled her and bent to capture her mouth.

Caitlyn responded hungrily and wrapped her arms around Ruth. She ran her palms up and down Ruth's back as they kissed.

Ruth slipped her tongue inside, indulging in the feel of Caitlyn's chest heaving against her naked breasts. Even though they had just started, Caitlyn's nipples were already rock-hard.

Breaking the kiss, Ruth slid down Caitlyn's body and lay against her. "Your breasts are delectable." She cupped them and relished their weight and softness in her palms. When she kissed the generous swell above the nipple, Caitlyn groaned.

Ruth licked and teased the top of the breast, taking her time, then grazed the hard peak with her tongue.

Caitlyn gasped and clung to Ruth's shoulders. Her hips rose, and wetness brushed Ruth's skin, making her sigh with pleasure.

Amazing. Every sign of Caitlyn's enjoyment increased Ruth's confidence. She took the nipple into her mouth and sucked. When Caitlyn responded with breathless moans, she sucked harder and nipped with her teeth.

"Oh my God." Caitlyn's chest heaved. "Do that again."

Ruth complied, savoring the taste and feel against her tongue. She caressed Caitlyn's belly and hips, then slid her hands beneath Caitlyn to squeeze her ass.

Caitlyn let out a surprised, high-pitched cry. She giggled and covered her mouth.

"Don't." Ruth squeezed again, slowly this time. "I love the sounds you make." She placed kisses in a trail down Caitlyn's belly, enjoying every twitch and moan in response.

Caitlyn spread her legs in invitation, but Ruth wanted to go slow. She kissed above the mound of Caitlyn's sex, then down her leg to the delicate flesh of her thighs. Her skin was slick and warm, and the temperature in the room seemed to climb.

"I want you." Caitlyn's voice was breathy. "Oh Jesus. God."

"I can tell." Ruth stroked the curls from the outside before gliding deeper, gently brushing around the edges and near the clit without touching it.

"Please," Caitlyn whispered.

"Soon." Ruth traced Caitlyn's slick opening with her finger. "Okay to go inside?"

"Definitely okay."

Ruth entered her with a single finger, finding it glided easily. She looked up to check Caitlyn's comfort.

Caitlyn met Ruth's gaze with a dreamy smile. "It feels really good. You can use two."

"Eventually." Ruth took her time and moved slowly, luxuriating in the intimate connection. After a few minutes, she added a second finger and thrust deeper.

Caitlyn arched and gasped, pushing against Ruth's hand. "Oh fuck. That feels good."

"*You* feel good. So wet and ready." Ruth moved slowly, then faster and deeper. At last, she leaned in to part the curls with her tongue. Her thighs squeezed as she tasted Caitlyn for the first time. *Incredible.* She licked along the edges of Caitlyn's clit, letting her tongue swirl and dance. When she gently pressed the center, Caitlyn's leg kicked the air.

"I'm going to—Oh fuck. Right there. Don't stop." She clenched and curled forward, then shuddered and collapsed.

Ruth felt the orgasm all around her fingers. When the tremors subsided and Caitlyn lay still, she gently slid them out and cleaned them on the sheet. She blotted her mouth and then moved up the bed to wrap her arms around Caitlyn.

Caitlyn was still catching her breath. "God. That was awesome."

"It was." Ruth held her closer, luxuriating in the feel of Caitlyn's loose, uncoordinated limbs lolling against her. The memory of Caitlyn moving against her, surrendering all self-consciousness and control filled her with wonder. "I'd say our first time was a success."

Caitlyn shifted and returned the embrace. "It was a success from the moment you got naked with me. Failure isn't a thing—not when we're together and loving each other."

The word *loving* filled Ruth with warmth. It wasn't the big *I love you,* but the way Caitlyn had cherished every inch of her made her feelings clear. They were falling for each other. "You're right." Ruth looked into Caitlyn's eyes and stroked her cheek. "Thank you."

"Thank you for trusting me." Caitlyn ran her fingers through Ruth's hair. "I know it's not easy for you to be vulnerable, and it means a lot."

"You're right; it's not easy. But you're worth it." As the words left her lips, Ruth flashed back to the first time she'd said those words to Caitlyn. Since then, everything had changed, but it was still true. What they had together was worth it.

Caitlyn's eyes were misty as she broke into a smile. "So are you." She kissed Ruth's forehead. "You know, I have zero issues with lube if you'd like to try penetration sometime."

"Yeah?" Ruth looked up to meet Caitlyn's gaze.

"Absolutely. In fact, I have some at home that smells like raspberries."

Ruth's chest swelled. Somehow, she'd found someone who accepted every part of her without judgment. She'd never dreamed that someone who had committed identity fraud at her workplace could be the person. Yet against all reason, it had worked out.

The next morning, Caitlyn awoke in a tangle of sheets with her arm slung over Ruth's boobs. She lifted her head from Ruth's shoulder and rubbed her eyes with her other hand. "Have you been watching me sleep?"

Ruth, lying comfortably on her back, watched with an amused smile. "A bit." Her hair was a mess, falling in three different directions.

Caitlyn's heart squeezed. *Ruth looks so cute with messy hair.* She wished she had her phone to take a picture. But maybe they'd have other mornings like this, until she knew all of Ruth's looks by heart. The thought made her warm and mushy.

Ruth ran her fingers along Caitlyn's arm. "I didn't want to disturb you. And I suppose I wanted to savor the moment."

"Aww." She removed her arm and scooted upward for a kiss.

"How long can you stay today?" Ruth's tone was neutral, but hope glittered in her eyes.

She wants me to stay. Caitlyn kissed her again. "As long as you want."

"I was thinking we might go out for breakfast, to spare you from my cooking. Or brunch, I suppose—it's already past ten."

"Oh wow, I can't believe we slept so late. It's a good sign, actually. In the past, I've had trouble sleeping next to another person, but it seems like I made myself right at home. Anyway, I'd love to go to brunch. But my clothes…" She pointed to the floor where her leggings and sweater lay in a heap.

"You can shop in my closet. We're not the exact same size, but we're close enough to share clothes."

"It's true." Caitlyn looked down at the borrowed T-shirt she'd slept in. "A nice perk of dating a woman."

They showered and then took Ruth's car to Maria's Café, a popular brunch destination in the artsy district of Linvale.

Caitlyn wondered if Ruth would keep her distance in public, but to her surprise, Ruth took her hand as they walked through the door. When Caitlyn shot her a questioning look, Ruth merely winked, confirming it was no accident.

She's amazing. Caitlyn knew that Ruth was private, especially around colleagues. The public acknowledgment of their connection touched her deeply.

The waitress led them to a small table near the front, in full view of most of the restaurant and anyone who happened to pass by the windows. Ruth accepted the table with a smile, apparently unafraid to be seen by all of Linvale.

After ordering coffee, they held hands across the table while they each looked at the menu.

"What do you like best for breakfast?" Caitlyn asked. "Sweet or savory?"

"I'm a huge fan of both, so it's always hard to decide."

Caitlyn was also torn between various egg combos and decadent French toast. "Why don't we get one of each and share?"

"What have we here?" a sneering voice interrupted.

Caitlyn jumped and turned her head to see Steve Stubbons approaching the table. *Oh shit.* They'd agreed not to hide their relationship, but Caitlyn couldn't help her nerves. Why did Steve have to be the first to find out?

"Oh great," Ruth muttered. She dropped Caitlyn's hand and sat up straight, pushing her shoulders back. "Hello, Dr. Stubbons."

"Well, this is a surprise." Steve leered at Caitlyn. "I didn't realize you two were friends. Or should I say, more than friends? Don't think I missed you two holding hands."

Caitlyn's pulse pounded, but she did her best to appear nonchalant as she squinted at him. "I'm sorry? Who are you?" She turned to Ruth with a quizzical expression.

Ruth regarded Steve with total composure. "Dr. Stubbons, I'd like you to meet Caitlyn."

"Nice to meet you." Caitlyn offered her hand and a polite smile.

"Huh?" Steve's face contorted in confusion.

"Caitlyn is Chloe Taylor's sister." Ruth turned to Caitlyn. "He teaches at Pulaski."

"Oh, gotcha." Caitlyn dropped her hand to her lap. "What do you teach?"

Ignoring the question, Steve glanced between them with a deepening scowl. "You're trying to tell me that this"—he jabbed a finger in Caitlyn's face—"isn't Chloe?"

"We're twins, in fact," Caitlyn said. "Don't worry, people mix us up all the time."

He fixed his gaze on Ruth. "Do you think I'm an idiot? This is obviously Chloe. I'd recognize her anywhere. You're on a brunch date with your ex-assistant, which makes me wonder if you were involved with her when she worked for you. That's an ethics violation, which is probably why you've concocted this ridiculous lie."

As Steve ranted about Ruth's relationship with "Chloe," Caitlyn felt herself calming down. After all, she *wasn't* Chloe. Her anxiety turned to excitement as she sensed an opportunity to ruin his day. "Excuse me." Caitlyn reached for her wallet. "I don't know why you're talking to Ruth this way, but I can show you my driver's license." She slid it out and held it up. "I'm not Chloe. I'm her twin."

"Huh?" He sputtered as he scanned the ID. "Bullshit. You just went by a different name." Doubt had crept into his voice.

Caitlyn pulled out her phone and quickly tapped to a photo of her and Chloe at Christmas, the same one she had shown Ruth on the day she'd finally come clean. She held up her phone again. "See? Twins. I'm not Chloe."

Steve's mouth worked as he scrutinized the photo, but no sound came.

Ruth crossed her arms. "I'll let you get back to wherever you came from. Thanks for saying hello."

Steve glared at them one last time before stalking away without a word.

Caitlyn giggled. "I have to admit I enjoyed that."

"Not as much as I did."

Caitlyn held up her coffee mug. "To a lovely brunch."

Ruth clinked hers against Caitlyn's. "Cheers."

Chapter 26

CAITLYN WAS ON HER KNEES, scrubbing the floor in a ratty tank top and pajama shorts, when someone knocked on the door.

What the hell? No one was supposed to come this early. It was Ruth's first time meeting her mom after five months of dating, and she still had almost two hours to make sure everything was perfect.

She pushed to her feet, dropped the sponge, and went to answer the door.

Ruth stood before her, dressed in a crisp blouse, jeans, and a bomber jacket with coiffed hair and a bottle of wine clutched to her chest. "Hi." She looked Caitlyn up and down, pausing on the pajama shorts with their pattern of smiling cartoon coffee cups on a faded pink background. "Interesting outfit."

"I'm still cleaning. I thought you weren't coming until later?"

Ruth shrugged off the jacket and stepped inside. "I thought you could use some help."

Caitlyn accepted the wine. "You're not wrong, but what about the Patriots game?" Ruth *never* missed her favorite NFL team.

"This is more important," Ruth said firmly.

Caitlyn leaned in and kissed her, enjoying the taste of minty mouthwash and lip balm. "That's really sweet of you. I don't want you to mess up your outfit, scrubbing, but maybe you could help me set the table?"

"Of course." Ruth hung her coat and followed Caitlyn to the kitchen. "Ooh, I like this." She inspected the glass serving dish Caitlyn had set out. "Fancy."

"Well, I'm a proper adult now." Caitlyn grinned.

"Absolutely." Ruth turned hesitant. "Your mother doesn't mind—?"

"I told you, she doesn't care that we're different ages. She and my dad were the exact same age, and look how that turned out. She just wants me to be happy." Caitlyn ran her fingers down Ruth's arm. "And I am."

Ruth kissed Caitlyn's cheek, then found her lips.

They shared a warm, languid kiss until Caitlyn pulled back. "I should start getting ready. Actually, can you do something while I'm in the shower?" She gestured to the pot on the stove.

Following Caitlyn's gaze, Ruth tensed as fear flickered in her eyes. "You want me to cook?"

"Oh God, no." Caitlyn laughed. "I know you better than that. It's supposed to simmer for forty-five minutes. Just watch it to make sure it doesn't boil. That's when the bubbles—"

"I know." Ruth playfully swatted Caitlyn's arm. "Consider it handled."

"You're the best." Caitlyn started toward the bathroom, then turned back. "Oh, and put the Patriots game on. I know you want to."

Ruth bit her lip guiltily. "Actually, they were tied when I left, so if you really don't mind..."

"The game was *tied*? And you still came here?" Caitlyn backtracked for one more kiss. "I don't deserve you. Now go turn it on." She shooed Ruth toward the television.

As Caitlyn stepped into the shower, a guttural howl drifted over from the living room. The Patriots must have scored.

She's so cute. Caitlyn hoped her mom would see Ruth's good qualities. As for Ruth and Chloe, she just hoped they could get through dinner without any sarcastic remarks.

———————

Ruth wasn't nervous. After all, she was the president of a college. She'd given talks to diverse audiences and charmed countless colleagues and stakeholders. Making conversation with her girlfriend's mother and sister would hardly be a challenge.

In fact, when Melinda and Chloe Taylor entered the apartment, Ruth rose to her feet with perfect elegance and greeted them with a steady voice.

"Hi, I'm Melinda Taylor." Melinda had curled her gray hair and pressed her slacks. She stepped forward and shyly offered her hand. "I've heard so much about you from both of my girls."

"You have?" Ruth had the sudden fear that her hands were clammy. She rubbed her palms on her pants before taking Melinda's hand. "I mean, that's good." She laughed too loudly. "Er, I hope it's good." So much for keeping her cool.

"Yes, all good things. Caitlyn just adores you," Melinda said.

"Mom." Caitlyn blushed.

"Well, it's true." Melinda shrugged. "And these past few months—well, it's the happiest I've seen her in a long time."

"I'm glad." Ruth breathed a small sigh of relief. Despite Caitlyn's many assurances, she had worried about Melinda's opinion. "She makes me happy too." She snuck a glance at Caitlyn, who beamed back at her with rosy cheeks.

Chloe hovered behind Melinda. "Um, hi."

Ruth faced Chloe—the real one—for the first time since their meeting at the park.

Chloe wore smoky eye makeup with bold lipstick and a tight navy dress. As Ruth studied her, Chloe fidgeted and darted nervous glances at Caitlyn.

It was hard to believe Ruth hadn't noticed the switch. They looked similar, but hardly identical. Now she would know right away that she wasn't looking at Caitlyn. "Hi, Chloe. It's good to see you again."

"You too." Chloe offered an awkward, but hopeful smile. "Caitlyn said that, you know…"

Ruth's lips twitched. "That I wouldn't bite your head off?"

"Something like that," Chloe said sheepishly.

Caitlyn stepped between them. "She won't. Ruth and I have moved on."

"That's right," Ruth said. "I'd like to get to know you as Caitlyn's family—and you too, Melinda."

"Thank you," Chloe said. "I'm really glad we're doing this and that I have a chance to get to know you outside of work."

"We didn't talk much when you worked for me," Ruth said. "That was my mistake. This is a fresh start for all of us."

"Okay, cool." Chloe grinned. "It's so funny how it all worked out, huh? Almost like the universe brought you and Caitlyn together through me."

Caitlyn shot Ruth an anxious look.

"Indeed," Ruth said smoothly. "The universe works in strange ways."

"Why don't you sit down?" Caitlyn gestured at her unusually spotless living room. "I'll get drinks."

"And I'll help to carry them," Ruth said.

Melinda and Chloe walked over to the couch, while Ruth followed Caitlyn to the kitchen.

"The universe, huh?" Ruth said with an amused smile.

"Thank you for being so cool about this," Caitlyn said. "It means a lot to me."

"I do want to get to know them," Ruth said. "I mean it. They're your family, and that means they're important to me."

"Thank you." Caitlyn squeezed Ruth's arm.

"Besides, Chloe brought us together. And I understand your mom helped too. How can I be mad when the outcome is so wonderful?"

Caitlyn glowed as she leaned in and planted a kiss on Ruth's lips.

"I love you," Ruth said. "Just so you know."

Caitlyn gasped and stepped backward. "You do?" Her eyes were round as saucers.

Ruth's blood ran cold. Was she alone in her feelings? "I'm sorry." Her voice sounded robotic. "It just slipped out. I guess it's too soon. And the timing"—she gestured toward the living room, where Chloe and Melinda were chatting—"wasn't great. I'm sorry."

"No!" Caitlyn's head whipped back and forth. "Don't be sorry." She embraced Ruth and then left her hands on Ruth's shoulders when she pulled back. "You surprised me. But I love you too. Of course I do."

"You don't have to—"

Caitlyn's lips crushed into hers, muffling the rest of the sentence. She pulled Ruth close and deepened the kiss, chest rising against Ruth's breasts with each hard breath.

The warmth radiating from Caitlyn's body filled Ruth down to her core. She could feel the certainty in Caitlyn's strong arms as they pressed their bodies as close as physics would allow. There was no question. *This is love.*

Epilogue

Seven months later

CAITLYN SURVEYED THE AUDIENCE GATHERED in the lobby of Pulaski's student union. The small crowd of faculty, staff, and students took up most of the chairs that had been arranged for the event. She spotted at least two reporters, armed with cameras and notepads.

Ostensibly, Caitlyn was there to support Dr. Tomlin. But as she watched from behind the podium, her entire focus was on Ruth in her formfitting suit and low heels. Since her stint at Pulaski, Caitlyn had missed watching Ruth in president mode. It was as hot as ever.

Ruth stepped up to the podium and waited for the audience to settle. "Thank you for coming. My name is Dr. Ruth Holloway—"

Someone in the back hooted, and a few people clapped.

"Thank you," Ruth said dryly. "I'm excited too."

Caitlyn could only see the back of Ruth's head, but she could imagine Ruth's raised eyebrow.

Ruth cleared her throat. "I am honored and thrilled to formally announce our new partnership with Linvale Community College. From this moment on, students who maintain a 3.0-grade average are guaranteed admission to Pulaski upon completion of their associate degree. We also have new transfer agreements for twelve LCC courses—in addition to the many courses already covered under the Illinois Articulation Agreement. This initiative will increase our enrollment, but more importantly, it will benefit our community."

A smattering of applause broke out, and soon most of the crowd had joined in.

"I'd like to thank Eli Tomlin for his partnership and friendship, in addition to the faculty at both institutions who worked hard to make these transfer agreements happen." Ruth shot a quick glance at Caitlyn. "I'd also like to acknowledge Dr. Caitlyn Taylor, the LCC director of research, who was instrumental in making this partnership a success. Some of you may remember Caitlyn's sister, Chloe, who once served as my executive assistant. No, you're not seeing double—those two are actually twins."

A few people chuckled, and several faculty and staff peered curiously at Caitlyn. According to Ruth, word of their relationship had spread fast after the encounter with Steve Stubbons, but most thought they were getting their first glimpse of Ruth's girlfriend.

Beverly smiled warmly, while Alice looked annoyed. Gary appeared intrigued.

Miguel shot her a conspiratorial wink.

"With that," Ruth said, "I'll turn it over to Dr. Tomlin, who will explain some of the details." She shook his hand before stepping to the side.

As Dr. Tomlin addressed the crowd, Caitlyn's phone buzzed in her pocket. She pulled it out and found a text from Miguel:

Twins, huh?

Caitlyn wrote back,

Admit it. You love being in on the secret.

He sent a smug-looking happy emoji in response.

After the event, Caitlyn hung back while Ruth greeted the faculty. She wanted to talk to some of the people she knew from her summer at Pulaski, but, of course, she couldn't—she wasn't supposed to recognize anyone.

Maggie approached her with a warm smile. "Hi, I'm Maggie, the director of research. I know your sister."

"Nice to meet you." Caitlyn admired Maggie's new haircut; her unruly, red curls had been trimmed to a chin-length bob.

"I'm not sure if she ever mentioned me. She probably didn't. But Chloe helped me a lot when she was here. She taught me some skills that I still use every day."

"That's great." Pride bloomed within her. *I was a good teacher.* "I'll tell her I ran into you."

"So you're a researcher too? I guess a love of data runs in the family."

Caitlyn stifled a laugh as she imagined Chloe's reaction to that comment. Before she could respond, Joe and Kimberly walked up behind Maggie.

"Wow!" Joe gawked openly. "You look exactly like your twin."

"Yup. We're identical."

"Incredible," Kimberly said. "I'm Kimberly. I teach political science, and I met Chloe several times. She was very impressive!"

"Yes, Chloe has many talents," Caitlyn said.

"We were all sorry when she left so abruptly," Joe said. "Where did she end up?"

"Oh, she's working for a property company now—in logistics. But I know she enjoyed working here, and she misses everyone at Pulaski." *Almost* everyone.

"We miss her too," Maggie said. "Please tell her we said hello."

"I definitely will."

A few yards behind them, Dr. Tomlin signaled to her.

"Excuse me," Caitlyn said. "My boss needs something. It was great to meet all of you."

Dr. Tomlin gave her a warm smile. "Everything went perfectly."

"I agree. And I'm so happy to see reporters covering the event."

"I'm going to head back to the office, but you can stay if you want. Have some refreshments, network. Take as much time as you like."

Caitlyn very much wanted to network—with one person in particular. "Thanks! I appreciate that. I'll text you when I get back."

She wandered toward the refreshment table, then jumped when a firm hand gripped her shoulder.

"Hey, Caitlyn," Miguel said.

Caitlyn whirled around. "Hey!" She grinned. "How are you?"

Miguel beamed. "I'm good. Really good."

"Oh yeah?" Caitlyn eyed him curiously. She'd seen Miguel smile many times, but today he appeared radiant.

"I got a new job," he whispered.

"What?" Caitlyn gasped. "In Canada?"

He nodded. "University of Toronto. I'll teach four classes per semester, with the opportunity for annual renewal. It's not tenure-track, but…"

"But you'll be with Preston." Caitlyn's heart squeezed.

Miguel nodded. "He's already scouting apartments in Toronto."

"Oh, I'm so happy for you." She gave him a long hug. "Congratulations."

"Thanks." He grinned. "Most academics won't see it that way, but I know it was the right decision."

"You chose love." Caitlyn couldn't stop smiling. "And I can tell from your eyes how happy you are already." She gave him another hug. "You won't regret it."

They broke apart. "You're looking happy yourself," Miguel said. "I take it you're glad you stuck around?"

"I'm so happy." Caitlyn snuck a glance at Ruth, who was chatting with a group of faculty. "Professionally and personally."

"That's wonderful. I should head to my next class, but it was so good to see you."

"You too. We should all hang out before you leave."

"Absolutely," Miguel said. "And hey, maybe one day you can visit. Toronto's got touristy things. You could meet Preston."

"Count on it." Caitlyn squeezed his arm.

As they parted, Caitlyn looked around the reception. Assured that no one was watching, she kept going and slipped out the side doors. Then she crossed the courtyard and headed to the administrative office building where she'd spent her summer.

Nostalgia washed over her as she walked down the long hallway to the presidential office suite.

Chloe's replacement, an older woman with a tight bun and floral-print reading glasses hanging on a chain, glanced up from her computer. "Yes?"

"Hi, I'm Caitlyn Taylor. You must be Betty. Ruth told me to wait in her office."

"Yes, I'm Betty York." She frowned. "But I can't let you into Dr. Holloway's office when she's not here."

"Oh, of course. I'll wait out here, if you don't mind." Caitlyn plopped into one of the chairs. She pulled her phone from her purse and texted Ruth:

I'm at your office. Betty is making me wait outside.

The response came a minute later:

Good. Can't have just anyone traipsing into my office. I'll be there soon.

Caitlyn scrolled through her email until she heard the door. She looked up, but it wasn't Ruth—it was Piper.

Piper looked her up and down. "Caitlyn. Good to see you *again*."

They hadn't seen each other since Caitlyn left Pulaski, back when Piper still believed she was Chloe. Caitlyn shifted under Piper's incisive gaze and straightened in the chair. "Hello." She tilted her head in a subtle nod toward Betty to remind Piper that they weren't alone.

Piper crossed her arms. "You're waiting for Ruth?"

"Yes. She's on her way."

"Okay. I'll stop back later, then. I'm sure she will want to show you around her office—since you've never seen it before." Piper winked before she turned and walked out.

Caitlyn's shoulders relaxed as the door swung closed. Perhaps the wink meant she had Piper's blessing.

A few minutes later, the doors opened again, and Ruth breezed in. "Thanks for waiting. You've met Betty?"

Caitlyn stood. "Yes, we've met."

A smile played on Ruth's lips as she turned to Betty. "You know, Caitlyn's sister used to have your job."

Betty's eyes widened. "Is that right? Let's see, her name was Chloe, right? When I first got here, folks were always asking me what happened to her."

"Yes, Chloe Taylor. I'm her identical twin."

"Oh really? So she looked just like you?"

"Mmm-hmm," Ruth said. "A *remarkable* resemblance."

"Well…good." Betty seemed a bit lost. She probably wondered why her predecessor's twin sister was there.

"Come on in," Ruth said to Caitlyn. "Betty, please block my calendar for the next hour."

Overcome with déjà vu, Caitlyn followed her into the office and closed the door behind them.

As soon as the door clicked shut, Ruth strode toward her and captured her mouth with a plundering kiss that left her breathless.

"Mmm." Caitlyn stepped backward, her ass bumping against the door. "I've always wanted to kiss you in your office."

"Always?" Ruth teased. "You mean, ever since we met?"

"Well, perhaps not on the very first day." Caitlyn recalled Ruth's impromptu rant about full-time faculty hires. "But it wasn't long before I started to notice your...good qualities." She trailed a finger down Ruth's jawline, all the way down to her cleavage.

"I believe you got an unexpected view of my qualities when you walked in on me changing my top."

"Oh yes." Caitlyn held Ruth's waist. "Nothing could have erased the image from my brain. I wanted to push you backward onto the conference table and have my way with you."

"Well. That would have been inappropriate." Ruth brushed Caitlyn's hair from her face. "I don't have relations with my employees."

"Good thing I was never your employee." Caitlyn leaned in for another kiss.

"Uh-huh. And it's a good thing you never impersonated my assistant for three months and altered the course of my entire presidency."

"Yes, I'm so glad I didn't do that." Caitlyn pulled Ruth closer.

Ruth held her tight. "I'd say it's the best thing that never happened to us."

Other Books from Ylva Publishing

www.ylva-publishing.com

The Love Factor
Quinn Ivins

ISBN: 978-3-96324-377-6
Length: 215 pages (75,000 words)

Molly is almost thirty, bored, and less into her PhD than her sexy, closeted statistics professor, Carmen, an icy woman with strict standards and no interest in dating students.

As they work together to expose a scandal, the chemistry builds, making for a dangerous equation.

A smart student-professor romance filled with nostalgia, politics, and the forbidden thrills of lesbian love in the '90s.

Just a Touch Away
Jae

ISBN: 978-3-96324-711-8
Length: 339 pages (120,000 words)

A professional cuddler and an aloof workaholic inherit a building together, but there's a catch: before they each get their half, they have to live together for ninety-two days.

An enemies-to-lovers lesbian romance with an ice queen whose frosty facade is melted by the power of touch.

The Number 94 Project
Cheyenne Blue

ISBN: 978-3-96324-567-1
Length: 288 pages (100,000 words)

When Jorgie's uncle leaves her an old house in Melbourne, it's a dream come true. Sure, No. 94 is falling apart, and she has to deal with her uncle's eccentric friends. But she'll do it up, sell it, and move on.

What she hasn't counted on is falling for Marta, who's as embedded in Gaylord St as the concrete Jorgie's ripping up.

Renovation takes a sexy turn in this light-hearted lesbian romance.

Her Royal Happiness
Lola Keeley

ISBN: 978-3-96324-601-2
Length: 276 pages (100,000 words)

When out British royal Princess Alice meets an opinionated single mother, the encounter goes viral. So when Alice later has to ask the education specialist for her expert opinion, it's awkward. Well, until they discover how beautifully they click together. But keeping a secret isn't easy when you're in the world's most visible family…

An opposites attract, charming royal romance with a dash of fake dating.

About Quinn Ivins

Quinn Ivins has been addicted to romance since she was a teenager, when she stayed up on school nights to read more *X-Files* fanfiction.

Now finally done with school after 27 years, she has published three lesbian romance novels. Her second book, *Worthy of Love*, won the 2022 Goldie award for Contemporary Romance: Mid-Length.

Quinn lives in the United States with her wife and son.

CONNECT WITH QUINN

Website: www.quinnivins.com
E-mail: quinn.ivins@gmail.com
Twitter: @quinnivins
Facebook: www.facebook.com/quinn.ivins.9
Instagram: quinn.ivins

Something's Different
© 2022 by Quinn Ivins

ISBN: 978-3-96324-738-5

Available in e-book and paperback formats.

Published by Ylva Publishing, legal entity of Ylva Verlag, e.Kfr.

Ylva Verlag, e.Kfr.
Owner: Astrid Ohletz
Am Kirschgarten 2
65830 Kriftel
Germany

www.ylva-publishing.com

First edition: 2022

Credits
Edited by Sandra Gerth and Sheena Billet
Cover Design and Print Layout by Streetlight Graphics

Made in the USA
Las Vegas, NV
24 January 2023

66149552R10177